C460355596

KT-175-809

# SPECIAL MESSAGE TO READERS

**THE ULVERSCROFT FOUNDATION**
**(registered UK charity number 264873)**
was established in 1972 to provide funds for
research, diagnosis and treatment of eye diseases.
Examples of major projects funded by
the Ulverscroft Foundation are:-

* The Children's Eye Unit at Moorfields Eye
  Hospital, London
* The Ulverscroft Children's Eye Unit at Great
  Ormond Street Hospital for Sick Children
* Funding research into eye diseases and
  treatment at the Department of Ophthalmology,
  University of Leicester
* The Ulverscroft Vision Research Group,
  Institute of Child Health
* Twin operating theatres at the Western
  Ophthalmic Hospital, London
* The Chair of Ophthalmology at the Royal
  Australian College of Ophthalmologists

You can help further the work of the Foundation
by making a donation or leaving a legacy.
Every contribution is gratefully received. If you
would like to help support the Foundation or
require further information, please contact:

**THE ULVERSCROFT FOUNDATION**
**The Green, Bradgate Road, Anstey**
**Leicester LE7 7FU, England**
**Tel: (0116) 236 4325**

**website: www.foundation.ulverscroft.com**

David Bell was born in Cincinnati, Ohio. He studied English at Indiana University, then worked a series of odd jobs — waiter, bartender, book store clerk, telemarketeter — in a series of odd places — Shreveport, Louisiana; Savannah, Georgia; Washington, D.C. After five years of that, he decided he had had enough of the real world and went to graduate school at Miami University in Oxford, Ohio, where he received his M.A. in creative writing; this was followed by a Ph.D. in American literature and creative writing from the University of Cincinnati. David is currently an assistant professor of English at Western Kentucky University. When he is not teaching or writing, David watches lots of movies and reads lots and lots of books. He also enjoys walking in the cemetery near his house with his wife, writer and blogger Molly McCaffrey.

You can discover more about the author at www.davidbellnovels.com

# THE HIDING PLACE

Twenty-five years ago, four-year-old Justin Manning disappeared. Two months later, his body was found in a shallow grave in the woods, shocking the small town of Dove Point, Ohio. Janet Manning has been haunted by her brother's death since the day she lost sight of him in the park. Now, a detective and a reporter are asking questions, raising new suspicions and opening old wounds. But if the man jailed for the murder is innocent, who did kill Justin? Janet thought she'd put the past and guilt behind her. But now the truth about her brother is heartbreakingly close — has she the courage to find it?

DAVID BELL

# THE HIDING PLACE

*Complete and Unabridged*

# CHARNWOOD
Leicester

First published in Great Britain in 2013 by
Penguin Books
London


First Charnwood Edition
published 2014
by arrangement with
Penguin Books
London

The moral right of the author has been asserted


Copyright © 2012 by David J. Bell
All rights reserved

A catalogue record for this book is available
from the British Library.


ISBN 978–1–4448–1801–7

C460355596

Published by
F. A. Thorpe (Publishing)
Anstey, Leicestershire

Set by Words & Graphics Ltd.
Anstey, Leicestershire
Printed and bound in Great Britain by
T. J. International Ltd., Padstow, Cornwall

This book is printed on acid-free paper

SOUTH LANARKSHIRE LIBRARIES

For Molly

# Prologue

*What do you remember from that day, Janet?*

Janet remembered the heat. The way it shimmered in waves in the distance, making the edges of the trees, the cars in the parking lot blurry and indistinct. Wherever she stepped, the grass crackled or the dirt puffed. The heat rose from the ground and scorched her feet through the soles of her cheap plastic shoes.

She was seven years old and in charge of her baby brother for the first time ever.

Janet watched Justin. She thought of him as a dumb four-year-old, a silly kid with a bowl of blond hair and a goofy smile. He sat with the other kids in the sandbox, scooping piles of sand into mounds with his hands, then smoothing them over. Back and forth like that. Sand up, sand down. Dumb and pointless. Something little kids would do. She watched him. Carefully.

But no, that wasn't right. That wasn't right at all . . .

Justin wasn't silly. And he didn't smile all the time. He was a quiet kid. A loner. He sat in the sandbox alone that day. And he didn't smile much. Not much at all. No one in her family smiled much, not when she looked back on her childhood . . . or even her life now.

What did she remember from that day? What did she really remember? It was so hard to —

Michael showed up.

1

She remembered that.

Michael showed up, her seven-year-old play-mate, the boy from the neighborhood and school. Their parents were friends. They played together all the time. Her boyfriend, she liked to think and giggle to herself, although they never touched each other. Never hugged or kissed or held hands. They were too young for that, too young for a lot of things.

But Michael showed up wearing denim shorts with a belt like a long rope and sneakers with holes in them. His hair hung in his face, and he brushed it out of his eyes constantly. He lived on the other side of the park. And so Michael called her name, and when he did her heart jumped and she turned away from the sandbox and the swings and the other kids. And she followed Michael wherever he went. Across the play-ground, over the baseball diamond, over by the trees. She followed him.

Is that all she did? Run across the playground?

It was enough. She let Justin out of her sight. Dad was at work and Mom was at home, and Mom let them go to the playground alone that day for the first time ever, but it didn't seem like a big deal. The park was near the school and the church and the other kids would be there, other kids they knew and even some parents. And all Mom said on that day when they left the house was, 'Janet, don't let Justin out of your sight. He's a little boy . . . '

But she did. She let Justin out of her sight.

Did she see the man?

Janet can't say anymore. She's seen his face so

many times. At the trial. In the newspaper. The mug shot. His face stoic, his eyes round, the whites prominent. His full lips, his black face. Not really a man. Now when she looks at the face, she sees a kid. Seventeen when he was arrested, but tried as an adult. He would have looked like an adult back then, that hot day in the park . . .

But she doesn't know if she saw him.

Other people did. Adults and kids. He was in the park, talking to kids at the sandbox and the swings. He carried Justin, according to some of the witnesses. He paid special attention to her brother, they said. Walked around with him. Talked to him. Lifted him on his shoulders.

For years, Janet thought she saw that, thought she remembered that. The young black man with the frizzy hair and the dirty clothes carrying her brother on his shoulders. Justin's blond head up high, almost as high as the top of the swing set. Justin parading around like a champion. Being tricked by this man. And then being taken away.

But she doesn't really remember that, does she?

She thought there was a dog. A puppy. It ran through the park, and Justin ran after it.

Is that what happened? Is that how Justin got away?

*What do you remember from that day, Janet?*

She can't be sure anymore. Not after twenty-five years.

She isn't sure she saw the man that day. But she wishes she had. She wishes she knew.

And she really wishes she had kept her eye on

3

Justin, like she was supposed to.

She didn't see the man and she didn't see Justin.

And when it was time to go home, when Janet finally did look around and try to find her brother, he wasn't there. The adults became hysterical and the police arrived and people asked a lot of questions, but none of it mattered.

Justin was gone. Long gone.

# 1

Janet hid the morning paper from her father. She saw it when she'd come downstairs, and even though she knew it was coming — knew for close to a week that an interview with her brother's murderer would be on the front page — the sight of it, the sight of his face, hit her with the force of a slap. And then she thought of her dad. His anger, his roiling emotions at the mere mention of Dante Rogers. She folded the front page in half, with Rogers's face inside the fold, and slipped it beneath a chair cushion.

Janet heard water running in the bathroom down the hall, then her father's feet on the hard wood. She was breaking her own rule. When she'd moved back in with her father after he'd lost his job, she'd made a silent vow not to be his household servant. She wouldn't become some version of a substitute wife to him — cooking, cleaning, laundry. But on certain days, she made exceptions. She took out eggs, cracked them into a skillet, and watched them sizzle. Summer work hours at the college left her just enough time to do it — and it might take the old man's mind off his troubles.

'Where is it?'

Janet turned. Her father, Bill Manning, filled the entrance to the kitchen. He was still tall — over six feet — but since being laid off he had gained about twenty pounds, mostly in the stomach and the face. He'd been out of work for nearly two years, ever since the recession had hit and his company, Strand Manufacturing, 'went in a different direction,' which meant laying off anyone over the age of fifty. Twenty-seven years working in product development and then an unceremonious good-bye.

Janet recognized the foolishness of trying to hide the paper. She pointed to the chair. Bill picked up the paper and sat down. Janet put the eggs in front of him.

'I thought you said you wouldn't wait on me,' he said.

'I felt like it.'

'You felt sorry for me,' he said.

Janet didn't answer, but there was some truth in what her father said. Years ago, he'd lost his son and then his wife. Then came the recent job loss, and Janet moved in to help make sure he didn't lose the house. Her father might be reserved and distant — difficult even — but she never outgrew the desire to protect and help him. And that desire only became stronger as her father grew older. He was sixty-two and starting to look his age.

'Jesus,' he said. He folded the paper, snapping the pages into place with a flick of his wrists, and leaned close to read the story. 'Not even at the top . . .'

Janet knew what the story said. Her brother had disappeared twenty-five years ago that day, and the local paper was running a couple of stories to commemorate the anniversary. The first one detailed the life of Dante Rogers, the man convicted of killing her brother. Paroled three years earlier, slowly adjusting to life back on the outside, working part-time at a church on the east side of Dove Point, Ohio . . .

While her dad read the article and cursed under his breath, Janet turned to the sink. She ran a rag over some dishes from the night before. 'Today's our day, remember?' she said. 'The reporter is coming over at two. I'm leaving work early — '

The paper rustled and fell to the floor. When Janet turned, her dad was cutting into his eggs, shoveling them toward his mouth with machine-like quickness. He paused long enough to ask a question. 'Do you know what I think of all this?' he asked.

'I can guess.'

He pointed to the floor where the paper rested, the article about Dante Rogers facing up. 'This article — it's like they want me to feel sorry for this guy. It reads like he got some kind of a bum rap because he went to jail for twenty-two years for killing a kid — '

'Did you read the whole story?' Janet asked.

Her dad kept chewing. 'I already lived it.'

Janet leaned back against the counter and folded her arms across her chest. 'He still says he's innocent,' Janet said.

Her father's eyes moved back and forth, giving him the look of a caged animal. His cheeks flushed. 'So?' He looked down at his plate, pushed the remains of the egg around, making a runny yellow smear. He didn't look back up.

'He says — '

'I don't want to hear it,' he said, dropping his fork. 'He just wants sympathy from people. Probably living on welfare.'

Janet took hold of the belt of her robe. She worked it in her hands, fingering it, using it almost like rosary beads. 'If it makes you feel any better, I don't really want to tell my story to the reporter either,' she said.

'I know the story. Rogers killed my boy. That's it.' He pushed away his plate and rose to his feet. The first year after being laid off, her dad dressed just like he did when he went to work — shirt and tie, neatly pressed pants. The past year had seen a change. He no longer dressed first thing in the morning and went days on end without shaving. He stopped reading the classifieds a few months earlier.

'Then I guess it's silly for me to ask if you want to do anything special today?' Janet asked.

'Anything special?'

'For the anniversary of Justin's death.'

'Have I ever before?' he asked. 'Have you?'

Janet shook her head. She hadn't. Every year, she tried to treat the day like any other day. She tried to live her life, work her job, and raise her daughter.

'Then there's your answer, I guess,' he said. 'What time's that reporter coming over?'

'I just said. Two o'clock. So, are you going to talk to her?'

He left his dirty dishes on the table. 'I've got nothing to say to any of them,' he said. 'Nothing at all.'

8

# 2

Ashleigh sent Kevin a text: *Where R U?*

She waited near the swings, the sun high overhead prickling the back of her neck. It was just eight thirty and already hot enough to send sweat trickling down her back. Ashleigh scuffed her sneakers in the dirt and checked her phone.

No response yet.

Where was he?

She watched the little kids scream and play. They ran around like monkeys, their mouths open, their hair flying. They never tired or stopped. Ashleigh felt something swell in her throat, an emotion she couldn't identify. She took a deep breath, like she needed to cry, but swallowed back against it, choking it down. She turned away. She couldn't watch the kids anymore. They looked so vulnerable, so fragile, like little glass creatures.

*This is the park*, she thought. *This is where it happened.*

Kevin came out of the trees. She recognized his loping gait, his broad shoulders. He wore his work uniform — black pants and a goofy McDonald's smock. He'd decided to grow his Afro out over the summer, and it made him seem even taller. Ashleigh took another deep breath, collected herself before Kevin arrived.

'Hey, girl,' he said.

'Thanks for writing back.'

9

'I got called in.' He pointed at his shirt. 'I have to be there at ten.'

'That's bullshit.'

Kevin shrugged, casual as could be. 'I have to earn my keep.'

'Let's get going then. These kids bug the shit out of me.'

★ ★ ★

They didn't talk much. Ashleigh imagined that the parents on the playground — the ones who always came to watch their kids, whether they knew what had happened there twenty-five years ago or not — had noticed the two of them: a tall black boy and a short white girl, walking side by side. She'd known Kevin for three years, ever since the first day of junior high, when they'd sat next to each other in history class. At first she thought he was dumb, maybe even retarded. He was so big, so quiet. Then she noticed the jokes he cracked at the teacher's expense, his voice so low only she could hear.

'What's your plan?' he asked.

They came out into the neighborhood that bordered the park. It was opposite where she lived with her mom and grandfather, and a little nicer too. She supposed it was upper middle class as opposed to simply middle class. Bigger houses, nicer cars. A neighborhood where no one got laid off.

They walked past older homes with nice yards. Retirees lived there, old people who spent their days digging in their gardens and sweeping their walks. If a piece of trash ended up in the yard, they'd probably call the police.

'I don't have one yet,' Ashleigh said.

'You usually have a plan for everything.'

'I don't for this.'

They reached Hamilton Avenue, a major road dotted with strip malls and gas stations.

Kevin said, 'So you're just going to go up to this dude and say, 'Hey, what do you know about my dead uncle?''

'Be quiet.'

Ashleigh looked down the road. She saw the bus.

'If I go with you ... ' Kevin sounded uncertain. 'I'm going to be late for work. I'll get written up.'

'Then don't go,' she said. 'Make hamburgers for strangers. Forget about all those football games I went to with you.'

'Come on, Ash. My dad says if I don't have a job this summer, he's going to kick me out of the house.'

'And remember how I helped you proofread your history term paper? Heck, I proofread all of your papers last year.'

'You're going to throw that back at me?'

'I'll go alone. The guy's probably not dangerous.'

'You know how my dad is,' Kevin said. 'He's old-school. He worked his way through college, so he thinks I need to earn my keep.'

The bus pulled up, air brakes exhaling. The diesel stank, burned Ashleigh's eyes. When the door rattled open, she didn't even look at Kevin.

She just climbed on and dropped her coins into the slot, where they rattled like loose teeth. She moved down the aisle and took a seat, staring out the window and watching the traffic go by.

She picked up movement at the front of the bus, something in her peripheral vision.

'Hey,' the bus driver called.

It was Kevin. He ignored the driver and walked right back to Ashleigh's seat.

She looked up into Kevin's face. A cute face, she had to admit. Beautiful eyes. A little puppyish.

'What?' she said, trying to sound mad.

'You really want to do this?' he asked.

'Yes.'

'Come on, goddamn it,' someone yelled from the back of the bus.

'I have one problem,' Kevin said to her.

'What?'

'Can I borrow fifty cents?' he asked, smiling.

She reached into her pocket and handed him the coins.

# 3

Janet tapped lightly on Ashleigh's door. Nothing. Then she knocked again, using more force.

'Ash?'

The knob gave as she turned. Janet stepped into the darkened room and saw that Ashleigh was already gone, so she pushed the door open all the way. It wasn't unusual for Ashleigh to leave the house early. Not unusual at all. She'd be with Kevin most likely, or sitting at the library thumbing through books and magazines. Kevin. Ashleigh didn't bring him around much anymore, not since they'd moved in with Bill. But the two spent all their time together. Janet tried not to pry, tried not to be a nosy mother, but she wondered sometimes. Did her moody daughter have a boyfriend? That at least was a normal concern for a mother to have, worrying about her daughter's dating life. The other things Janet worried about were a product of her own childhood, and they made her heart flutter . . .

It's okay, she told herself. It's okay to let her out of the house. She's not a child — she's fifteen. She won't get taken and it'll be okay.

Janet reminded herself to breathe. She'd half entertained the notion of taking Ashleigh out to lunch or shopping, something to break the usual routine and mark the importance of the day. But Ashleigh was living her life, just the way Janet wanted her to. Why burden her or anyone else?

13

Janet turned her attention to the things in the room. She had to give Ashleigh credit for something else — the girl knew how to keep order. No teenage mess in that room. The bed was made, the closet closed. Janet went over and opened the blinds. The light fell across a neat row of photographs on the shelf above Ashleigh's bed. The photos were all familiar. Janet and Ashleigh at a school awards ceremony. A portrait of Janet's mother — high school graduation? — the grandmother Ashleigh never knew. And on the end, facing the light, the last portrait of Justin ever taken, the one that ran in the newspaper and on TV during the summer he disappeared. Janet picked the photo up, ran her hand across the dust-free glass.

Janet had once asked Ashleigh why she kept a portrait of her dead uncle above her bed. The girl just shrugged.

'It's the past,' she said. 'Our past. And isn't the past always with us?'

Janet shivered. Out of the mouths of babes . . .

She went to get dressed for work.

★ ★ ★

Janet had begun working at Cronin College fourteen years earlier. She'd started in the mailroom just after high school, sorting packages alongside work-study college students from all over the country. Ashleigh was a year old then. Janet didn't think she could work, raise a baby, and attend college, but she took the job at Cronin with an eye toward bigger things. She

14

knew — *knew* — her daughter would go to college someday, and employees of the college received a huge tuition break. Janet even planned on getting a degree herself and had taken classes over the years as she worked her way from the mail processing center to the copy and print center to the chemistry department and finally to her current position working for the dean as office manager, overseeing a staff of five. She loved her job. She loved supporting herself and her daughter with her own work. She even enjoyed knowing that her job and salary helped her dad hold on to her childhood home.

But she didn't love her job the day the story about Dante Rogers ran in the paper.

As soon as Janet walked into the office, she knew everyone had read about it. Nobody said anything — at least not right away. But she could tell by the looks on their faces. Her coworkers smiled at her, but they weren't happy smiles. They were forced, toothless, the heads cocked to the side a little, the lips pressed tight. *Oh, you poor thing*, the smiles said. *The tragedy. You were there that day* . . .

You were supposed to be watching him . . .

In the break room during lunch, Madeline Hamilton, the office's resident busybody, approached Janet, sitting down next to her and casually removing a soggy sandwich from a plastic bag. Madeline had known Janet's mother, had landed the job in the dean's office with Janet's help. Janet knew Madeline's interest wasn't casual, and Janet even found herself happy to see the older woman cozying up next to her. She hoped someone

15

would break the tension, pop the black balloon that seemed to be hovering over her head.

'So,' Madeline said, drawing out the *O*, her tiny mouth formed into a similar, circular shape. Madeline didn't bite into her food. She raised her right hand and fussed with the pile of bright red hair on the top of her head. 'Crazy day for you, huh?'

'Do you want to ask me something about the story?' Janet said.

Madeline took a bite of the sandwich and gestured with her free hand. 'If you need someone to talk to . . . ' she said, the free hand floating in the air, a heavy, fleshy butterfly. 'I've always thought of you as family. And I know today's that awful anniversary. Are you going to the cemetery or anything?'

Janet shook her head. She had a Diet Coke and a bag of pretzels in front of her. She'd eaten two pretzels and barely touched the drink. 'They're interviewing me today.'

'Oh, really,' Madeline said. She wiped her mouth and set the food aside, shifting to all-business mode. 'But you read that story? The one today?'

'Yes.'

'Can you believe he's still here in Dove Point? Just living here? Among all of us?'

'Where is he supposed to go?' Janet asked.

'I'd think he'd want to live anywhere but here.'

'His parents are dead. He lived with his aunt . . . back then. But she's dead, too.'

'See,' Madeline said. 'No ties here. He could just pick up and move anywhere.'

16

'You make it sound so glamorous. He's an ex-con. What's he going to do? Besides, I don't think he's going to hurt anybody.'

'He's already killed two people,' Madeline said. 'First Justin and then your mother. She'd still be with us if not for the grief.'

Janet didn't disagree. Her mother never recovered from her brother's death. Diabetes-related complications, they'd written on the death certificate nearly eighteen years ago. Janet knew the truth — her mother had died of a broken heart. But Janet just couldn't summon the same anger toward Dante Rogers that everybody else did.

'Don't you feel sorry for him?' Janet asked. 'Even a little? He looks so pathetic, so empty.'

'Sorry for him?' Madeline fanned herself with both hands. She looked like she was choking. 'Sorry? For a killer? He better hope he doesn't come my way or cross my path. I can't be held responsible.'

Janet checked the clock. She needed to get back to her desk. The dean's office didn't rest in the summer, despite the shorter hours. In fact, summer brought more work. Annual reports, budgets, faculty travel arrangements. But she wasn't ready to go back.

'Do you ever wonder?' Janet said. She knew her voice sounded dreamy, distracted. She didn't know what she wanted to say. She didn't know if she should even give voice to her thoughts.

'Wonder what?' Madeline asked.

'The way he maintains his innocence, even after all this time. He has no reason to. He's

17

already done his time.'

'Remember what was lost,' Madeline said. 'Your mother never had the life she wanted because of that man. And neither did you. You've been without a mother for eighteen years because of that man.'

'I'll see you later, Madeline.'

'You call me and tell me how it went when you're finished.'

Janet left without agreeing to make the call.

★　★　★

But Janet didn't go back to work. She took the back stairs down to the parking lot. She stepped out into the hot day, felt the wave of humidity wash over her. The trees just beyond the parking lot were a rich summer green and the traffic on Mason Street just off campus hummed back and forth, the steady rhythm of Dove Point's life. When she needed a break from work, a moment alone or a moment to think, she came to the back of the building. No one else ever went there unless they were coming or going from their cars. Janet knew she could steal a quiet moment.

She noticed the man almost immediately. He stood by a parked car, watching her as she stepped outside. The man was tall and lean like a runner. He looked to be the same age as Janet, and despite the heat, he wore jeans and a long-sleeve button-down shirt. Even though about two hundred feet separated them, Janet could sense the piercing nature of his eyes. Was he a faculty member, perhaps someone newly hired she had never met? She thought of turning away, of simply stepping back inside Wilson Hall and going back to work, but something about the man's posture and the way he held his head looked familiar to her. She had seen this man before — hadn't she? — but not for a long time.

And then he raised his hand and made a waving gesture, beckoning her to him.

# 4

The bus carried them five miles west and let them out near an abandoned shopping mall. As the bus pulled away, Ashleigh pointed and walked forward, Kevin following. Ashleigh had printed a map the night before and studied it enough so that she wouldn't need to refer to it again. They were still on Hamilton Avenue but took the first right and headed north for a few blocks, back into a run-down neighborhood, one her grandfather would call 'hillbilly.'

Kevin hadn't said much on the ride over. He'd left her to her thoughts, one of the reasons she liked him so much. He'd heard it all before, listened to her stories and plans, patiently and without judgment. He knew what these trips meant to her — 'her escapades,' he called them — and went along with her as both companion and protector.

Ashleigh found the street she wanted — Lemongrass — and turned left. The apartment complex came into sight, a series of gray buildings with little landscaping or color to break up the monotony. Even the cars in the parking lot looked dingy and old, their fenders rusting, their mufflers sagging. She stopped, and Kevin stopped beside her.

'Well?' he said.

She shrugged. Her heart rate had picked up and she felt a tingling down the length of her arms, the mixture of excitement and fear she always felt on these escapades. But it was even greater this time.

*This is really it*, she thought.

'We're going to have to look at mailboxes or just knock on doors,' she said.

And hope.

'Okay,' Kevin said. 'But if I'm doing all this, you need to be writing the history paper for me.'

Ashleigh didn't move. She stayed rooted to the spot, her feet like concrete.

'Well, boss?' Kevin said. 'What do you say?'

Ashleigh had had one glimpse of this person, one fleeting look at a face on a darkened porch. Like a picked scab, she'd kept it alive and fresh, a fixed point around which the last few months of her life had revolved — the man who'd shown up one night claiming to know something about the murder of her long-dead Uncle Justin. Claiming that Dante Rogers was not guilty . . .

She took a deep breath and shivered.

'Okay,' she said. 'Let's go.'

\* \* \*

Three months earlier, the man had come to their house in the middle of the night.

Ashleigh didn't know if the sound of his knocking had stirred her, or if her mother's voice had brought her out of sleep. But she'd woken up. She'd gone down the stairs, wearing a long T-shirt that hung below her knees, and stood in the darkness of the hallway, listening to the muffled voices from the front porch. The night

21

was cold. She shivered.

Her mother cried.

Most of the words her mom spoke were indistinct, coming as they were between choked, halting breaths. But Ashleigh understood the important ones. The ones she never forgot.

'Justin,' her mother said, over and over again. 'Are you sure? How do I know this isn't a joke? Tell me what you know — tell me right now.'

And when Ashleigh heard that name spoken and her mother's pleading, she too began to cry. Her chin puckered, and hot tears fell down her face.

She saw the man through the open door.

He wore his blond hair short, almost a buzz cut. The scruff on his face tried to make a beard, and in the bright shine of the porch light, Ashleigh saw dark circles under his eyes, like he hadn't slept well in weeks. He seemed gaunt, undernourished.

'No, no,' the man said, his voice husky. 'I can't stay. I have to go. But don't call the police. Don't get them involved.'

'But why?' her mom asked.

'Soon,' he said, backing away. 'You'll know it all soon. I promise.'

He was gone. Out of sight and into the darkness.

Her mom called to the man — once and then twice. She held out her hand toward the dark, a desperate, grasping attempt to hold the man and keep him from going away. But he was gone.

Ashleigh didn't think. She didn't process the information or make a conscious choice. She simply turned and ran up the stairs to her room and slid under the covers before her mother could see her.

Ashleigh sat in the dark, listening. She expected the police to come. She anticipated sirens and reporters and commotion. But none of it happened. Fifteen minutes later, she heard her mother's slippers trudging up the stairs. Ashleigh took the photo of her uncle off the shelf. She held it in the air so the moonlight through the window illuminated the smiling face of the little boy.

He said he knew something. The man on the porch knew something.

She desperately wondered what it could be.

* * *

She and Kevin stood side by side, examining the rusted mailboxes. Ashleigh held her finger in the air as she passed over the names, looking for one that said 'Steven Kollman.' Many of the boxes hung open, their doors broken and loose. Old flyers and pieces of junk mail littered the floor. In her mind's eye, she saw the man from the porch. He'd worn a red T-shirt with an atomic symbol on the upper left side. Her mother wouldn't know what the shirt meant, even if she had been clearheaded and in the best frame of mind. As emotional as she had been on the porch, Ashleigh guessed there was no way she could have processed what the man wore in such detail. But Ashleigh knew what the shirt meant

— every nerdy high school kid in town would. Atomic Tom's Comic Book and Card Company, a small store in a dingy strip mall where Ashleigh and Kevin sometimes hung out.

A week after the man's appearance on the porch, Ashleigh had gone to Atomic Tom's and asked about the guy. He didn't work there. Atomic Tom had only two employees — Tom himself and his cousin Dirk, a shaggy-haired guy who tipped the scales at close to three hundred pounds. Dirk liked Ashleigh and Kevin. He joked around with them, called them 'Little Salt' and 'Big Pepper,' and Kevin sometimes brought Dirk shakes and French fries. When Ashleigh asked about the man and described him, Dirk eventually pieced it together and told them he thought the guy they were looking for worked as a dishwasher at Mi Casita Mexican restaurant.

It took Ashleigh a few more weeks to even go to Mi Casita, and then another few weeks of cautious questioning of the employees there. The man didn't work there anymore, but she learned his name — Steven Kollman — from one of the waiters. And eventually a friendly hostess told Ashleigh she thought she knew the apartment complex where the man lived. Steven Kollman had moved by the time Ashleigh went to that address, but one of his neighbors speculated about a new address, where Ashleigh and Kevin were standing.

'Why would he just show up here now?' Kevin asked. 'What's changed?'

'That's what I intend to find out.'

'Isn't he afraid of getting caught?'

'Caught at what?' Ashleigh asked, turning her head toward him. 'Knocking on doors in the middle of the night?'

Kevin shrugged. She could tell he wanted to be supportive, but he also had more to say. 'Messing with people, I guess.'

Ashleigh ignored him and kept looking.

'I mean,' Kevin said, 'if this ends up being the guy who came to your house, you're sure we don't want to call the police?'

'I'm sure.' She heard the sound of her voice, the way it snapped out like the lash of a whip. Kevin shrugged again, giving in to her wishes. She knew he just wanted to protect her. She tried to soften her voice. 'His name isn't here.'

'Okay,' Kevin said. 'What now?'

Ashleigh started up the stairs into the building. 'Come on. We're going to look,' she said. 'Sometimes people have their names on their doors. Or maybe we'll ask someone else.'

They checked all the doors on the first floor. A couple of names but not the one they were looking for. The hallway smelled dirty and musty, an accumulation of cooking odors and unclean apartments. Ashleigh could only imagine the dust and filth behind the walls. The dirty diapers and greasy stoves, the overflowing garbage cans and dusty corners. Better to think about those things than the task at hand, which made her heart skip and stutter like a damaged DVD. She led Kevin to the second floor, where they again checked all the doors.

Nothing. One more floor to try.

The stairs squeaked and rattled beneath their feet. With every step, Ashleigh gripped the railing tighter, a layer of sweat between her skin and the cold metal. She reached the top and saw the door of the first apartment on the right stood open. She stopped. She felt Kevin behind her, his feet still on the stairs. A plunger, a bucket, and a wrench sat in the hallway just outside the door. Even though she doubted Kevin would speak, she still held her finger in the air, asking for silence.

She wanted to leave. She wanted to back down the stairs, pushing Kevin ahead of her, and go. But she couldn't. Instead, Ashleigh willed herself forward and peered into the apartment. It looked cluttered and dirty, the floor covered with papers, the furniture rickety and worn. She knocked on the open door, and a pudgy middle-aged man came out of the kitchen. His thinning hair hung in limpid strings, and his thick glasses clung to the tip of his nose so precariously Ashleigh wanted to reach out and push them back up where they belonged.

'Help you?' he said. His face brightened a little, and he brushed some of the strands of hair into a semblance of order. Then his eyes moved over Ashleigh's head. He saw Kevin, and his face fell a little. 'You have to be eighteen to rent,' he said. 'And married. I don't rent to couples who aren't married.'

'I'm not looking to rent.' *God, I hope I never have to live in a place like this.* 'I'm looking for

26

someone. A guy named Steven.'

The man's face pinched up like he had finally caught a whiff of the smells that permeated the building. 'Steven Kollman?' he asked.

She nodded. She didn't know if she could speak.

'He's not home,' the man said. He reached up and used the back of his hand to wipe sweat off his forehead. 'I'm the building manager. Just fixing a leak in the kitchen, although why I'm fixing it for him I'll never know.'

Ashleigh took a step back. 'I guess I'll come another time.'

'Are you a relative or something?' the man asked.

Ashleigh looked back at Kevin. She shrugged. 'Kind of.'

'He's two months late on his rent, so if you see him before I do, you should tell him to get his act together.' The man looked pleased with his tough talk. 'Hey, if you're a relative, maybe you know someone else who can pay the rent for him?'

'I don't think so.'

'Anybody can pay it, you know.'

'Sure,' Ashleigh said, backing down the stairs.

The man's brow furrowed and he scratched at his head. Then his face brightened. 'Maybe that guy who came to see him the other night,' the manager said. 'Do you know him?'

'A guy?' Ashleigh said. 'What guy?'

'I figured maybe he's a cousin or a brother or something. He seemed to have a little more class than Steven.' The man wiped his nose with his hand. 'Sounded like they were arguing.'

'I don't think I know him,' Ashleigh said.

'Maybe Steven owes him money too.'

'I guess I don't know about that,' Ashleigh said, and she and Kevin left the building.

# 5

'Michael?' Janet said, moving closer. 'Is that — Michael?'

When she said his name, he pushed himself up off the car. He didn't smile, but his eyes brightened. 'Hey.'

'It's you,' Janet said. 'It's really you.'

They came within arm's length of each other, and the awkward moment descended in which she didn't know if they were going to hug or if he even wanted to hug her. But he held out his arms, so she went for it, felt herself folded up against his body, triggering, as if by raw instinct, a flash of heat on the back of her neck and a tingling of desire in the pit of her stomach. She inhaled his rugged scent — a touch of sweat and a tangy cologne or deodorant.

When the hug broke off, she examined him up close in the sunlight. It had been how long? Five years? More? He looked thinner, older, the lines at the corners of his eyes and on his forehead more pronounced and deeper. But he finally smiled, and the old Michael was there, the one from childhood and high school. The Michael she really knew. And that familiar desire was there — desire for him — as strong as it had been in the past.

'I didn't know you were back,' Janet said.

'I wanted to see my mom,' he said.

'Did you just get back?'

'It's been a little while.' He seemed evasive, which told Janet that he'd been back longer than he wanted to let on. 'A few weeks or so.'

'What have you been doing? Where were you living? We heard you might have been in Chicago for a while.'

'I don't want to keep you from work,' he said.

Janet made a dismissive wave toward the office. 'They don't need me now,' she said, feeling awkward, like a teenager again. She didn't know what to do with her hands, so she crossed her arms, then uncrossed them. She did this twice. 'Why don't you come in and we can talk somewhere?'

'I won't keep you,' he said.

'Okay. But you were in Chicago?'

'That was a couple of years ago,' he said. 'I was on the West Coast for a while, then Columbus.'

'You were in Columbus?' Janet said. 'Just an hour away?'

'The last year or so,' he said. 'I was working for this guy, but — the economy, you know?' He looked around the lot, not letting his eyes rest on Janet.

'But you're here now,' she said. 'For a while?' She heard the hopeful, almost pleading tone in her voice and didn't like it. But she couldn't help it. She'd be lying to herself and anyone else if she said she wasn't thrilled to see him, if she said she didn't think, from time to time, about the possibility of Michael Bower coming back to Dove Point for good.

'There's another reason I'm back,' Michael

said. He turned to face her. 'Do you know what it is?'

'Your dad?'

Michael frowned. 'No, not him.' He shook his head. 'Twenty-five years, Janet. I know the date. I saw the paper today. Twenty-five years.'

'I didn't know if you'd remember,' she said.

'Of course. I was there.'

'I know,' she said. 'It's just — we've never really talked about it, you and I. But there's a reporter coming over to interview me after work today. They're doing another story.'

'How are you doing with all of this, Janet?' he asked. 'I thought you might need the support. You shouldn't have to go through it alone, you know.'

'You should come to the house today,' Janet said. 'The reporter asked me if I was in touch with you. We can do the interview together.'

Michael looked away again, but this time he glanced behind her. She turned to follow his gaze and saw Madeline coming out of the back of the building, her hand raised to shield her eyes from the sun.

'There you are,' Madeline said. 'I thought you'd run off. The provost's office is on the phone. They need you.'

'Okay. Just a minute.'

'I think they have a question about the budget.'

Before Madeline went back in, she cast a last, long look at Michael, and Janet knew she'd have more questions to answer about the man in the parking lot.

31

'I have to go,' Janet said. 'But come to the interview. Really. You must be thinking about this a lot. We can talk about it.'

'You must think about it a lot, too,' Michael said. He stared at her, studying her face. 'What do you remember from that day, Janet?'

For a long moment, Janet stared at him. Her mouth was dry, and the sounds of the passing cars amplified, like rushing wind. Before she could say anything else, Madeline stuck her head out the door and called her name again.

'You'll come today, right?' Janet asked. 'Two o'clock.'

'We'll talk,' Michael said.

Janet looked back once before she entered the building, but he was already gone.

# 6

As the nearly empty bus brought the two of them back near their homes, Ashleigh thought about the size of Dove Point, Ohio. Not really big enough to be called a city, and yet not really small enough to be called a town. According to her ninth-grade civics class, about fifty thousand people lived there. Most of them worked at the university or the medical center complex or the handful of factories that dotted the perimeter of Dove Point like beads on a bracelet.

Had she really come that close to the guy from the porch? Had she almost found the needle in the haystack?

Kevin stretched across from her. His long legs spilled off the end of the seat, partially blocking the aisle, and she could tell by the way he chewed his thumbnail that he was anxious.

'They won't fire you for being late once,' she said.

'I know. I really wasn't thinking about that.' He straightened up and scooted over to the seat on the aisle, making sure he wouldn't have to raise his voice to be heard. One old woman rode at the front, her little rolling grocery cart close by her side as if it contained gold. 'What are you going to do now?' he asked. 'I mean, you didn't really prove that's the dude who came to your house in the middle of the night.'

She didn't hesitate. 'It's him,' she said.

'Really?'

'Really. It's him.'

They stopped at a light, the engine rumbling in idle. The air-conditioning worked hard to keep them cool, and Ashleigh pinched the fabric of her T-shirt between two fingers and tugged it back and forth, adding to the breeze.

'Do you think this guy might be getting ready to leave town? Not paying rent, not hanging around. Do you think he heard someone was asking about him?' Kevin asked, his voice low. 'Maybe the people you asked at his old job told him.'

'What was I supposed to do? Ignore it?'

'No, no.' He held out his hands. He was placating her, which always made her even more angry. 'I'm just saying, this guy — if he really knows something — doesn't want to spill it yet.'

'He showed up at our door.'

Kevin raised an index finger. 'In the middle of the night.'

'He said he'd come back.'

'But he hasn't yet. He could be in trouble with the police. He could be scared. Think about how you would feel if someone came around asking questions about you. You'd freak out. He doesn't know who you are, does he? Or what you want.'

'Fuck you.'

'Ash, come on — '

'You heard me. Fuck you.'

The old woman at the front of the bus turned, her lips pursed. Ashleigh swallowed hard, felt her anger rise.

'Don't be like that,' Kevin said. 'But if we'd

34

told the police or an adult, maybe they could have . . . I don't know . . . handled it better.'

Ashleigh pulled the bell. 'This is your stop,' she said.

The motion of the bus stopping rocked Ashleigh in her seat. She heard Kevin stand up and take two steps up the aisle.

'Hey,' he said. 'You coming?'

'You know where I'm going,' she said.

'You want me to come with you?' he asked.

She didn't respond. Kevin was keeping the bus waiting, but he said one more thing.

'I'm just worried that this guy might be trouble. What if he's dangerous? What if he wants to hurt you or your mom for some reason?'

Ashleigh heard him. His words registered within her, but she didn't give him the satisfaction of seeing any response. She stared straight ahead and froze him out until he turned and pushed through the side door of the bus, leaving her alone.

★  ★  ★

Ashleigh knew where her uncle had died. She'd been there many times. The Norbert Rovin Memorial Park sat two blocks north of their house, the house Ashleigh shared with her mother and grandfather, the house her mother had grown up in. Adjacent to the park stood a thick cluster of trees — several acres' worth. The land for the park had been set aside not long after the town's founding, and over the years houses and neighborhoods sprung up around its

35

border. Kevin lived with his family on the opposite side of the park from Ashleigh, which made it a convenient meeting place.

Ashleigh walked the two blocks from the bus stop to the park. She knew — seemingly since her birth — that her uncle had been murdered in the woods near their house. Over the years, a process of eavesdropping on adult conversations combined with her own investigations at the local library had allowed Ashleigh to know the facts of her uncle's death as well as anybody else. Her Uncle Justin had gone to the park with her mom on a hot summer day. Eyewitnesses — both adults and children — remembered seeing a young black man in the park talking to some of the children, including Justin. When her uncle disappeared, the police made a sketch of the man and searched for him. Volunteers and professionals combed the woods near the park, then expanded their search to remote areas around town — ponds and culverts and abandoned houses. While the search for the boy — or his body — went on, police began to learn more about the man in the sketch. A woman came forward four weeks after the disappearance and told police her nephew — seventeen-year-old Dante Rogers — liked to go to the park Justin had disappeared from. She also said he had been acting strangely since the boy's disappearance, and had even started collecting newspaper articles about the case. When the police investigated Rogers further, they found he had once been arrested — as a juvenile — for improper contact with a child. They took him

36

into custody, where he denied his guilt.

That summer had remained hot. For the six weeks after her uncle's disappearance, the Midwest baked under record heat. The search parties tailed off. Then the weather broke. The temperatures cooled and the area was soaked with several days of heavy rain. Hoping the weather change might aid the search, the volunteers looked again, starting in the woods near the park. Apparently, the recent rain had disturbed the earth enough to reveal the skeletal remains of her uncle, who had been buried in a shallow grave in the woods near the park, not far from a walking path. Police charged Dante Rogers with the second-degree murder of Justin Manning.

As long as Ashleigh could remember, she had asked her mother to show her the place where the crime had occurred. As a child, Ashleigh couldn't articulate why she wanted to see that spot. She just knew she felt curiosity about it. Only as she grew older did she feel she fully understood the fascination that place held for her.

It was simple, really: everything for her family had changed that day in the park. If her uncle hadn't been killed, if her mother hadn't been there . . . who knows how things would be different? Would her grandfather be less distant and cold? Would her mother be stronger and have a more fulfilling life?

Her mom took her to the crime scene once and once only. Ashleigh was nine and had been bugging her mother to take her there. Her mother always refused. She didn't give Ashleigh good reasons for not doing it — she just flat out refused. But one day Ashleigh asked, and her mother — somewhat reluctantly — agreed.

'I'll show it to you,' she said. 'But then that's it. I don't want to hear about it anymore.'

Ashleigh knew — even as a child — that she had probably just worn her mother down. Ashleigh possessed a rare persistence, a determination that she sometimes believed could chip away at glaciers if she set her mind to it.

But, looking back, Ashleigh wondered if her mom wanted to tell Ashleigh something by taking her to that place. Did she want — symbolically or psychologically or emotionally — to pass a torch to her daughter, even though she was only nine years old?

Whether her mother intended it or not, Ashleigh felt that is what had happened that day. Her mom rarely spoke of her uncle's murder, but Ashleigh became fascinated by it. She went to that place in the woods as much as she could — sometimes once or twice a week. Ashleigh couldn't say for sure why she went. She liked the isolation, the quiet, and the mystery. It was her place, a hiding place. And being there didn't creep her out or scare her. What was scary about it after all? The body was long gone, and except for the occasional drug arrest or fight between teenagers on the basketball court, nothing dangerous ever happened in the park.

Ashleigh walked past the playground where she'd started her day. More kids were playing there than early in the morning. The swings were filled, the chorus of kids' voices and screaming rose like a million crickets. It almost hurt her ears. Parents watched from the side, chatting with each other or else talking on cell phones. If they noticed Ashleigh at all — any of them — they likely dismissed her as a typical moody teen, sulking along the edges of the park in her dark T-shirt and dirty jeans. Ashleigh knew appearing disaffected had its advantages — people tended to leave you alone.

She easily found the path through the trees and started toward the place where her uncle had died. The growth was thick from summer, the trees a vibrant green, the mosquitoes and gnats swarming around her face and hands. She thought about Kevin's words on the bus. She'd been pissed at him before, usually over some minor slight that only Ashleigh understood. She knew she had a tendency to lash out at people — especially those closest to her — and then later regret it. She never really *apologized* to Kevin. She never actually said the words 'I'm sorry' to him. She didn't need to. She'd go to him after one of her blowups and say, 'Kevin, about that thing earlier . . . I mean . . . I didn't mean . . . I wasn't exactly . . . ' And then he'd laugh at her and she'd know she was forgiven.

He was usually right about most things. So she wondered, *Is he right about this? Did I blow it by not getting the cops involved?*

*Could this weird guy from the porch really be dangerous? Could he hurt someone — even Mom?*

She reached her destination. She knew it

because first she passed a tiny pond, one that the police had searched right away looking for her uncle's body, and then the path opened up just a little, spreading out for about ten yards and becoming a small clearing. She knew Uncle Justin's remains had been found just to the west of that open clearing, several yards into the woods where the undergrowth grew thick in the summer heat. The place looked like — nothing. She wondered every time she came how many other people trudged through here — bird-watchers, hikers, teenagers looking for somewhere to smoke or drink or fuck — without even knowing that someone's life, a child's life, had ended on that very ground. It seemed like something should mark the locale — a plaque or a marker or something. But the only plaque to her uncle was in the cemetery — a small, simple one. She never went there. If the soul was separate from the body, then what was the point of going to where the body was buried? More than likely, he was there in the woods — or his spirit was — if spirits or even God existed the way everyone seemed to believe.

Ashleigh sat on a stone at the edge of the clearing. It had a smooth top, perfect for sitting. The day her mom brought her here they didn't do or say anything. Ashleigh expected her mom to want to pray or at least make some sort of statement about what happened, but she had kept her mouth shut. She stared at the ground, her lips pressed into an odd shape, and after about ten minutes said to Ashleigh, 'Come on, let's go home.'

As far as Ashleigh knew, her mother had never gone back to the woods. And as Ashleigh sat there in the clearing, listening to the chirps of the birds or the occasional distant shout from the playground, she knew she saw that as a weakness in her mother, this refusal to take things head-on and really deal with them. And Ashleigh believed her mom had done nothing to find out more about the man who'd shown up on the porch that night. She hadn't pursued him or investigated him in any way, leaving the burden to fall to Ashleigh. And Ashleigh couldn't help but judge her mother even as she tried to help her.

She clenched her fists, squeezed them as tight as she could until her fingernails dug into the skin of her palms. She believed the man who came to the door that night really knew something, and being so close to finding the key, so close to bringing home the answers her mother needed almost hurt —

She would do it her way. She'd find the answers everyone needed.

Ashleigh loosened her grip. When she was a kid and she felt this way — scared, nervous, alone — her mother told her to pray. It worked back then. She slept with a rosary under her pillow — one that had belonged to her grandmother — and fingered the beads when she heard noises in the house and couldn't sleep. But that hadn't worked for years, not since long before that man showed up in the night promising to return. Ashleigh still went to church. Her mom dragged her early every

41

Sunday morning and every holy day, and they sat on the side near the front. Ashleigh went through the motions of the Mass, repeating the words and standing up and kneeling without even thinking about it. She suspected most people in the church were doing the same.

She believed her mom's conviction, though. Her mom went through Mass with her eyes closed and her head down, and after Mass they never failed to go to the front and light a candle, slipping a dollar through the slot as a donation. When she was little, Ashleigh used to ask whom they were lighting a candle for, and her mom always gave the same response: 'My brother.'

Ashleigh shut her eyes in the clearing. She heard the distant hum of a leaf blower, the rustle of the tall trees as the breeze picked up. But she kept her eyelids closed. She watched the weird starburst patterns that exploded on her retinas, shifting swirls of green and red. She mouthed one word:

'God.'

She felt nothing. She felt alone. She didn't even feel connected to the trees and the grass. Did praying even matter? Did all the time she and her mom spent in church really amount to anything? It all seemed like a fantasy. And Ashleigh wondered if there had really been a man on the porch that night speaking to her mother. Had she dreamed it? A child's dream? She'd never spoken to her mother about it, so how did she know it really happened?

'God?'

Nothing.

She opened her eyes, and it took a moment for them to adjust to the bright sun. Impulsively, she raised her right hand to her mouth, kissed it, and then cast the 'kiss' toward the ground where her uncle's body was discovered, a gesture that felt a little childish and immature. She'd never done anything like it before, but something about the gesture just felt right, almost required.

Ashleigh pushed herself to her feet. She knew she had to get home. She knew the reporter was coming by their house, and her mother had begged her to be there for the interview. 'It sends the message that we're all united in this,' she had said.

But Ashleigh couldn't convince herself to believe that either. It too felt like a fairy tale, a child's myth. Her grandfather never spoke about his dead child or dead wife, and the man barely gave the time of day to Ashleigh or her mother. Ashleigh couldn't say why, but she even felt a distance between herself and her mother. She thought about it often, searching for the source, and could only conclude that it had to do with the sadness of her mother's life, the black cloud that seemed to hang over everything the woman did. Ashleigh knew a better daughter would have reached out to her mother, talked to her about it, and tried to be the support system she so clearly lacked. But Ashleigh couldn't bring herself to do that. She feared the wellspring of emotion that might pour out if the two of them even tried to talk about something real. Instead, Ashleigh decided to take the indirect approach. She'd find the man from the porch, and in the process, she'd find the truth about her uncle's death. That would help her mother. That would put everything back on track.

When she first heard the twig snap, she assumed she had made the noise. Ashleigh looked down and saw that she was standing on dirt with no twigs nearby.

The noise came again, and when Ashleigh looked up, toward the same path to the clearing she had just come down, she saw the man looking at her, his body frozen in place next to the pond. A green scum was growing across the surface of the still water.

She recognized him. Didn't she?

He was black. His eyes were large, the lids heavy and droopy. The man looked tired. Not like someone who hadn't slept well, but rather like someone who had been knocked around, someone whose life had encountered a series of wrong turns and dead ends. The man's eyes widened when he saw Ashleigh. He looked guilty, as though he had been caught doing something he shouldn't be doing. Ashleigh didn't think — didn't know if — the man would even recognize her.

But she knew him. She had seen his picture in the paper that very morning.

'Hey,' she said. Her voice sounded low, tentative. She felt as if she were in a dream, the kind in which she would try to cry out but her voice wouldn't make a sound. To prove this wasn't a dream, she spoke again, her voice finding itself and rising louder beneath the trees. 'Hey.'

The man started backing away. He held up one hand, the palm toward Ashleigh. She thought he wanted to say something but could manage only the gesture. And what did that gesture say to her?

*Stay away from me.*

No, that wasn't it, Ashleigh decided. It was something else, something more benevolent.

*I'm sorry.* Is that what it said? *I'm sorry.*

The man turned away and started jogging. He didn't move fast. Ashleigh took several steps after him but then just as quickly stopped. Why would she run after him? What would she do if she caught him?

What could she have to say to Dante Rogers, the man who'd killed her uncle?

# 7

Detective Frank Stynes brought his car to a stop, then checked his face in the rearview mirror. *Sick*, he thought. *I look sick*. The air-conditioning in his city-owned sedan was on the fritz, so he drove to the Mannings' house with the windows down, the hot summer air swirling through the car, rearranging his remaining strands of hair into a comical mess on his head. Without fail, his allergies kicked in with the arrival of the first official day of summer. The whites of his eyes were more pink than anything else, and the tip of his nose was red from repeated blowings. A good day to meet the press and pose for photos, he thought as he climbed out.

Stynes couldn't remember the last time he had been to the Manning place. Five years, maybe seven. Whenever Dante Rogers had been up for parole the last time, and Stynes had gone over to brief them all on what to say before the board. Whatever he told them or whatever they said worked — for a time. But after twenty-two years of being a model prisoner and repeated claims of being a born-again Christian, Dante was released back into the community. And so Stynes came to the Manning house one more time — probably the last — to commemorate the twenty-fifth anniversary of the murder of a four-year-old.

Stynes's right hip creaked as he climbed out of the car. He needed to have it replaced — so his doctor told him — and he planned to have it done as soon as he retired. He'd do that in two years, when he turned fifty-seven. He'd opted to stay in for the full thirty. He told himself because he wanted the full pension and then some, but he knew the truth. Some people looked forward to traveling after retirement. Others to gardening or time with the wife and kids. Stynes had been a widower for four years, no kids. He hated to travel and paid a neighborhood teenager to cut his grass and pull weeds out of the cracks in the sidewalk. As far as he could tell, all he had to look forward to in retirement was a new hip.

The Mannings lived in a decent middle-class neighborhood in Dove Point, one planned and built in the sixties that had always housed schoolteachers and bank managers and sales-people. Kids ran or rode their bikes through the streets, and everyone spent their weekends grilling burgers or washing their cars. Janet Manning told Stynes she had moved back in because her father was contemplating early retirement. Stynes read between the lines of what she said, and he understood. Her dad — a guy a few years older than Stynes — had been laid off and didn't think he could find another gig. *At least you have that going for you, Stynes,* he said to himself. *Bad hip or not, no one is forcing you out.*

Stynes climbed the steps to the porch, and just a few seconds after he'd hit the bell, Janet Manning opened the door.

'Hello, Detective,' she said, stepping back so he could enter. The living room caught a lot of light through the open curtains, and the place looked clean and orderly. Stynes assumed the woman's touch — either Janet or her daughter or a combination of both — kept the house looking in good shape, but then stopped himself for being sexist. Maybe her dad liked to keep a neat house? Maybe he spent his enforced retirement vacuuming and dusting? The thought depressed Stynes more than he could have anticipated. He caught a quick flash of himself tending to his own little house — cooking meals on one burner, washing one dish and one cup in the sink . . .

Maybe he could land a private security job or do some consulting once the hip was fixed . . .

'So,' he said, 'you're back in the old homestead.'

'The house you grow up in always seems like home, doesn't it?' Janet said. She looked trim and fit in her work clothes, and despite the grim news they discussed, her voice and movements possessed a lively energy. 'And with me working so much, and Ashleigh in her teenage years, I thought it would be good to have another parental influence around.'

Stynes nodded, but he could tell Janet wasn't fully convinced by what she was saying. He'd always liked Janet Manning. Even as a kid, in the swirl of her brother's disappearance, she seemed pretty tough. As a seven-year-old, she didn't cry or act scared when they interviewed her in the wake of the disappearance. Over the years, she always put on her best face and marched to the parole hearings without hesitation. Stynes knew her mother had died about seven years after her brother, and somewhere along the way Janet ended up pregnant and raising a kid by herself. He never knew — and never asked — who the father was. But she worked and supported herself, and Stynes sensed a measure of ambivalence about moving back into her childhood home. No independent person wanted to move back in with Dad. They did it, but they didn't like it. Stynes concluded that if he'd had a daughter, he'd want her to be like Janet Manning.

Janet pointed to an overstuffed couch, so he sat. The TV played a political show with the sound down, the screen dominated by a wildly gesticulating host in a tricornered colonial-style hat. 'Dad watches that junk,' she said, turning the TV off. She sat in a love seat perpendicular to the couch.

'You've done all this before,' Stynes said, 'so I don't see that I have to give you any pointers.'

'About that,' Janet said. She scooted to the edge of her seat. She rubbed her hands over the tops of her knees as though trying to generate heat. 'Do you think — I mean, why am I doing this? Rogers is out now, and everything is over. Do I really have to do more interviews?'

'You don't have to do it,' he said. 'No one can make you.' She nodded a little, so Stynes went on. 'People in Dove Point remember the story. We haven't had many murders here since I was on the force. Certainly none involving children. I encouraged you to do this when the reporter called because I think it's important we remind people of what has happened and what can happen, even here. To be honest, this is twenty-five years. It's probably the last time you'll have to do this.'

Janet still looked distracted. She nodded, as though she understood everything Stynes said and as though it made sense to her, but something told him it wasn't all getting through. He watched her and realized how young she really was despite all she'd lived through. She was only in her early thirties, a young woman from where Stynes sat, staring down the barrel of retirement.

'If you want,' Stynes said, 'you can beg off. I'll deal with the reporter.'

'I don't want to inconvenience anyone.'

'Is something wrong?' Stynes asked. 'You really seem to be struggling with this.'

'Do you think — ?' She stopped. She stared at a fixed point somewhere in the space between her and Stynes. 'I guess that article about Dante Rogers got me thinking.'

'About what?' Stynes waited. Janet didn't answer. 'Are you afraid? Do you think he's going to hurt you or your family?'

'No, not that,' she said. 'He looks so pathetic in the picture.'

'That's what twenty-two years of being in prison for killing a child will do to you.'

Stynes hoped that he could turn the conversation in a different direction, move the focus to the punishment of Rogers rather than

Janet's doubts or anxieties about the past or the present. But who was he to think he could play psychological mind games with the family member of a crime victim? Stynes was who he was — an aging detective in a midsized Midwestern town, a guy who had investigated three murders in almost thirty years as a cop. He too had seen the pathetic picture of a doughy, paunchy Dante Rogers in the morning paper, and like Janet Manning he even felt the questions rise in his own mind: had this guy really lured a little kid away from a playground and killed him? Unlike Janet Manning, Stynes was supposed to know better. Regular-looking people committed awful crimes every day. Appearances didn't tell the whole story. They never did. Circumstantial or not, Dante Rogers was guilty. He had served his time.

But Stynes held his own doubts, had held them for the past twenty-five years. Sure, they'd done everything right while they investigated the crime, and the case — circumstantial though it was — held enough water to put Rogers away. Stynes fell back on an old trick, one that had served him well ever since the jury returned with a conviction against Dante Rogers: he told himself to forget about it, to not dwell on things from the past that didn't need to change. It was over, long over. More important, it was time for everyone to move on.

'Maybe if you think of this as the last time you have to answer these questions, it will make it easier,' Stynes said.

Janet nodded but didn't seem convinced.

'You know, Janet — ' Stynes began. He shifted forward on the couch. He'd always wanted to say something to her but never felt the time or moment was right, even when she was a kid. He decided to take his chance. 'No one blames you for what happened. It wasn't your fault.'

Janet looked surprised by what he said. Her eyes widened a bit, and Stynes worried he'd overstepped his bounds and said the wrong thing.

'Thank you, Detective,' she said.

'I hope you don't mind me saying so,' he said. 'I've worried sometimes — '

Janet shook her head and smiled, and Stynes saw the smile contained a hint of bitterness.

'I'm not worried about that at all, Detective,' she said. 'In fact, these days, that's the least of my concerns.'

# 8

Janet let the reporter in and wondered if some kind of mistake had been made. The girl — woman? — looked too young to be a newspaper reporter unless it was for her high school paper. The only difference between the whip-thin blonde girl entering her living room and Ashleigh's friends from Dove Point High was her clothes, which looked impeccably professional. Knee-length skirt, white top, black pumps, and a leather bag to match. The girl — *woman* — introduced herself as Kate Grossman of the *Dove Point Ledger*, and she apologized for being late, even though she wasn't.

Stynes stood and shook hands with Kate, and they all settled into their seats. Kate sat on the opposite end of the couch from Stynes, and Janet noticed the detective take a quick, admiring peek at the reporter's backside before she sat down. Janet looked at the reporter and then at Stynes. The contrast was striking. The reporter looked to be fresh out of college. Her hair was long and yellow and shined with such good health that Janet involuntarily raised a hand to her own hair and touched her split ends. Detective Stynes looked older than Janet knew him to be. His hair was thin and wiry, and his small physique and below-average height — Janet guessed he was about five feet seven — made him seem more like a high school math teacher than a police detective. He walked with his shoulders slumped a little, as if some unseen weight rested there, pushing down ever so slightly. But she liked him. He tried to reassure her. He just didn't understand — or *know* — everything she knew.

'I'm so glad you took the time to talk to me, Mrs Manning,' Kate said. Her eyes widened when she spoke, as though every word lifted her to a new level of excitement.

'Miss Manning,' Janet said. 'Or Ms. Just not Mrs — I've never been married.'

'Right. Of course.' Kate placed a handheld tape recorder on the table.

'Excuse me,' Stynes said. 'It was Richie LaRosa who covered this story the last time there was a parole hearing.'

'Mr LaRosa?' Kate said. She put on an exaggerated frown. 'He's taking an early retirement, even though he's only in his forties. A lot of the more experienced reporters at the paper are.'

'Oh,' Stynes said.

Kate shrugged. 'I begged my editor to let me cover this for the paper. It's my first big story. Shall we begin?'

Kate's sorority-girl good cheer had already irritated Janet. Shall we begin? Let's sing a song! Let's talk about your awful personal tragedy!

'Miss Manning — '

'Janet's fine.'

'Great,' Kate said. They were old friends already. 'Okay. Janet, is your dad, Bill Manning, is he going to talk to us today?'

'I don't think so.'

The young woman frowned a little. 'Is it too hard for him to talk about it?' she asked.

'Something like that.'

Not only would Dad not talk, but Michael wouldn't either. Janet checked her watch. Just after two. He could still show, she told herself, but even as she had the thought she doubted it.

Stynes stepped in. 'I've found over the years that Janet is an excellent advocate for her family. She was always very eloquent before the parole board.'

'Well, Janet.' Kate leaned forward a little. 'Can you talk a little about what it's been like to live without your brother all these years?'

Janet took a deep breath. What had it been like? She'd managed to control — most of the time — the fantasies she used to indulge in, the ones in which she imagined Justin hadn't died and had instead spent the last twenty-five years growing up, maturing, becoming the young man — and brother — Janet wanted him to be. A college graduate, a businessman, a husband, a father . . .

'I think about it every day,' Janet said. 'I guess I feel like I've been cheated out of something.'

'All those years?'

'Yes. My whole family. I have a daughter who will never know her uncle. I wanted her to know him.' Janet cleared her throat. 'She said she'd be here today . . . She must be running late.'

'Are your memories clear of what happened the day Justin disappeared?' Kate asked.

*What happened that day, Janet?* Michael had

asked. She wanted to say she was surprised he didn't show up for the interview, but she wasn't. Reliability and predictability had never been his strong suits. Janet learned that early on, during childhood. Why would anything change now, all these years later?

But why show up at her job, asking that question?

*What do you remember from that day, Janet?*

'I can't forget,' Janet said. 'It's something I'll never forget. My mom sent us to the park to play, just the two of us.'

'Was that unusual?' Kate asked.

'Yes, it was,' she said. Then she added, 'That was the first time that ever happened.'

'Why do you think she did that?' Kate asked.

Janet had been wondering the same thing for twenty-five years. And she had never asked her mother. 'Maybe she just needed some time alone. She thought we were old enough to go to the park alone and give her a little break. There were a lot of people there.'

Kate nodded. *Go on.*

'We played,' she said. 'We ran around. We went on the slides. We went on the swings. There were other kids there, and a lot of parents. We weren't alone. And Michael showed up, and we all played together.'

'This is Michael Bower?' Kate asked.

'He was my best friend.' Janet decided not to mention having just seen Michael and asking him to come to the interview. 'His parents and my parents were friends, so we played together a lot.'

'Now, at some point, you saw Dante Rogers there, right?'

'Yes,' Janet said. She didn't think about her answer. She had said the same thing so many times over the years — to the police, to the prosecutor, to other reporters and the parole board — that she didn't even have to think about it. She just said it — yes. But had she really? Did she know anymore that she had seen Dante Rogers in the park?

'You saw Dante with your brother, right?'

Yes, she did. Janet closed her eyes for just a moment, and she saw the image: the park on that hot summer day. And there was her brother with a black man she had never seen before. That picture was always there in her mind, available for easy summoning.

But did she really see it? How could she know after all this time? And why would someone else — the man on the porch — claim to know otherwise? And why would Michael ask that question at work?

What do you think really happened that day, Janet?

Janet opened her eyes. 'A lot of people saw Dante in the park that day. He was there, and so were we.'

'And let me just be clear,' Kate said, 'Dante has never denied being in the park when Justin disappeared. Never.'

'But he denies killing Justin.'

'I totally understand that this is tough,' Kate said. *Totally.* Kate shifted in her seat a little, scooted closer to the edge of the couch, so that

Janet thought Kate might reach out and take her hand. 'Now, do you remember what happened next? I mean, when did you notice that Justin wasn't there?'

Janet found herself easing back a little, away from Kate. Something about Kate's behavior seemed too familiar, too cloying, and she knew the young woman just wanted to get a good story. She probably hoped Janet would cry so the opening line of the feature would read, *Through heavy tears, Janet Manning remembered her brother today . . .*

'I'm not really sure about that part.'

'Did you notice it, or did someone tell you?' Kate asked.

'I'm just not sure,' Janet said. 'I know Michael was there. I know I must have mentioned it to Michael. Then a bunch of adults were there. My mom. Michael's dad. All of the adults and the police and the reporters . . . ' She felt the tears misting her eyes, saw the room swim in her vision a little. She fought back against them, refused to give in. *Don't be an ass,* she told herself. *You're not saying anything new here.* She took a quick swipe at her eye with the knuckle of her right index finger, then straightened up. She saw Kate clearly in her vision. 'He was just gone then. Gone.'

Kate nodded. Her mouth was pressed into a tight, sympathetic line. *I feel your pain,* the young reporter's look said. *I get it.*

But she didn't. It was just an act, and Janet knew it. Just like all the people at work and in the town and even Detective Stynes. None of them really understood it. Only Michael. He was there . . .

'Why don't I turn to you then, Detective,' Kate said. 'I really appreciate the two of you talking to me together — '

'I want to say one more thing,' Janet said.

Kate nodded. 'Of course.'

'I've been meaning to say this for a while, so I want to say it now. I hope you can work it into the story.'

'I'll try.'

'I do have one regret about all of this,' Janet said. 'It's that my mother and brother aren't buried next to each other. We buried Justin in one part of the cemetery, and when Mom died there weren't any plots next to Justin. And we can't afford to move him. I want to see that done someday. I know she'd want it that way. They both would.'

Kate kept right on nodding. 'That's really powerful,' she said. 'And I totally get it. I'll try to work it in.'

'Thanks,' Janet said.

'Okay,' Kate said, turning to Stynes. 'I guess it's your turn now.' She gave him a flirtatious smile. 'Was this a tough case to investigate?'

'Of course. The disappearance or death of a child is always difficult.'

'Right,' Kate said. 'And have there been a lot of cases like this in Dove Point? I just moved here from Oxford a year ago.'

'We've been fortunate,' Stynes said. 'Major crimes aren't a big problem in a city this size.'

59

'You must not have been a detective for very long,' Kate said.

'Only about a year. I'd been on the force longer than that.'

'And what was the key to solving the case and making an arrest?' Kate asked.

Janet watched Stynes while he answered the questions. He seemed thoughtful, almost professorial as he spoke, but she detected something beneath his words, something that always seemed to lie beneath his speech and his gestures. The man seemed, for lack of a better word, tired. Weary, Janet guessed would express it better. Early in the morning, in the middle of the day, whenever she saw Detective Stynes he looked like a man weighed down by something, and that force seemed to be drawing his facial features a little lower, adding slack to the skin around his jaw, slowing his legs when he walked. Janet knew he didn't have a wife — at least he never mentioned one — and no children. She wondered if that weight had to do with his personal life, or was it something else?

'Like we just heard,' Stynes said, 'Janet was there in the park that day, and so was her friend Michael Bower. They were both small children themselves. Seven years old. But they *did see*' — Janet noticed the emphasis he placed on those words — 'a man talking to Justin. So they told us, and we had a sketch artist draw a composite of the man they saw. We circulated that through the media. Dante Rogers's aunt — he was living with her at the time — thought the sketch bore a strong resemblance to Dante and called us. We went and talked to him and found out he was at the park that day.'

'And I understand he had a stash of child pornography in his room,' Kate said, her reporter eyes narrowing just a little at the mention of the juicy detail.

'We did find some pornographic materials in his room,' Stynes said, his voice level. 'He also had a prior arrest for improper contact with a minor child. In addition to the pornographic materials, Dante had a collection of newspaper clippings about the case. And his aunt said his behavior had changed after Justin's disappearance. He had become withdrawn, moody, paranoid.'

'Janet said that there were a lot of adults at the park that day,' Kate said.

'A number of adults testified to seeing Dante in the park that day. They saw him talking to Justin and some of the other children.'

'But Dante always said he was innocent, that he didn't hurt Justin.'

'Dante still says he's innocent,' Stynes said. 'I read your story this morning.'

Kate's cheeks flushed, and she suppressed a little smile. But the gesture almost seemed too practiced, too awshucks. Could someone train her body to blush at will?

'I'm so glad to hear that. This is my first big series, and I'm kind of nervous about it.'

'It's my experience, Miss Grossman, that whether you catch someone drinking and driving or you're dealing with Dante Rogers, people almost never admit what they did wrong. If they did, we'd have a more efficient justice system.'

'Right.' Kate leaned back in her seat and raised her pen to her mouth. She chewed on the end, her straight white teeth taking a few quick chomps on the plastic. Janet sensed Kate had something she wanted to say but wasn't sure how to say it. She removed the pen from her mouth and looked at Stynes. 'Okay, so like I said, I just moved here to Dove Point. This is my first job. But I've noticed that there really aren't a lot of black people here in Dove Point. Right?'

'It depends on how you define 'a lot,'' Stynes said. 'We're kind of a smaller town.'

'Do you remember, Detective Stynes, if anybody on Dante's jury was black?'

Stynes took a long moment to answer. 'I don't think so.'

Kate nodded and chewed the pen again. She wore a look that said, *Isn't that interesting?* She probably dreamed she could win a Pulitzer for exposing racism in the jury selection procedures of a sleepy Ohio town.

'He had a lawyer defending him,' Stynes said.

'A public defender, right?' Kate said.

'That's usually the case for people in Dante's situation.'

'You mean people without a lot of money?' Kate asked.

'I guess that's what I mean.'

'And I know . . . ' Kate tapped the pen against her wrist. 'I know Dante's lawyer asked for a change of venue and was denied.'

Stynes didn't respond.

'Do you know how much experience his

public defender had?' Kate asked.

'I wouldn't know.'

'Well.' Kate reached out and picked up the tape recorder. 'I think I have enough for the story now.' She turned the recorder off and dropped it and her pen into her oversized bag. 'I do appreciate the time you took to talk with me. If I need anything else, I can just call you guys, right?'

'Let me be clear about something,' Stynes said.

Kate stopped what she was doing and gave him her full attention. Stynes didn't raise his voice or lose his cool, but he did seem determined to speak his mind to Kate Grossman.

'We did a solid investigation here,' he said. 'We had the witnesses, and it went to a jury. It even stood up on appeal.'

Kate nodded. 'I know, Detective. It's my job to ask these questions.' She reached into her bag again and brought the tape recorder back. 'Do you want to say something else on the record? I can add it.'

She flipped the switch and held it out toward Stynes, who looked at the recorder like it might bite him. He cleared his throat and leaned forward.

'The world was a better place with Dante Rogers behind bars,' he said. He punctuated his words with a quick nod.

Kate recognized her cue, shut the recorder off, and put it away.

Janet didn't know if Kate picked up on what

she had — a key element of Detective Stynes's final statement. He'd said the world was a better place with Dante Rogers behind bars.

Given the chance to say so definitively, he didn't say he thought Dante Rogers was guilty. He didn't say that at all.

# 9

Stynes walked Kate to the door and watched her stroll down the walk — her young hips moving back and forth — and climb into a new red Honda Civic. A graduation gift from Dad, Stynes figured, watching her drive away. Most of the reporters he knew drove older cars held together by rust and prayer. One more reason to resent her, even if she did look good both coming and going. A rich college girl turning over the race card. Stynes felt his back molars grind against one another. *Let it go. Let it go.*

He turned to say good-bye to Janet and found her standing right behind him in the doorway. Before he could say anything, he saw the look in her eyes. Something pleading, almost fearful.

'Don't worry about that stuff — '

She cut him off with a nod of her head. Toward the porch. She wanted to talk outside.

Stynes held the door, and they stepped out into the heat of the late afternoon. The sun glanced off the chrome and glass of the parked cars. The street shimmered. Stynes didn't sit, but Janet did. She settled into a lawn chair and looked up.

'I just wanted to talk about all of that,' she said, pointing toward the general area where Kate's car had been parked.

'Like I said, don't worry about it. She's just a kid trying to make a name for herself. She thinks a race angle might play big in a story like this. Little does she know people in Dove Point would rather attend free colonoscopy day at the hospital than dwell on racial issues. It probably won't even get into the story. I know the features editor at the *Ledger* — '

'I don't mean the race stuff,' Janet said.

Stynes shifted his feet. He wore a suit coat over a polo shirt, and he felt the sweat forming on his back. He had about two hours of paperwork to do back at the station, and he wanted nothing more than to get home in time to watch the Reds play the Cardinals. For the first time in years, the Reds had a prayer of reaching the playoffs, and Stynes wanted to enjoy it. The simple things, he called them. The simple things.

'Which stuff do you mean then?' he asked. 'You just mean her questions? Did they upset you?'

Janet turned her head and looked over her shoulder to the front door, wanting to make sure her dad wasn't there listening. When she was satisfied he wasn't, she spoke in a low voice. 'She seemed to be suggesting that Dante Rogers is innocent,' Janet said.

'No, she wasn't — '

'And I was wondering the same thing,' she said, her voice still low but forceful. 'Did you have enough to convict him?'

'We did convict him.'

'But like Kate said, in Dove Point — '

'Hold on.' Stynes held both hands out in front of him like he wanted to push something away.

66

The sweat ran faster down his back and sides and suddenly the thought of his air-conditioned office seemed even more appealing than Kate Grossman's backside. 'Don't let this girl get into your head. The story this morning, this interview — it's all just talk. It doesn't change the past.'

Janet nodded. She looked mollified, and Stynes took quiet pleasure in having found the right words for the right situation and shutting things down effectively. He sometimes thought the ability to talk, to placate, to smooth ruffled feathers in the heat of the moment was the most useful skill any cop or public servant could have.

'Janet, call me if — '

'Was the evidence against him just circumstantial?' she asked.

Stynes deflated. *So much for my placating skills*, he thought.

'This isn't *CSI: Dove Point*. We don't have oodles of DNA and fiber evidence when someone commits a crime here. Usually, someone knows the person or knows someone who knows the person, and nobody is surprised when they find out who did what to whom. Now, we had witnesses who saw Dante with your brother, including you, and we had the pornography and the newspaper clippings, the prior arrest, and the testimony of his aunt. Twelve citizens of this community listened to the evidence and rendered a verdict. Who cares if they were white or black?'

Stynes waited again while Janet processed his words. He thought he'd made another good pitch, but while Janet didn't say anything else, she didn't look at peace with his explanation.

'Janet?' Stynes asked. 'Is there something else at play here? Why are you so worked up about this?'

Janet looked back to the door again, her lips pressed into a tight line.

'Is this about your father?' Stynes asked. 'Is he upset about something?'

She turned back around, shaking her head. 'It's something you said. Or didn't say, I guess.'

'What did I say?'

'When that reporter asked you about Dante's trial and conviction, you didn't say he was guilty.'

'Yes, I did.'

Janet shook her head with more force, like a dog in the rain. 'You said the world was a better place with him behind bars.'

'What's the difference?'

'You didn't say he was guilty.'

Stynes raised his hand to his forehead. He wiped droplets of sweat away, then brushed his fingertips against his pant leg. Wasn't it the same thing? Wasn't it the same thing as saying he was guilty?

'Maybe it was a mistake to have you do this interview,' Stynes said. 'Maybe it's just bringing up unpleasant memories for you. Like I said, this is probably the last time you'll have to do this. Maybe it just needs to be over for all of us.'

'Were there other suspects?' Janet asked. 'Was there anything that indicated it wasn't Dante?'

'Has someone been talking to you about this?' Stynes asked. 'Is it Dante? Did he try to talk to you? Because the conditions of his parole — '

'No.'

'I can't help you or even protect you if you don't tell me.'

Janet took a long time to answer, but then she shook her head. 'There's nothing wrong, Detective. No one is bothering me.'

'You're sure?'

'I am.'

Stynes paused, examining her face. She didn't reveal anything. She didn't crack or speak. If there was something going on — and Stynes suspected there was — she wasn't ready to give it up to him. Not right then. Stynes checked his watch and told her he had to get back to the station.

'But you know how to reach me if you need something, right?'

'I do. Thanks.'

Stynes went down the walk, his mind turning over the events of the past hour. Not just the reporter's questions but Janet's as well. His own doubts were stirring, like silt in the bottom of a clear streambed.

*And how do you plan to navigate these troubled waters, Stynes? What are you going to do?*

# 10

Ashleigh walked home from the park. She took the long way, exiting the park closer to where Kevin's family lived than on the side near her own house. She wanted the extra time to think. She ignored the heat and let her mind work, trying to process what she'd seen — *who* she'd seen — in the middle of the woods.

As soon as Dante ran off and disappeared from sight, Ashleigh regretted letting him go. She wished she had continued after him, running hard so she could catch up and ask him what he had been doing at the place her uncle died. The question circled in her brain. And even while she thought about it and imagined catching up to the man, a more rational, more logical voice spoke in her brain as well: What would you do if you caught up to him? Tackle him? Punch him? Take him to coffee? What would a fifteen-year-old girl do with a convicted murderer?

Ashleigh put her hair up as she trudged along in the heat. The sun beat against the back of her neck, but she minded that less than the stickiness of the sweat that plastered her hair to her skin. She passed quiet homes that looked cool and comfortable. She thought about the air-conditioned comfort inside them — and she also thought about the normal lives their inhabitants led. No one behind those doors and windows was caught up in pursuing crazy leads in a twenty-five-year-old murder. Were they?

But Ashleigh knew the truth. No, they might not be doing that exactly, but every home contained some craziness. She knew that from the kids at school. Alcoholism, abuse, infidelity. Her friends saw it all. Despite all her complaints about her mother and grandfather, they didn't subject her to anything awful. But, still, a murder in the family past stood out as pretty crazy . . .

She hadn't even called or texted Kevin. She would eventually, but she didn't want to call him at work, especially if he'd already been made late by their trip to Steven Kollman's apartment.

And then there was the other part of it.

She felt a little weird — sometimes — talking to Kevin about Dante Rogers because of one simple fact: Dove Point contained a fair share of racist assholes. No, nobody burned crosses on anybody's lawn. And plenty of black people — including Kevin's dad, who handled all the IT for a bank — held prominent positions in town and did very well, but Ashleigh knew the truth. Most people didn't feel comfortable seeing a black guy and a white girl hanging around together. She could tell the way some of them — friends of hers from school and even once a science teacher — asked a question:

Are you and Kevin dating?

She and Kevin were *not* dating — they were just friends. But Ashleigh thought about dating Kevin all the time. She liked to look at his face when he didn't know she was watching, and she enjoyed the electrical charge that coursed through her body if they inadvertently brushed their arms against each other. But they weren't dating. They hadn't even come close. Ashleigh's mom and grandpa acted a little weird whenever Kevin's name came up, but Ashleigh knew that wasn't really about race. She understood that the adults in her family were more worried about her going out and getting knocked up like her mom did in high school.

But sometimes she worried about what Kevin thought. He always acted like he didn't mind. He made jokes all the time about his race, going so far as to refer to the two of them as the 'salt and pepper twins' when they went places together, but she absolutely didn't want him to ever think the views of certain narrow-minded and stupid people in the town had somehow become her own. She didn't want to suffer guilt by association, so sometimes she avoided the topic of Dante.

The house came into view, and every time it did, Ashleigh's heart dropped a little. It wasn't a bad house. The rooms were big enough, and her mom and grandpa did a decent job of keeping it in shape. But it wasn't *her* house. For the past three years, she and her mom had rented a cute little bungalow near downtown on Park Street. The morning sun lit Ashleigh's bedroom there, and they lived side by side with young couples and college kids. At least once a month, Ashleigh asked her mother why they couldn't just move out and get their old place back, just the two of them. Her mom always explained that this was a financial decision, that when Grandpa lost his job he needed help in order to keep the family

72

home. *And besides, Grandpa needs us,* her mom would say. *We're all he's got.*

Ashleigh never said it out loud, but she thought it: He doesn't have me. Only a few more years, and I'm off to college. Ohio State. Miami. Cincinnati. Bowling Green. As long as it's college and as long as it's away.

Ashleigh entered the dark, quiet house. No surprise. Her grandfather liked to keep the place closed up and sealed. Like a bank vault. Or a morgue. Both Ashleigh and her mom went around behind the old man, opening blinds he closed or pulling open curtains he'd yanked shut. Ashleigh liked windows and air and light. The house on Park Street had had all of those things.

She stopped in the kitchen for a quick glass of water, then planned on slipping up to her room. She hoped her mother wasn't home, that she wouldn't have to face the usual interrogation. Her mother's questions were the bane of her existence. *Where were you? Who were you with? Why did you go there?* She knew her mom was still a little freaked by her uncle's death, but come on. *I'm fifteen. Fifteen.*

Ashleigh could just imagine her mom's response to where she'd just been. *First I tried to find the creepy guy from the porch. And then I saw the guy who killed your brother — at the crime scene.*

'Ash?'

Ashleigh froze, the glass of water halfway to her mouth. Her mother must have been upstairs, maybe even napping. Ashleigh wanted to slip away, but knew she couldn't.

'I'm here,' Ashleigh said, giving in. As much as her mom annoyed her, Ashleigh found it hard to be outright mean to her. Or ignore her. If they were all her grandpa had, Ashleigh knew she was all her mom had.

Her mom came into the kitchen. She was wearing a T-shirt and sweatpants and looked tired. Maybe she had been asleep. Her hair looked flat, her face without makeup.

'Where were you all day?' her mom asked.

'I was with Kevin.'

'Where?'

Ashleigh sighed. She took a long drink of water, then filled the glass again.

'Don't sigh,' her mom said. 'Where were you?'

'We went to see a friend, but he wasn't home. So then Kevin had to go to work, and I came home.'

'You've been gone since before I went to work.'

'Mom, please? It's summer. You said as long as I kept my grades up — '

'Do you know why I'm mad at you?'

'Mad at me?'

Her mom's brow was furrowed, the lines at the corners of her mouth deepened and exaggerated. She looked ugly when she was like this. She looked like life was chiseling its marks onto her face.

'You were supposed to be here today,' her mom said. 'That reporter came by.'

Shit. The reporter.

'I forgot.'

The words sounded hollow even to her own ears. Her voice came from far away, its sound tiny, like a little kid's. *Shit*, she thought. *I really forgot.*

'I don't think you appreciate what this means to me,' her mother said. 'To have this reporter come here and to have to talk about those things. Your grandpa doesn't want to talk about them, so I count on you.'

'I said I was sorry, Mom.'

Ashleigh saw the tears forming in her mother's eyes, little pools of water that threatened to spill. Her mother rarely cried. And whenever she cried, Ashleigh felt the same way. She'd do anything on earth to stop it from happening.

But the tears didn't spill. Instead, her mom seemed angry, ready to lash out.

'I swear, Ashleigh, I'm the only one here who really cares about this family. The only one who cares about what happened in the past and who cares to do anything about it now. Do you know how frustrating that is for me?'

The only one who cares about what happened in the past? The only one who cares to do anything about it now?

Ashleigh felt her own anger rise. She slammed the glass on the counter, creating a mini geyser of water. It drenched her hand and the counter.

'You've got a lot of nerve saying that to me,' Ashleigh said.

'Don't act that way.'

'What are you going to do about it?'

'You can't talk to me that way.'

'You're the one stuck in Dove Point, living in

75

the same house you grew up in,' Ashleigh said.

Ashleigh regretted the words as she said them, but she couldn't stop. And when they came out, her mother lifted her hand to her own mouth, reacting as though she'd been slapped.

'Ashleigh,' she said. All she managed, her voice just above a whisper.

'Mom, I'm sorry — '

Then the tears really did come. Her mother turned away, went up the stairs and back to her room, leaving Ashleigh behind.

And as soon as she was gone, Ashleigh knew what she wanted to say to her mom. What she should have said:

*If you really knew what I was doing today . . . And if only you knew I was doing it all for you. Only for you.*

# 11

The call came just after nine in the evening. Janet was in her bed, the TV playing low. They were all in their rooms in the house, each of them isolated and locked in their own worlds. Janet let the phone ring. She figured it was a call for Ashleigh. No one ever called Janet or her dad.

But the phone kept ringing. Either Ashleigh was wearing her headphones in her room and couldn't hear it, or else she was letting it ring as a protest in response to the fight.

Janet answered.

'Hey,' the still familiar voice said. 'It's me.'

'Michael?'

Her heart started to thump. She felt almost breathless.

'What are you doing?'

'Watching TV.' She regretted the admission. So mundane. 'I mean, there's a movie.'

'I was hoping we could talk more,' he said.

'Sure.' Janet reached over and muted the sound. She sat up. 'Do you want to come over? We could sit on the porch.'

Michael laughed a little. 'I'm guessing your dad is home, right?'

'He is.'

Janet understood. Her dad wasn't a fan of Michael. He still thought of Michael as the shaggy-haired, partying wild man from high school. And Ashleigh's father, Tony Bachus — now married and living in Florida — hung out with Michael all the time back then. Her dad associated the two boys so closely that neither one was allowed on the Manning property after Janet became pregnant.

'I was thinking of neutral territory,' Michael said. 'Do you know the coffee shop downtown? It's open until eleven in the summer.' His voice carried mystery, like he knew things others didn't know. Even something as trivial as the coffee shop hours. 'Can you meet me there?'

Janet didn't hesitate. 'I'll be there in fifteen.'

★   ★   ★

But when she stepped outside, into the hot, still night, something felt different. Too calm. Too quiet. Janet stopped in the driveway, halfway between the house and the car, the keys dangling from her hand. She listened.

At first, she heard nothing but typical night sounds. The chirps of the crickets, the soft hum of a neighbor's air conditioner. She waited and started to tell herself that she was being paranoid, that her stressed-out and emotionally tired mind was playing tricks on her, but then she heard it. Two quick sounds close together, the muffled thump of leather hitting the ground.

Footsteps? Someone running away?

Janet turned her head toward the back of her dad's property where the sound seemed to originate, but it was dark and her eyes hadn't adjusted to the night. She strained her eyes, squinting.

Had she heard anything at all? Had it just been a dog, a jogger, a falling branch?

Janet turned back to the house. She went to the back door and gave it two solid tugs. It was locked. Dead-bolted. She looked up at Ashleigh's window, where the light still burned. Janet considered going back inside and staying home, where she belonged, but she cut the thought off before it took root. Who said she belonged at home? Janet had never wanted to be that person — that woman — and she turned away from the house and back to the car, knowing her father was home with Ashleigh.

Janet hadn't told anyone she was leaving. She left a note on the kitchen counter. *Back in a bit*, it said. She felt guilty being so abrupt, but a part of Janet was still angry with her daughter. Typical teenage boundary pushing, she knew, but how dared the little snot mouth off like that?

Ashleigh wasn't the only one who could act immature, and immature was the right word for it. Janet felt like a teenager again, sneaking out of the house to see Michael. Jumping when he called, her body filled with a buzzing intensity at the sound of his voice. She felt it again that night as she drove away from the house — the same feeling she'd had in the parking lot. A pleasant tingling, the hint of possibility.

A traffic circle formed the center of Dove Point's downtown. Like spokes on a wheel, four main streets radiated out, and businesses, all of them locally owned, ringed the circle. At night,

79

parking was easy, and Janet found a spot two doors down from the coffee shop. She paused in the car, checking her face in the lighted vanity mirror behind the sun visor. Before leaving the house, she'd brushed her hair, trying desperately to bring it to life, and dusted some makeup across her face. She thought she looked tired, her eyes still a little puffy from crying, but a part of her didn't care. This was Michael. He knew what she looked like. He knew who she was.

Still, she reached into her purse and pulled out a lipstick. It belonged to Ashleigh. Janet wasn't sure how it ended up among her things. Maybe Ashleigh had left it in the bathroom once, or maybe Janet had found it sitting on the kitchen counter and tried it on herself. It didn't matter. Janet almost never wore lipstick, but she opened the tube and ran some across her lips, then blotted with a Kleenex. She studied herself again. A nice touch, even a little sexy. She was trying.

But before she slipped out of the car, Janet pulled out her phone. She sent a text to Ashleigh: *How are you?*

Janet waited twenty seconds for a response: *Um, fine. Why?*

Janet wrote back: *Just checking*. And got out of the car.

Two teenagers, a giggling young couple, came out of the shop as she went in. They looked to be close to Ashleigh's age, and probably attended Dove Point High with her. The kids looked so healthy, so happy, so all-American in their earnest devotion to each other. So normal.

Would Ashleigh ever know that worry-free life? Would the weight of all that had happened to their family always burden the girl?

Michael waved when she came through the door. He was seated at a table halfway back in the little shop, a steaming mug in front of him. He gave a quick tilt of his head, the smile she always remembered spreading across his face. Janet went over. She settled into the seat across from him and ordered hot tea from the waitress.

'You got out past the old man,' Michael said.

'Like being a kid again.'

Michael smiled. The tea came, and she took a tentative sip. It warmed her, but not as much as knowing that she and Michael shared a past, one that extended to the present. 'He really never did know everything that went on right in front of him,' Michael said. 'Out of sight, out of mind.' He shook his head. 'I remember the time he caught us taking a fifth of whiskey from his liquor cabinet. He acted shocked that we even wanted to drink.'

'I don't think he'd care if you came over now,' Janet said. She opened two packs of sugar and dumped them into the cup. 'It's Tony he's really mad at. You know, he still doesn't remember to send Ashleigh a birthday card every year.'

'Do you ever talk to him about it?'

'No way. My dad is the closest thing to a male role model in Ashleigh's life. He's certainly not perfect, but he provides something. Some stability, I guess. He's like a rock that's always there. That's part of the reason I moved back in with him. Of course, Ashleigh doesn't seem to

81

need much of anything.'

'She doesn't see Tony?' Michael asked.

'She doesn't even ask about him,' Janet said. 'She understands who he is and the role he's played in her life so far. I've raised her to be self-sufficient. Too self-sufficient sometimes.'

'And she never says she misses him or wants to see him?' Michael asked.

'She's pretty strong-willed. And quiet. I'm trying to figure out if she has a boyfriend.'

'Really.'

'She has a guy friend she used to bring around all the time. They'd play games at the house, watch TV. Now they spend all their time together, but she never brings him to the house. Makes me wonder.'

'Maybe they're just being teenagers.'

'Or maybe the kid's afraid of my dad.' She stirred and sipped again. 'How about *your* dad? How's he?'

Michael's face changed. Like someone dropped a curtain or threw a switch, the happiness that had been there since she walked in the door evaporated.

'We're not really talking right now,' he said.

Janet studied his face longer, waiting for more. She noticed the flecks of gray at his temple, the sprinkling in the stubble on his chin.

'Sorry,' she said.

'It's fine, you know,' he said, recovering some of the life in his eyes. 'He and I just don't agree about the world. We never have. I accepted it a long time ago. He just can't get outside his world, you know? He's trapped in it. He only sees the things right before him, this conventional life he leads as a bookkeeper. And anything outside of that is invisible.'

'A lot of parents are like that.'

'I was in Portland for a while.'

'Oregon?'

Michael nodded.

'Wow,' Janet said. 'I've never been.'

'I met a lot of people out there who think for themselves, who aren't hung up on all the little things people are hung up on here. People like my dad. Everything here is so stuffy. I don't know how long I can stay.'

Janet felt her heart drop at the words. She took a drink of the still too hot tea. 'Portland,' she said. 'You know, it's been a few years since I've even had a call or an e-mail from you. At least once a year I'd hear something from you, even just a lousy Christmas card. You even used to come back here from time to time. I was trying to remember how long it's been since I've seen you. Wasn't it Christmas about five years ago?'

'I know,' he said. 'I've had a lot on my mind. I've been distracted.' He smiled at her, and she knew he hoped that would make everything better. 'I'm here now.'

'And how's your mom?' she asked.

'She's okay,' he said. 'She's lost weight, you know, a lot of weight, and she has high blood pressure.'

'I see her from time to time around town. She's always so nice and asks about me and Ashleigh.'

'The years have been hard on her.'

'She's never married anyone else, has she?'

'God, no,' Michael said. 'The divorce ripped her up.' He shook his head. 'She hasn't been the same since.'

'My dad either,' Janet said. 'Since Mom died.'

Some kids at the next table were playing a game. It involved stacking wooden blocks as high as they would go and then gently trying to pull out the ones at the bottom without toppling the whole structure. Jenga? Was that it? One of the kids sent the whole pile down, a great tumbling of wooden pieces across the table and onto the floor. They all groaned and laughed. And again Janet thought of Ashleigh. Such a serious kid. How often did she laugh like that?

'I couldn't make it today,' he said. 'I know you wanted me to see that reporter, but I couldn't make it.'

Typical Michael. He wouldn't apologize for not showing up. He'd just say he couldn't make it.

'I wanted to talk to you about that,' she said, thinking back on Stynes's words. She'd been turning them over ever since the detective left and coupling them with the words spoken by the man on the porch that night.

'I said I just couldn't make it.'

'I don't mean that,' she said. 'I don't care about that. The reporter was just a little college girl. She wanted to score some kind of big scoop, I guess. She was annoying and pretty.'

'Pretty?' Michael perked up.

Janet knew he was joking, but she still felt a twinge of envy. He was free to come and go. If he wanted to give Katie College Girl a call and ask her out, he could. He wasn't beholden to anyone, unlike Janet.

'I meant to tell you how good you look,' Michael said.

'Me? Right now?'

'You look young,' Michael said. 'You haven't changed that much since high school really.'

Janet felt her face flush. 'Anyway,' she said. 'I wanted to talk to you about what you said today on campus. You asked me what really happened at the park that day, and I just wanted to know what you meant by that. Why did you ask me that question?'

Michael looked around, his eyes restless like they were in the parking lot. This evasiveness was a new trait. When they were kids, Michael didn't look away from people. He didn't avert his eyes from things. If you asked him a question, he answered it.

Janet waited until he was ready to talk, the clacking of the wooden Jenga pieces and the teenage conversation the only sounds she noticed.

'You think about that day a lot, don't you?' he asked.

'I do.'

He looked away again, eyes restless still. 'I do, too,' he said. 'Almost all the time lately.'

'Why? Did something change?'

'My parents getting older, I guess. Thinking about that and the anniversary got me thinking about it. I can't think about home without thinking of that day.'

85

'That seems normal to me.'

'I guess a lot of people around here think about it,' he said. 'That's why they did the newspaper stories, right? How did that go with the reporter?'

'It was a little tough talking about it,' she said. 'I didn't expect it to be. I really didn't. I hadn't talked about it since the last parole hearing, I guess. I don't talk about it with Dad. Or with Ashleigh.'

'Did you read the story about Dante Rogers?' Michael asked.

'Yes. Did you? Did you have the same reaction I had?'

'What was that?'

Janet tried to think of what she wanted to say, but there seemed to be only one way to say it. 'I felt sorry for him.'

Michael was nodding. 'Exactly,' he said. 'I felt that, too.' He licked his lips and leaned in, lowering his voice. 'And I couldn't help but think he's a victim, too.'

'How?'

'It's the system, Janet,' Michael said. 'A black man like Dante in a town like this — what chance does he have?'

'That's what the reporter was asking about today.'

'Was she?'

'Yes.'

'I wish I'd been there now,' he said, shaking his head. The waitress came and brought refills. Coffee for Michael, hot water and a new tea bag for Janet. When the waitress was gone, Michael continued. 'We put him there, Janet,' he said. 'We threw him into that system.'

Janet had never thought of it that way. She told the truth to the police when she was a child. She saw that man in the park, and when they asked, she told them. She had never stopped to consider everything else that went along with it. She'd been a kid then, only seven. She didn't think of the larger implications.

'I asked you that question on campus because I really wanted to know,' he said. 'What do you remember from the park that day? What did you see?' Despite the importance of the question, he didn't seem to want an immediate answer. He pressed on. 'I'm not sure anymore what I saw. I know what I told the police, and I know they acted on it. And I know they arrested Dante and put him on trial. But I'm not sure anymore if I remember what I saw, or if I remember what I think I saw. I don't know if I can trust my own memory anymore.'

'Michael, I have something very important to say about that.'

'When I was in Portland and again in LA, I took some recreational drugs to try to regress my memories back there. I did some hypnosis, too, with a therapist, but I didn't trust it. I didn't think I could really get back to that place.'

Janet was ready to jump out of her chair. 'Michael,' she said, 'I need to tell you something.'

'What?'

'There's a man,' she said. 'And this man came to my house. And he says he knows what really happened in the park that day.'

Michael froze in place for a long moment, his lips slightly parted. 'What do you mean?' he finally asked.

She told him the story of the man coming in the middle of the night, appearing on the porch out of the blue and spinning his strange tale. Janet told Michael that she kept waiting for him to come back, to explain what he meant by his cryptic words, but that so far he hadn't returned. While she spoke, Michael listened. He didn't interrupt, and he didn't ask questions. He just listened, his face rapt. Janet knew that not only would Michael be fascinated by the story, but he would listen to her without judgment. He wouldn't laugh. He wouldn't call her crazy. She knew this about him, and so he became the first person she had ever told.

'That man on the porch,' she said. 'Sometimes I think he's just like that day in the park. Sometimes I can't really believe that he came to the door. I'm the only one who saw him. I don't know him. He didn't give me anything. He appeared like a ghost. In fact, I know I'm overreacting, but I thought I heard someone in the yard when I left the house tonight. I almost didn't come because of it. I thought it might be that man and maybe he meant to hurt someone. Ashleigh. Or me.'

'But you came.'

'I figured I was being silly. And I just texted Ashleigh in the car, and she's okay.'

Michael shook his head. Just a little, but the shake was there. He looked surprisingly agitated.

'See, you need to forget about this guy,' he said.

'Why?'

'He sounds like a kook. Aren't you worried he's dangerous? Coming to your house in the middle of the night? What if he is sneaking around the yard? What if he's crazy?'

The same thoughts occupied Janet's mind at least once a day. She wasn't naive. She knew sickos got kicks from tormenting the families of crime victims. She knew strange men shouldn't be knocking on the door in the middle of the night.

'I know,' she said.

'Did you call the police?' Michael asked.

'The guy said not to.'

Michael looked satisfied, his point made. 'See.'

Janet felt uneasy leaving the house sometimes, wondering if the man watched what she did, making sure she didn't contact the police. Did he see Stynes at the house that very day?

'Forget about this guy, Janet. He's a creep. Tell me, answer the question — what do you remember from that day?'

Janet looked down. An oily sheen had formed on the top of her tea, swirling around in the wake of her stirring. Janet had been asking herself this question — really asking it — for the past three months, ever since the man appeared on the porch raising questions of his own.

'It was hot. Very hot.' She looked up at Michael, and he nodded. So she went on. 'And Justin and I were there first. We were playing in the park, and then a little while later you showed up.'

'See, I don't remember that, but I believe you. I thought I was there the whole time.'

'It wasn't long before you came,' she said. 'I remember what you were wearing. I can see that. Shorts and a long belt.'

'I remember that belt.' He smiled.

'Yeah. It was goofy.' Janet paused a moment, then went on. 'I saw Dante with Justin. I saw him talking to him. And I think I saw him carrying Justin on his shoulders. Way up high.'

'Right. I thought I remembered that, too.'

'But you don't?'

'I don't know,' he said.

'What do *you* remember?'

He paused a long time, drawing the moment out like a good actor would. He rubbed his chin with his right hand. 'I think Justin ran away. Don't you? I think I remember him running into the woods.'

'Are you sure? I don't remember him running away. I don't really remember anything that happened after he was on Dante's shoulders. I don't even know what order those memories come in.'

Michael had a look of focus on his face. He didn't seem to hear Janet's words. 'I think he ran away and into the woods. There was a dog in the park, not much bigger than a puppy. And a bunch of the kids were playing with it. And Justin was fascinated by that dog.'

'He loved dogs,' Janet said. 'I remember that. He wanted one. We both did, but my parents didn't want one. My dad always said he'd end up taking care of it.'

'That dog ran off into the woods eventually. And Justin went after it, trying to catch it. And I have a very clear memory of running after Justin, like I wanted to bring him back to where he was supposed to be.'

'Was it in the direction . . . they found him back there . . . ?'

'It was,' Michael said. 'He ran toward the woods where they found his body, and I went that way, too.'

'And what happened?'

'I went into the woods after him,' Michael said. 'I remember going down that path, past that little pond, following him. I remember the voices from the playground growing fainter and more distant.'

'You were in the woods right then, right before . . . '

A long pause settled over the conversation. Janet didn't realize it, but she had gathered a paper napkin into her hand and was slowly, surely grinding it between her thumb and forefinger, turning the napkin into small, pulpy balls that littered the tabletop. When she noticed the mess, she stopped and brushed the napkin pieces aside, behind the little dish that held sugar packets and artificial sweeteners.

Janet looked at him. 'What is it, Michael? What did you want to tell me?'

'I told you I've been to therapy to try to remember things about that day.'

'Sure.'

'There's something I've been able to remember, something I've never told anyone else.'

91

'What is it?' she asked.

He swallowed once, his Adam's apple bobbing. Janet became aware of the tension in her own muscles. They felt taut as steel cables waiting for Michael's words.

'I think my dad was there in the woods that day. I saw him when I went in there after Justin and the dog.'

The noise in the coffee shop stopped. People were still moving. The waitress wandered from table to table. The teenagers nearby continued to play. But Janet didn't hear them. She concentrated on Michael's face, locked in on him as she processed his words.

'But that's not possible, Michael,' Janet said. 'Your father wasn't there. He wasn't in the park that day. Or in the woods.'

'He was, Janet. I can picture it.'

'What was he doing?' she asked.

'I don't know. That part isn't clear. But I feel very certain about this, Janet. My father was there in the woods. He was there the day Justin died.'

Even though she hadn't seen Michael for years, since he'd moved away immediately after high school, and even though they had rarely spoken in that time, Janet still trusted Michael almost as much as anyone else she knew. She felt she could tell him anything, and he would listen without judgment.

'Michael.' She picked up another napkin and went to work on it. 'There's something I want to say, too, something about Justin.'

The room still felt still and quiet, a bubble that

enclosed them both. Michael nodded, encouraging her to go on.

'That man who came to the house,' she said. 'His face — it's frozen in my mind. All I have to do is close my eyes, and I can see him. Every detail, even though I only saw him once.' She stopped working on the napkin. 'There's something familiar about his face. The shape of it, the color of his hair. The shape of his eyes and the prominence of his chin. I see my dad there, Michael, when I think of that face. I see Justin.'

'Justin?' Michael looked confused. 'Where are you going with this?'

'Michael, sometimes I think, I really, really think that man who came to the door? I think that man is Justin. He didn't die that day in the woods, and he's back to tell us all what happened.'

'Oh, Janet,' he finally said.

'You think I've lost it. You think I'm mad with grief and guilt — '

'No, no, I didn't say that at all. I think it's natural that you have a lot of emotions connected to this, Janet. It's a huge rent in your life.'

'But?'

She felt her cheeks flush — embarrassment this time and not desire. How awful to be embarrassed in front of Michael. She didn't want that. Never that. Even after all those years, she still couldn't help but feel he was the cool kid she had to impress.

'Think about what you're saying,' he said. 'You saw this man once.'

'How is what I'm saying any less valid than what you said about your dad?'

'There was a body, Janet. They found a body in the woods. Right in those woods Justin ran into. I'm not trying to be dismissive, but is it really possible?'

Michael's words restored some reality. They were a splash of cold water against her face. What was she thinking? Michael was right — they'd found a body. They'd had a funeral. Everyone else had moved on, years ago.

What had she seen in that face? A real resemblance? Or did she simply see what she wanted to see? Could her memory of that man's face be trusted any more than Michael's memory of his father in the woods?

Janet felt tired all of a sudden. The day had whipped her — the reporter, Michael's return, the conversation with Stynes, the fight with Ashleigh. Work waited for her in the morning, and she contemplated doing something she never did — taking a personal day and spending the entire day in bed.

She knew she wouldn't. But it sounded tempting.

'I should go,' she said. 'It's late.'

Janet dug in her purse for her wallet. She tossed some bills onto the table, intending to cover the cost of Michael's coffee as well as her tea.

'We can talk about this more, Janet. I want to.'

'Of course.'

'I think we both have a lot we're working through from that day.'

94

'I'll call you,' Janet said.

She stood up, expecting him to walk out with her or at least make sure she made it to her car safely. But Michael stayed seated. As she turned to go, he signaled the waitress and asked for a refill.

# 12

The desk officer approached Stynes, who was hunched over his keyboard entering reports from the last two days. He hadn't had a spare moment to get caught up, and he'd entered the station that morning — early, before anyone else had arrived — with only one thought in mind: *Give me some peace and quiet.*

The desk officer approached cautiously. Stynes saw her coming out of the corner of his eye, but he didn't look up. He was hoping she wouldn't notice him and would just walk past. She was a new recruit, kind of timid, and Stynes didn't know her name yet.

'Detective?'

'I died and didn't leave a forwarding address.'

'Excuse me?'

Stynes looked up. The girl was pretty, but so, so young. Another reason to retire. When the new recruits looked like high schoolers, it was time to go. 'Wishful thinking on my part. What is it?'

'There's a woman here, and she needs to see a detective.'

Stynes pointed to the computer. 'Does this promise to be as fascinating as yesterday's stolen purse or last night's vandalism at the school?'

'She says she has a complaint about Dante Rogers,' the young officer said.

'Dante Rogers?'

'Yes, sir. You know, he's the guy — '

Stynes held up his hand, cutting off the rookie's words. 'I know who he is.'

Stynes had spent the past two days going about his business as a cop, all the time trying to reassure himself that there was nothing to what the reporter had said, nothing to Janet's nervousness and doubts. But here was Dante Rogers — again — and he seemed to be falling into Stynes's lap, insisting on being heard.

The day did just get a little more interesting, he thought to himself.

★ ★ ★

Stynes drove east out of downtown, taking High Street, one of the four spokes off Memorial Circle. For a short time he passed businesses — a pizza parlor, a Laundromat, a bike shop — then his car rattled over an uneven set of railroad tracks, traveled down an incline, and — presto — he entered what passed for a black neighborhood in Dove Point. Literally and figuratively, at least in the minds of most of the town's white citizens, the wrong side of the tracks.

There was truth to back up the belief. More crime happened on the east side — East Dove Point, as some had taken to calling it. A public housing project as well as a collection of run-down low-rent apartment complexes meant a lot of transients, a lot of comings and goings and drugs. A murder was still rare, but assaults and gun-related crimes were up. What was that

97

movie? The one with the crazed killer — *No Country for Old Men*. Stynes felt that way when he drove over to the east. He was too old for this shit and thankful he had only a couple of years to go. He couldn't imagine what East would look like in another decade.

Stynes made two turns, a right and a left. He knew everyone in their yards and on the street corners made him out as a cop. Even the little kids. The shiny car, the white man in a shirt and tie. They looked at him like he was an alien, the contempt dripping off their faces. Stynes stopped in front of the Reverend Fred Arling's First Church of Zion, a low brick building with an overgrown yard that looked no more like a church than Stynes's car looked like a fighter jet. A sign out front advertised the upcoming sermon: WHO IS YOUR BROTHER? WHO IS YOUR NEIGHBOR?

Before Stynes climbed out of the car, his cell phone rang. He recognized the number and answered.

'I was just thinking of you,' he said.

'Why?' the familiar voice answered.

'I was thinking about being old and retired, so naturally I thought of you.'

'Fuck you.'

Terry Reynolds was Stynes's first partner. They'd worked the Justin Manning murder together. Stynes would never say it out loud — certainly not to Reynolds — but he owed his former partner a great deal. He learned more about being a cop just from watching Reynolds work than from anything else. Reynolds had been retired for close to eight years. He'd remarried and spent his days playing with his grandchildren and digging in his garden.

'Guess where I am?' Stynes asked.

'A home for bald-headed perverts?'

'I'm at Reverend Arling's Zion Church.'

'Jesus. Did you do something wrong in a previous life?'

'You know who works here, right?'

'Did you get a message saying I wanted to play Trivial Pursuit over the phone?'

'Your boy, Dante Rogers.'

A long pause. Stynes could hear Reynolds breathing. 'Really,' he said. 'Shit, I saw in the paper he was working in a church, but I didn't put it together that it was that one.'

'Someone came in today and filed a complaint about him.'

'What did he do? If he violates, we can send his ass right back — '

'That's what I'm here to find out, boss.'

'I never understand why these guys don't move out of state. Everybody in fucking Dove Point knows who he is. If he sneezes on somebody they're going to call the cops.'

'I was planning on calling you when I was done here,' Stynes said. He looked out his window. Two kids went by on the same bike. One of them pedaled while the other perched on the back. They laughed when they saw Stynes. 'I was going to give you an update on Dante, and I wanted to talk to you about some other stuff. You have any time?'

'I have nothing but time, unless Jeannie sends

me to the store for a loaf of bread.'

'Or more adult diapers.'

'I saw that story in the paper yesterday, the one with you and the Manning woman.'

'Yeah?'

'Nice of the reporter to make the whole town look racist.'

'She's a kid.'

'I don't miss that shit, I tell you.'

Stynes gathered a pad and pen from the center console and slipped them into his jacket pocket. 'I've got to go in here now,' he said. 'But I'll call you later. We can get together.'

'Sure,' Reynolds said. 'And give Reverend Fred a message from me.'

'What would that be?'

'Tell him I said, 'Fuck you.''

★   ★   ★

The Reverend Fred Arling stood six feet tall and was rail thin. His mostly gray hair had receded half the distance across the top of his large head. He opened the side door wearing a black suit, white shirt, and narrow black tie. He looked at Stynes over the top of small gold reading glasses and smiled.

'Detective.'

'Reverend.'

'Here to be saved?'

The reverend stepped back and showed Stynes down a short hallway into a small room that served as an office. The room was surprisingly clutter free — as opposed to Stynes's own desk, which swam in paper — and smelled like it had just been cleaned. A new laptop sat open on the desk, and next to it was a well-worn, leather-bound Bible.

'Are you running a special?' Stynes asked.

'Always.'

The two men sat on opposite sides of the desk. The reverend's posture made him seem even taller than he was, and Stynes wondered what it was like for a member of his flock to sit down in this room seeking guidance or forgiveness.

'I understand you have Dante Rogers working here,' Stynes said.

'Let me guess,' the reverend said. 'A woman named Letitia Myers came to see you.'

'Go on.'

'Sister Myers read the newspaper story about Dante, saw that he was working here in my church, and — how do you white folks say it — had a cow?'

'She doesn't think a convicted child killer should be working in a church around small children.'

'Did she accuse Dante of something?'

'Not directly.'

'Are you here to arrest him?'

'Not yet. But just being around small children could be seen as a violation of his parole. There are restrictions on where he can go and what he can do.'

The reverend removed his glasses and leaned forward, folding his hands on the desk. 'Let me explain something to you, Detective. Do I look like I'm stupid? Do you think I'd let a man who might harm children, or harm anyone, around my congregation?'

'Why is he working here?' Stynes asked.

'Detective, I'm sure you can imagine what it would be like for a middle-aged black man, three years out of prison, with no education and not much in the way of smarts to begin with, to try to get a job? Don't you think a church like mine has a role to play in making a brother's life a little more tolerable? I counseled Dante when he was in prison, and then I continued that work after he got out. About a year ago, I gave him the chance to work at the church part-time, and he never, ever works with or around children. Now, I didn't make a big deal out of him working here. I didn't exactly tell any members of my congregation he was doing it. I figured if he wasn't working with the congregation, then no one needed to know.'

'You might want to reconsider that stand,' Stynes said. 'You're just going to get more complaints. I know you're not a for-profit operation here, but how are you going to keep the donations flowing in with someone like Dante around?'

'I have a higher calling to answer to.' The reverend raised his right index finger and scooted back.

'Is he here?'

'*He* is everywhere.'

'I mean Dante. And keep in mind his parole officer already told me he's working here today.'

The reverend shrugged. 'Then I guess this humble servant of the Lord has no choice but to

102

let you by. Dante is back in our literature room right now, stuffing envelopes. When he's finished, I'm going to treat the brother to lunch and a little Bible study. If you or Sister Myers object, I can't change that.'

'I would like to talk to him,' Stynes said.

'Two doors down on the left,' the reverend said, pointing. 'And go easy, Detective. Dante is a little skittish.'

Stynes stood up. 'Dante remembers me,' he said. 'And don't I look like a gentle man?'

'Do you want to investigate a real crime, Detective?' the reverend said. He pointed to his computer. 'Three hundred dollars missing.'

'From where?'

'From my accounts,' he said. 'We're a small church here, and we can ill afford to lose even a small amount of money.'

'Sounds like you need better bookkeeping software,' Stynes said.

★   ★   ★

Stynes found Dante hunched over a stack of envelopes and paper. Two large folding tables filled the center of the room, both of them covered with church flyers and literature, but Dante worked alone. The room smelled musty, like a long-closed closet. Dante didn't look up when Stynes came to the door.

Stynes had seen the photos of Dante in the paper, but they didn't convey completely the toll the years had taken on him. At the time of his arrest, Dante's body had possessed a leanness.

He looked like someone who ran track or cross-country. But there was nowhere to run in prison. Even though he was only forty-two, his face bore enough lines to make him appear ten years older, and a puffy double chin hung beneath his gray stubble. His shoulders were slumped. He seemed to be concentrating with great force on each individual task he performed in the 'literature room.' Fold. Stuff. Seal. Dull work, but Dante made it look particularly arduous, like each piece of paper weighed fifty pounds.

'Dante?'

He stopped what he was doing and slowly turned his head toward the door. His eyes had always been big, but they looked sad and pathetic after the prison time. A whipped dog's eyes.

'Do you know who I am?' Stynes asked.

'Yes, sir.'

'Tell me. Who am I?'

'Cop.'

'You know why I'm here?' Stynes asked.

'Checking up on me.'

Stynes came into the room and sat down across the two tables from Dante. Dante followed Stynes's movement with a slow turn of his head and a wary tracking of his big eyes. Stynes pointed to the piles of paper.

'You like doing this?' Stynes asked.

Dante shrugged. 'It's okay, sir.'

'Reverend Fred treat you okay?'

'Yes, sir.'

'You messing around with any little kids?'

Dante's head jerked higher. His eyes widened. 'Oh, no, sir. No, sir. Not at all.'

'Lot of little kids in this neighborhood,' Stynes said. 'I saw them when I came in. A lot of little kids come to the church. Sunday school. Bible study. Youth groups. This seems like a nice hunting ground for a guy like you.'

'Reverend Fred doesn't let me around the children,' Dante said. 'I don't want to be around them.'

'Oh, come on, Dante. I'm not an idiot. I know what you did in prison all those years. You didn't sit around working through your problems and developing coping mechanisms, did you? You sat around fantasizing about getting out again and getting to where you'd see more little kids. You built up twenty-two years of frustration in there, and now you need to let it out.'

'No, sir. I became a Christian in there. I studied the Bible. I learned to deal with my problems.'

'You admit you have a problem?'

'Had, sir,' Dante said. 'Had.'

For the first time, Stynes saw some life flash in Dante's eyes, a hint that more brewed beneath the surface than was immediately apparent. His answer possessed a sharpness that his other speech lacked.

'You don't want to relive the past?' Stynes asked.

'No, sir.'

'You talked to that reporter. Katie What's-Her-Face.'

'My PO wanted me to do that,' Dante said.

105

'And I thought I could give my testimony in there. Did you read it? I testified. I spoke about how God has helped me.'

'You said you're innocent.'

'We're all guilty of something. Only God can judge.'

'Don't bullshit me, Dante,' Stynes said. 'You said in that story you didn't kill Justin Manning. Is that part of your testimony? Not taking responsibility for what you've done?'

A long pause. Dante considered Stynes from behind the sad eyes. He still held an envelope in his right hand. 'I didn't kill that boy,' he finally said. 'But I've done other wicked things. My interview in the paper was about that.'

'You mean the little kid you diddled before you killed Justin Manning?'

Dante held the envelope in the air between them. 'If you don't mind, sir, I'd like to get back to work.'

'Do you really know why I'm here? Do you know what prompted this visit? Some biddy from this church came to me and complained about you. She said she didn't like the idea of a kid killer and a pervert working in a church. Now what do you think about that?'

'Like I said, only God can sit in judgment.'

'Don't you just want to admit it now?' Stynes asked. 'They can't do anything else to you. You've already done your time. But don't you want to give that family some peace? The Mannings? I saw them just yesterday, and they still wonder about what really happened in that park. They have questions. Wouldn't God want you to just step to the plate and come clean? Wouldn't he want you to say, 'Yeah, I did it, and I'm sorry.' Couldn't that be part of your testimony?'

Dante put the envelope down. He used his hands — the fingers long and thin — to straighten some of the stacks before him. He didn't look at Stynes.

'I'm sorry for that boy's family,' he said. 'I really am. I pray for them and for that boy.'

'Justin Manning. He has a name.'

'I can't admit to something I didn't do.'

'Why don't you sue us then? You were wrongly convicted. Take us to the cleaners. Get a bunch of money and move to the Bahamas.'

'I don't need earthly treasure,' Dante said. 'And besides, I did commit wickedness and needed to be punished for it. Like Christ on the cross, I accepted my punishment.'

'Oh, Jesus, Dante,' Stynes said. 'You're really shoveling it.' Stynes shook his head. The man still didn't meet his eye, and Stynes figured he had pushed about as hard as he could push against someone so obtuse, such a true believer. 'I'm going to have to notify your PO that you're getting too close to little kids,' Stynes said.

'He knows I work here.'

'I'll do it just to be a dick. The PO will probably call you in for a piss test. They like doing that to ex-cons, even ones who don't do drugs. He'll probably even search your room. You better hope you stashed the porn in a good hiding spot.'

'I'd like to get back to work now, sir.'

Stynes went to the door. He looked back one more time.

'Think about doing that, Dante,' he said. 'Think about stepping up and giving that family some peace.'

Dante resumed stuffing envelopes. He didn't even look up.

*   *   *

Stynes stopped by Reverend Arling's office on the way out. The reverend had his head bent over the computer screen, the glasses again perched on the end of his nose. He looked up when Stynes knocked on the doorjamb.

'Ah,' the reverend said. 'Done hassling the brother, are we?'

'His PO might come by and follow up.'

'There's nothing to find.'

'I have a feeling that if you keep Dante around, there will just be more of these visits.'

'Jesus ate with the lepers and the tax collectors,' the reverend said. 'I can handle one wayward brother in my church. But you know what is interesting, Detective? You come here to hassle Dante, but does anyone hassle you about what ran in that newspaper story?'

'What do you mean?'

'I mean that Dante has done his time, paid his debt, but still you come around. Meanwhile, no one questions that all-white jury, that circumstantial evidence at the trial. Why isn't Dante afforded the same consideration as a white police detective?'

Stynes had a lot of things he could have said, most of them not appropriate for the confines of a church. He chose to walk away. 'Save it for the pulpit, Reverend.'

'That's right,' Arling said. 'Walk away. You won't even address the crime being committed against me. This hard-working church's dollars being siphoned away.'

But Stynes was through the side door and on his way to the car. The heat pressed against his scalp and the back of his neck. He opened the car door, slipped off his jacket, and tossed it onto the backseat.

Three hundred dollars? Was it worth it to go back for three hundred dollars?

'Shit.'

Stynes reached into the backseat and grabbed his pen and pad. He walked back to the church, the sweat popping out on his skin.

He couldn't wait for the day he could just walk away and stay away.

# 13

Janet spent her morning at work and the day before that *not* thinking about Michael. She attended a campus-wide meeting of office managers. She met with her boss, Dean Higgins, briefly about writing ad copy in order to hire two new work-study students for the fall semester. She answered the usual never-ending stream of e-mail.

And in spare moments — a short bathroom break, a quick visit to the break room for a cup of yogurt — she pushed Michael out of her mind, reminding herself always that she was no longer sixteen and no longer looking to date the coolest guy in school. Sure, Michael still looked good despite the signs of aging and, sure, she still turned flutter-hearted just being in his presence. But Janet knew who she was — a working single mother with a larger mission in life, one that didn't involve men. She needed to worry about raising her daughter, excelling at her work. Moving forward.

And while she — mostly — managed not to think about any romantic possibilities with Michael, she couldn't stop thinking about what he'd told her and she'd told him:

Michael thought he saw his father, Ray Bower, in the woods the day Justin died.

In and of itself, Janet wouldn't have thought much of the revelation. The Bowers lived close to the park, so maybe Ray was there. Or Michael could have been mistaken, conflating some other memory from his childhood with the day Justin died.

But Janet had told Michael about the man from the porch, and if there was someone else — even this man from the porch — who claimed that the events of that day didn't happen the way everyone thought, then maybe there was something to it, something to be explored more fully.

And Janet hadn't even spent much time factoring in the questions asked by the newspaper reporter —

'There you are.'

Janet looked up from her desk. Her mind was drifting too far, letting thoughts that didn't belong at work grab too strong a hold in her brain.

Madeline stood before her, and as strange as it seemed, Janet wanted to thank her for the diversion, for getting her mind away from problems she couldn't solve.

'Here I am,' Janet said.

'You seem distracted,' Madeline said. 'Ready for lunch?'

'Lunch?' Janet looked at her desk calendar. *Lunch with Madeline.* Once a week the two of them walked to the student center together and either grazed the salad bar — if they were being good — or joined the students in eating the hamburger and fries special if they felt indulgent. Janet suspected today would be a hamburger and fries day.

She needed it. Hell, she even thought she deserved it.

'Let me grab my purse,' Janet said.

They walked across the mostly quiet midsummer campus. Scattered students went by, those taking summer classes, and occasionally they passed a faculty member in their warm-weather wardrobes — shorts and Birkenstocks, pale legs flashing in the sun like the bellies of beached fish. When she felt she had the time, Janet took classes. She had completed half the hours required for a bachelor's degree in history and needed to get back to it. Ashleigh would be gone in a few years, off to college herself, and Janet considered her next, longer-term life project. Finish the bachelor's and then what? Try for a master's? Why not?

'I can't stop thinking about that article.' Madeline held her hand over her heart, like she was about to pledge allegiance. 'Heartbreaking,' she said. 'Just heartbreaking. I had no idea your mother and brother weren't buried next to each other.' Madeline acted as though she should have been consulted about it because she — and she alone — could have prevented it in the first place. 'What are we going to do about this?'

'We?' Janet asked.

'Yes. Have you looked into moving one of them?'

'Justin would have to be moved. The plots on either side of him are taken.'

'Okay. And there's an empty spot next to your mom?'

'Yes, but it's not that easy. You need to pay for

the reburial. You have to buy a new casket.'

'We do have wet weather here. That can cause damage.'

'Believe me, I've looked into it, and we can't afford it right now. It's just — it's a dream, that's all.'

★   ★   ★

They ate their burgers at a small table out of the way. The food tasted better than it had any right to. Janet knew she was feeding her emotions, but she didn't care. Like she said to herself, she deserved the little indulgence. Janet ate quickly, not saying much, which she knew would activate Madeline's radar.

It did — in the form of a motherly hand on Janet's arm.

'Honey,' Madeline said, 'I saw who was in that parking lot the day before yesterday. I know who you were talking to. Is he back in town for good?' Madeline asked.

'I don't even think he knows the answer to that question.'

'He was always a good-looking one.' Madeline sighed as though Michael were the great lost love of her life. 'I know you always had a thing for him.'

'Every girl in the school did.'

'So.' Madeline grinned like a naughty child. She scooted forward in her seat. 'You can tell me. Did you and he ever — you know? When you were young?'

Janet smiled. Despite Madeline's busybody

tendencies, Janet liked having a friendship with an older woman. She liked to imagine that her relationship with her own mom would have developed this way as they both grew older — shared confidences, passed on wisdom. Would she have that with Ashleigh someday? Janet wondered. She knew mother-daughter relation-ships changed with time and the easing of adolescent tensions, but it was hard to picture herself engaging in girl talk with Ashleigh. Did Ashleigh engage in girl talk with anyone?

'No,' Janet said. 'Never. I wanted to. As long as I knew him, ever since we were little, I wanted to be his girlfriend. But I always just followed in his wake, I guess. It would have been awkward, I suppose, with our families knowing each other so well.'

'But not impossible.'

'Not for me,' Janet said. 'But he had plenty of girls to choose from. I settled for' — she paused, trying to think of a number that summed things up — 'fiftieth best, maybe?'

'Let's not even talk about Tony. Please? I mean, he gave you a beautiful daughter and all, but that's just called being a sperm donor.'

'It was a little more fun than that, as I recall,' Janet said, causing them both to laugh.

When they collected themselves, Madeline pressed on. 'So what is Michael doing back in town then? He's barely shown his face around here over the years, and all of a sudden he's back.'

'He lost his job,' Janet said.

'There's a lot of that going around.'

'And he's worried about his mom. I guess her health isn't great.'

'Rose Bower,' Madeline said. 'A very sweet lady.'

'I think he's also thinking about the twenty-fifth anniversary as well,' Janet said. 'Maybe he just wants to be someplace familiar for a change, around people he knows.'

'Maybe,' Madeline said. 'But if he's looking for a port in the storm, be careful.'

Janet rolled her eyes. 'How about one night's shelter?'

'I told you, I'd introduce you to my nephew in Dayton. He's recently divorced and looking to date again.'

'You never give up, do you?'

Madeline finished her fries. 'No. And you shouldn't either.'

But Janet didn't hear Madeline's last comment.

She saw a movement across the room. A man in a blue shirt. She didn't know why this person caught her eye among all the others. But he did. Janet got a quick glance, a brief look before he slipped back into the crowd and out of the cafeteria. The man looked back once before he left. He looked right at Janet.

She recognized him. The short blond hair, the thin frame.

She blinked her eyes but knew the truth: it was him — the man from the porch.

# 14

Stynes saw Reynolds in a corner booth of Judy's Grill, a Dove Point diner and local landmark. For close to seventy years, city council members and county commissioners gathered in the booths, making deals and pulling strings over eggs and coffee. Stynes and Reynolds used to eat there at least once a week. They liked the food and the cheap prices. And they liked to make fun of the self-important politicians.

Reynolds drank from a tall glass of soda as Stynes approached. Stynes noticed that his former partner's hair looked thinner, the skin of his scalp touched with pink from time in the garden. Reynolds chewed on an ice cube as Stynes sat down. He wore a few days' worth of gray stubble.

'Nice to see you, handsome,' Reynolds said.

'Some of us still have to work,' Stynes said.

'I waited to order. You know I'm diabetic now. I have to eat regularly to keep my blood sugar right.'

'Is that why you're drinking a Coke? Your blood sugar?'

'Fuck me,' Reynolds said. 'It's *Diet* Coke.'

Stynes ordered a patty melt, fries, and regular Coke. Reynolds winced as he listened to the order, then asked for a turkey club and a salad.

When the waitress was gone, Reynolds said, 'How was Reverend Fred?'

'Full of God's love. He has his dress over his head about an error his bookkeeper made.'

'Guy has a bookkeeper?' Reynolds asked. 'Isn't that place worth about fifty cents? It's in East for Christ's sake.'

'He's trying to properly render unto Caesar, I guess.'

'He's given sanctuary to more mutts,' Reynolds said. 'Every guy we've ever arrested over in East has passed through Reverend Fred's church at one time or another. Somebody ought to bring him in.'

'For what? Having a messiah complex?'

Reynolds rubbed his hand over his stubble. 'And now he has Rogers there. Jesus.'

'I saw him.'

'Rogers?'

'In the flesh.'

'What the fuck kind of work is he doing?'

'He's the right reverend's administrative assistant and Bible study partner apparently. He was stuffing envelopes when I saw him. Looks like he's aged forty years since he went away. I mean, the guy really looks like shit. He must have had hell's own time inside.'

'Good. I hope someone tore him a new rectum.'

The waitress brought the food. Stynes salted his fries. He was blessed with good genes. No blood pressure or cholesterol problems. He'd never smoked. Reynolds had gone through hell quitting cigarettes fifteen years earlier, and he was still kicking at sixty-eight.

'Look at this shit,' Reynolds said, nodding

117

toward his plate. 'I might as well be a vegetarian.' He took an unenthusiastic bite of his salad. 'What did Dante have to say for himself?'

'Not much. Says he's a born-againer, found Jesus on the inside and did time for his wicked, wicked ways.'

'He confessed?'

'Not to the Manning murder,' Stynes said. 'I think he's just admitting he's a perv, you know?'

'That's headline news.' Reynolds grabbed the salt and sprinkled a liberal amount on his salad and sandwich. 'Speaking of which, what gives with that article? This little bitch trying to stir the pot or what?'

'She's trying to make her bones.'

'I bet the Reverend Fred ate it up with a knife and fork.'

'He did manage to bring it up,' Stynes said. 'Acted like we'd railroaded Dante.'

'Pissant.'

They chewed their food in silence for a while. Silverware clinked against dishes, and a low murmur of lunchtime conversation filled the air. A busboy went by with a huge tub of dishes. Stynes watched him go through the swinging doors into the kitchen, then spoke up.

'You know,' he said, 'do you ever think about that case? The Manning case?'

'From time to time,' Reynolds said. 'I've got grandkids that age. If one of them disappeared that way — Jesus. I don't know how the Mannings function day to day. I'd be ready to tear the world down.'

'Their life isn't a bed of roses.'

'No shit.'

'Seriously, though, do you ever think about how we ended up getting Dante in the first place?'

Reynolds stopped chewing. He leveled his gaze at Stynes from across the table. 'You mean by investigating?'

Stynes considered dropping it. Reynolds was retired and likely not to be a receptive audience. But if he didn't ask the guy he respected most in the world, who was he going to ask?

'We had witnesses,' Stynes said. 'The kids and the adults in the park. And we had his aunt, and the porn and the clippings about the case. Did we have enough? I mean . . . talking to Dante Rogers today, hearing what he had to say . . . And talking to the Mannings, too . . . There might be something there — '

'Okay.' Reynolds dropped his fork with a loud clatter. It dropped off the table and onto the floor. He made an exaggerated show of picking up his napkin and wiping it across his mouth. 'I know what this is,' he said. 'I've seen it before. You've got, what, two years to retire?'

'About that.'

'Okay, and you're getting old, right? Pushing sixty? And you're looking back over everything and you're saying to yourself, 'Well, what did I do right and what did I do wrong? And does any of it amount to two farts in a windstorm?' Right?'

Stynes didn't answer, but Reynolds's insights struck a chord. Stynes knew he was reassessing, summing up, looking forward to life in retirement. And what waited for him there? Reds games on TV six months a year and *Gunsmoke* reruns in the winter.

'You know what you need to do? You need to get remarried. Look at you.' Reynolds signaled the waitress and received a new fork. He started eating again. 'Look at you. Widowed. No kids. No dog or cat. And you're looking down retirement like it's the barrel of a gun. Get outside yourself a little bit. You're still young. You can still get it up. Find a nice schoolteacher who's about to retire. Ride off into the sunset together.'

He paused to chew. Stynes thought he was finished with his rant, but Reynolds leveled his butter knife, pointing it right at Stynes's chest, and said, 'This shit ain't going to fly with me, okay? I'm not digging into the past and thinking about all the shitheads I put away. This Dante, he got what he deserved. Right? Don't go there.'

Stynes worked on his fries. He nodded, absorbing Reynolds's words, letting them rattle around in his brain. As expected, Reynolds didn't want to hear it, and maybe his old partner was right. Why dig into the past just because Dante Rogers looked like a pathetic piece of shit at the Reverend Fred's church?

'That's the longest we put anyone away,' Stynes said. 'I mean, outside of guys who pled or were obviously guilty.'

'You did good,' Reynolds said. 'You were young, but you did good. You worked well with the Mannings and those little kids. It worked. I only wish the asshole had gone away longer. I wish we'd made it first degree. They were still frying bastards back then. He could have ridden the lightning. *Zap*. Then we're not having this talk.'

'And you'd be missing me,' Stynes said.

'Bullshit.' Reynolds threw the last bite of his sandwich into his mouth and wiped his hands. 'Listen to what I said. Retirement can be a bitch if you don't have something to do.'

Stynes sipped his drink, drained it down so only ice was left in the glass. 'Do you remember something about that case?' Stynes asked. 'The testimony of those kids. When we talked to them at the park, they told us two things. Yes, they told us they saw Justin with Dante and all that. But they also told us that Justin had run off into the woods, alone, chasing a dog or something. But that night when we talked to them, neither one of them remembered that part of it. All they wanted to say was that they saw Justin with Dante. Nothing about the woods.'

'So? They're kids. Remember Elizabeth Smart? Her kid sister sees the guy come into the room and take Elizabeth. Nine months later, she wakes up one day and says, 'Hey, I know who it is.' Nine months. They're kids. Little kids. Who knows how their minds work? And other people — other adults — saw Dante at the park.'

The waitress brought the check, and Reynolds pointed to Stynes. 'It's his turn. I'm on a fixed income.'

Stynes brought out his wallet and put a twenty down with the check. The waitress collected it and brought him change. 'Look,' he said. 'There were a lot of adults in the park that day. We talked to all of them, but we pretty quickly started looking for a black guy and dropped any other thoughts because of what those kids said at night, how adamant they were that night. Adamant. Right?'

Reynolds didn't respond, so Stynes counted out the tip and went on, his voice lowered.

'Who commits most crimes against children?' Stynes asked.

'More Trivial Pursuit?'

'You know as well as I do — sixty-eight percent of the time it's a parent or family member, right? We may not have known that as much back then, but we sure as hell know it now.'

Reynolds made a circular motion with his hand. *Go on.*

'And who had access to those kids before we talked to them?'

'We talked to them right in the park and they mentioned Dante, right after it happened.'

'There was a lot of heat on us. Hell, there was heat on every cop in America back then. Crime was up all over. If something happened, everybody freaked out. They acted like the world was ending. Maybe we didn't pay enough attention to what was said in the park because of the chaos that day. The body was found in the woods, and that's the direction those kids pointed us to initially.'

'We searched there,' Reynolds said. 'Hell, we searched those woods multiple times. We dragged that little pond, turned over every rock.

122

We had to wait for Mother Nature to give that kid's body back to us.'

'Didn't you think there was something . . . *off* about Bill Manning? We talked about it at the time.'

'Yeah, his kid was missing. That's enough to make anybody off.'

'Are you going to give me another lecture on how I don't understand what he went through because I never had kids?'

Reynolds almost smiled. 'I'll let it go.'

'Seriously, there was something going on there, right?' Stynes asked.

Reynolds leaned back. 'You mean because of what the Mannings said that day?'

'Yes,' Stynes said. 'In the morning, right after Justin disappeared, Mrs Manning, Virginia Manning, told us that her husband *didn't* go to work at his usual time that day. She said that he stayed home, which was unusual. But that night, when we went back to the house to talk to them again, she had changed her tune. She said her husband *did* leave for work at the usual time, that everything was normal in the morning, and he didn't come home until they found out that Justin was missing. She called him at work and told him.'

'I remember all this, Stynes.' Reynolds pointed to his head. 'I've still got it together up here.'

'Well?'

'Well what?'

'When someone contradicts themselves, we see it as a red flag. We push harder.'

123

'It *was* a red flag,' Reynolds said. 'We both saw it that way. We talked about it then, remember?'

'Yes. And you told me to let it go, to back off the Mannings.'

'Damn right.'

'You said they were scared and upset, and it wasn't unusual for someone like Mrs Manning to get her facts mixed up.'

'It's called being compassionate,' Reynolds said. 'Good cops do that. They know how to treat the victims of crimes.'

'But didn't we turn away from them too quickly?' Stynes asked.

'Too quickly?' Reynolds asked.

'Yeah.'

'As I recall, you pulled Mrs Manning aside for a little heart-to-heart the night her kid disappeared, didn't you? You asked her all about this, right? As I recall, you did it without my permission. And what happened?'

'She stuck to the story,' Stynes said. 'She said she mixed things up in the morning because she was upset.'

'There you go,' Reynolds said.

'But was it enough? Couldn't we have pushed them just a little more?'

'Let me ask *you* something, since you're so fond of these trivia questions. Who commits most of the violent crimes in Dove Point? And where do most of the violent crimes take place?'

Stynes paused, letting Reynolds's words sink in. 'Jesus, Terry. Are you for real?'

'I'm talking numbers, Stynesie.'

'You're saying that blacks commit most of the

violent crimes, and most of them take place over in East.'

'Amen, brother.'

'So that's why we looked so hard at Dante Rogers and let the alibi from the Mannings go?'

'We had the witnesses against Dante,' Reynolds said. 'Against the Mannings we had what? A woman's hysterical story about her husband?'

'And the tendency of kids or anyone else to be killed by people they know.'

Reynolds shook his head. 'I don't see it, Stynesie. Take my advice — get a hobby. Become one of those Walmart greeters. Do something. But I have to get out of here — '

'What about Scott Ludwig?' he asked.

Reynolds tightened his jaw, as though biting back on something.

'Ludwig was there,' Stynes pressed. 'He was doing that nature walk or whatever for a group of kids. But he left without talking to us. As soon as trouble went down, he was gone. And nobody saw him or could find him.'

'That's not a crime.'

'It is damn weird if a crime has been committed, and he was at the scene. He's always been an odd duck — '

'Also not a crime. Look at you.'

'We should have looked at Ludwig harder. We both know that.'

'I don't.'

'You don't? I guess Dante made a more vulnerable target, didn't he? He wasn't white and from a prominent family — '

125

'Hey,' Reynolds said. The word came out so loud it seemed to surprise even Reynolds. Other diners turned to look, and Reynolds ducked his head a little, gathered his cool. But he didn't cool off. He pointed at Stynes and said, 'Listen, you want to carry around some bullshit guilt and doubts, that's fine with me. But you do it alone.' Reynolds looked around. The other diners were back to their own business — or at least pretending to be. He turned back to Stynes. 'You can accuse me of a lot of things, but I wouldn't dump a case because someone has money. You bring me one shred of proof, one piece of evidence that Ludwig or anybody else did anything to that Manning kid, and I'll change my mind. Otherwise, put it in the win column and let Dante Rogers live out his crappy life over in East like the puke that he is.'

Stynes hated himself for feeling chastened, like a little kid scolded by his dad. Reynolds had that effect on him. Always.

But at some point, everybody leaves home . . .

'I'm going to talk to Ludwig, Terry,' Stynes said. 'And Bill Manning. I have to.'

Disgust dripped off Reynolds's face as he pushed himself up from the table and left Judy's without saying good-bye.

# 15

Janet knew she was acting distracted. She didn't tell Madeline who she had seen — *might* have seen? — but she abruptly announced her intention to head back to the office, leaving Madeline to hustle to keep up.

In the bright sunlight outside the student center, Janet looked left, then right. She saw scattered people — individuals and groups — but no sign of the man from the porch. No sign of a blue shirt or the short-cropped blond hair. Why was he there if he only wanted to slip away without speaking to her?

'Hon? Is everything all right?'

Madeline came alongside of Janet, a little out of breath. Janet didn't know what to say. She couldn't tell her the truth, of course, so she nodded.

'Fine,' Janet said. 'I just — I want to get back and get out of this heat.'

'If you keep moving that fast I'm going to faint on the sidewalk.'

'Sorry.'

As they walked, Janet paid more attention to the surroundings, to every figure that passed through her line of sight, every tree or car someone might be hidden behind. Madeline talked — something about her son and his decision to get a tattoo — and Janet interjected some mindless yeses and noes as she saw fit.

But she kept looking for the man, and as she looked, her anxiety level rose.

What if Michael was right? What if the man intended to do her some kind of harm? He'd shown up in the middle of the night and adamantly insisted she not tell the police.

Who would make such a request but someone who was in trouble?

Janet started to reach for her phone, to call home and tell her dad to be careful if a strange man came to the door. She could even call or text Ashleigh and tell her not to leave the house —

But she didn't.

If the man wanted to hurt someone or do her family harm, wouldn't he have done that already? He knew where they lived. He knew he'd hooked Janet with his appearance on the porch and the promise of more information to come. And did she need to make Ashleigh any more agitated with her than she already was?

Then Janet saw the man again. He stood on the left side of Wilson Hall as they approached the front of the building. He leaned against the trunk of an old and richly green maple. They locked eyes, but the man made no gesture toward her. He didn't summon her with a wave or acknowledge her at all.

But he watched her. He didn't avert his eyes.

Madeline continued to talk. Janet doubted she had even seen the man, or if she had she would figure he was a student or maintenance worker or other campus visitor.

Janet felt a chill, a quick frosting inside her chest. She knew she could just walk into Wilson, sit at her desk, and go about her day. She could call campus security and report the man. She could have done any of those things.

But she didn't.

She wanted to talk to the man. She wanted to find out what he knew.

She turned to Madeline at the entrance to the building.

'I'll be right inside,' Janet said. 'I have to do something.'

Madeline saw the man then. She looked to the man and then back to Janet, her face full of questions.

'Go on. I'm fine,' Janet said.

Madeline didn't look like she believed her, but she did — reluctantly — go inside the building.

★ ★ ★

The man wore his hair short, buzzed almost to his scalp. He didn't appear to be losing his hair, but he wore it that way. He wore baggy jeans and mud-splattered work boots. His blue T-shirt advertised a local food bank. If he felt scared or nervous about talking to Janet, he managed to keep it hidden.

When Janet reached him, she didn't know what to say. Her legs felt light and hollow. She wanted — needed — to sit down.

'Hello,' the man said.

'How did you know I worked here?' she asked.

'I read that article in the paper,' he said. 'I

tried to come by yesterday to talk to you, but couldn't make it.'

'You came by here?' Janet asked. 'To campus?'

The man didn't answer.

'Did you come to my house? Last night in the dark? Were you there?'

'I'm here to talk to you now,' he said.

'Are you here to tell me what I want to know?' Janet asked. 'What do you know about Justin's death?'

The man looked around a little, as though he thought someone might be listening. 'Can we talk somewhere?'

'We can talk here,' Janet said. 'Now tell me what you know, or I'll call the police on you. If you think you can come by my house — '

'I just want to sit down somewhere and talk.' He looked behind him. About fifty feet away sat a shaded bench, a donation in the name of some long-dead alum. 'Can we sit over there?' he asked. 'For just a few minutes.'

Janet looked over at Wilson Hall, to the first-floor windows where the dean's office was housed. She saw Madeline looking out, not even pretending to be subtle. Janet gave a little wave to her, trying to let her know that, at least for the moment, everything was okay.

But was it?

She didn't see the harm in staying close. And she knew Madeline was on alert.

'Let's go,' Janet said. 'But I don't have a lot of time. I'm at work.'

They walked to the bench. Janet looked around before she sat, making sure of her surroundings. She didn't see anyone else nearby. She took that as a good sign. She felt better thinking the man was alone and not accompanied by others.

They settled on opposite ends of the bench, and Janet studied his face, matching to the memory she carried from that one night on the porch. Her recollections seemed surprisingly accurate. The man did carry the features she remembered, the ones that she associated with Justin. The shape of his eyes — round like her father's. And like hers. The chin that came to a sharp point — kind of but not exactly like her mother's. Janet studied his features so long it took her several moments to realize how rapidly her heart was beating. She wiped a drop of sweat off her forehead with a shaking hand.

'Do you need something to eat?' Janet asked. 'Do you need help?'

He smiled a little. It made him look young, almost childish.

'Why would you think I needed something to eat, or help?' he asked.

'I don't know,' Janet said. 'I don't know where you've been or what you've been doing. You might be in trouble.'

'Do you remember me, Janet?' he asked.

'I'm trying to figure that out.' She tried to keep her voice level. 'Who are you?'

'I lived here in Dove Point when I was a kid. I have to admit I didn't really like it very much.'

'You didn't like Dove Point?'

'I guess I didn't like being a kid,' he said. The man smiled a little, but it looked forced, like some pressure existed behind his lips he was trying to hold in. 'People control us when we're kids. They hold us back. They do things to keep us in line.'

'I wish you'd tell me what you know about Justin.'

The man looked at Janet, considered her. 'I didn't always meet people who had my best interests in mind when I was a child. It wasn't easy at all.'

'I'm sorry.'

'My mother died. My father didn't care.'

'I'm sorry. My mother died, too.'

'Yes,' he said. 'I saw that in the article. That must have happened after I left town.' He looked around again. His lips were dry and cracked. They looked painful to Janet. 'I thought that was . . . particularly sad.'

'Why?'

'Mothers.' He shrugged. 'Are you and your daughter close, Janet?'

Janet squirmed in her seat. 'I'd prefer you didn't ask or talk about her.'

The man shrugged again. 'The newspaper mentioned her. It must be difficult — '

'You need to tell me what you came to tell me, or I'm going to leave. I might leave anyway, but I'll leave even sooner if you don't start telling me about Justin. You said you knew something.'

'I do. But I have to tell you something about me first.'

'Why? What's the connection between you and Justin?'

He held up a finger, asking for patience.

Janet wanted to bolt. She shifted her feet. But she couldn't bring herself to do it. She couldn't walk away from him. Janet told herself she needed to let go of the notion that this man was Justin — but she couldn't. His face, the similarities ... the hints he dropped in conversation ... There was something there.

'We're a lot alike, Janet. You and I. We share certain experiences from our childhoods. We've both lost things. Precious things. Pieces of our families and of ourselves.'

'Because we both lost our mothers? What does this have to do with — ?'

'You lost a member of your family,' the man said. 'He was taken away.'

'What do you know about that?'

'I was taken away from my family,' he said.

'What do you mean?' she asked.

'I was taken away from them,' he said. 'Taken.'

'Kidnapped?' Janet's control slipped. She moved closer to the man. 'Who took you? You mean in the park?'

'I've seen you, Janet. Your house, your family.'

'You have been to my house — ?'

'I never had that. A home like that one.'

'Why didn't you? Do you mean the house I live in? Is that what you're talking about? Tell me.'

She reached out and took his hand. Squeezed it inside her own. The man didn't return the squeeze, but he didn't back away or seem put off. He left his hand in hers for long moments, their flesh touching. *Connection*, Janet thought.

There was something there, something she felt about this man —

Janet couldn't stop herself.

'Justin?' she said. 'Is it you? Justin?'

The man's eyes widened. He did pull back. His hand slipped out of Janet's as he stood up.

'Not yet,' he said. 'Not yet.'

'Now,' Janet said. 'Tell me what you know. We've been waiting a long time.'

But the man was backing away from the bench, his pace increasing with every step. He turned and started jogging away, across the quad.

Janet didn't think. She simply acted.

She kicked off her shoes and started after the man, running through the dry grass. She thought she'd never catch him, but he didn't seem to be running all out. She closed the gap between them quickly, reaching out her hand until she took hold of his shirt.

Did he want to be caught?

He stopped running, and Janet stopped next to him. She was out of breath from the short, intense burst across the quad. She hadn't done anything like that in years. It felt like being a kid again. Running, chasing, tagging —

Janet looked the man right in the eye, worked up the ability to speak.

She managed to get a fractured, breathless sentence out.

'Tell me what you know,' she said.

'We need to be closer before I can tell you,' he said. 'We need to know each other better.'

'Bullshit. You're a liar, and I'm calling the

police. My friend is probably calling the police right now. She probably saw me running after you.'

The man shook his head. 'That won't help,' he said. 'That won't do anyone any good at all.'

He started running again, faster than before and away from her. He didn't look back.

Janet didn't go after him this time. She was too tired. She couldn't will herself to give chase.

But she managed one more word. She called it but doubted the man heard her.

'Justin!'

He kept on going.

*   *   *

When the man was gone, his body disappearing out of sight as he ran across the quad, Janet didn't know what to do. She noticed her legs were shaking, her knees loose as though someone or something had removed the tendons and ligaments that held them in their proper place.

She needed to sit down.

Janet went back to the bench she had sat on with the man and let her body fall onto it. Her back thumped against the wood slats. At another time, it might have hurt, but Janet didn't even notice the contact.

It couldn't be, she told herself. It couldn't be.

Michael was right. There was a body and a grave and a funeral.

Justin was gone.

So then why did this man come to Janet saying

135

Justin's death didn't happen the way she thought it happened — the way everyone thought it happened? And why did he say he knew her but wouldn't give his name?

Janet's mouth felt dry. She needed water. But she couldn't move. She sat on the bench, staring at the grass.

What did it all mean?

A hand touched her shoulder. Janet whipped her head around.

'Hon? Are you okay?'

It was Madeline. She looked down at Janet, a confused and concerned look on her face.

'What?' Janet asked.

'Are you okay? Are you hurt? Did that man do something to you?'

'I'm fine.'

'Do you want me to call campus security?'

'No,' Janet said. Her voice came out strong and harsh, like she was correcting a child. She moderated it when Madeline looked like she'd been slapped. 'It's okay. Thanks. I'm fine.'

Madeline sat down on the bench close to Janet.

'Hon, who was that man?' she asked.

'He was — he just wanted money.'

'He's a beggar?'

'I guess,' Janet said.

'But you ran after him. You looked like you knew him.'

'I thought he needed help.'

Madeline didn't look convinced. Her brow furrowed. 'I saw things getting weird between the two of you, so I came out. I heard you say something to him when he ran away. I heard your voice.'

'I told him to go away.'

'You said a name, Janet. You called him by a name.'

'I didn't. I don't know the man's name.' Janet patted Madeline on the knee, a gesture of thanks. 'He just freaked me out, but I'm fine. Let's go back to work, okay?'

# 16

Stynes recognized the symmetry of it all. He'd started his day in East, easily the worst part of Dove Point. He headed west in the late afternoon to the neighborhood a few blocks outside of downtown where the oldest and nicest houses in Dove Point stood. Those homes didn't change much, nor did the types of families who lived inside them. The names changed in some cases, and generations came and went. But by and large the occupants were still doctors and lawyers, prominent insurance agents and bankers. The homes rarely sold, and when they did, they went for a price that Stynes could only dream of spending.

He followed West High Street three blocks away from the circle and turned onto Washington. The home he sought sat on the corner, a large redbrick colonial complete with white columns and two even rows of windows — one upstairs and one downstairs — that bounced the late-afternoon sun back off themselves, making it impossible to see anything inside. Stynes took the three steps up the front walk, then another three across the porch. Someone liked to mow the grass and pull the weeds, and it looked like they did it with a ruler. Not one blade of grass appeared to be taller than another. Not one weed grew. The petunias and geraniums in the window boxes conceded nothing to the summer heat and dryness. They looked like they spent their days in a greenhouse.

Stynes rang the bell. Unannounced visits were touchy. They tended to make people feel like the police suspected them of something, leading to defensive behavior. It also meant they could hide out in an upstairs room and simply pretend they never heard the bell. But Stynes prided himself on his patience. He could come back if he had to.

He didn't have to.

He didn't even have to ring again. The door opened revealing Scott Ludwig, the object of Stynes's quest. The middle-aged man wore a white summer suit and panama hat as though he were about to stroll the grounds and inspect the cotton crops. He used a cane for support on his left side and didn't appear at all surprised or concerned to see Stynes on his porch. He squinted at Stynes and seemed to want to treat the visit of a police detective as a game.

'I know you, don't I?' Ludwig said.

'We've met before.'

'Help me remember,' he said. 'Give me a hint. The gallery walk? The hospital fund-raiser?'

'The police.'

Ludwig's eyes opened wider, a look of exaggerated shock. 'Oh, my,' he said. 'You must have a badge then, hmm?'

Stynes reached into his coat pocket and showed Ludwig the badge. Ludwig barely looked at it, then stepped back.

'You may as well get out of that beastly heat,' he said. 'Unless this is a brief visit.'

'I could stand to cool off,' Stynes said.

'Fine. I can't stand for very long, so come in.'

Ludwig turned to the right, leading Stynes into a sitting room. It was painted white with bookshelves all around. The large windows let in a flood of light, and Ludwig pointed to a chair that left Stynes squinting into the sun and Ludwig backlit against a window. Stynes perched on the edge of the chair while Ludwig sat, laying his cane at his feet.

Ludwig took a long time to adjust himself. He shifted his weight one way and then the other, grimacing every time he moved. The man looked thin, almost bony. His crisply ironed white shirt hung loose on his midsection. His skin was pale, with a touch of pink on the cheeks and nose. He didn't remove the hat, even indoors, and Stynes noticed that no hairs stuck out from the sides. Not a single stray strand showed itself. His hair must have been as neatly combed into place as the lawn, or he didn't have any left.

When the man was finally settled and most of the grimacing over, Stynes spoke.

'You don't seem alarmed about a detective showing up at your door,' Stynes said. 'Does this happen all the time?'

'What's your name, Detective?' Ludwig asked.

'Stynes. Frank Stynes.'

Recognition crossed Ludwig's face. He rolled his eyes theatrically. 'Oh, that's where I know you from. Oh, Lord. It has been a long time, but now I get it. I saw you in the paper this week talking about that awful story.'

'You didn't answer my question,' Stynes said.

Ludwig offered a forced smile. 'No, Detective, it's not typical for the police to show up at my door. I was trying to be polite by so readily inviting you in. What do you want to know, Detective?' he asked, his voice and demeanor weary. 'I'd offer you something, by the way, but the help is gone, and since my mother died only a year ago, I'm not used to playing host.'

'I'm fine. So you read the paper and you see that there's been some renewed interest in the Manning case.'

'You know, Detective,' Ludwig said, shifting again. He closed his eyes with the pain he seemed to be feeling. 'You may have noticed I'm not doing well. I'm in a lot of pain as the result of a recent illness. Maybe I could come to the station sometime when I'm feeling better, and we could have a nice long talk. I could bring my attorney with me.'

'You were at the park that day because you were conducting some sort of nature walk. Is that right?'

Ludwig sighed. 'Yes. I'm sure you recall I taught biology at Dove Point High for thirty years. I used to keep myself busy in the summers by volunteering to lead nature walks in the park. You know, we'd walk around and I'd point out the plants and the trees and the butterflies. It was free, and it got the kids out of their parents' hair for an hour or so. The kids loved it. We covered this all back then, you'll recall.'

'And now refresh my memory — what did you see that day? The day Justin Manning disappeared.'

'Oh, my.' Ludwig sighed again. 'You seem determined to ride this hobbyhorse one more time, don't you? What happened to your partner? That unpleasant man?'

'He retired.'

'Hmm. Aren't you getting close to that? You can't be but a few years older than I am.'

'That day at the park. Did you see anything?'

'Do you promise to leave if I answer the question?'

'Maybe.'

'Then it's worth a try. Like I told you then, I didn't see anything. I was there getting ready for the walk. I always met the kids at that main picnic shelter. There were a lot of people in the park that day, both children and adults. As I recall, I was running a little late, so I was focused on my work. All of a sudden, a flurry of activity broke out. A large group formed in the center of the park near the swing sets. Panic seemed to be spreading. I thought someone had fallen and injured themselves. Then the police came.'

'And where were you when the police came?'

'You know this, Detective.'

'Humor me. I'm getting old, and I forget sometimes.'

'I wasn't there when the police arrived,' Ludwig said.

'You weren't there.'

'I went home. When I saw the commotion and knew something bad had happened, I went home. I could tell the nature walk was going to be canceled, so they didn't need me.'

'Some kids were left waiting at the shelter. You didn't even bother to see that they had rides or anything.'

'The park was full of police officers. I figured the kids would be safe.'

'I don't think the parents agreed with you. Did they?'

'Parents can be so overprotective sometimes.'

'So they did mind?' Stynes asked.

Ludwig sighed. 'Well, the park service didn't let me do any more nature walks that summer, if that's what you mean.'

'You know what's weird?' Stynes said. 'And I really did forget this detail after all these years, but when I looked at my notes it came back to me. You left your car at the park. You were in such a hurry to get out of there, you walked off and left your car just sitting there. Why did you do that?'

'I said I — '

'And when we tried to come here and talk to you, you weren't home. It took four hours before we got ahold of you here. And no one knew where you were or what you were doing during that time.'

Ludwig didn't say anything. He opened his mouth a little and looked at Stynes expectantly. Finally, he said, 'Do you want me to answer these questions? Or are they accusations?'

'Where were you?'

'I was just walking.'

'Just walking?'

'Just walking.'

'And I guess you were alone?'

'Did I mention, Detective, that I'm recovering from surgery? Prostate cancer. I get tired easily, so I'm probably going to have to ask you to leave.'

'That's fine.' Stynes thought the man's face looked even paler than when he'd first entered. And the conversation didn't appear to be leading anyplace productive. 'Were you alone?'

'I was. When I came home after my walk, my mother told me you'd been here. And I contacted you right away and answered all of your questions.'

'Fair enough.' Stynes stood up. When Ludwig started to reach for his cane, Stynes waved him off. 'I can show myself out. Thanks.'

'As you wish,' Ludwig said, although he looked relieved. 'How is this Manning family holding up, Detective? I read about them this morning.'

'The years have made them pretty strong.'

'Give them my best, if you don't mind,' Ludwig said.

But before Stynes left the room, he asked Ludwig one more thing. 'You've never been married, have you, Mr Ludwig?'

'Is that a crime?' Ludwig asked. 'I know how my life must look to someone outside of it. Unmarried old bachelor who lived with his mother all those years. Took kids on nature walks at the park. But don't forget, I taught in the schools here for thirty years. My record is impeccable. I'd never harm a child.'

Stynes pointed at the cane. 'I hope you feel better.'

'I hope *you* feel better, Detective,' Ludwig said. 'It looks to me like something pretty serious is bothering you.'

# 17

In the late afternoon, when the heat of the day started to ease, Ashleigh received a text from Kevin.

*I'm done. Where R U?*

She wrote back: *Going 2 park. Meet me there.*

Ashleigh wore olive-green shorts and a black Rolling Stones T-shirt she'd bought in a thrift store. She pulled a lightweight zippered sweatshirt from her closet, not because she was cold or expected to be but because she liked the feeling of long sleeves, of being a little covered up. She stepped into sneakers and went downstairs.

The old man sat in front of the television, getting his daily dose of Fox News. He looked up when she came into the room, his face almost expectant, like he might just be happy to see her. But the look fell just as quickly.

'I thought you were your mom,' he said.

'I'm not. Is she home?'

'She's still at work,' he said. 'They keep her hopping there, I guess.'

'She likes it.'

'Have you noticed anything different about her?' her grandpa asked. 'Ever since the reporter and all these things started happening she's been a little off.'

'This stuff probably just freaks her out,' Ashleigh said. She could tell the old man didn't really get it. He looked confused, like he couldn't grasp why someone would feel upset by reminders of a family tragedy. 'Doesn't it freak you out a little?'

The old man looked away. Ashleigh thought he wasn't going to answer her, that he was just going to pretend he didn't hear the question or something, but finally he said, 'It's best for everyone to not revisit those kinds of things from the past.'

Ashleigh didn't say it, but she thought it: *Things from the past? Your son's death is a 'thing from the past'?* She wanted to just walk away, to leave the old man to sit in his house and stew in his own thoughts. But she felt compelled to push him just a little, if only to defend her mom.

'But it is hard,' Ashleigh said. 'For all of us.'

'You weren't even born,' he said. 'Just don't worry. We can't sit around and fall to pieces about it.'

'I don't think Mom's falling to pieces.'

The old man chose not to respond to that comment. He watched the TV, the images from the screen flickering across his glasses.

Ashleigh shrugged. She didn't have time for him anyway. 'I'm going out. Tell Mom I'll be back later.'

'Where are you going?'

Ashleigh froze in her tracks. The old man never worried about where she was going. The two of them seemed to have an unspoken agreement — neither one asked what the other was doing. Her grandpa left both major and minor decisions about Ashleigh's life to her mother. Ashleigh suspected — although she didn't know for certain — that her mom had laid that out as one of the conditions for the two of them moving into the house. To his credit, her grandfather managed to leave her alone, a far cry from her childhood when visits to his house — the house she currently lived in — meant a steady stream of corrective advice from how to chew her food to the proper way to hold a pencil. Ashleigh would never admit it out loud — and certainly not to her mother or grandfather — but she kind of missed his involvement in the things she did. Sure, he annoyed the crap out of her when she was little, but she liked having his gruff, raspy concern as a part of her life.

'I'm meeting some friends at the park,' she said. 'Bye.'

'Hold it,' the old man said, his voice rising.

She looked over at him in his chair. He was wearing a Cronin College T-shirt, something her mom had gotten during homecoming week, and the same khaki pants he seemed to wear every day. His feet were bare, and his face looked puffier, heavier. Being out of work meant he sat around the house more, eating instead of working. It made Ashleigh a little depressed to think about it.

'That boy, you know — Kevin,' he said.

'What about him?'

'Is he in the park?'

'Yes.'

He looked back at the TV, but Ashleigh could

tell he wasn't finished asking her questions. She shifted her weight from one foot to the other. *Get on with it.*

'Are you . . . going with him?' he finally asked.

'Going with?' Ashleigh said. 'You mean, am I dating him?'

The old man just nodded. He couldn't even say the words.

'No, Grandpa, I'm not going with him. We're just friends. From school.'

He nodded his head a little, eyes still on the TV. Some tension seemed to ease out of his face.

'Do you not like Kevin because he's black?' Ashleigh asked.

Her grandpa's head whipped around so fast she thought he might have injured himself. 'What makes you think that?' he asked.

'I don't know. I just think there are a lot of racists in Dove Point.'

'Well, I'm not one of them,' he said. He didn't turn back to the TV but kept his eyes on her. 'I just think you're a little too young to be . . . keeping company with any boys, regardless of their skin color.'

'I'm fifteen, Grandpa.'

'When I was fifteen, I had a job. I worked.'

'Mom said — '

'I know,' he said. 'As long as your grades were high, you didn't have to work this summer. You'll get into a good college someday. You do want to go to college, right?'

'Definitely.'

'Good.' He examined Ashleigh carefully, looking her over, his eyes traveling from her head to her feet. 'You look like your grandmother did, you know that? She was skinny like you.'

Ashleigh felt uncomfortable under the old man's gaze. She put her hands in the pockets of her sweatshirt. She guessed he was being nice, trying to compliment her.

'Did you know Grandma when she was fifteen?' she asked.

The old man looked surprised by the question. But he seemed to be giving it some thought. 'I knew her then. We went to school together. But we didn't go together until after high school.'

He offered nothing else, so Ashleigh said, 'I'm going to go. Tell Mom for me.'

'You look like her, too. Your mom. You're the spitting image of her when she was in school. And you're smart like she was. Good grades. Your mom got good grades, up to a point.'

'You mean up until I was born?' Ashleigh said.

'Now don't take it that way,' he said. 'I just don't think you should be spending a lot of time with a boy. You should be worried about school.'

'So I don't get knocked up?' Ashleigh asked.

His eyes narrowed. She thought he might give her a lecture on the proper way to talk to one's grandfather, but he let it go. He said, his voice a little weary, 'Just do the right thing.'

Ashleigh looked at the door. She wanted to go, but she said one more thing. 'Do you know why I'm not going to get pregnant, Grandpa?'

He reluctantly asked, 'Why?'

'Because I don't want to get stuck in Dove Point the rest of my life.'

When Ashleigh reached the park, her heart sank. 'Shit.'

She saw Kevin, but he wasn't alone. He stood by a bench at the baseball diamond, and three other kids hovered around him, sitting and standing. Ashleigh knew who they were. Todd, Sarah, and Kelcey — three other kids from their class. Kevin and Todd were friends from grade school, and Todd had started dating Sarah during the spring. Kelcey hung around and made Ashleigh want to punch things.

Ashleigh wished she could turn around and go back. But she'd been seen. And she hadn't talked to Kevin since she saw Dante Rogers in the woods. She wanted to tell him — almost did a few times — but it didn't seem right to share something like that by phone or text. She wanted to tell Kevin in person.

Except they weren't alone.

Ashleigh walked up, hands in pockets.

'Hey, girl,' Kevin said. 'I was just telling them about this dude who came into McDonald's today. We messed up his order, so he got all up in the manager's face. He was like, 'If you don't fix this for me, I'm going to fuck this place up.' We were in the back rolling.'

His voice trailed off at the end. Ashleigh saw the other kids looking at her and not Kevin. They seemed to be expecting something from her.

'I guess you had to be there,' Kevin said.

It was Kelcey, of course, who spoke up on

everyone's behalf. 'We saw your family in the paper,' she said.

'And?' Ashleigh said.

'My God,' Kelcey said, eyes widening, mouth open so far Ashleigh could see her fillings, 'we had no idea that happened to your family. No idea. That is totally wild that your uncle died like that.' She looked to the other two. 'Did you guys know?'

They both shook their heads, but Todd said, 'My dad remembered it. I told him I went to school with you, and he was like, 'Whoa, I remember when that kid was killed. We were so fucking scared there was a madman on the loose.''

Ashleigh looked at Kevin. They made eye contact, and he understood. 'Anyway,' he said, 'we don't have to talk about all this.'

'No, of course not,' Kelcey said. 'Of course not. Unless Ash wants to talk about it, and then we'd all listen, wouldn't we? I mean, it's cool whatever you want to do. I think if I had a big tragedy in my family I'd want to talk about it.'

Sarah shrugged and Todd nodded.

'Kelcey?' Ashleigh said. 'Do you pay any attention in school?'

'What?'

'I said, do you pay any fucking attention in school?'

'Ash — ' Kevin said.

'It's a question,' Ashleigh said. 'Just a question.'

Kelcey sat there with her mouth half open, the fillings in her back teeth smaller but still visible.

'I pay attention,' Kelcey said.

'If you did, instead of sitting there texting or chewing gum or twirling your hair with your finger, you'd know that someone dying isn't a tragedy. A tragedy is when a noble character falls as the result of a fatal flaw. It provides catharsis and pleasure to the audience to watch it happen. Do you feel catharsis or pleasure reading about my family?'

'Come on, Ash — ' Kevin placed his hand on Ashleigh's arm, calming her down and leading her away.

'Fuck you, Ashleigh,' Kelcey said. 'God. We're just trying to be nice and ask about your family. But if you want to keep being the little moody girl, go ahead.'

'I can be the moody girl and you can be the dumb girl — '

By then, Kevin was applying more force, guiding her away from the baseball diamond and out of the park. She let herself be led because she realized she'd finally get to talk to Kevin alone.

★   ★   ★

They walked out of the park side by side. They didn't talk to each other. Ashleigh kept her head down, her hands in the sweatshirt pockets. She didn't look at Kevin but felt him by her side, a solid, reassuring presence. She didn't pay attention to where they headed, didn't care. She felt the anger at Kelcey — and all the stupid people she knew — course through her body.

She hoped the walk would cool things down, let the steam of her rage dissipate.

When she looked up again, they were at Clark Street Junior High, the place where Ashleigh and Kevin had first met before they'd moved on to high school together. They still didn't speak. They knew where to go without words, so they walked to the side of the school building and over to the old playground. Ashleigh went right for the swing sets, with Kevin following, and they sat next to each other, each on their own swing.

After a long few moments, Ashleigh spoke. 'You look like an idiot, you know that?'

The swing was too small and too low to the ground for Kevin. It forced his knees up high, making him look like some kind of contortionist. 'No,' he said. 'I'm cool.' He spread his arms wide. 'Look at me, I'm cool.'

Ashleigh swung a little, a gentle back and forth. 'Don't tell me I shouldn't have yelled at Kelcey,' she said. 'I know you want to tell me that, so just don't.'

'I won't.'

'She's a fucking airhead.'

'I know. But in her own way, she was trying to act concerned.'

'I thought I said not to tell me that.'

But she wasn't really mad. The anger — at least at Kelcey — was gone. Ashleigh continued to rock. She looked at the old school building, the dirty bricks, the huge windows. It seemed so long ago that she was a student there, even though it had been just over a year.

'What are you so pissed about?' Kevin asked.

'I'm not pissed,' she said.

'That wasn't pissed?'

'I mean I'm not really mad about that.' Ashleigh slowed her movement on the swing. She scraped her feet against the ground, felt the bark and twigs against her feet. 'I'm mad at my mom and grandpa. But that's not really bothering me either. I just wanted to tell you something. I'm not mad. I just wanted to talk.'

'What's up then?' Kevin asked.

But Ashleigh didn't feel ready to talk. Not about all of that — her uncle, the murder. The man in the woods. Not yet.

'Do you remember playing kickball and dodgeball here?' she asked.

'Sure. It was kind of fun.'

'I hated it,' Ashleigh said.

Kevin laughed.

'Seriously, I hated it,' she said. 'I thought nothing would ever be worse than being in grade school or junior high and having to do what everybody told me to do. I couldn't wait to get to high school, you know? I thought I'd be a grown-up then.'

'Are you a grown-up?'

'No. Things are just as bad. And now I can't wait to graduate and go to college.'

'The grass is always greener,' Kevin said. 'But aren't we supposed to be happy and carefree? Aren't these the best years of our lives?'

'Right,' Ashleigh said. She kicked at the dirt, then made a circular pattern with her foot. She knew Kevin was watching her. She felt his eyes on her even when she wasn't looking at him.

'The other day when you got off the bus, I went on to the park.'

'I figured you were headed there, that you were in the mood to be there.'

'Something happened.'

Kevin looked concerned. Protective. 'What happened?'

'I saw someone.'

'Who, Ashleigh?'

She didn't answer right away.

'Who did you see?' Kevin asked.

'Dante Rogers. The guy who killed my uncle.'

'He was in the park?'

'He wasn't just in the park. He was at the place where they found my uncle's body. He was right there.'

'He was there when you were there? Just the two of you in the middle of the woods?'

'Yes.'

'Were you scared?'

Ashleigh thought about the question before she answered. 'Not scared. Uneasy, I guess.'

'What the hell was he doing there?' Kevin asked.

'He was just standing there. He came walking up, and he looked surprised to see me, like he'd been there before and was always alone.'

'Did you talk to him?'

'I tried.' Ashleigh thought back to the scene in the clearing, the way Dante just ran away from her, as though she had something wrong with her. 'He bolted. As soon as I went toward him, he ran.'

'He didn't say anything?'

Ashleigh shook her head. The sun had fallen farther, and near the low ground beneath the hedge that separated the school from the road, fireflies began to blink on and off.

'He held his hands out,' Ashleigh said. 'He looked like he wanted to say something, but he didn't. He looked scared, I guess.'

'Weird.'

'Why would he go there?' Ashleigh asked.

Kevin shrugged. 'Maybe he's been going to that spot in the woods ever since he got out.'

'But if you go to the place where you supposedly murdered someone, doesn't it mean you're guilty?'

'If you're going there and no one's making you go there, yes, it does suggest guilt.'

Ashleigh didn't say anything else, but she again felt Kevin staring at her. Studying her.

'Ash, why do you care about that? Wouldn't you be happy to know that Dante really killed your uncle? It would mean they convicted the right guy, and he did his time.'

'I don't know . . . '

'You don't know?' Kevin asked. 'Are you mad because he didn't go to jail long enough?'

'Not that. I don't really care about that. I'm not like those stupid people who live for revenge, who foam at the mouth if they think someone should have gone to the electric chair.'

'Then what is it?'

Ashleigh watched the fireflies and tried to think of the right words.

'I want the story to change,' she said finally. 'My whole life, that's been the story. Dante

Rogers killed my uncle. He went to jail. My grandmother died from grief. All of that happened before I was born, but I've lived with it my whole life. It's been a black cloud over my head and the whole family.' She turned to him. 'But when that guy showed up at the house saying the story wasn't true, that something else happened to my uncle, I felt something change. I don't know . . . There was a chance.'

'A chance to change the story? Your family's story?'

'Yes.' She kicked at the ground. 'When that guy — Steven — first showed up, I thought he just meant that Dante didn't kill my uncle the way they said he did. Or maybe he just meant that Dante didn't kill him and someone else did.'

'But?'

'But what if he means something more? What if he's trying to say that my uncle didn't die? What if he's still alive?'

Kevin took a deep breath. 'Holy shit, Ash. You don't know that. You don't have any evidence for that.'

'I know. But there's something happening with this guy. I can feel it.'

She knew Kevin would understand. She wanted to tell him because she knew he would get it without a lot of explanation. They *got* each other. Sometimes she thought he was the only person who got her.

'It makes sense,' he said. 'I understand why you want to find this guy and talk to him. But there's one potential problem with all of this.'

'What's that?'

'What if you find out something different did happen, just like that guy said, and what if it ends up being worse than what you know now?'

As quickly as Ashleigh wanted to celebrate her friendship with Kevin, she just as quickly wanted to curse him. Being friends with him — and maybe being good friends with anyone — meant that he knew exactly how to cut to the heart of a matter, even if it meant saying something Ashleigh didn't want to hear.

'It can't be,' she said. 'Anything is better. My mom, you know? She's living her life and everything, but has anyone ever needed a different story more than her? Hell, sometimes — and I can't believe I'm going to say this — but sometimes — '

'You even feel sorry for your grandpa.'

'Yes.'

Kevin laughed. Ashleigh spent so much time complaining about the old man that she knew it struck him as funny to hear her express any sympathy for him. But she really felt that way. He might be a grumpy old man, but he was her grandfather.

'So, what are you going to do next?' Kevin asked. 'Call the police, I hope.'

'And report a guy hanging out in a park?'

'A murderer, Ash. If he's out, he's on parole. He can't just go wherever he wants or do whatever he wants.'

'How do you know what he can and can't do?' she asked.

Kevin chuckled. 'I'm black, Ash. I may be middle class and respectable, but black men

159

don't grow up not knowing about these things. If he's out on parole, I guarantee he's not allowed to come near your family or that park. He could get sent right back to jail.'

'I won't call the police on him,' she said.

'Then what?'

'I'm going back,' she said. 'I'm going back to talk to Steven Kollman.'

# 18

Stynes called into the station before he left his house for his noon-to-nine shift. He spoke to the desk officer and asked if anything was brewing in Dove Point that morning, anything that required his immediate attention. He waited while the officer checked, and while he stood there he looked down at his little notebook. He revisited the details that Reverend Fred had provided — six times in the last eighteen months money had disappeared from the church account. Not big amounts. They all ranged between three hundred and eight hundred dollars. The money always returned, usually without the reverend having to say anything to his bookkeeper.

But still, the reverend wondered, where was that money going?

The desk officer came back and told Stynes all was clear.

'I'm going to be checking on a complaint from the Reverend Fred Arling,' Stynes said. 'It shouldn't take long.'

He hung up and took a last look at the name of the bookkeeper before he left the house.

Ray Bower. Michael Bower's father.

Could it just be a coincidence?

★ ★ ★

A converted Cape Cod with a wide front porch housed Ray Bower's bookkeeping office on Lincoln Street, just two blocks off the circle. Stynes stepped into what had once served as the living room of the home. A large desk and a photocopier took up most of the space, and the young woman behind the desk took up the rest with the size of her smile.

'Can I help you?' she said.

The woman, who looked to be about twenty-five, wore her hair pulled back into a businesslike ponytail. Stynes made a point of not staring at the exposed skin where her black V-neck shirt dipped low enough to reveal a strip of black bra. A large bouquet of flowers took up one corner of the desk.

'Is Mr Bower in?' Stynes asked.

'He sure is. Did you have an appointment?'

'No,' Stynes said. 'I just wanted to talk to him.' Stynes decided to cut to the chase. He reached into his jacket pocket and pulled out a small leather billfold. He felt a little like a cliché from a TV show, letting one half of the billfold fall open, revealing his shiny gold badge. 'Is he in?'

The smile remained in place but the wattage dimmed. She stood up. 'Just one second. I'll tell him.'

She went through an open door at the back of the front room, one that must have led to the original kitchen. She disappeared inside, and Stynes heard their murmured voices while he looked around at the Rotary Club plaques and citations from the Dove Point Small Business

Association that decorated the walls. It took less than twenty seconds for the girl to come out.

'You can go right on back,' she said.

'Thanks.'

'Would you like some coffee or something?'

'No, thanks. I won't be long.'

Stynes tried to remember the last time he had seen Ray Bower. He didn't know the man outside the confines of the Manning case. If it hadn't been for the death of Justin Manning, Stynes doubted he would know the man at all. From time to time over the years, they may have crossed paths in the grocery store or at a Dove Point High basketball game, but if they said more than three words to each other, Stynes couldn't remember them. Every once in a while, Ray Bower sprang for ad time on a local radio station, and some of those commercials slipped through the filter that ordinarily blocked such things from Stynes's consciousness. The name always conjured up brief thoughts of the Manning case, but those thoughts never coalesced around Ray Bower in any meaningful way.

As Stynes entered the room, the man stood up, removed his half-moon reading glasses, and came around the desk to shake hands. He'd grown thick over the years. His big belly hung over his waist, pushing against the yellow polo shirt he wore and forcing the belt on his khaki pants lower. His hair had turned completely gray but still remained full.

'Have a seat, Detective,' he said, returning to his spot behind the desk.

Stynes sat and brought out his notebook. 'I'm sorry to walk in on you like this, but I was in the neighborhood.'

'It's no problem.' Bower tossed the glasses onto the scattering of papers on his desk. 'You do have my curiosity piqued, I have to admit. It's been a long time since we last crossed paths. I hope it's nothing as serious as that.'

Stynes smiled. He could picture Bower bellied up to a table at the local country club. Not Indian Lake, the most exclusive club, the one that only Dove Point's richest residents could afford. More likely Bower would pay the dues at Rolling Hills, the older and less exclusive club, the one that a middle- to upper-middle-class bookkeeper could afford to join. He would be perfectly at ease drinking beer with the boys after a long round, his face florid from the sun and the alcohol, telling jokes and complaining about the national debt or the tax code or the way kids today just didn't understand the meaning of hard work and sacrifice.

'I'm happy to say it's not nearly as serious as the Manning murder.'

Bower nodded. He did look relieved. 'Good.'

'One of your clients is the Reverend Fred Arling, right?'

Bower made no effort to conceal the eye roll. 'Yes, the Reverend Fred. I've been doing his books for about ten years. Not much money there, but, you know, it's a service. Sort of like a lawyer doing pro bono work.'

'You do his books for free?' Stynes asked.

'No, no. He's just not a very big client, that's all.'

'Has he ever complained to you about missing money?'

Bower rolled his eyes again. 'Only every week for the last three years — Cindy? Cindy?' The girl appeared in the doorway, her face open for whatever task the boss would assign. 'Can you get me the Reverend Fred's folder, please?' When she was gone, Bower pointed to his computer and said, 'Some of this stuff is still easier to look at on paper.'

'I get it,' Stynes said. 'I hate computers.' He looked around. No pictures of a wife or kids or grandkids. Stynes tried to remember if Bower was still married to the same woman. He didn't wear a wedding ring. But even if he was divorced, why no pictures of his son, Michael? Wasn't that Small Businessman 101? Scatter the place with pictures of your family so everyone thinks you're a regular guy?

'I don't even have a cell phone or one of those BlackBerry things,' Bower said. 'If they can't reach me here, they don't need me, right?'

'I hear you,' Stynes said. 'They make me carry one.'

Cindy breezed back in carrying a manila folder. She brought it around behind Bower's chair and, while moving about as close to the man as she possibly could, laid it open on his desk. Stynes saw she wore a gold engagement ring on her left hand.

'He needs a phone,' Cindy said. 'What if there was an emergency or something?'

165

Stynes started to see the picture developing. Cindy did everything but give Ray Bower a kiss on the cheek.

'Thank you, Cindy,' Ray said.

She picked up on the hint and left the room.

Ray flipped the folder open when she was gone and let out a long sigh. 'Let's see,' he said. 'The Reverend Fred.'

'I'm not looking for every detail of his financial holdings,' Stynes said.

Bower didn't look up from the file. 'You couldn't do that without a subpoena anyway.'

'I just want to know if there's validity to his complaint, or is it just a misunderstanding.'

Bower looked up. 'Of course there's no validity to the complaint,' he said. He leaned back in his chair, the springs groaning as he adjusted his weight. 'The Reverend Fred is a little too literal-minded to understand the way business works. He thinks if a certain amount of money is in his account at one point during the month or a quarter, then that amount is always going to be there.'

'Shouldn't it be?'

'A few years back, a rich elderly woman who had been going to Reverend Fred's church for about forty years up and died. Classic little old lady who lived frugally and tucked her money into nice safe investments and drove the same car for thirty years, and when she died she had a decent amount socked away. She didn't have any kids, so she left the money to Reverend Fred's church.'

'What's he doing with the money?' Stynes asked.

'I know the place looks like a rat-trap, but he did use the money for some capital improvements. He put a new roof on. Bought new Bibles and pews. Cleaned up some debts. About what you would expect.'

'So what's the problem?' Stynes asked.

'None really. I set the money up in a mutual fund for him. Pretty safe stuff, enough to generate a little income and build a nest egg.' Bower rubbed his right eye. 'Of course, the economy went off the cliff a couple of years ago, and even people who invested in safe stuff lost a chunk of change.'

'And so did Reverend Fred.'

'He did. It'll come back eventually, but he blamed me for it. Thought I should have been even safer and more conservative than I was.'

'Should you have?'

'A guy in my business can always be safer,' Bower said. 'But you can be so safe sometimes you're not doing anybody any good. At some point, you might just want to stuff the money under your mattress, you know?'

'And is this the root of the reverend's complaint?'

'Every time he gets a quarterly report and the account has lost a few hundred bucks, he calls me up and accuses me of ripping him off. Usually, by the time the next report comes along the money is made up again. Sometimes he makes a lot more, and then he cools down. He's a hothead.'

'Why doesn't he fire you?'

'Like I said, I'm cheap. And so is Reverend

Fred. The better question is why don't I dump him. He's a permanent headache.'

'And why don't you?' Stynes asked.

'I have to be honest, I kind of like the guy,' Bower said. 'I disagree with everything he believes, and he's a pain in my ass, but he's entertaining. I don't get much entertainment in my line of work.'

Stynes closed the notebook but didn't get up. 'Yeah, I kind of agree with you, Mr Bower.' Stynes hooked his pen back onto his shirt pocket. He didn't look at Ray Bower when he said, 'How do you feel about Reverend Fred hiring Dante Rogers to work at his church?'

'He did what?'

'Don't you read the paper?' Stynes asked.

'You mean those articles about the murder?' Bower said. 'I didn't read them. I try not to relive that stuff. I have a lot of bad memories from that time.'

'Dante works at the Reverend Fred's church,' Stynes said. 'I saw him there just yesterday.'

Bower's lips pressed together. His face darkened. 'I didn't know that. As far as I'm concerned, they shouldn't allow that bastard back into society at all. He killed a kid. And he's a pervert.'

'He did his time.'

'Not enough. Not enough at all.'

'You seem pretty angry about it still,' Stynes said, although Bower's anger possessed a practiced, almost scripted quality that Stynes had seen before. People often felt they had to display their anger in a predictable fashion, the

168

way they saw people on TV do it to reporters and news anchors. They worried if they didn't express anger and outrage in its proper, acceptable forms, others would feel they were heartless and unfeeling. Stynes filed the response away in the back of his mind. 'You know the Mannings pretty well, right?'

'Sure.'

'Still see them?'

'Not really.' Bower seemed to want to stop his answer right there, but Stynes just kept watching him, waiting. After a few moments, Bower gave in to the stare down and continued. 'Our kids played together when they were little. The kids grew up. The parents drifted apart. That murder took a big toll on Ginny Manning.'

'That's Justin and Janet's mother?'

'Yes. Virginia. People called her Ginny if they knew her well.' The tension around Bower's jaw eased a little. His eyes lost their focus for just a second as he appeared to think about something. Then he said, 'That boy's death killed her. It really did.'

'That's what people say.'

'After the murder, things weren't the same. How could they be?'

'Indeed. It must have been scary for you. Michael was there that day.'

'I feel like we dodged a bullet.'

'What is Michael doing these days?' Stynes asked.

'He's back in Dove Point.'

'He is?'

'He's been back about six weeks.' Something

else took over Ray Bower's face as he talked about his son. It wasn't the look of a proud father, someone who glowed because the prodigal son had returned to the fold. He looked confused more than anything else, like he had things he wanted to say about Michael, but couldn't be sure if they were the correct or appropriate things to say to a stranger about one's child. 'He lost his job apparently, over in Columbus. He's back here figuring out his next move. To be honest, I'm not really sure what his plans are.'

'It must be nice to have him here.'

'Sure, yeah, it's great.' Again the words seemed forced. So did the smile. 'He's staying at his mom's house.'

'Well,' Stynes said, 'I've taken up a lot of your time.'

'It's not a problem,' Bower said. 'I'll call Reverend Fred later today and smooth his feathers. Although that Rogers thing . . . '

He let his voice trail off.

Stynes pushed himself up from the chair and reached across the desk to shake Ray Bower's hand. 'I guess you don't see much of Bill Manning either?' he asked.

Bower looked surprised by the question. He let go of Stynes's hand.

'No, I don't. Like I said, we're not close anymore.'

'You think Justin's death affected him as much as Virginia?' Stynes asked.

Ray Bower seemed to think his answer over carefully. 'Bill is a tough nut to crack. I'm not sure he ever let on how he felt about anything.'

'Strong, silent type?'

'Well, you know him. If you can figure that man out, Detective, you're a smarter man than me.'

'How do you mean that?'

Bower rubbed his chin. 'I'm not sure he ever felt anything for anybody. If he did, he kept it hidden. His wife, his kids, his friends. I don't know what goes on inside him.'

'Thanks,' Stynes said. He stopped at the door to Bower's office. 'By the way, congratulations.'

'What's that?'

Stynes pointed to his own — empty — ring finger and then pointed behind him in Cindy's general direction.

Ray Bower's face flushed even more than it did at the mention of Dante Rogers. He ducked his head a little in an aw-shucks, you-got-me kind of way.

'Yeah,' he said. 'It's going to be a small wedding.'

'You could do it while your son's in town,' Stynes said.

Bower looked as though that notion had never occurred to him. 'Yeah, we'll see.'

On the way out, Stynes congratulated Cindy. She insisted on showing him the ring, which he complimented appropriately. He excused himself and left the building before she launched too deeply into a rundown of her plans for the wedding, which seemed more elaborate than what Ray Bower was considering.

# 19

Ashleigh slept poorly, her dreams populated by weird, shifting images of Dante Rogers and the man from the porch. She felt unrested and anxious when she opened her eyes just before nine o'clock, knowing that today she would go back to the apartment complex to find Steven Kollman. The kids she went to school with talked about feeling the same way whenever a test approached. Some of them took pills for it. Anti-anxiety. Antidepressants. Tests and school never ruffled Ashleigh. She carried an unspoken contempt for the kids who relied on pills to get through their days.

But she suddenly felt different about that. If a pill had been within her reach, she thought she might have taken it.

She checked her phone and saw a text from Kevin.

*Meet at Macs at noon. Have 2 wk brkfst.*
Noon?

Ashleigh almost screamed. They were supposed to go at ten, and now he couldn't go until noon. She shut the phone without responding, flopped back onto the bed, and stared at the ceiling.

Waiting. Why was she always waiting?

★　★　★

She walked to McDonald's around eleven, after spending the morning trying to distract herself by drawing out every task she performed. Slow breakfast. Slow shower. She even sat and listened while her grandpa lectured her for fifteen uninterrupted minutes on why the Reds would never win the World Series with their current manager.

As she walked along the hot road, she thought about what lay ahead, and her nerves jangled even more. She remembered everything Kevin had said at the park and on the bus the other day.

What if the guy was dangerous? What if he was crazy?

Ashleigh read the news on the Internet. She loved the 'News of the Weird' feature, the bizarre stories compiled from around the country and around the world. Construction workers with nails through their heads, enormous chain reaction car accidents in the fog, babies switched at birth who end up marrying each other.

But some of the stories disturbed her, even with her appetite for strangeness. Serial killers, young girls held hostage in basements, doctors who raped their patients.

What if she ended up in one of those stories? The girl killed by a creep who claimed to know something about her uncle's murder.

She took a few deep breaths, told herself she couldn't let those thoughts take over her mind. She didn't need pills. She wouldn't let her mind twist her into knots.

She decided to eat while waiting for Kevin. At

eleven fifteen, the restaurant remained relatively calm. A few of the old men who gathered for their morning coffee and biscuit still remained. Ashleigh took some sort of comfort from their presence. They seemed like part of the order of the town, like the monument to President Grant on the courthouse lawn or the Fall Festival in October. Their number never decreased. Even when one of them died, another old guy showed up, keeping the number of the group about the same. A part of her wished that her grandpa would come and join them, that he would leave the house a little more and talk to somebody. But he didn't seem to be the type of man who could even stand to talk to other men. Ashleigh just didn't know if he'd always been so closed down, or if her uncle's death sealed her grandpa off from the rest of the world.

Kevin worked in the back, so Ashleigh didn't see him. She ordered Chicken McNuggets, fries, and a Coke and took her tray to a table in the corner. The lunchtime crowd would arrive soon, goofy-looking businessmen in their starched white shirts, mothers pulling a train of kids behind them. She wanted to stay out of everyone's way and eat in peace. She wanted to think about and prepare for seeing Steven Kollman.

What would she say to him?

She decided to be direct, to just ask him what he knew. Just say it straight out.

*Listen, dude, I don't mean to freak you out or*

*anything, but I've got to know what you know. And if you don't know anything, leave my mom alone . . .*

She had a mouthful of McNugget and her eyes on the parking lot when Kevin slid into the booth across from her. Ashleigh jumped a little, lost in imagining the scenario at the apartment complex.

'Easy, Ash. It's just me.'

He smiled wide. Ashleigh had to admit she was happy to see him, even if he did make her jump.

'Are you the fry guy today?' she asked. 'These McNuggets are a little dry.'

'I'll tell the chef.'

'I was just thinking about Kollman, and what I'm going to say to him.'

'About that . . . '

Ashleigh understood what his words meant.

'About that?' she said. 'What are you doing?'

Kevin held his hands out. Placating. Ashleigh hated being placated.

'It's just a delay,' Kevin said.

'A delay?'

'Two people called off,' he said. 'They need me to stay through lunch.'

'We made these plans.' She didn't want to sound whiny, but she was pissed, and her voice rose beyond her control. 'You know how important this is.'

'I know, I know. But the other day when we went to see this guy, I showed up late and got written up.'

'So?'

'So my dad knows the manager. They're friends from the Optimists Club or something, and my dad gave me this big bullshit talk about not being late again.'

'You won't be late,' Ashleigh said. 'You're already here.'

'I feel like I can't say no,' Kevin said. 'And my dad said I need to save money for a car in the fall. It's just until three. Then we can go.'

'Three?'

'Hell, the guy probably isn't even home. We went in the morning last time and he wasn't there. He probably works somewhere, so if we go later we'll catch him. Makes sense, right?'

Ashleigh looked back out the window. A minivan and an SUV pulled in. Any minute and they'd start spilling kids out their sides, the parents irritable, the kids little eating machines. What Kevin said made sense, but she didn't want to wait.

*We made plans.*

'Fine,' she said. 'Work until three.'

Kevin didn't say anything. He looked around the restaurant.

'What?' Ashleigh asked.

'You know, other people have things going on in their lives. I'm offering to go with you. It will just be later.'

'Fine.' She took a long drink.

'I know what that means,' he said. 'You're pissed. I get it. I get how much this means to you. But we have to compromise sometimes, you know? Like you going to football or basketball games when I know you don't want to. Now I'm

176

asking you to wait for me. Jesus, just once could you give somebody a break? Could you? Like Kelcey in the park. Why lash out at people who mean well?'

Ashleigh didn't meet his eye. He'd never spoken to her like this, and it brought an unnatural burning to her eyes, something that made her feel like a little kid.

But she wasn't going to cry.

She wasn't going to show it.

'It's fine,' she said. 'Just work.'

But Kevin didn't leave. He reached across the table and squeezed her hand. 'Come on, Ash. I'm sorry — '

She pulled her hand away. 'It's fine. Go.'

He leaned back. 'We can do it at three. You can hang out at the library or back home, and we can leave right at three.'

'Okay,' she said. 'Really.'

She offered nothing else, so Kevin went back to work. She finished eating alone.

★   ★   ★

The bus dropped Ashleigh at the same stop as the other day — Hamilton Avenue, a few blocks' walk from Steven Kollman's apartment complex. She stepped out into the heat, the crappy food from McDonald's heavy in her stomach. She'd left the restaurant without talking to Kevin. She'd handed the woman at the cash register a note, written on a thin paper napkin.

*Going to library. See you at 3.*

By three, Ashleigh expected — *hoped* — to

177

have everything with Steven Kollman wrapped up. She could go back and meet Kevin and tell him what had happened. She could do it on her own.

But as she walked down the sidewalk toward the street where the apartment complex sat, she started to doubt the wisdom of what she was doing. What was she going to do — a skinny fifteen-year-old girl armed with scraps of information? What would she do if the guy was a rapist or a killer?

But she wouldn't turn back. Couldn't and wouldn't.

It meant too much and she'd waited too long.

Ashleigh remembered the building. The cooking smells in the hallway were worse than what she ate at McDonald's. Everyone seemed to have their TVs blaring. She didn't want to think about what went on behind all those doors, the empty, boring lives led by people with nothing better to do than watch TV all day.

But was her grandpa any different? And what right did she have to come down on these people so hard? Maybe they were like her grandpa and had lost their jobs or had someone close to them die, leaving them to fend for themselves.

Ashleigh stopped on the first landing. She knew she judged others harshly, even went so far as to look down on anyone she considered stupid or ignorant — and as far as Ashleigh was concerned, that meant a lot of people.

But what if Kevin was right? What if she never gave anybody a break? Her mom, her grandpa, Kevin, Kelcey, the kids at school. People she didn't even know as she walked through her life. Maybe this guy, Steven Kollman, was one of those people. Someone who had been dealt a bad hand, never given a chance by the world, and so he ended up living in a dumpy apartment building in Dove Point, Ohio.

Ashleigh hoped to find out soon enough, so she resumed her climb up the stairs.

She had taken just a few steps when she heard the whooshing sound. It repeated itself rhythmically — *whoosh whoosh whoosh*. Ashleigh couldn't place it, but it sounded like it was coming from the top floor, where Steven Kollman lived. She moved past the second landing, and the noise increased. When the third floor came into sight, Ashleigh had a pretty good guess as to what the noise was.

Steven Kollman's apartment door was wide-open. Three large dark garbage bags sat just outside of it. They looked to be filled to bursting. Every time the *whoosh* sound came again, a puff of dust and dirt came out the door of the apartment like a little cloud. Someone was cleaning Steven's apartment. Really cleaning it.

Was it Steven?

Or . . .

The sweeping stopped, and the familiar head of the building manager popped out of the apartment door. For a short moment, it looked like he didn't know who Ashleigh was and wanted to ask her what she needed. But then recognition spread across his face. His eyes brightened and his eyebrows raised behind the loose-fitting glasses.

179

'Oh, it's you,' he said. 'Steven's . . . what? Are you his cousin or something? I forget.'

'Something like that,' Ashleigh said.

'Where's your friend?' he asked.

'Oh, he's at work.'

She regretted telling the truth as soon as the words came out of her mouth. She should have thought on her feet and told a lie. She could have said he was in the car or waiting outside or on his way to meet her. But the man now knew she was alone. She was halfway up the staircase, between the third and second floor, so the manager and his blandly happy face loomed above her. He came all the way out and set the broom down, leaning it against the wall. He wore a red T-shirt and great blotches of sweat encircled the area of his armpits.

'Is Steven home?' Ashleigh asked.

The man wiped his hands together, trying to clean the dust or dirt off. 'You're too late,' he said. 'Or he's too late really. He never paid me the back rent he owed, so I left him an eviction notice. Late last night, I see him carrying some stuff out to his car. You know, a suitcase, a couple of boxes. I asked him what he was doing, and he said he was moving out, but he had the back rent for me. Next thing I know, he's driving off.' The guy shrugged. 'He never came back, the bum.'

'You don't know where he went?'

'Sweetie, if I knew that, I'd find him and send the marshals after him. I see this all the time. There are a lot of crummy people in the world.'

Ashleigh didn't know what to think. She felt relief, yes. All the fears and anxieties she carried with her, all the worries about what might have gone wrong if she did end up talking to Steven Kollman eased and allowed her to breathe more freely than she had all day. On the other hand, a crushing disappointment lurked beneath everything. What was she going to do if Steven was gone? Everything — *everything* — she'd hoped for about finding this man and helping her family was gone. She had fallen back to zero.

'Didn't he tell you he was leaving?' the man asked.

'No,' Ashleigh said.

'He didn't tell anyone in the family?'

Ashleigh shook her head.

'See, that's crummy.' He pushed his glasses up.

Ashleigh agreed. It was.

'That guy came back looking for him.'

'What guy?' Ashleigh asked.

'Remember?' he said. He sounded frustrated, like Ashleigh should know exactly what he was talking about. 'Last time you were here I told you that another guy came to see him and they had an argument. Remember?'

Ashleigh did, once he mentioned it. 'Sure. Okay.'

'That guy came back, too, looking for Steven.'

'And you don't know who this guy is?' Ashleigh asked.

'I'm not a secretary.'

'I thought maybe he left a note or something.'

'He didn't. He just left. And that's all I know.'

But she couldn't turn away. She remained on the stairs with one hand holding the banister.

'What's going to happen to all his stuff?' she asked.

The man turned and looked into the apartment door, appraising the contents of the room. 'The apartments come furnished, so none of that is his. I guess I'm lucky he didn't try to swipe it. The rest of the stuff is just junk. Papers and bills and stuff. It all gets thrown out.'

'Thrown out?'

'What am I supposed to do with it? Make a scrapbook for him? Store it?'

'Let me come in and see it,' Ashleigh said.

The man looked surprised, like someone who finds a forgotten twenty-dollar bill in his pants pocket.

'You want to come in? Here?'

'If you're just going to throw the stuff away — '

'Of course. Come in.'

He stepped back and into the door of the apartment, and while he moved he reached up with both hands, attempting to smooth the ragged strands of his hair down against the skin of his scalp. Ashleigh knew she was taking a risk. Her mom had already given her more than one talk about men — the kinds of situations to avoid, the times to turn and run. Mom wouldn't approve of this one, Ashleigh knew. Being in an apartment with a strange older man. Alone.

But Ashleigh put it all aside. The guy looked so pathetic, so nerdy. And how would she live with herself if she came this close and didn't take the opportunity? She may never have the chance again to learn something — *anything* — about Steven Kollman.

Ashleigh went the rest of the way up the steps to the third floor. The manager held out his hand.

'I'm Nick,' he said, his body filling the doorway. 'Nick Reeves.'

'Ashleigh.'

She took his dirty hand reluctantly, but tried to conceal her disgust. His skin was wet and clammy. Ashleigh wanted to wash the feeling off right away but didn't see any graceful way to do it.

Ashleigh followed Nick inside and looked around. A few boxes sat on the floor, their tops open. Junk filled them. Papers, magazines, plastic cups and dishes. A few pieces of clothing. Ashleigh noted that Nick didn't shut the door behind them, and that brought her a small measure of relief. She thought again of what Kevin said about giving people a break. Shouldn't she give Nick a break as well? Maybe he was just a harmless nerd, a middle-aged guy who didn't know how to act around women of any age.

'Is this all there is?' Ashleigh asked, pointing to the boxes.

'There's the trash in the hall,' he said. 'But that's basically it. I already cleaned out the bedroom. Are you looking for something in particular? There wasn't any jewelry or pictures, if that's what you're looking for. I wouldn't throw someone's pictures away, and I'd sell the jewelry for the back rent. I'm allowed to do that.'

'I don't know what I'm looking for,' Ashleigh said, bending down near the first box. 'I don't know. And it probably isn't here anyway, whatever it might be.'

'That doesn't really make sense.'

'No, it doesn't,' she said.

She took handfuls of the paper and paged through them, letting each piece drop away to the bottom of the box when she saw it wasn't important. And none of it was important. Junk mail, mostly. The same crap that filled their mailbox at home, the stuff everyone on earth must throw away but companies still felt compelled to mail.

'Where do you go to school?' Nick asked.

'What?' Ashleigh turned her head.

Nick still stood there, just a few steps away. She had assumed he would go back to his cleaning and leave her alone, but he hadn't. He seemed to be waiting on her, like he thought she might need something that only he could deliver.

'Your school?'

'Dove Point High,' she said. 'I'm going to be a sophomore.'

'DPH? I went to Dove Point West — you know, out in the country.'

Ashleigh waited to see if he wanted to say anything else, but he didn't. In fact, Nick turned away a little bit and looked around the kitchen of the apartment. Ashleigh could see dishes piled in the sink and some garbage in the corner. He still needed to clean there.

She turned back to the papers and picked up her pace. She didn't know how long she could stay in this little crowded room with Nick. She shuffled the papers quickly, almost not paying attention to what passed her eyes.

'Are you going to drive next year?' Nick asked.

'Sure. I guess so.'

She kept looking at the papers.

'You'll turn sixteen, right?'

'In April.'

'You can drive then.'

'Sure.'

*Wait!*

She picked up the paper she had just discarded.

Across the top it said: 'Clerk of Courts, Franklin County, Ohio.'

*Franklin County. Columbus.*

Ashleigh scanned the paper. A few words jumped out.

Assault . . . second degree . . . warrant . . .

And then she saw it — the name on the court summons:

*Justin Manning.*

Her hands shook.

'Holy fuck!'

Ashleigh didn't know if she said the words out loud or in her head. It didn't matter. They sounded like a scream in her own mind.

For what felt like forever she just sat there, the paper raised to her eye level. She stared at the paper, made sure she really saw what she thought she saw.

It was there. Her uncle's name in this man's things.

Then the hands were on her. From behind,

185

Nick's sweaty, greasy hands. They fumbled across her breasts, brushed against her face. She felt his hot breath on her neck as he wrapped her up, tightening his grip around her so it was difficult to move at all.

Ashleigh made a sound. Somewhere between a scream and a gag. She didn't think it was very loud, so she made it again even louder.

But who would hear her in the shitty building with everyone staring at their TVs?

She dropped the paper and remembered something her grandpa had taught her: if someone grabs you from behind —

Ashleigh brought her right arm up as far as it would go, then swung it back, her elbow aimed for Nick's gut like a missile. She connected, felt the rush of air that came out as Nick said, 'Ooof!'

Ashleigh slipped away as he loosened his grip. She turned. Nick still stood between her and the door, but he was doubled over, his eyes closed tight. She swung her foot high and caught him in the chin. Her shoe against his face made a satisfying smack. She didn't wait to see the damage done or how he reacted.

She didn't care.

She ran. Her shoes pounded down the stairs. Pounded and pounded.

She ran and ran until she looked back over her shoulder and couldn't see the building anymore.

# 20

Rose didn't know Janet was coming. Janet went to call Michael before she left work, then realized he had never given her his cell phone number or even an e-mail address. She didn't know what he did with his days. Maybe he looked for work in Dove Point, a thought that caused an unreasonable flutter of emotion to rise in Janet's chest. He hadn't said any such thing, but that didn't stop Janet from hoping he might stay and settle down. In the immediate moment, she just wanted to talk to him, to hear his voice. She wanted to tell him about seeing the man again, this time on campus. And she wanted to tell Michael she wasn't crazy — the man probably had been creeping around her house two nights earlier.

So when she couldn't reach him by cell phone, she decided to just stop by. Rose's number was in the phone book — she found it with no trouble — but Janet didn't bother to call in advance.

Rose Bower lived north of Dove Point's city limits. Everyone called the area Baileytown because the Bailey Foundry operated out there and most of the people who lived nearby had worked for the company. The foundry had closed when Janet was in high school, not long before Ashleigh was born, but the name Baileytown remained. The foundry still remained as well, its gates padlocked, its vacant and unused buildings slowly and inevitably crumbling.

As far as Janet knew, Rose had never worked for the foundry. She'd split from Michael's father when Michael was fourteen, so she must have moved to Baileytown then because of the cheap rents that were available as the foundry's workers moved out. Janet remembered going to Rose's house in high school either to pick up or drop off Michael. Rose always showed a great deal of interest in Janet. She used to ask Janet about school as well as her future plans, and when Janet talked about going to college and having a career, Rose nodded affirmatively as though that was the exact right thing to do. Janet chalked Rose's interest up to the woman's overall benevolent nature, but also supposed that she saw Janet as a kind of surrogate daughter. Rose never had a daughter of her own, and with Janet's mother gone, it seemed like a natural fit.

But Janet stopped going to Michael's house once she became pregnant.

Janet dealt with the shame of her pregnancy at school about as well as could be expected. As her stomach grew, and as she faced the stares and occasional comments from her classmates and teachers, she allowed herself to feel a measure of pride in the pregnancy. She knew some of the other girls were jealous and wanted nothing more out of life than to begin having children, so Janet managed to convince herself that she was doing something special and unique.

But those thoughts — and years later, Janet

knew they were just a defense mechanism, a form of self-preservation — didn't carry over to facing Rose Bower. Of all the people in her life outside of her father, Janet hated the thought of letting Rose Bower down. A woman who'd always asked about Janet's career ambitions, a woman who seemed to be pushing Janet to be better, wouldn't understand how she'd managed to get herself knocked up. Janet didn't know the answer to that question herself, so she simply avoided the Bower house from the day she learned she was pregnant.

Which is not to say Janet hadn't seen Rose over the years. Dove Point was too small of a town to not occasionally run into somebody. As Janet drove away from campus and across town on Old Hanover Road, she tried to remember the last time she'd seen Rose. They'd run into each other once at the funeral of the former principal of Dove Point High, an event everyone in town seemed to have passed through. And Janet could recall a few encounters in the grocery store, most recently . . . was it five years ago? Ashleigh was still young enough to want to tag along to the store with her mother, and still young enough to answer an adult's questions without rolling her eyes or sighing. Even then, five years earlier, Rose's frailty had struck Janet as somewhat disturbing. The woman seemed to be diminishing into herself, becoming just a shell of what she once was. How much more diminished would she be now? Maybe some part of Janet needed to see Rose again, to let the woman know Janet was doing okay, that she was making it despite becoming a mother while still in high school. And Janet could see how Rose was doing too.

The streets of Baileytown looked even worse than Janet remembered. Plastic toys and junked cars littered the yards she drove past. Children played in the street under the suspicious eyes of parents who were smoking or drinking. Janet felt grateful to have a job, to have a life with future prospects. If she'd married Tony Bachus back in high school, would she be living on one of these streets? Would she have popped out more kids without regard for how to provide for them? One kid proved to be work enough . . .

Two window air-conditioning units stuck out from the side of the dirty white house. The paint was peeling in large chunks, and the house appeared not to have been painted in the fifteen years since Janet last visited. A neighbor's dog barked from a fenced-in yard, its white teeth visible like angry knives. Janet knocked on the rickety screen door, which despite the heat was all that stood between the natural elements and Rose's living room. The sun was still bright outside, but Janet leaned close to the screen in an attempt to see into the house. No lights were on, and the curtains looked to be drawn against the heat.

Janet knocked again. 'Hello?'

'Yes?'

The voice sounded faint but close. Was she right in the living room hidden from Janet's sight?

'Hello? Rose?'

'Yes?'

Janet heard a rustling, and then the woman appeared in the doorway. It took a moment, but a smile spread across her face.

'Do you remember me, Rose? It's Janet Manning.'

'Of course, of course.' She unlatched the screen door's eyehook lock and stepped back to let Janet in. 'I know you, honey. Come in.'

While Janet looked at the furniture — which also hadn't changed in fifteen years — Rose Bower scurried around opening the curtains and letting in daylight. Despite the furniture's age, the house looked clean and well organized, as though someone took pride in its appearance.

'I'm sorry to just show up like this,' Janet said.

'I'm glad you did,' Rose said. 'Sit, sit.'

Janet chose the end of the floral-patterned couch and took her first good look at Rose Bower in the daylight. She looked even thinner and more frail than the last time. Janet reminded herself that the woman standing before her was roughly the same age as her own parents — about sixty — because anyone else would have guessed she was closer to eighty. Deep lines creased her face — did she smoke? — and her hair looked thin and brittle, brushed back into place and held by a series of bobby pins. A gray housecoat hung loose on her body, and when Rose sat down — resuming her spot in a recliner near the couch — she let out a long breath, as though the effort of standing up and opening the door and the curtains had cost her a great deal. She didn't offer to get Janet anything.

'Are you looking for Michael?' Rose asked.

'I am. But I was also hoping to see you.'

'He's not here, Janet. I don't know where he is today.' She pointed vaguely toward the front door. 'He said he had some business to attend to, but he didn't tell me what it is.'

'Is he looking for a job?'

Rose's face brightened considerably. 'Do you think he might be? Here in Dove Point?'

Janet wished she'd kept her mouth shut. She didn't want to give Rose false hope that her son might be home to stay. Janet knew well the difficulties of false hope.

'I don't know, Rose,' Janet said, scrambling. 'How are you doing?'

Rose smiled without showing her teeth. 'I'm okay. I'm doing okay. I don't work. I don't do much, to be honest.'

'The house is clean.'

'I manage to do that. It's an old habit I can't let go of.' She looked around the small room with pride. 'How have you been? You must be working still. Or did you . . . ?'

Janet caught her drift. 'No, I'm not married. I still work at Cronin. I manage the dean's office. I've been doing that the last three years.'

'And your daughter? Ashleigh, right?'

'Yes. She's good. She's very smart, and she knows it. She's fifteen, and I imagine she's as challenging as any fifteen-year-old can be.' Janet paused a moment thinking of all she had to protect Ashleigh from. Not just the usual stuff, but all the other things like the man from the porch. Janet had been crazily vigilant in the

192

house the previous two days, making sure every door and window was locked. 'We moved back in with my dad. He lost his job.'

'He did? You mean Strand laid him off?'

'Yes.'

'Oh. He was a company man. I thought he'd be there forever.'

'Times change,' Janet said. 'Anyway, we're all together in the old house now.'

Janet expected Rose to comment on that, to offer something about the good old days, but she didn't. Maybe Rose wished she could have the same thing — Michael move in for good, a grandchild or two to look after and celebrate.

'Have you seen Michael since he's been back?' Rose asked.

'We had coffee the other night. We just talked.'

'I kept telling him to call you when he came back, but he must have taken his sweet time. You were always such good friends. To be honest, I always hoped the two of you would . . . you know, get together at some point.'

Janet's face flushed. She looked away for a moment.

'I'm sorry if I was rude — '

'Oh, no,' Janet said. 'It's not that.'

'I shouldn't have said that. I embarrassed you.'

'It's okay, Rose.' Janet looked back and smiled. 'I always hoped the same thing when we were in high school.'

'I could tell. He had all those girls following him around. His groupies, I used to call them. He liked a certain kind of girl, you know. The showy ones, the wild ones. And there was the best one right under his nose. You.' She paused. 'You don't ever hear from that Tony Bachus, do you?'

'Not much. He sends money for Ashleigh when he can. Or when he feels like it.' Janet waved the thought of Tony away with her right hand. 'I haven't needed him.'

'You haven't, that's right.' Rose mirrored Janet's gesture of dismissal. 'He was never any damn good. I don't even know why Michael was friends with him. He hung around with some real dolts in his time.'

Janet laughed.

'You know,' Rose said, 'I sometimes wonder if he's gotten any better. Did he tell you anything about what he was doing in Columbus?'

Janet recognized the position she was being put in. Rose wanted information, and since she didn't think she could get it from her son, she intended to pry it out of Janet. Janet had to applaud the strategy. If Ashleigh brought any of her friends around, or if her few friends — besides Kevin — were less reticent and angsty, Janet might have used it herself.

'I thought he was working there,' Janet said.

'Maybe.'

'Maybe?'

'I think he asked his dad for money a few times,' Rose said. 'I don't know, but that's the impression I got.'

'Didn't he lose his job?' Janet asked.

'Sure. But I don't know when. I thought maybe you did.'

'We didn't talk about it,' Janet said. 'Is something wrong?'

Rose didn't answer. She pressed her lips tight, as though she wanted to keep whatever she had to say bottled up.

'It's okay if — '

'This phone call came here,' Rose said. 'And I don't know what to make of it.'

'Was it about his job?'

Rose shook her head. She lowered her voice when she spoke, even though no one else was around.

'Who was it?' Janet asked.

'It was a detective from the Columbus Police Department. She called here looking for Michael. She wouldn't tell me what it was about when I asked. She just said she'd call Michael back.'

'When was this?' Janet asked.

'A few days ago.'

A few days ago. *Before* Michael came and saw Janet at work.

'Did you ask him about it?' Janet asked.

'I gave him the message, but he just grunted. Then he went outside and used his cell phone.'

'To call the detective?'

'I assume.'

Janet leaned back. 'Maybe it was just something simple. Maybe someone broke into his car or something.' Even as she said the words, she doubted they were true. He'd come to her worked up about his dad's possible role in Justin's death — and this happened after he spoke to a detective. 'It's probably nothing,' she

195

added, hoping her voice sounded convincing.

'I hope you're right.'

'Michael's never been in trouble.'

Again, Rose pressed her mouth shut.

'Has he?'

Rose reached up and fiddled with one of her bobby pins. 'You know, things didn't always go well for Michael when he was out on the West Coast. His jobs . . . well, he still didn't tell me everything, of course, because he didn't want me to worry. But he had rough times.'

'Really?'

'He tried more than one thing, more than one career.'

'A lot of young people do that. They try to find themselves.'

'I guess. What do I know? I've always been here. But a mother worries, you know?'

'Sure.'

Janet tried to process what Rose told her about Michael's life out west. She tried to make it match with the picture she had carried with her since high school graduation and Michael's departure from Dove Point. In that picture in Janet's head, Michael worked in an exciting job and lived close to the beach. He was carried along by a tide of good times and good friends, and yes, Janet had to admit, she always imagined a swarm of good-looking California women. Liberated, tan, educated. And not tied down in Dove Point, Ohio. Even having the information that contradicted that picture didn't change the way Janet thought about Michael's time in California.

'You're not saying Michael was in trouble with the police out west, are you?'

'If he was, I wouldn't know.'

'Was he? Do you know something?'

'I don't know,' Rose said again. 'But when the police call the house looking for your child, you wonder.'

Janet thought of Ashleigh. Of course, Janet thought. She knew exactly what Rose meant.

'I understand why you'd be worried,' Janet said. 'If I talk to him, and if it seems natural, I'll ask him about it.'

'I'm not asking you to spy — '

'I know,' Janet said. 'I want to talk to him again anyway.'

Rose's face looked a little dreamy. Janet wondered if she was falling asleep or losing focus because of her age. But she spoke through the dreamy look.

'You know,' she said, 'Ray was the golden boy too when we met. Football player and all of that. Everybody's friend, everybody's drinking buddy. Lots of girls wanted him, but I got him . . .'

Her voice trailed off, even though there seemed to be more to say. Janet leaned forward.

'And?'

'Michael and his father have a lot in common,' she said, her eyes still distant. 'Sometimes I worry about how much they have in common.'

# 21

A pull-down ladder at the end of the hallway provided access to the attic. Janet hadn't been up there for a few months. Every so often, a wave of nostalgia and regret washed over her — took hold of her really — and at those times she comforted herself by looking at old photos of Justin and her mother. It eased her mind knowing the mementos were stored just above her, like a savings account she only occasionally withdrew from.

Janet always worried she wouldn't be able to pull the ladder down by herself. She came home from Rose's feeling more tired than usual. The past few days' events — the encounter with the man on the quad, the trip to Rose's house — had left her drained, and she resisted the urge to crawl straight into bed with the TV for company. She needed a pick-me-up, a little lift, so she gave the short pull string two good tugs and brought the ladder down with a groaning, whining protest. She unfolded the wooded contraption, breathing in dust, and hoped — like she always did when she stepped onto it — that it would still hold her weight. *I'll never reach Memory Lane if I break my neck on the way . . .*

She started to climb. More than simple, painful nostalgia drove Janet forward. A sharp purpose guided her to the attic — she wanted to look at pictures of Justin and her mother and even her father as a young man and determine if a resemblance really existed between them and the man from the porch. She needed to study those pictures, to contemplate them. She couldn't trust her memory to do the work for her anymore. Her memory — her heart — wanted it to be true so bad she couldn't rely on it.

The ladder shook and squeaked beneath her weight, but it held. A lone bulb on a cord illuminated the slanting roof, the thick tufts of insulation. Janet always feared bats and mice and bugs. She once heard a story about a woman in Dove Point who'd found a rattlesnake nesting in her attic. But that couldn't be true, could it? The obvious irrationality of the story aside, Janet shivered despite the heat in the enclosed, musty space. *Quickly*, she told herself. Quickly.

Janet knew where the box was kept. She remembered the days and weeks after her brother's funeral, waking during the night to the sound of creaking footsteps in the attic. Terrified, she'd pull the covers to her head, thinking the same man who had killed her brother had come into the house looking for her.

But it wasn't a stranger. It was her mother. Eventually, Janet screwed up the nerve to investigate and she found the ladder to the attic pulled down. And she heard the sobs echoing in the unfinished empty space. Her mother crying over mementos of her murdered child. Photos, clothes, crayon drawings. When she was old enough, Janet made the trek up those stairs too — always when her parents weren't home — and relived her brother's short life through the contents of that one box.

She turned to the right, to the corner of the attic where the box always sat. She didn't see it right away. She couldn't imagine anyone else in the family had been up in the attic moving things around, certainly not her dad. Would Ashleigh go through these things? Janet pushed some boxes aside, felt a layer of dust against her skin. A small lump of panic rose in her throat, almost as though she had swallowed the very dust she was kicking up as she moved around the attic. The box was always in that corner. Always. Before her mom died it had been there, and after her mom died it remained.

Janet moved around the room, her actions becoming more frantic and panicked the longer she looked. It couldn't be gone because it held everything. Everything that was left —

She made a circuit of the room, opening every box. Then she did it again, and by the time she finished the second go-round she was crying. She wiped the tears away, felt them mix with the gritty dust that coated her face.

'No,' she said. 'No.'

She must have missed it, must have passed it by as she tried not to lose control of her emotions. But something told her that wasn't the case. She knew it was gone, gone, gone.

Janet stood still in the middle of the attic, the roof support beams just above her head. A bright spark of anger and frustration ignited in her gut. She left the attic, back down the rickety stairs, not worrying at all on the descent if the ladder would hold her weight or not. When she hit the bottom she went right down the stairs again to the first floor, where she heard the TV playing, the usual late-afternoon news drone that her father couldn't seem to get enough of.

Sure enough, she found him in his chair, his eyes a little glassy from the tranquilizing nature of the TV set. He didn't bother to look up when she came into the room. He kept his eyes on the screen as if Janet wasn't there.

'Dad?'

He still didn't respond.

Janet reached down for the remote and turned the TV off.

'Hey.'

'Dad, I need you to listen to me. I need to ask you something.'

'What's wrong?'

'There was a box in the attic, a box of things from Mom and Justin.'

'I don't — '

'You know goddamn well what box I'm talking about,' she said. 'It's been there forever. I know you like to pretend you don't know about things like that, but I know you know what I'm talking about. I'm not the only one who used to hear Mom go up there at night and cry. I know you remember that.'

Her dad looked away, back to the blank TV screen.

'Dad, that box is gone. What happened to it?'

'It's dark up there.'

'Dad, there are only three of us in this house. I know I didn't move it and I know Ashleigh didn't. So I'm asking you.'

He remained silent for a long time. Janet decided to wait it out, to stare him down and not give him a chance to turn away or say something off the subject. She just waited.

It took a long time, but her dad finally spoke. 'It's gone,' he said.

Janet didn't process the word. She waited another beat, then said, 'Gone? Do you mean it's missing?'

'I mean it's gone,' he said. 'I threw it away.'

Whatever anger Janet felt when she entered the room left as soon as her father's words registered in her brain. In place of the anger, an emptiness grew, spreading through the inside of her body like expanding warm air, filling her and driving everything else away. She felt hollow.

'Why . . . ?'

He finally looked at her.

'It's time to move on,' he said. 'It's been time to move on for a while, but now it's really time. As long as that stuff sat up there, as long as we could go up and look at those things whenever we wanted to, then we couldn't go on. So I made the decision to get rid of it.'

'It wasn't your decision to make.'

'When you moved out and grew up, it was okay to have it there. I thought it was good for you to have your own life. But when you moved back in, you started going up there again.' He shook his head. 'And now all this stuff this week. It's not good for any one of us.'

'That's what we had left of your wife and son.'

He didn't say anything for a long time. And then, his voice flat and without emotion, he said,

'It's over, Janet. It really is.'

He reached for the remote and turned the TV back on.

Janet started to walk away, knowing she'd been dismissed. But she stopped immediately. She wasn't ready to walk away.

Janet came back and took the remote again. She turned the TV off and stood over her dad's chair.

'Dad, I need to ask you something.'

He reached for the remote. 'Give me that.'

Janet took a step back but held on to the remote.

'I need to know why you don't care about our family's past,' she said. 'What's going on?'

Her dad looked puzzled. What she said wasn't registering.

'You never want to talk about the past. You never want to talk about Mom or Justin or about what happened. Why is that, Dad? You couldn't even come out of your room and talk to that newspaper reporter who came here. You couldn't even make that much of an effort about your family. Why?'

'I'm not a woman,' he said. 'I don't live in the past.'

'Oh, no.' Janet raised her finger and wagged it in the air between them. 'You're not going to pull that one on me.' She took a step closer and studied his face. Janet understood something then, something she'd thought about many times but had never given clear voice to: she really didn't know her father. Or, to be more accurate, she'd never been allowed to know her father. He

203

never opened up, never revealed anything of himself. Even standing over her mother's grave, he never shed a tear, never gave voice to what he felt or lost.

What else could there be inside the man? What didn't she know?

'Dad, can you look at me and tell me what your problem with the past is? What is it that you really don't want me to know?'

Janet tried to put her father's reticence together with the events of recent days — the man on the porch, the anniversary of the murder, Dante's maintaining of his innocence, the newspaper stories. Michael's return and questions.

What didn't she know?

'Dad, just tell me. Is it something about Justin? Do you know something? Because I've been starting to think — some things have been happening . . . '

Her dad looked over and they locked eyes. For a brief moment, an understanding passed between them, something that placed them on the same wavelength for a split second. Together, they had moved closer to something, closed the gap that had previously existed.

But her dad didn't say anything.

And before Janet could say more, the doorbell rang.

'I don't care about the door,' she said. 'I'll ignore it. This is important — '

'No, get it,' he said. 'Just go get it. I told you, I'm done with talking about all of this.'

# 22

Ashleigh ran until her heart nearly burst. She always ran well in gym class, even better than the girls who played on the school's sports teams. She was light and fast and never tired.

But she finally ran out of gas two miles down Hamilton Avenue. She stopped running and stood in the middle of the sidewalk, her hands on her knees, her breaths coming in great huffing bursts. She looked at her shoes and wouldn't have been surprised to see the rubber of the tread smoking, she'd been going so fast. She straightened up, placed her hands on her hips, and started walking, hoping to cool down and breathe like a normal person again. Spots swam before her eyes. She hoped she wouldn't faint.

*The fucking creep. He touched me. My breasts* —

No. Wait. That didn't matter.

It really didn't matter.

The name — the name on that ticket or whatever it was —

Justin Manning.

Her uncle, who was supposed to be dead for twenty-five years. He was alive? He was alive!

Her mind raced faster than her heart. She couldn't make any sense of it.

Ashleigh looked behind her. She really didn't think the creep from the apartment complex would be following her. He was probably scared, probably still doubled over from her elbow and her kick. She'd never hit anybody, never even been close to a fight. Hell, she'd never had a guy touch her like that, either a creep or a guy she liked. But as she thought back over the scene in the apartment, she felt less scared and more exhilarated. A smile grew across her face, and she wanted to laugh.

Had she really just kicked that guy's ass?

The return bus came along Hamilton. Ashleigh waited until traffic cleared, then managed to jog across the street. Her muscles burned from the exertion and her legs felt rubbery. She'd never been so glad to see a bus. If it hadn't come, she wasn't sure she could walk all that way, several miles. She needed to sit, to ride. To think.

She took a seat near the back. The air-conditioning was almost too cool, too intense. But she welcomed it. She fanned her face with someone's discarded newspaper. The bus was mostly empty in midafternoon, just a few old ladies and their rolling shopping baskets, a mother with a baby near the front.

Ashleigh thought about what she'd seen on that paper —

Her uncle's name. Did she really see it? Or did she want to find something so much she imagined the name?

No, no, she said. She saw it. She knew she saw it. He'd come to their house in the middle of the night. He'd told her mom he knew the truth about what really happened to Justin.

And he was Justin?

Who else could he be?

Ashleigh reached up and rang the bell when they were just half a block from the stop. She was so distracted she almost forgot, and the bus lurched as the air brakes whined. The bus driver, a middle-aged guy with greasy hair, looked in the giant rearview mirror at the front and shook his head at her. She didn't care. She needed to get off the bus. She had cooled off; her breathing was normal again.

She had things to do.

She had to talk to Kevin first.

★  ★  ★

'You did what?' Kevin said.

His manager had let him out of work early, Kevin told her. He'd walked to the library looking for Ashleigh and didn't see her. So he texted her — at least three times. Getting no response, he returned to McDonald's, where Ashleigh found him waiting in a booth, two hamburger wrappers and the remnants of an order of fries scattered before him. He looked up in anticipation, but then Ashleigh sat down and told him where she'd been.

'I had to know,' Ashleigh said. 'I couldn't wait.'

'You went there alone? To that strange dude's apartment? Jesus, Ash.' He looked to the ceiling, as if he wanted divine intervention. 'Did you do that because you were mad at me about what I said earlier?'

'I told you — I just couldn't wait. I've been looking forward to this a long time. I couldn't just sit in the library and pretend to read a book.'

Kevin almost smiled. 'You've got balls, girl. I'll say that for you. Damn.'

Ashleigh took Kevin's drink, shook it, and when she heard liquid slosh in the bottom of the cup, drew from the straw. She swallowed, then said, 'If you think that was ballsy, let me tell you what happened while I was there.'

Kevin listened while Ashleigh told the story. When she told him she went into the vacated apartment, his mouth fell open a little. Ashleigh didn't pause. She didn't want him to be able to interject. And it wasn't the most important part of the story.

She watched him carefully as she told him about the letter with her uncle's name on it. As she said that, his mouth fell open even more. Something lit up in his eyes, something between joy and fear — she couldn't tell which.

'Holy shit,' he said. He looked around the restaurant, which was fairly empty. He said it again. 'Holy shit. Ash, you were right. You found something.'

'I know.'

Ashleigh tried to contain her own joy and enthusiasm, but her heart raced, and this time not from the adrenaline of the run and the close call with the creep, but instead from the pure joy of accomplishing something she'd set out to do. She felt like a little kid. If she'd let herself, she could've screamed and squealed with joy.

'Did you take the letter?' Kevin asked. 'Where is it?'

A thin shadow of disappointment fell over

Ashleigh. She'd dropped the letter. When the creep took hold of her, she let it go. Why couldn't she have held on to it? If only —

'I don't have it,' she said.

'You don't? Didn't the apartment manager let you take it?'

'Kind of . . . ' She told him the story of the guy talking to her about school and trying to act like they were friends. Then she told Kevin about the sudden grab around her middle, the fumbling hands, the fight —

'No,' Kevin said. The response was simple, direct. She knew what it meant. Kevin was pissed. 'He touched you.'

'He tried to,' she said. 'Well, he did. He put me in a bear hug. But I got away.'

Kevin started to slide out of the booth. 'I'm going back.'

'No.'

'Ash, that little creep. That asshole. I'm going to — '

She reached out, placed her hand on his. 'Stop. It doesn't matter.'

'It matters. I'm calling the police. Then I'm kicking his ass.'

'No, wait.' She kept her hand on his. She had to admit, she liked seeing this side of him — protective, passionate. He wanted to stand up for her, exact justice on someone who had wronged her. Ashleigh didn't want him to follow through on his threats. She thought that her own defense of herself was good enough. But it felt good to have Kevin on her side. 'Forget about that guy. We have something bigger to deal with, remember? This guy.' She lowered her voice even though no one was nearby. 'The guy from the porch. He says he knows something about my uncle's death. Well, now we know what he knows. He *is* my uncle.'

Kevin sat back in the booth, letting the news really sink in. While he sat there for a moment, still and quiet, Ashleigh noticed that they were still holding hands. Well, not really holding hands, but her hand rested on top of his — and neither one of them bothered to slide their hand away.

'But all that stuff,' he finally said. 'The body they found. The body they buried. It doesn't make sense.'

'I know,' she said. 'But what else could it be?'

Kevin looked thoughtful again. He leaned forward, his hand still underneath hers. 'I know you're not going to like this,' he said. 'But we're going to have to do something now.'

Ashleigh was already a step ahead of him.

And she agreed.

'I know,' she said. 'We're going to have to tell my mom.'

# 23

Janet took a few deep breaths and then opened the door to Detective Stynes. She thought she knew what he was there for. He had heard about the man from the porch. Someone had called to report him — maybe even Madeline, maybe someone else at work — and Stynes was at the house to ask Janet what she knew about the man.

And if he came in asking questions about the man, her dad would hear. Everyone would know the secret she'd been carrying with her.

Janet gathered her wits and decided to keep Detective Stynes out on the porch and handle the situation out of her dad's earshot, but Stynes changed things by saying, 'I wanted to talk to your dad for a few minutes.'

'My dad?'

'Is he home?' Stynes asked. 'I'm sorry I didn't call.'

'He's here,' Janet said, but she didn't turn or make any effort to call for him. She hoped that by standing in the doorway long enough Stynes would feel compelled to explain the purpose of his visit. But apparently the detective possessed better waiting skills than Janet. He wore a patient look on his face, his eyes calm, his expression mild. He looked like a man without a care in the world — and all the time to pass. 'Come on in,' Janet finally said.

The detective followed Janet inside, where

they found her dad standing beside his chair, the TV turned off. His face still looked agitated from their argument, and before Janet could say anything, her dad said, 'I don't want to hear about all of this stuff anymore, Janet. I'm just tired of it.'

'It's Detective Stynes,' she said. 'And he says he needs to talk to you.'

Stynes nodded to her father, ignoring his complaint. For his part, her dad looked surprised and rendered speechless by the detective's appearance. Janet wasn't sure anyone could look good or react well when the police unexpectedly showed up on their porch.

'Is something wrong?' her dad said.

'No,' Stynes said. 'Do you mind if I sit?'

He didn't wait for an invitation. He took a spot on the end of the couch, and with nothing else to do that seemed reasonable, Janet and her dad sat down as well, her dad back in his chair and Janet on the opposite end of the couch from Detective Stynes.

'Like I said, Mr Manning, I'm sorry I didn't call. But this shouldn't take long.'

'This? What's this?'

Stynes reached into the inside pocket of his sport coat and brought out a small spiral-bound notebook. Then he brought out a pen and clicked it with his thumb. While Janet watched, she couldn't help but think his movements and gestures had become practiced and meaningful over the years. He wasn't just taking out a notebook and a pen — he was stalling, drawing out the moment so the person on the other end of his questions grew more nervous and agitated as he waited.

So then why was he giving this treatment to her dad?

Did Detective Stynes suspect her dad of something, possibly some involvement with Justin's death? Janet felt a hint of outrage start to grow, but just as quickly reined it in. Why would it bother her to see Detective Stynes think that when she had just been thinking the same thing minutes earlier?

'As I'm sure you know,' Stynes said, 'there's been a lot of attention focused recently on Justin's death.'

'Okay,' her dad said.

'I've been going over the case notes from back then,' Stynes said. 'It's a bad habit I have. Rethinking things, second-guessing myself. Maybe it's something that happens with age.'

Stynes seemed to be waiting for an answer, so her dad provided one.

'Maybe,' he said. He looked uncomfortable to Janet's eyes. Tense and nervous, and Janet felt sorry for him. No matter what might or might not transpire between them, he was her father, and she didn't want to see him made to squirm.

'Detective, can you tell us what this is about?' Janet asked. 'You know my dad. He doesn't like to talk about these things. That's why I spoke to the newspaper and not him.'

'I understand,' Stynes said. 'But this isn't for the newspaper. This is just for me. I promise I'll be quick.' He flipped through the notebook, found the page he wanted, and looked up. 'I'm curious about your recollections of the day Justin disappeared. Specifically, that morning. Did anything unusual happen before you knew he was gone?'

Her dad shifted his weight in the chair, his posture gaining rigidity and energy. He sat up straighter, making it clear that he was taller than Detective Stynes by at least four inches. 'I answered all these questions twenty-five years ago,' he said. 'I sat right in this house the day Justin disappeared and I told you everything I could. So why are you showing up here now and asking me these things?'

Stynes didn't show any concern. He wasn't intimidated. 'I'm asking you these things because I'm a police officer, and we like it when citizens cooperate with the police. But, okay, I understand that it seems a little strange for me to show up now and ask a question like that.'

'Yes,' Janet said. 'It does.'

Both men looked at her, but she didn't feel embarrassed. Her heart rate started to rise, and her hands, which were clasped together in her lap, felt moist from sweat.

Stynes looked back to her father. 'When we interviewed you right after Justin disappeared, you told us that you went to work as usual that morning. You worked for Strand, right?'

'Right.'

'And that night, when we talked to you again, you said the same thing. You said you got up at the usual time and got ready and went to work as usual. I guess your wife called when she realized

Justin was missing, and you came home from work. Right?'

'I don't see the problem,' he said.

'Well, we spoke to your wife that morning, of course, and then again that night.'

Stynes stopped speaking. He let his words hang in the air between the three of them. Again he seemed to be waiting for something. When no one said anything, Stynes went on.

'That night, she told us that you had gone to work that morning like any normal day. But that morning, when we came and spoke to her, she told us that you hadn't gone in to work at your usual time. That you'd stayed home, and you were here when Justin disappeared and not at work.'

Janet almost gasped. She sucked a large gulp of air into her lungs and felt it catch there like an obstruction. It took a long moment for her to be able to breathe again, but the men didn't seem to notice. They were staring each other down, their eyes locked.

'She made a mistake,' her dad said.

'You know that?'

'She was upset when Justin disappeared. She made a mistake. I don't see why that's such a big deal. You talked to her about it that night. Here she was racked with grief over her missing child, and you just wanted to pick her words apart like she was a criminal.' He paused. 'She was very upset that day.'

Stynes nodded. 'Right. Of course. People do make mistakes in stressful situations. And if we checked the records out at Strand to see what time you arrived at work, they'd confirm that you were there?'

'I don't know what they would confirm after twenty-five years,' her dad said. His voice sounded less steely, less certain.

Stynes held her father's gaze for a long moment, then tapped the little notebook with his index finger. 'Well, I guess I'll have to see.'

'What do you mean?' Janet asked.

'I mean I might go out to Strand tomorrow morning to take a look at their records.'

'And,' Janet said, 'what if the records say my dad didn't go to work that morning, if such records even exist after all this time? What if they say he wasn't there? What happens?'

Stynes smiled, his eyes still on her dad. 'One old cop will have his curiosity satisfied, I guess. I'll just file it away in the drawer of oddities I keep in my mind.' Stynes stood up and tucked the notebook back into its pocket. 'I told you it wouldn't take very long.'

And that was it? Janet thought. But what did it mean? She tried to wrap her head around Detective Stynes's visit, but she could reach only one conclusion: Stynes had suspicions about her father, and he was following up on them.

It was as though Stynes had tapped into the dark thoughts growing inside Janet . . .

'Let me ask you something, Detective,' her father said.

Stynes stood still, looking down on her dad, who remained in his seat.

'Yes?'

216

'Have you investigated a lot of murders over the years?'

'A few.'

'And other crimes? Robberies? Rapes?'

'Of course.'

'Do you pay these kinds of visits to the parents of those victims, or am I just special?'

Stynes considered this and said, 'Some things stay with us longer than others, I guess.'

# 24

Stynes expected to hear the door slam at his back, but it didn't. Instead, Janet Manning came through the door behind him and out onto the front porch. Stynes stopped at the edge of the steps and looked back, surprised to see the woman standing there, arms folded, lips pressed tight.

Stynes thought he might have overplayed his hand. What did he really have to go on anyway? In the confusion of events in the aftermath of a kidnapping, two children jumbled their stories and a distraught mother misspoke about her husband's whereabouts. Was it worth chasing and waking ghosts over things like that?

He wondered if Janet was going to chew him out for the indelicacy of his visit, coming as it did just days after the twenty-fifth anniversary of her brother's murder. She would have a point, Stynes admitted to himself. But then again, Bill Manning did act a little off balance about the question of his whereabouts that morning. Did it mean anything? Or did the guy just feel ambushed by a twenty-five-year-old question?

Janet didn't say anything. She stood on the porch looking into the distance, toward where a neighbor washed his car, the hose creating a fanning spray of water in the sunlight.

'Did you want to ask me something, Janet?' Stynes said.

It took her a moment, but she spoke without facing him. 'What was that about, Detective?'

'I was following up on something related to your brother's case,' he said.

'After all this time?'

'I think we both know time doesn't matter so much with this case.'

'Why didn't the police follow up on this back then?' she asked. 'If someone gave conflicting stories twenty-five years ago, why didn't you explore it?'

Stynes saw Reynolds's face in his mind's eye, heard his claim that Mrs Manning's story didn't matter because we all knew who committed most of the crimes in Dove Point.

'It was determined at the time that your mother was simply confused about the course of events,' he said. 'Your parents were distraught, obviously, and those of us investigating the case decided we didn't want to push them. We felt we had more evidence pointing in the direction of Dante Rogers. We have to make those judgments during an investigation.'

She turned to face him. She studied him.

'You don't think Dante did it, Detective, do you?'

Stynes wanted to tell her. He wanted to admit his doubts about his performance on the case all those years ago, that he should have worried less about his stature as a young detective and more about finding the truth, whatever it was. He recognized that of all the people he knew — Reynolds, his fellow officers, his few friends and acquaintances — Janet Manning might be

219

the person he was most likely to tell what he really thought about Dante and what Stynes had come to think of as his alleged role in the crime. But Stynes knew he had already tipped his hand too much. Janet Manning wasn't a dummy. She only needed to listen to the questions Stynes directed at her father to know that there was suspicion in that direction, that a follow-up on the man's whereabouts meant Stynes harbored some doubts about her father and the events of that morning.

'What do you remember about that day, Janet? Do you remember talking to me in the park?'

Her mouth twisted a little as she thought. She shook her head. 'Not really. It's fuzzy. I know the police were there. I remember seeing the police cars at the park, more than one of them.'

'But you don't remember what you said?'

She shook her head. 'I've read about it in the paper so many times that I know what I said, but I don't remember saying it.'

'Do you remember talking to us that night? Here at the house?'

'I don't know. I really don't. I just remember a lot of people coming and going. I remember feeling empty all the time. Justin was gone, and something wasn't right. But I can't look back there and tell you what I was thinking.'

'It was confusing.'

'Yes. I know Michael came over one night and we played together. The adults were in another room, I guess.' Janet smiled, almost laughed.

'Why are you smiling?' Stynes asked.

'Michael.'

'What about him?'

'I cried for him. Not for Justin.'

'What do you mean?'

'I cried because I wanted to see Michael and play with him. I guess my parents didn't think I needed to be playing or goofing around, you know? I don't know if that was the first day or later. But somehow Michael ended up coming over to our house and we played together.'

'He was here that night. I remember that.'

'It must have been then. I just remembered that,' she said. 'I hadn't thought of that for a while.' She shook her head a little. 'But that's about it.'

'I heard he's back in town.'

'Michael?'

'Yes.'

'He is.'

'Have you seen him?' Stynes asked.

'A few times. Why? Do you want to talk to him?'

'It doesn't matter,' Stynes said. 'But if you think of anything else about that day or that time — anything at all — you let me know.'

'It's funny, Detective,' she said. 'I always told myself when I was growing up and then when I left home that I wouldn't be defined by that day in the park. I saw what it did to my mother, and to a lesser extent my father.'

'Why a lesser extent for him?' Stynes asked.

'He's a man, I guess. He's always kept things inside and been hard to reach. But my mother was very open and loving until Justin died. She lost something then, some spark of life.' Janet

221

sighed. 'Anyway, I said I wasn't going to be like them, looking backward all the time. I had a daughter to raise, and I sure as hell wasn't going to let her get dragged into all of this.'

'Sounds like a good idea,' Stynes said.

'And if it's such a good idea,' Janet said, 'why are we all standing in the same place, in the same town, at the same house, still talking about that day twenty-five years later?'

# 25

Despite Kevin's long legs and height advantage, he struggled to keep up with Ashleigh on the way to the Manning house. She no longer felt the aftereffects of the run from the apartment building. Quite the opposite. Both her body and her mind felt renewed in some way, as if energy were shooting through her and lighting up the cells and circuits of her body.

Had she done it? Had she found her uncle?

Could she make everything okay for her family again?

They didn't speak much on the way. Ashleigh kept her eyes focused on the walk ahead, imagining as they went along the look on her mother's face when she told her about the man. Even her grandfather, a man who showed no emotion about anything — not even his own dead son — might lose control of himself and be forced to admit that something more than extraordinary had happened.

'Hey,' Kevin said.

Ashleigh kept walking.

'Ash? Hey.'

'What?' she said, stopping.

'Are you sure you want me to go with you?' he asked.

'What?'

'Me,' he said. 'Should I tag along here? Your grandpa isn't exactly a fan of mine, and if he's been asking if we're dating — '

'Just come,' she said, starting to walk again. 'What do you mean, he's not a fan of yours?'

'I don't want him getting pissed at me, you know? Just because you and I have been hanging out.'

'He won't care.' Ashleigh slowed down and looked at Kevin. 'We're about to tell him his son is still alive. Don't you think that trumps everything else?'

Kevin nodded, although he didn't look entirely certain.

Ashleigh tugged on his arm. 'Come on.'

Ashleigh's mind continued to race. Would they all jump in the car and drive to the man's apartment? No, they couldn't do that. He was gone. Plus, the creepy manager would be there. Ashleigh decided not to tell her mom about that part of the story. She didn't want the two things mixed up — the discovery of her uncle's whereabouts and the pervert groping her. No, they wouldn't drive right over there. But they'd have to do something, right? Celebrate or something?

What on earth did people do when something like that happened?

Did stuff like that ever happen to anyone else on earth?

Ashleigh saw the house ahead, and slowed her pace a little. She started to re-imagine the scenario of telling them, and wondered what would transpire as the weeks passed. What if they did meet the man, and he really was her uncle? What would happen then? Would he move into the house with them? Would he come over for Thanksgiving and Christmas?

Was he even right in the head, wandering around in the middle of the night, knocking on doors and not identifying himself?

'What's wrong?' Kevin asked.

'Just thinking.'

'They'll probably just call the police and let them handle it,' he said. 'It'll be okay.'

How did he do that? How did he always read her mind that way?

'Okay,' she said. 'Okay.'

They drew closer to her grandfather's house. Her mom was on the porch, and Kevin said, 'Who's that dude?'

'Where?'

'The one going to his car.'

Ashleigh saw who Kevin was talking about. 'It's Detective Stynes,' she said. 'You know?'

'The one who investigated your uncle's murder?'

'What's he doing here?' Ashleigh asked. 'Do you think he knows about the guy? Do you think they found him?'

'Maybe he came back here,' Kevin said. 'Your uncle or whoever he is. Maybe they all know everything.'

But Ashleigh got the feeling that wasn't the case. Her mom saw her and came down off the porch, a worried look on her face. She looked back and forth between Kevin and Ashleigh, waiting for an explanation.

'What happened?' she said. 'I can tell something's wrong.'

Ashleigh opened her mouth to speak, but then —

Everything caught up to her. The fight with Kevin, the groping by the manager.

The letter with her uncle's name on it.

And everything else — the weeks of looking for the man. The years of her mom's unhappiness over her brother's death.

It was all there — inside Ashleigh's throat. A giant ball of emotion.

She started to cry.

But Ashleigh didn't just cry. She heaved, a great outpouring of tears and giant breaths that seemed to come from the deepest center of her being and jolted her entire body with convulsions. Through the scrim of tears, she saw her mother's face, even more concerned. Scared, even. Her mother looked at Kevin, seeking an explanation.

'What's wrong?' she kept saying. 'What happened?'

Kevin wouldn't say anything. She knew he wouldn't. This was her news to share, her prize to bring home. He put his hand on her back and rubbed it gently.

'Ash, it's okay,' he said. 'Tell her. Just tell her.'

'Tell me what?'

And then Ashleigh saw the cop coming over from his car. He must have seen the show she was putting on and decided he couldn't just walk away from a citizen in distress. But the sobs kept coming, so she tried to talk through them.

'I'm . . . okay . . . '

Her mom placed her hands on Ashleigh's

upper arms. 'Tell me, honey.'

'I'm okay . . . It's . . . I found . . .'

'You found?'

She lost control for a minute, then managed some deep breaths, which slowed the pace of her crying. She looked around, saw everyone's eyes on her, even the cop's.

'Justin,' Ashleigh said.

'What?' her mom said.

'Justin,' Kevin said. 'That's what she's talking about.'

'Justin?' her mom said. 'What about Justin? Honey, what about Justin?'

Ashleigh swallowed again, another deep breath.

'I found him, Mom. I found Uncle Justin.'

# 26

Janet guided Ashleigh into the house, followed by Kevin and Detective Stynes. The girl still huffed and hiccupped, but seemed to be on her way to calming down. Ashleigh had cried a lot as a baby, but not much since then. While Janet went to the kitchen to get a glass of water, she tried to remember if she'd ever seen Ashleigh cry so hard.

But she understood. Something big had happened.

Something about Justin.

When Janet returned to the room, her father was there. He must have been down the hall or in the bathroom when they'd first come into the house. He looked like all men look in the presence of a crying female — perplexed, a little lost. Janet handed the glass of water to Ashleigh, who was sitting on the couch alone. The other two men — Kevin and Stynes — weren't much more help, although Janet could see the concern on both of their faces.

'What's going on now?' her dad said.

'She found something, Dad. Something about Justin.'

He didn't say anything. He just looked even more confused.

Ashleigh drank the entire glass of water and took two deep breaths. 'I'm okay,' she said. 'Really. I'm sorry.' She looked around the room at everybody. 'I just kind of lost it for a minute. It's been a crazy day.'

'It's okay,' Kevin said. 'We don't care.'

'Why don't you just tell us what happened, honey?' Janet said. 'Start from the beginning. You said you found something out about Justin . . . '

'I didn't find something out,' Ashleigh said, her voice, even in this time of great stress, still laced with the contempt only a teenage daughter can have for her mother. 'I found *him*. He's alive.'

A stillness fell over the room. Janet moved over to the couch and sat down next to Ashleigh. She took the girl's hand in her own. 'Why don't you tell me about it?'

Ashleigh looked around the room at the other expectant and curious faces. Janet could read her mind — cop, emotionally distant grandfather, friend, and mother. Did she really want to tell the story to this eclectic cast? But Ashleigh had always been a brave girl. Not particularly effusive or outgoing, not always even warm. But she was brave. So Janet watched as her daughter took another deep breath and said, 'Remember that guy who came to the door in the middle of the night?'

Janet felt her mouth fall open. 'How do you know about that?'

'I saw it. I heard you talking to him, so I came downstairs and saw the whole thing. I looked at him carefully and remembered him.'

'And you found that man?' Janet asked.

'*He's* Uncle Justin,' Ashleigh said.

'Hold on a minute,' Stynes said. 'I'm a step behind here.'

'Me, too,' her dad said.

And Janet saw the trap she herself had stepped into. In order for Ashleigh to tell her story, Janet was going to have to admit the secret she'd been holding back from the police, in particular Detective Stynes. Rather than let Ashleigh stroll through that minefield alone, Janet stepped forward.

'Okay,' she said. 'I think I need to provide a little background about this, before Ashleigh goes on.'

So she did. She told Stynes and her father about the visit in the middle of the night by the man claiming that Justin's death hadn't happened the way everyone thought it did. She told them that she'd wanted to call the police, but the man told her not to, so she didn't.

'Did he threaten you?' Stynes asked.

'No, he didn't,' Janet said. 'I mean, not directly. He may have been coming around the house other times. During the night.'

'During the night?' her dad said.

'Just let me explain,' Janet said.

Janet went on to tell them about the months she'd waited for the man to come back — and that he finally did come back, just a few days ago on campus. But the man refused to say who he was or what he really wanted.

'He just said we knew each other in the past and that he knew something about Justin's death. Something that no one else knew about the way it happened.' Janet swallowed. She felt the eyes on her, especially Stynes and her dad. 'I have to be honest. Ever since that first night he showed up here, I've had a . . . wish, I guess you would call it. No — more than that. A belief is what I think it is.'

'A belief about what?' her dad said.

His voice surprised Janet. It was unlike him to speak up about something so deeply personal in front of people he didn't really know.

But could she really say he felt anything about Justin deeply? Did he?

She looked at her dad when she spoke. 'I've started to believe that he is Justin. That Justin is still alive, and he didn't die in the park that day. And now he's back.'

Her father simply looked away. He turned his eyes to the floor and didn't speak.

It was Stynes who filled the quiet space.

'Leaving aside the question, for now, of why your mother didn't call the police and notify us about this man,' he said, 'I'm curious to know how you, Ashleigh, came to believe that this man is your uncle. Did he tell you this?'

'I went to his house — '

'You went to his house?' Janet said.

The gust of fear that swept through Janet in that split second almost forced her to reach out and grab hold of Ashleigh, tuck her into her arms, and hold her tight. Her daughter, out in the world, chasing after a strange man. A man who'd made Janet uneasy in a bright, public place. No matter who he was, the thought of Ashleigh's exposure to the man, her vulnerability in such close proximity to him — or someone like him — terrified Janet.

But she swallowed the fear, and the impulse to grab her daughter. She listened, her hands clenched in her lap, while Ashleigh told the story of tracing the man through the comic store and the restaurant he worked at to the first apartment complex and then the ratty apartment complex a few miles away.

'He says his name is Steven Kollman,' Ashleigh said. 'That's the name everyone knew him by.'

Stynes looked at Janet. She read the look on his face. *Does that name mean anything to you?*

Janet's mind swirled. Did it? Was there familiarity there? Or was it like the man's face — a place she saw familiarity because she wanted to?

Janet shook her head.

'How did you come to decide this man was your uncle if he used another name?' Stynes asked.

Ashleigh looked over at Kevin. Something passed between them, an unspoken understanding. Kevin nodded his head to Ashleigh. *Go ahead*, he was telling her. *It's okay*.

Janet's clenched fists grew tighter while Ashleigh spoke of going into the abandoned apartment. She heard the words about the court summons with Justin's name on it, but when Ashleigh told the next part of her story, the part about the man's hands on her body — touching her, groping her, assaulting her, for the love of God — Janet felt a sharp pain at the base of her neck. She placed her hand back there and rubbed.

*It's okay,* she told herself. *You raised a strong girl. You raised a fighter.*

And she did. Janet saw the hint of pride on Ashleigh's face as she talked about fighting the man off, kicking him, punching him. *That's my girl,* Janet wanted to say, but knew it would only embarrass her daughter. But she felt it. *That is my girl, the fighter.*

'Detective,' Janet said. 'I trust that whatever else happens the police will be paying a visit to this pervert's apartment.'

'Of course,' Stynes said, but he was clearly more interested in Ashleigh's story about Justin. 'You didn't see anything else? Pictures, other mail? Anything?'

'That's all. I wish I'd held on to the letter,' Ashleigh said, sounding almost apologetic. 'If only I'd kept it.'

'That's fine, Ashleigh,' Stynes said. 'You did fine.'

'I guess that's why I cried when I walked up here,' Ashleigh said. 'I knew I'd found something important.' She looked at Janet, this time without the contempt or averted eyes that were the moody teen's trademark. 'I knew it was important to you, Mom. I was happy and sad at the same time. It was everything all mixed up.'

Janet couldn't play it cool any longer. The emotion took control of her. She leaned in and took her daughter in her arms, wrapped her up the way she wanted to — not out of fear or anxiety, but out of pure, unadulterated love and appreciation for this girl.

'The detective's right, Ashleigh,' Janet said. 'You did do good. I love you, and I'm glad you're safe.' She held on. 'You're a sweet, crazy girl.'

'It's okay, Mom. Jeez.'

But Ashleigh's voice, even muffled by Janet's hug, didn't sound annoyed or exasperated. She took the warmth and let her mom hold her as long as she wanted.

# 27

Stynes didn't know what to think. He had come to the Manning home to investigate a loose end from twenty-five years ago. Why had there been a contradiction between the account of Manning's whereabouts given by his wife and the account given by Manning himself? Was Bill Manning home that morning or not?

It had come up twenty-five years earlier, as he and Reynolds investigated the case. They had talked about it at length. In the end, Reynolds had told Stynes to let it go, to not worry about a small and understandable contradiction in one person's story when there was enough evidence to convict someone else, someone much more likely to have committed the crime. Someone the wrong color, Stynes realized . . .

But there Stynes sat, still inside the Manning house, and Ashleigh Manning, a fifteen-year-old girl, had revealed what might just be the smoking gun.

Was Justin Manning still alive?

Stynes looked around the room and saw Bill Manning turn and leave. He disappeared down a hallway, probably toward a bedroom or bath-room. Overwhelmed? By guilt, or something else?

First things first, Stynes thought. *Easiest* thing first. He pulled out his phone and called in the assault on Ashleigh Manning committed by the apartment manager.

'You don't know the creep's name, do you?' Stynes asked Ashleigh.

'Nick something,' she said, then went on to give a solid description all the way down to the scent of his breath. Stynes also requested a crime scene unit be sent to the apartment formerly occupied by Steven Kollman/Justin Manning. He asked for prints to be taken and any evidence that remained to be tagged and inventoried. When asked if a warrant was in order, Stynes said, 'The guy didn't pay his rent and vacated the premises. We don't need a warrant. Tell them I'll meet them there in a little bit. And I need you to run two names for me.' He gave them the names of the two men he was — might be — pursuing. The two ghosts who were now permanent residents of his brain. Steven Kollman and Justin Manning. 'Anything that pops, let me know.'

He put the phone away and sat in the chair Bill Manning had occupied earlier, back when Stynes believed in his gut the man was involved with the death of his own son.

And now?

He couldn't believe that Justin Manning was still alive after all these years. He'd watched them remove the kid's body from the woods, saw the skeletal remains and the wisps of blond hair still attached to the skull.

'Janet, can you tell me anything else this man said to you? Anything at all?'

He watched Janet think, her hand still

clutching her daughter's. 'He told me that he lived in Dove Point, and he didn't like it,' she said. 'He said he was taken away from his family — he definitely said that. That's one of the things that made me think he was Justin. Somebody took him away from his family.' She lifted her free hand to her chest. 'My God, where has he been all these years? Has he been lost or homeless? I asked him if he needed help when I saw him on campus. He looked a little . . . ragged or dirty, I guess. Not dirty like he didn't have a place to live, but just like he's had a rough time. If it was Justin . . . he was there, right there in front of me.'

'But he didn't tell you he was your brother?' Stynes asked.

Color rose in Janet's cheeks. 'I did something weird,' she said. 'I called him 'Justin.' When he started to leave, I called out that name to see how he would respond.'

'And?' Stynes asked.

'He said something like, 'Not yet.' Whatever that means.'

Ashleigh looked at her mom and said, 'So maybe he's going to tell you soon. Maybe he can't right now.'

'Why would he not be able to?' Janet asked. 'Does someone want to hurt him?'

'Was there anything else, Janet?' Yes, Stynes was more involved with this case than any other. He could admit that to himself. Then all the more reason to remain sharp, to not let the emotion of the Mannings possess him and interfere with finding out what he needed to

237

learn. 'Anything he said or did that might be pertinent?'

'I don't know.'

'Did he talk about anything from your childhood? Did he ask about your parents or other family members?'

Janet swallowed. She lowered her voice. 'He said his mother was dead. And that his father didn't care about him.'

Even Stynes felt a chill on his neck when he heard that. The room grew quiet. Someone needed to break the tension, and to his credit, the kid, Kevin, did.

'Detective?' he said.

Stynes looked up.

'Didn't you do a DNA test on the body you found in the woods back then? Or something?'

'We didn't do DNA testing back then. I know it's hard for you kids to understand, but it just didn't exist.'

Ashleigh said, 'I always hear about bodies being checked with dental X-rays.'

'Your uncle was so young when he died that he'd never had dental X-rays taken.'

'Then how did you know it was him?' Ashleigh asked.

Stynes resisted the urge to tell the two teenagers to keep their mouths shut and quit bothering the grown-ups. But they were right. People were going to be asking the same types of questions once the news broke. And it would break. Yes, it would.

'Justin disappeared from that park,' he said. 'We found the body of a child in the woods near that park. The remains were the same approximate age and size as Justin Manning. We had a suspect. We had witnesses, including Janet here. That's how we make a case.'

But the words didn't ring true as they came out of Stynes's mouth. He felt like an actor reading from a script he thought was terribly written. None of it made sense. None of it at all, unless Stynes believed that this Kollman/Manning guy was just a nutjob who wanted to harass the family of a crime victim.

But Stynes had never heard of such elaborate manipulation. If the guy was just a nut, he was so far out there the scale would need to be recalibrated.

Stynes stood up. 'I have to go. We're going to head over to this Kollman guy's apartment, see if there's anything else we can use to help establish his real identity. I suspect he doesn't mean to do any of you any harm. If he wanted to, he would have done so already. But I'm going to ask the officers who patrol around here to keep a special eye on this house. You never know. At the very least, he's probably guilty of harassment and identity theft. If he comes around, call us.'

Janet looked at Stynes. 'What if he needs our help?' she asked. 'Are you saying I should not have contact with the man who might be my brother?'

'I'm asking you to be careful, Janet. Just be careful.'

'Detective?' Janet said.

'Yes?'

'The other day with the reporter and then

239

tonight — I was right, wasn't I?'

'About what?'

'You don't think Dante did it.'

Stynes couldn't lie. But he wasn't ready to admit anything because too many things were coming at him at once.

'Let's just say, things appear to be in a state of flux right now. And do me a favor? Keep the doors locked. And if anything happens after I'm gone, make sure you share it with me this time.'

# 28

Janet went down the hall to the closed door of her father's bedroom. Everyone else had left — Stynes to pursue evidence against both the man who'd assaulted Ashleigh and the man who might be Justin, Kevin back to his home and his family. Janet thought about leaving the old man alone, leaving him to stew in the bedroom with his own miserable thoughts, whatever they might be.

But she couldn't just walk away from him. Something had changed, something profound. Justin might be alive. And in the wake of their earlier conversation, the one in which the darkest thoughts Janet had ever experienced about her father came to her mind, she felt a need to see her father's face, to know how the news Ashleigh brought home affected him.

She heard the TV playing through the closed door. When she and Ashleigh had moved in, her dad had immediately gone out and bought his own television for the bedroom, something that allowed him to retreat from the shared living space of the house and be alone. He'd done this with more and more frequency in the six months since he'd stopped actively looking for work. And until that night, Janet rarely disturbed him. She rapped lightly, expecting an immediate response. But none came.

She knocked louder.

'Dad?'

Still nothing.

She placed her hand on the knob but didn't turn it. Even as a kid, she wouldn't have gone into her parents' room when the door was closed. She couldn't bring herself to do it as an adult. And a part of her felt relief. If he wanted to lock himself away, that was his problem.

But she'd let him off the hook so many times, given him so much space just to make his life easier and less confrontational. And, Janet had to be honest, to make her life easier as well. She didn't want to tap into whatever the old man was thinking, so she avoided it. But the time for avoidance was past.

She made a fist and used it like a club, rapping against the door. The volume on the TV dropped and the door opened. Her dad stood there, still dressed, but his hair mussed in the back.

'What are you doing?' he asked.

'I want to know what you think of all this now,' she demanded.

'Oh, Janet — '

'No, you can't just turn away,' she said. 'Tell me something about tonight. What do you think about the fact that Justin might still be alive? Just say something.'

'I think it's unfortunate that all of this is stirring your fantasies,' he said.

He tried to close the door, but Janet put her hand out and stopped it.

'This isn't going to go away, Dad. We're in the middle of it now, and we're going to know something. Finally. We can't avoid it.'

He met her eye and stopped trying to close the door. 'I know that as well as you do, Janet.'

She let go of the door and straightened up. They stared at each other across a distance that felt much greater than the physical space separating them.

'I have to go somewhere tonight,' Janet said.

'So go.'

'I wouldn't go anywhere if it wasn't important,' she said. 'But there's someone I need to talk to.'

'The cop?'

'No. Michael Bower.'

'Jesus.' He rolled his eyes. 'What's he doing in town?'

Since the real explanation seemed too complicated, Janet made it short and sweet. 'He's visiting his mother. And I want to talk to him about everything that's been happening. He's a good friend, Dad.'

'That cop said not to leave the house.'

'He said to be careful,' Janet said. 'I'm just going to see Michael — that's it. But I didn't want to leave without talking to you.' She lowered her voice. 'I'm worried about Ashleigh. I *don't* want her leaving the house.'

'So? Tell her.'

'I will, Dad. But I'm asking you to help, too. That man, he's been hanging around our house. Make sure Ashleigh doesn't go anywhere. Can you do that for me? Or do it for her if that makes it easier.'

His face lost some of its hard edges. He nodded. 'But you shouldn't be out running around either. Who knows what this maniac is doing.'

Janet recognized that her father had just issued the strongest statement of concern he could muster.

'Thanks, Dad.'

He left the bedroom door open but turned the sound on the TV up without saying anything else.

★ ★ ★

Janet stopped outside the door to Ashleigh's room, which was, as usual, closed and probably locked. Janet tried to remember when Ashleigh started retreating to her room and shutting herself in. Had she been eleven? Twelve? Janet remembered the disappointment she felt when Ashleigh began locking herself away. Janet had hoped that she would have a few more years of a preteen daughter, a little more time before the full force of adolescence hit the house. But that wasn't to be. Ashleigh walked her own path and kept her own counsel.

Obviously.

Janet didn't know whether to be impressed or terrified that her daughter had managed to keep such a huge secret for so long. Well, she thought, raise an independent kid and suffer the consequences.

She knocked on the door and wondered why she was always knocking on someone else's door inside the house. Did they ever come and knock for her? Or was she always the one reaching out?

Janet thought she heard Ashleigh say she could come in, so she did, only to be greeted by a scrambling on the bed.

'Jesus, Mom,' Ashleigh said.

'I thought you said to come in. I'm sorry.'

Ashleigh tucked something away beneath her pillow, a scrap of paper or a note. Janet wouldn't have been able to tell what it was anyway, but if Ashleigh felt better hiding it, so be it. Probably a love note from Kevin, if Janet had to guess.

Despite her secretive nature, there were times Janet saw Ashleigh as the kid she still was. Lying on the bed, wearing a pair of shorts and a loose T-shirt, Ashleigh looked small, vulnerable even. Janet couldn't forget the danger the girl had found herself in earlier that day and decided right then that she wasn't going to leave the house, that Michael could come here or they'd talk on the phone or something. But she couldn't leave her daughter alone. Not so soon.

'What?' Ashleigh said.

'It's nice to see you, too.'

Ashleigh smirked. 'I mean, what are you doing here?'

'Remember when you came home today and you were so sweet and emotional and vulnerable? Remember that girl?'

'You're not funny, Mom.'

'I thought I was,' Janet said. 'I was coming to tell you that I was going out for a little bit, but I changed my mind.'

'So you're coming to tell me that you changed your mind?'

'I guess.'

Ashleigh looked at the clock, then back at her mom. 'It's almost nine. Where would you go anyway?'

'I was going to see a friend of mine.'

Ashleigh looked even more puzzled. Janet understood that the notion that her mother had friends, let alone friends she would socialize with on a weeknight, seemed too much to imagine. Real friends? People she had fun with? No way.

'Michael Bower,' Janet said. 'You know who he is, right?'

Ashleigh perked up, suddenly interested. 'Your friend,' she said. 'He was in the park that day.'

'That's right.'

'Why aren't you going to see him?'

Janet came farther into the room, stopping at the foot of Ashleigh's bed. 'Honestly?'

'Honestly.'

'I don't want to leave you,' Janet said. 'Not after today. I just don't think it would be right.'

'Does he know anything about what happened to Justin?' Ashleigh asked.

Janet wasn't sure how to answer that. 'He certainly has some questions about what happened that day.'

'Then you should go.'

'Why are you so certain about this?'

'What if he knows something? What if it helps?'

What if he does? But everything Michael said ran counter to what they'd found out earlier. Michael thought his father was involved in the crime, not that Justin was still alive. But Janet also knew that a part of her — a bigger part than

246

she cared to admit — wasn't just going out to discuss Justin's disappearance with Michael. She wanted to see him and would have whether there had been a break in the case or not. The news about the case just gave her a bit of cover when she showed up at his house asking to see him.

'I don't know,' Janet said.

'Mom, I'm not a kid. Look at what I did today.'

*That's what worries me*, Janet thought. Ashleigh didn't quite know the location of the line between stupid and brave.

'Grandpa's home,' Janet said. 'I told him I was going out and to keep an eye on you.'

'I'll bet he's thrilled.'

'He'll keep an ear out. He likes you.'

'I'll probably be asleep in an hour,' Ashleigh said. 'It's been a long day.'

Before Janet left, she said, 'It was nice of Kevin to come home with you today.'

Ashleigh nodded.

'Maybe we should have him over for dinner some night. You two used to spend a lot of time together at our house, but now I hardly ever see him.'

'This isn't our house,' Ashleigh said.

'It *is* our house. Now. And I grew up here. What do you say? Should we have Kevin over for dinner some night? Maybe play a game or something? I feel like I should see more of him since you two are so close.'

'I can tell you're fishing,' Ashleigh said. 'We're just friends.'

At the door, Janet stopped and looked back.

'Hey,' she said. 'Are you worried about me? The police said I should stay home.'

Ashleigh gave Janet a long look. She really seemed to be considering her mother, weighing her pros and cons and making a balanced judgment.

'I think you'll be okay.'

'Because I'm tough like you?'

Ashleigh tried to hide the little smile that grew across her face. 'No, because there are cops outside and if the bogeyman tries to get you, they'll save the day. You'll be fine.'

Janet smiled. 'Are you sure *you're* okay?'

'I am. Are you?'

'Yes, I think I'm getting there.'

★   ★   ★

It was high summer, and even after nine o'clock in western Ohio a faint tint of pink remained at the horizon. They were just past the longest day of the year, and as Janet stepped outside into the warm night, she was aware of the slow unwinding of the days, the sense that summer could go on forever.

But she was old enough to know that it wouldn't. Even then, the days were starting to reverse, the daylight growing incrementally shorter until it was time for Ashleigh to go back to school and time for the students to return to Cronin.

Would they know something by then? Would it all be resolved?

And if it was, what would life be like then in

the absence of mystery?

Janet fumbled for her keys and approached her car. She wondered whether it was even worth it to see Michael, to tell him about the events of the day. She knew she would, of course. She wouldn't be able to shut him out. But she also understood that he might not be ready to give her the kind of response she was hoping for. She wanted someone — Michael, in particular — to share her joy, her confusion, her fear, but he seemed too absorbed in his own feelings about his father to be there for anyone else.

Before Janet slipped into the car, headlights approached the house. The vehicle moved slowly, like someone searching for something. Janet felt her heart jump a little. As the car slowed even more at their house, she considered going back inside. But then in the disappearing light she saw the outline of the top of the car — a rack of lights and sirens.

Janet felt relief wash over her. The police.

They turned the interior light on in the car as Janet walked down the driveway. She leaned in, getting closer to eye level with the officer in the passenger seat. He was young, probably just out of college. His hair was cut short, making his head appear sleek and bullet-shaped.

'Evening, ma'am,' he said. 'Are you Mrs Manning?'

'Ms Manning.'

'Is everything okay here?' the officer asked.

'Yes,' Janet said. 'Why?'

She took a quick look at the cop in the driver's seat. A female officer, her hair pulled back in a tight ponytail. She nodded at Janet.

'No worries, ma'am,' the first officer said. 'Detective Stynes asked us to keep an eye on this house, so we saw you out here and wanted to check in.'

'I'm fine,' she said. 'We're all fine. My father and daughter are still in the house.'

'Just call us if you need anything.'

'Have you seen anything?' Janet asked. 'There's a man . . . '

'Detective Stynes told us. But we haven't seen anybody. We'll be patrolling all night.'

Janet felt relief as they drove away. Someone would be watching the house and the neighborhood once she was gone. She could put her mother's guilt and fears aside — to some extent.

Janet walked back up the driveway, heading for her car. The crickets in the grass started chirping in greater numbers, and a few stars, low and bright, emerged in the growing darkness. Janet looked up at the house one more time, saw the TV glow in her father's room, the soft light through the curtains in Ashleigh's. It looked so normal, so peaceful. But had it ever felt that way to her? Had it ever felt like a safe, normal home?

Her hand hovered above the door handle, but before she gripped it the voice came from the darkness next to the house.

'Janet?'

Her body spun halfway toward the sound, releasing the handle. For a moment, she thought she imagined the call, but then she saw the shape of a man emerging from the darkness, moving toward the car. Janet looked to the front door.

The angle of the man's approach meant that if she ran, she might not make it past him.

Was it him? Was it the man from the porch?

'Who's there?' she asked.

'It's me,' the voice said.

Then she saw it — the familiar thin frame. 'Michael?'

He came closer and smiled a little. 'It's me,' he said again.

'Jesus. I was on my way to your house.'

'My mom's house,' he said.

'Did you call here and find out where I was going?' she asked.

'No, I guess we're just on the same wavelength tonight.' He smiled, the wattage turned up high. 'There's something I want to do. It's easier this way.'

Janet's heart calmed down, the rhythm easing from the bass drum pounding when she heard that voice in the dark.

'The police were just here,' she said. 'They're watching the house. If they'd seen you creeping around . . . '

'I saw them,' he said. 'Why are they watching the house? Did something happen?'

'Oh, Jesus, Michael. So much. That's what I wanted to come and tell you.'

He placed his hand on her arm. 'Come on,' he said. 'Let's walk and talk at the same time.'

'Are you sure?' Janet stopped. Michael seemed distant, distracted. Despite the strength of the smile, something looked off. 'Is something wrong?'

He let out a long breath. 'I want to hear what

251

happened to you,' he said. 'And I have to tell you something. I just want to talk to you.'

So Janet followed along.

★  ★  ★

While they walked through the darkened streets, past homes that looked more comfortable with their porch lights burning and their kids tucked safely away in bed, Janet told Michael about the events of the day. She gave him a condensed version of Ashleigh's adventure to the apartment complex — leaving out the details of the assault. When she told Michael that the man had a court summons with the name Justin Manning on it, Michael continued to walk by her side, but he kept his face turned away. He hadn't said anything the whole time, hadn't so much as grunted or acknowledged that Janet was even speaking. She didn't know what to think or how to read his response, so when he continued to walk in silence for minutes after she stopped speaking, she said, 'Well, what do you think of all this?'

He still took his time answering. They continued walking at a slow, easy pace until Michael abruptly stopped and turned to face her.

'I think it's all bullshit, Janet.'

She stared at his face. They stood in the wash of a streetlight near the edge of the subdivision. Michael's jaw was set hard, his eyes cold. He'd shown a similar response to the mention of the man on the porch when they spoke in the coffee shop, but he seemed even angrier and more agitated hearing about the man using Justin's name. He still didn't speak, and Janet got the sense he wasn't ready to say anything else. But she wanted to hear from him. She'd sought him out for the sole purpose of sharing the news with him and seeing his reaction.

'Isn't this good news, Michael?' she said. 'Doesn't this give us hope? I thought you'd be thrilled.'

'I'm not.'

'Can you tell me why?'

He took a step closer to her and reached out with both hands. He placed them on her upper arms, a gentle, affectionate gesture. 'I don't want to see you get hurt, Janet. In any way.'

'You mean because this guy might be dangerous?'

'That may very well be,' he said. 'Some guy shows up spinning a tale about knowing the truth about the crime. But he won't tell you the truth about it? Or he won't go to the police?'

'Maybe he can't. Maybe he's not ready yet. Michael, I saw this man up close. I talked to him on campus. He seemed . . . disturbed in some way.'

'You see?'

'I don't mean he's dangerous.' Janet fumbled for the right words, but she knew that 'disturbed' captured it best. And she also knew she wasn't being completely honest with Michael. She didn't know that the man was harmless. When she heard that voice calling her name outside the house in the dark, and she thought it was the man from the porch . . . she did feel afraid. But if he wanted to hurt her, why go to such elaborate lengths to talk to her? Why not just do what he wanted to do? Something else was at play. 'I mean, Michael, that he's been through something. He has something wrong with him in terms of how he interacts with people. Maybe he's been homeless or abused.' She reached up to where his hands rested on her shoulders and took his hands in hers. 'Oh, Michael, what if it is him? What if it's really Justin? What if the whole last twenty-five years has been some kind of insane nightmare?'

'It hasn't,' he said, his voice flat. 'The last twenty-five years did happen. Your mother died, and my parents split up. And we . . . we lived with it all that time.' He let go of her hands. 'Whatever this man is up to won't change that, don't you see?'

Janet did see. She understood that the years and their toll wouldn't be erased. But she wasn't going to dwell on what had been lost. She couldn't bear it. Like those photos that her father threw away — they were gone. She could let them go as long as she could also look forward to something more.

And here it was — the something more. Her brother might be alive. He might be alive and living right there in Dove Point. All they had to do was find him and talk to him. Whatever she needed to do to bring him back into the family, she would do. No questions asked.

'Michael,' she said. 'I don't know what your life has been like over the last decade or so, but surely this could help, couldn't it? We could start to put some things back together.'

Michael turned away again. He looked into the distance and then Janet looked around as well. While they were walking and talking, she hadn't been paying attention to where they were heading. She had followed Michael's lead and concentrated on giving him a version of the day's events. So when she looked around and followed the line of his gaze, what she saw surprised her.

They weren't just on the edge of the subdivision.

They were across the street from the park. Michael reached out to her again, took her hand, and said, 'Come on, this is what I wanted to show you.'

# 29

When Stynes reached the apartment complex, the first thing he saw was two uniformed cops leading a sweaty middle-aged man out of the manager's office in hand-cuffs. The light was draining out of the day, but even in the glow from the parking lot lights, Stynes saw the man's pasty skin, the clammy sheen of sweat across his forehead. They stuffed the guy into the back of a cruiser but left the door open when they saw Stynes approaching.

'This is our guy?' he asked the officers.

'Indeed,' one of them said. 'Nicholas Reeves. Age thirty-eight. He says he's managed this complex for the last three years.'

Stynes leaned into the car, positioning his face about a foot from Reeves. 'So you like touching little girls, Nick?'

The man started crying right away. He squished his eyes shut and ducked his head and his body shook while he cried. Stynes noticed that Reeves's lip looked a little puffy and red, the result of being kicked in the face by Ashleigh Manning. Stynes thought the girl was nuts for doing what she did, but he had to admire her cojones. And he kind of liked seeing a guy like Reeves take a good shot to the face.

'Do you think this is going to make me feel sorry for you, Nick?' Stynes asked. 'This crying bullshit.'

The man still couldn't bring himself to speak, but he managed to shake his head. In truth, Stynes did feel a little sorry for the guy. He might be a creep and a pervert, but he still possessed a vulnerable humanity that Stynes couldn't ignore. And if he thought his life sucked while sitting handcuffed in the back of a small-town police cruiser, wait until he got a load of prison as a pasty, doughy child molester.

'She was only fifteen, you know that?' Stynes said. 'Fifteen. My socks are older than that.'

'I'm sorry,' Reeves said.

'What's that?'

'I'm sorry.'

'You're sorry? Yes, you are. But sorry doesn't feed the bulldog, does it?'

The man continued to weep, but his sobs were more quiet.

'Let me guess. I bet your apartment is full of porn and underwear you swiped from your tenants' apartments when they weren't home.'

'Don't tell my mother,' Reeves said. 'Can we just not tell my mother?'

'Does she read the newspaper? Because it will be in there under the heading 'Felony Sexual Assault.''

The man's head jerked up. 'Felony?'

'What do you think? You touch a little girl and we give you a break?'

'I just wanted to hug her,' he said. 'Just . . . feel her.'

'You're not supposed to do that with kids.'

'I don't mean that way.' Reeves took a deep breath. He tried to suck some of the snot on his

257

face back into his nose. 'I mean I just wanted some companionship.'

'You should have got a cat.'

Stynes reached into his back pocket and brought out an old handkerchief he sometimes remembered to carry. He balled it up, taking great care to cover the skin of his own hand, and wiped Reeves's nose back and forth, clearing most of the snot and tears. He tossed the handkerchief onto the ground.

'Thank you.'

'So, Nick, tell me about the guy who rented this apartment from you. You know, the apartment in which you sexually assaulted this girl today.'

Reeves took a long moment to answer. Stynes lifted his foot and gave Reeves a gentle kick in the leg.

'I'm waiting,' he said.

'Are you willing to work out a deal?' Reeves asked. 'I tell you what you want to know, so you go easy on me?'

'You watch too much *Law and Order*, Nick. How about you tell me what I want to know, and then I won't put you in a holding cell with a four-hundred-pound gay black man who likes pasty white guys? How's that for a deal?'

Reeves nodded. He understood.

'He rented the place three months ago. A three-month lease.'

'Is that standard?'

'We offer it when we have a lot of vacancies. The rent is more per month, but you get the shorter lease.'

'Go on.'

'He showed up and paid the deposit — that was just ninety-nine dollars — and the first month's rent. Then he didn't pay again, so he was going to get evicted, except the lease was up anyway. And when I told him he was being evicted, he just took some of his stuff and left.'

'He pay with a check?'

'Cash.'

'His name?'

'Steven Kollman.'

'You ever talk to him or find anything else out about him?'

'Is he in trouble?' Reeves asked.

'Not as much as you. Yet.'

Reeves stared straight ahead. He seemed to be thinking something over. 'I got kind of a weird vibe off the guy.'

Stynes looked at the two uniformed cops who were listening in. '*He* got a weird vibe off the guy.'

'Seriously,' Reeves said. 'He said he used to live here, and he was back in town to reconnect with his roots. That's what he said. We never talked after that until I evicted him.'

'How did he take the news of the eviction?' Stynes asked.

'Like it was nothing. Like I'd told him it might rain tomorrow. I don't think he cared. He just left.'

'Did this Kollman guy have any visitors? Did you ever see him with anybody?'

'Besides the girl from today?'

'Yes, besides the girl you assaulted. Yes. Any

other visitors or friends?'

'There was one guy.'

'Who was he?'

'Just some guy. He came by not long after Kollman moved in. I saw them talking outside the building one night. It looked like the other guy was kind of pissed at Kollman, but then they were okay, you know? The situation calmed down. And then just a few days ago, the guy came back one night. I saw him going into the building. I was cleaning up some trash out back, but it sounded like they were arguing a little. I mean, the voices were raised loud enough a couple of times that I could hear it outside.'

'What happened?'

'I was going to go up and knock on the door and ask them to keep it down. We try to run a tight ship here.'

'I can tell.'

'Thanks. But when I started over to the steps, the other guy was coming down and left the building. That was it.'

'What does this guy look like?'

'I didn't see him up close. That night on the stairs, I only saw him from behind. I was in the basement and he went out on the first floor.'

'What did he look like?'

'He was kind of tall and thin. He was dressed okay. Not like Kollman, you know? He always looked a little ratty. But this guy looked decent. Kind of middle class, you know?'

'Did you see his car?'

'No.'

'And was that the only visitor for Kollman?

No girls? Nothing?'

'Nothing else that I saw. I swear. He was quiet. He was a good tenant, except he didn't pay.'

Stynes straightened up. 'All right, Nick. Thanks.'

'What happens now?'

'A free tour of our justice system, courtesy of the taxpayers of Dove Point, Ohio.'

'Oh.' Reeves closed his eyes, and the tears started again. 'Please?'

'Get ahold of yourself.'

Stynes closed the door and turned to the two officers. They walked a few feet away.

'What's his deal?' Stynes asked.

'He's clean,' the one said. 'Not even a moving violation.'

'Really?'

'And we didn't find anything weird in his room. A little porn, but no kiddie stuff. No weapons or anything like that.'

Stynes nodded. 'He's all yours.'

'What do you think they'll do with him, Detective?'

'The prosecutor's office can sort it out, but I think he's looking at lewd conduct with a child. They'll threaten him with a felony, but he might get off with just a misdemeanor. And do me a favor? When you get him to the jail, let him wipe his face off.'

Stynes saw more uniformed officers a couple of buildings away. He walked down there and met a crime scene technician on her way out of the building.

'What's it look like?' Stynes asked.

The tech looked to be about twenty-five. Like the rookie cops, they grew younger and younger all the time. Sometimes Stynes felt as if the rest of the world were a film being shown in reverse, and everyone grew younger while he aged.

'Not much,' the tech said. She wore a Dove Point PD polo shirt. 'Your friend over there pretty well cleaned the place out. We've got a notice to hold the Dumpster. We can check it tomorrow in the daylight.'

'Prints?'

'A mess of them,' she said. 'It's a furnished apartment and not a particularly nice one. Every tenant for the last twenty years has touched every surface in there. We got some good ones, but there's no way to know if they're from your guy or not.'

'And that's it?'

'Pretty much,' she said. 'What did this guy do?'

Stynes looked up at the window of the apartment. 'Right now, I'm not sure.'

The tech shrugged.

Stynes asked, 'Is it clear up there? I can go in?'

'It's all yours.'

Stynes went up the stairs, trying to ignore the smells in the hallway, the cooking smells and body odor and dirty diapers. The door to the apartment stood open, and Stynes went in. Most everything had been cleared away. He wouldn't say the place had been cleaned, but there was no clutter or garbage present. If not for his arrest, Nick Reeves would be getting ready to rent this palace to the next lucky contestant. His arrest would likely cost Reeves his job.

Stynes looked around the place — kitchen, bathroom, small bedroom. He was on his way back to the living room when his cell phone rang. It was Dispatch.

'Detective Stynes? We found that detective in Columbus, the one you were asking about.'

'Great,' Stynes said. 'Let me get a pen.'

'He's on the line right now, Detective. I can put the call through to your phone.'

'Really?'

'Really. Stand by.'

The wonders of modern technology.

Stynes waited, listening to a couple of clicks. The dispatcher told him to go ahead. 'You're speaking with Detective Helton of Columbus PD.'

'Detective Stynes?' a surprisingly young voice said.

'That's me. Thanks for taking the call.'

'No problem. We're always happy to help out our brothers in the rural provinces.'

*Shithead*, Stynes thought.

'You're wanting to know about an assault case, one that involved a Justin Manning.'

'Yes, that's it,' Stynes said. 'I know it might be a long shot you would remember anything, but I wanted to try.'

'I've got the file and my notes here.' Helton hummed to himself while he apparently looked at the file. 'I do remember this. Kind of.'

'What happened?' Stynes asked.

'Standard stuff. Manning got into it with some

263

guy. There was pushing and shoving. I guess your boy Manning took a swing at the other dude and clocked him in the jaw. Guy wasn't really hurt, but he wanted to press charges. Misdemeanor assault. Manning didn't have a record, so he walked with a fine. Except he never bothered to pay the fine, so the warrant was issued. Happens every day in the big city. Why are you interested? What did Manning do?'

'Let's call it identity theft.'

'Well, I can send you a copy of this report if you'd like.'

'Thanks. That would be great.'

There was a long pause. Stynes thought the connection had been lost. He was about to ask when Helton spoke again.

'Shit,' Helton said.

'What?'

'This name. Manning. And Dove Point. I read about this.' Another pause. 'Shit. This guy's pretending to be . . . '

'That's what I'm trying to find out.'

'Trying? Isn't it obvious he isn't the kid? He stole a dead kid's identity.'

'That would be my guess, too. But we have to make sure.'

'I'm going to look at that story again.' Helton made the humming noise again. 'Yeah, I have in my notes that Manning seemed like an odd duck. He had that twenty-mile stare, you know? But that's half the perps we deal with here.'

Perps? Stynes thought. Did people really talk that way?

'If you could just send it on over.'

'You got it,' Helton said. 'And I guess an identity theft case is a nice break from prosecuting cow tippers?'

'Right,' Stynes said. He hung up, then added, 'Asshole.'

# 30

Ashleigh looked at the photos from the box under her bed. There weren't that many, which surprised her. Did people take many pictures back then? Her mom once explained that taking photographs used to be expensive. You had to bring the film to a place that developed it and then wait for the pictures to come back. You bought them whether they were any good or not. Sometimes her mom talked like she grew up in the nineteenth century.

But there were maybe only fifty photos total of her uncle. Some were posed portraits, the kind they took at the mall. Others were candid — birthday parties, Christmas. Ashleigh studied the portraits, trying to see a resemblance. But she'd seen the man on the porch for only a few minutes — and from a distance. What was she going to be able to see?

Someone knocked on the door again. Ashleigh sighed and threw the pictures back in the box, then slid it under the bed.

'Hold on,' Ashleigh said.

She made sure the box was hidden and opened the door. Except it wasn't her mom — it was her grandpa. He stood there in the hallway looking as uncomfortable as he always did when he came to her room. Ashleigh didn't know why he acted so weird about coming near her personal space — he'd raised a daughter before.

But the old guy always looked afraid when he stood in the doorway of her room, like he was expecting a training bra or a tampon to leap up and bite him on the neck.

'Hi,' Ashleigh said. 'Is something wrong?'

'Your mom asked me to check in on you.'

'I'm fine,' Ashleigh said.

She thought that would be it. Ordinarily that would be it, but for some reason her grandpa lingered around the door as if he wanted to talk or something. Except he didn't say anything. He stood there, hands in pockets. Ashleigh didn't know what to do.

'Are you watching the Reds game?' she asked.

'Oh, yeah,' he said. 'Seventh inning. They're winning. Do you want to watch the end of the game?'

'Um . . . '

'It's okay if you don't. I know you're not a big sports fan.'

'I guess I was going to read something,' Ashleigh said, although, in truth, she didn't have a new book to read and needed to go to the library. She just really didn't want to watch baseball with the old man. She'd done it before, and even with the game on to provide a distraction, sitting there with him felt awkward.

'That's okay.' But he still didn't turn away. 'Hey,' he said, 'I meant to ask you. When that man today tried to, you know, touch you?'

'Yeah?'

'You're telling the truth that nothing else happened, right?'

'I am, Grandpa.'

'Because that shouldn't happen to a young girl like you, and I just wanted you to know that it's okay.'

'What's okay?'

'If you want to tell me anything else.'

Ashleigh's cheeks flushed with warmth. She understood. The old guy was looking out for her. He was being protective. 'It's okay, Grandpa,' she said again. 'I told everything there is to tell. He didn't hurt me.'

He nodded, and Ashleigh thought she saw his shoulders lift a little with relief. 'Good,' he said.

'Grandpa?'

'Yeah?'

'You know how I got away?'

'How?' he asked.

'Remember you taught me once how to get away if someone grabbed me from behind?'

'I do,' he said. 'You used that?'

'I swung my arm back and hit him in the gut. And then, when he doubled over, I kicked him in the face.'

Her grandpa smiled bigger than she had ever seen him smile. 'I didn't even teach you that.'

'I know. I just did it.'

'Great.'

Then they didn't know what to say to each other again.

'Well,' he said.

He went back down the stairs. Ashleigh went into her room but didn't shut the door. She didn't return to the bed or look for a book to read. Without thinking of it too much, she left and went downstairs, following in her grandpa's wake. He was sitting in his chair, the baseball game playing at high volume. He looked up when she came into the living room, his face showing surprise. He appeared even more surprised when she sat down on the couch and looked at the TV, but he didn't say anything.

Ashleigh tried to decipher the action of the game. She read the score in the upper left-hand corner of the screen. The Reds appeared to be playing and beating a team from New York, one that wore orange-and-blue uniforms. The Yankees? Or was it the Mets? They were from New York, right? Otherwise, she couldn't follow beyond the basics — balls and strikes, outs and hits. When the players ran around the bases and things happened, she lost track of what it all meant.

During a commercial, her grandpa said, 'Your mom never liked baseball.'

'I don't really like it either,' Ashleigh said.

Ashleigh knew what he was thinking: *Then why are you sitting here?* But he didn't say it. During the next round of commercials, Ashleigh said, 'Grandpa, what do you think happened to Uncle Justin?'

He didn't look away from the TV. 'He's dead, Ashleigh.'

She didn't know how to respond. She'd expected some debate, some hedging of bets based on the events of recent days. But there was none of that — just a flat statement of fact.

'How can you be sure?' Ashleigh asked.

He still didn't look away from the TV. 'It's been so long,' he said. 'I just know it.'

269

The game started again, and one of the batters for the Reds did something impressive because all the fans were cheering. When it quieted down, Ashleigh said, 'Do you mean that because Uncle Justin is your son, you can feel if he's alive or not?'

'I'll say something about all of this.' He used the remote control to turn the volume down a little but didn't look at her. 'I have a feeling we're going to learn something in the coming days, all of us. Too many people are nosing around and getting worked up.'

'We're going to learn something about who really killed him?'

'Just something,' he said. 'Your mom told me tonight before she left the house that we were in the middle of all of this and we couldn't avoid it.' He turned the volume back up on the TV. The crowd cheered more. Someone had hit a home run. 'I think she's right.'

# 31

Michael led Janet to the opening to the path into the woods. She stopped there, peering ahead into the darkness.

'Why are we here?' she asked. 'Is this what you want to show me?'

'Yes.'

'Why here?'

'It's just . . . ' Michael searched for the right words. 'It will help to do it in there.'

Janet tried to remember the last time she had gone into the woods. She had been there only once since the day Justin died. When Ashleigh was small and asking questions about Justin's death, Janet had relented and took her into the clearing and showed her the spot. The place fascinated Ashleigh. She wanted to sit and pepper Janet with questions about the day Justin disappeared and died, but Janet made them leave before Ashleigh could say anything. It didn't feel right to Janet to be there. If she didn't want to be defined by the events that happened in that place, then there was no point in returning to it time after time. Likewise, she spent little time in the cemetery where her mother and brother were buried. She hoped they would rest together someday, if only for the symbolic nature of having them side by side — not because she wanted to spend every Sunday bringing flowers and tending to their graves.

So what did Michael want?

The night was dark. Her eyes had adjusted to the lack of light, which meant she could see about twenty-five feet in front of her.

'Michael,' she said, 'I don't like this place.'

He looked down at her in the darkness. He reached out a comforting hand, placed it on her upper arm again. 'I know,' he said.

'Then why are we here?'

'We're here because I learned something in therapy about confronting things from our past. Janet, did you ever talk about this with a therapist?'

'They made me talk to a school counselor when Justin died,' she said. She remembered the hours spent in the small office, the counselor a well-meaning but past-his-prime man with white hair and a polyester tie that Janet knew even at that young age was too far out of date. She told him what she thought he wanted to hear because she thought it would release her from the sessions sooner. *No, I'm not having nightmares. No, I don't obsessively think about my brother's death. No, I'm not scared in the dark.* And it worked. The sessions stopped, and Janet began the project — mostly on her own — of trying to be a normal kid again.

In the darkness, Janet studied Michael's eyes. Despite his touch and his smile, his eyes looked nervous and afraid. After all the years she'd known him, Janet couldn't reconcile the two images — the smiling golden boy she'd known both in fact and in memory and the man standing before her, a man in his early thirties who'd been a little battered by life. That one had become and fed into the other Janet understood on an intellectual level, just as she understood that the defensive seven-year-old determined to soldier on through her brother's death had become the woman at the head of the path. A little fearful and nervous and uncertain about how the events of the last few days were going to turn out — and what it all was going to mean to her.

'I need to do this, Janet,' Michael said. 'A therapist I saw in California encouraged me to come back to this spot. To be in it again. You know, I haven't been here since that day?'

'Is that why you're back in Dove Point? To do this?'

'I've been circling the issue for years,' he said. 'After California, I moved to Chicago, then Columbus. I kept getting closer.'

'Why do we have to do it in the dark? Justin didn't die in the dark.'

If he died at all.

'I need to share it with you,' he said. 'And this is our chance to do it without interruption.'

Janet looked down the path again, then up at Michael.

She nodded her head, and they started into the woods.

\* \* \*

They moved down the narrow path single file, with Michael going first and Janet following, holding on to his hand. Janet knew that kids

273

came to the park to have sex or drink or escape from the adult world that held them back, and it wasn't lost on her, as they walked through the woods, that if this scene were playing out sixteen years earlier — the two of them holding hands in the darkened park, heading to an isolated place — her entire body would have been thrumming with the electric pulses of desire. Even under the current circumstances, Janet felt some of that. She and Michael were together. They were touching. They were sharing something, just the two of them.

But Janet knew enough — had lived enough — not to give in to that feeling. Bigger things were happening. Much bigger.

Branches and twigs brushed against her arms and pant legs as they progressed down the path. Despite the heat and recent lack of rain, the foliage in the woods remained thick and lush. In the darkness, the leaves shifted and moved in the light breeze, their shadowy outlines tricking Janet's eyes with their movement, giving the impression of the presence of animals or people where there were none. She smelled the rich earth, felt the buzzing of flying insects that nipped at her face and exposed arms.

She couldn't turn back. Michael needed her. And maybe he was right. Maybe she needed to face this place again.

Michael turned back to her. 'It's right up there,' he said. 'Are you okay?'

'How do you even know where to go?' Janet asked.

'There's only one path through the woods over

here,' he said. 'Besides, I can just feel that this is the place. I know. Don't you?'

Janet didn't say it out loud, but she agreed. It did feel like the place. It really did.

Michael's pace slowed a few moments later. He came to an almost complete stop and shifted to the right, his hand still holding Janet's. She saw the dark outline of the little pond to the left, smelled the stagnant, boggy water. And then she saw the opening ahead of them, felt herself guided by Michael to the edge of the clearing where he stood by her side.

It looked the same as the last time, which had been how long? She tried to remember how old Ashleigh had been that day they walked down to the place her brother died. Ashleigh must have been about nine, which meant it had been six years since Janet had been to the spot.

'It's weird to think about, isn't it?' Michael said.

'What?'

'Someone died here. A life ended on this spot, and there's nothing to indicate that it ever happened. Anyone could walk through here. People probably do, and they just don't know the ground they're walking over.'

'There's no need for any marker,' Janet said. 'Everywhere you go someone's died there. Or had a relationship end or received bad news. If we marked all those places, the world would be full of nothing but awful reminders.'

Michael looked over at her, his face puzzled. Janet recognized that her statement revealed a

calmness and rationality that she didn't completely feel. But she did believe the sentiment she
expressed. Why should the rest of the world have
to be reminded of what happened to her family?
Why shouldn't the high school kids be able to
roll around on the ground and make out without
having to think about a death that happened
years earlier?

'Well,' Michael said. He took a step forward,
expecting Janet to move with him.

Janet resisted. 'No.'

'What?'

'I'm okay right here,' she said. 'On the edge of
the clearing.' She saw a flat rock to her left and
sat down on it, letting go of Michael's hand. 'I'm
okay here.'

'But — '

'Michael, I guess I'm starting to wonder if this
is a good idea. Being here. What are you trying to
achieve?'

He studied her for a moment in the dark, his
facial features obscured by the shadows. 'I'll
show you,' he said.

He moved out into the center of the clearing.
Janet thought he was going to stop in the middle,
as close as he possibly could get to the spot
where Justin's body was found. But Michael
didn't pause. He walked past that point and over
to the far side of the clearing. There, he turned
back to Janet and faced her through the murky
darkness, his body practically just another
shadow among the shadows.

'This is where I was,' he said.

Janet waited for an explanation, and when he

276

didn't offer one, she asked, 'What do you mean?'

'I think this is where I stood that day. The day Justin died.'

Michael closed his eyes, squeezed them tight, and he crouched down in the darkness, bending at the knees until he was in a squatting position. He covered his face with both of his hands.

Janet didn't know what she was supposed to do. She still didn't understand what Michael wanted from her. She waited while Michael remained in that position, his face hidden, his body quiet. Someone who stumbled upon him that way would think he was praying — or grieving. And maybe he was.

He finally shifted his hands from over his mouth and said, 'I can see it, Janet. That day.'

'I can see it, too. Always.'

'No, Janet.' His voice sounded harsh, impatient. 'I can see that day, of course. But I can see this spot. This very spot.' He slid his hands all the way off his face and shifted his weight. He leaned forward and rested on his knees, his body kneeling in the soft dirt. 'Remember, I followed Justin into the woods when he chased after that dog.'

'Sure.'

'And this is where he came. To this exact spot.'

'Are you saying you were here? You came this far into the woods?'

'Something's happened to me since I've been back in Dove Point. It's exactly what my therapist told me would happen. Since I've been here and living in this place, a flood of memories has come back to me. Everything. Smells and sounds and sights. I've been a little over-whelmed.'

'It's hard for me to really understand,' Janet said. 'I never left like you did.'

'Trust me. Memory is a powerful force.'

For a long moment, there were only the night sounds. Then Janet said, 'You told me in the coffee shop that you think you saw your dad in the woods that day. Did you see him here? In this clearing?'

'I went to our old house today, the one we lived in when I was a kid. You know, Dad has it on the market. I made an appointment with the real estate agent. I didn't tell Dad that I was doing it. He was at work while I went through with the agent. I'm not going to buy it, of course, but I wanted to see what the old place was like.'

'I didn't know he was moving.'

Michael made a bitter laughing sound. 'He's getting married. Did you know that? He's marrying his fucking secretary. Some girl younger than us, and he's marrying her.'

Janet thought of her own dad. She couldn't imagine him marrying again, or her reaction to it, but there were days she would gladly have accepted a twenty-five-year-old stepmother if it brought the old man out of his funk.

'It's been a long time for him — '

'No,' Michael said. 'No. I don't want to hear excuses for him. He left my mother. I know you went to the house the other day. I know you saw how she lives.'

Janet understood. She didn't know the particulars between Ray and Rose, but she understood that Michael would believe his mother had got the shaft. On the surface, it certainly seemed that way.

'So you went through the house?' Janet said, hoping to steer Michael away from the anger at his father and back to what he had to say about his memories and the clearing.

'I did.'

'You didn't tell your dad?'

'We're not really talking right now. I don't want to talk to him.'

'Okay.'

'It's funny. You're back in your house, and I went back through my house. Did we ever think we'd be doing that when we were sixteen?'

'We figured we'd be in New York or LA. At least one of us made it out.'

He made the bitter laughing noise again. 'For a while. Anyway, when I went through the house, a lot of things came back to me. The way I felt as a kid. The way I felt about my father. I opened up the medicine cabinet and saw his aftershave. I sat in the recliner he always sat in. I didn't tell the real estate agent who I was or that I used to live there. She probably thought I was nuts, wandering around so lost in my thoughts. And then, at the end, I just left. I didn't take her card or the sheet about the house. I just left.'

He scratched his nose. 'I feel like it made a lot of sense to go there like that. It served as preparation for the other things I needed to do. A warm-up exercise, if you will.'

'And what were you warming up to?' Janet asked.

'When I left the house and the real estate agent behind, I walked over to the park. I followed the exact course that he would have taken to get here. Out our backyard, through the neighbor's yard, and over to the path into the woods. I walked all the way back here, right to this spot.'

'And what did you find?'

'He was here, Janet.'

'Today?'

'Then. That day. He wasn't just in the woods. He was here. Right here.' He closed his eyes again. 'I can see him. I can see him in this clearing.'

Janet shivered. The sweat on her body seemed to have suddenly cooled. 'With Justin?'

'I don't know'

'Why would your dad be here in the first place?' Janet asked. 'Why would he just be walking through the woods in the morning?'

'I don't know that either.'

'It doesn't make sense.'

'It does if my dad was involved somehow. If he *did* something.'

'But what reason would he have for doing anything to Justin? Why?'

Michael shook his head. 'I don't know, Janet. I don't know any of it. I just know that something is wrong with my dad. He walked away from my mom. He walked away from his responsibilities as a father.'

'It doesn't make him a killer,' Janet said. 'And there's a guy claiming to be Justin running around town — '

'And the convicted killer says he's innocent,' Michael said. 'So if Dante Rogers is innocent, that means someone else committed the crime. Someone who was here and close. And my dad was here.' Michael pointed at the earth. 'He was right here.'

Something snuck up on Janet, a memory of her own. Except it wasn't from years past. It was from earlier that day.

'My dad,' she said.

'What about him?'

'I just found out today that my dad was home the morning Justin died. Not only was he home, but he . . . I don't want to say he lied, but he . . .'

'He what?'

'He told the police one thing about where he was that morning, and my mom said something else. But he was home that morning when he was supposed to be at work. Why would they both be home in the morning? Did you ask your mom about this?'

Michael shook his head. 'I can't. She's too fragile. She's not over the asshole yet. It's pathetic.'

Janet wrapped her arms around her body. She looked at the ground where her brother supposedly died. 'What happened here, Michael?'

'I don't know.'

'I don't even know if I'm supposed to trust these memories you're having,' she said. 'I can't remember what I did last week, and you're asking me to believe that you can remember something that happened twenty-five years ago, something you haven't clearly remembered until now. I don't know what to do with all of that. And the truth is I don't want to believe you. I don't want to believe that your father or my father had anything to do with Justin's death. I want to believe he's still alive, that the man claiming to be him is really him.'

Michael stood up. He came over, and Janet scooted to her left so he could sit on the rock next to her. Their legs touched, the fabric of their jeans rubbing against each other. Michael took her hand in his. 'That's what I'm here to find out. That's why I came back here.'

'They're looking for that man, Michael. The one who might be Justin.'

'He's not Justin, Janet.'

Janet pulled back so she could see Michael's face clearly. 'Why would you say that?'

'The answer is here,' he said. 'In this clearing. With my dad.'

'But you don't know that.'

'I believe it.'

'And you need me to believe it along with you?' Janet asked. 'That's why you brought me here today.'

'I do.'

Janet looked around at the darkened ground. That was always the thing with Michael, always the thing. He needed, and she ran along behind providing. Twenty-five years, ten years — nothing had changed.

'Okay, Michael,' she said.

'You believe me,' he said.

'I believe how important this is to you,' she said. 'I'm not sure I'm convinced of anything else.'

# 32

Stynes stayed up too late, then woke up too early. After returning home from the apartment complex, he checked his e-mail and downloaded a scanned copy of the police report on the arrest of Justin Manning. Stynes read it over several times, sitting at the small table in his kitchen. He made notes, but when his eyes grew bleary because of the late hour, he put it all aside and decided to deal with it in the morning.

Which meant he didn't sleep well. He stared at the ceiling for an hour before he drifted off. The time in bed, in his dark house, represented the first quiet moments he'd had since he'd gone to the Mannings' house in the afternoon. And every question that the day had raised swirled through his mind.

Was this man Justin Manning? Why was Bill Manning home that day? Why was money disappearing from the accounts at the church where Dante Rogers worked — accounts overseen by the father of one of the key witnesses against Dante?

*Why didn't you stand up to Reynolds back then? Would you be asking any of these questions if you had just stood up to your partner?*

He woke up sooner than he needed to as well, but took it as punishment for being in the middle of a case that should have closed twenty-five years ago. So he went in to work and reviewed the notes he'd made the night before. One thing stood out that merited further investigation: the man assaulted by Justin Manning worked for a child welfare office in Columbus. Why hadn't Helton mentioned that detail on the phone? Stynes located the office through a Google search and understood why Helton hadn't mentioned it — the assault hadn't taken place at the child welfare office. Stynes called the office, and after a series of transfers and relays through secretaries and assistants ended up speaking to the man named as the victim in the police report: Paul Downing.

When Downing came on the line, Stynes explained who he was and why he was calling.

'Oh.'

Downing sounded a little taken aback by Stynes's introduction. Wouldn't a social worker be used to getting calls from the police? Maybe just not about a case in which he was the victim . . .

'I'm just wondering if you could tell me about this altercation you had with Justin Manning.'

'It was hardly an altercation,' Downing said. 'Altercation suggests something mutual, like a fight. This was decidedly one-sided.'

Downing's voice sounded high and reedy. He expected the man to harrumph through the phone.

'So what happened?' Stynes asked.

'Well, Mr Manning came into my office seeking records and information about someone who had been in our foster care system many years ago.'

'Who?'

'Well, it's been a little while. I see so many names cross my desk.'

'He wasn't asking about himself?'

'No.'

'Was the name 'Steven Kollman'?'

'Yes, I believe that's it.'

'Okay. Go on.'

'I told him he couldn't just come in and ask for records for anybody and expect us to hand them over. Most of those records are sealed, and even if they aren't, someone would have to get a court order to have anything released to the public, let alone someone who didn't appear to be related to the individual in question.'

'Did he say why he wanted Steven Kollman's records?'

'No.'

'And did he give any identification saying he was Justin Manning?'

'Not to me, no. But I didn't ask for it.' He sniffed. 'I suspect the police saw his identification.'

'So you told him no, and he decked you?'

'He begged and pleaded for me to bend the rules, but I held firm. I just can't do anything like that. A few hours later, I was at a restaurant near work having a drink, and Mr Manning came in and confronted me. He asked for the records again, and when I refused him again, he did, as you so eloquently put it, deck me.

Someone called the police, and I filed the complaint.'

'Were you hurt?'

'Just my pride.'

'Did Manning threaten you or have a weapon?'

'The punch was threat enough. I didn't see any weapons.'

'How do you think he found you in this restaurant? Did you mention it in front of him?'

'It's near my office. For all I know, he just went to the places near where I work looking for me. There aren't many.'

'What's the place called?'

'Hathaway's.'

'Would any of your coworkers give that information out to Manning?' Stynes asked.

'Heavens, no. In this business, we do whatever we can to protect ourselves. As evidenced by Mr Manning's behavior.'

'Anything else you can think of?' Stynes asked.

'No, I haven't seen the man since.'

'After all this happened, did you look into the records of Steven Kollman? Just to see what might be there?'

'I didn't bother.'

'Can I check them out?' Stynes knew the answer but wanted to take a shot.

'You'd need a court order, too, Detective. It shouldn't be hard to get.'

'Of course.'

'Tell me, Detective, this Manning isn't some sort of serial killer, is he? I'd hate to think I'm in danger.'

'I guess we don't know what he is yet,' Stynes said. 'But I'd sure like to find out.'

Stynes hung up, then stood and walked to the desk officer.

'Covington?'

The eager young officer looked up. 'Yes?'

'Aren't you from Columbus?' Stynes asked.

'Yes, sir.'

'You ever hear of a bar called Hathaway's?'

Covington thought about it, her face puzzled. 'Hathaway's? It sounds kind of familiar.'

Stynes looked at the printed copy of the police report in his hand. 'It's on something called Bethel Pike.'

'Bethel Pike. That's on the west side of town.'

'You tell me,' Stynes said.

Covington chewed on the end of her pencil. 'Is this a little dive bar?'

'I don't know.'

'I think there's a place called Hathaway's on the west side. A little hole-in-the-wall.'

'You sure?'

'My uncle rides Harleys. He's talked about it.'

'Harleys,' Stynes said. 'So it has a pretty rough crowd?'

'I would think so. Mostly the shot-and-a-beer types.'

'Would you expect to see an effeminate social worker hanging out there?'

'Not if he valued his life.'

'Is it the kind of place you just stumble across, or do you have to know it's there?'

'You'd have to know it's there. I don't think they've invested in a very big sign.'

287

'Thanks, Covington.'

Stynes returned to his desk and called Helton's number. He didn't answer, so Stynes left a message asking Helton to call him back. If he'd worked a late shift the previous night, then he probably wouldn't be in early the next day. And even if Stynes had the guy's cell number, he wouldn't use it. Let the young guy sleep in. But just a few minutes passed before Covington came back and informed Stynes that a detective from Columbus was on the phone.

'Detective Helton?' Stynes said into the phone.

'No, this is Detective Bowling. Helton gave me your number.'

'Oh.'

'Helton isn't in until noon, but he and I talked last night, and I have some more information for you about the Manning case. Do you have a minute?'

'Of course.'

'Like I said, I talked to Helton last night in passing, and he told me you were dealing with some stuff from that Manning case. Were you on the case originally?'

'I was.'

'Damn. And here it is still coming back up for you. Anyway, I don't know if what I have to tell you is a big deal or not, but about six months ago a guy came into the station and asked to talk to a detective. He said he had information about a murder case. I was next up, so he ended up sitting at my desk and told me that he knew something about the Justin Manning murder that happened twenty-five years ago in Darke County.'

Stynes's blood grew a little colder. He swallowed and said, 'What did he say?'

'That's just it — he didn't have much to say. He said the crime didn't happen the way everyone thinks it happened, that an innocent man went to prison for it. This guy said his father was involved somehow, and he wanted to know what could be done about it.'

'Who was this guy?' Stynes asked.

'Well, that's just it. He wouldn't give me his name. He said he understood that he was making a pretty big accusation of murder, and he didn't know if he was really ready to step forward. He wanted to talk to a detective first and see what his options were.'

'He didn't give his name?'

'He wouldn't. I told him I needed a name if the conversation was going to go any further, so he said to call him Mr Jones.'

'Original. What did this guy look like?'

'Good-looking guy, early to mid-thirties. Seemed educated. And he sounded like he was from the Midwest.'

'That's all he said then.'

'I asked him what kind of evidence he had to back up his claim. I told him that he couldn't just suspect something and expect a twenty-five-year-old case to be reopened. He said it wasn't just a suspicion. He said he had memories, memories that had been lost to him but had come back over the years through therapy. He said he knew now that he had seen his dad in the vicinity of the crime scene when the murder happened.'

'And that's all he had?'

'That's it. Memories.'

'Was the guy a nut?' Stynes asked.

'You know, we have some cases based on that over here,' Bowling said. 'Apparently the current scientific evidence sees real merit in recovered memories. We have shrinks testify about it, and it's helped us win some cases.'

'No shit.'

'Sure. But since this guy didn't want to give his name or anything, it kind of makes me doubt his story.'

'Sounds more like he doesn't like or trust his old man,' Stynes said.

'Exactly what I thought.'

'Why didn't you call me back then?'

'Like I said, since the guy wasn't giving his name and seemed a little flaked out, I decided it wasn't worth bothering anybody with it. What could have been done if I had called you?'

Stynes knew he was right. And the news only added to the puzzle. Who would make such a claim in Columbus? Steven Kollman?

'Thanks for calling,' Stynes said.

'Helton tells me things are getting weird over there,' Bowling said. 'You've got a guy pretending to be the dead kid?'

'Looks that way.'

'The fun never ends, does it?'

'Hey, while I've got you on the line, what do you know about a dive bar called Hathaway's? Ever hear of it?'

'Sure,' Bowling said. 'A few years back we had to clean some drug activity out of there. It's that kind of place. Bikers and biker chicks. Why do you ask?'

'Our Justin Manning was arrested for assault there,' Stynes said.

'Most assaults there usually end with a knife or a gun.'

'Lovely place?'

Bowling laughed. 'Detective, as I'm sure you know, it's a lovely, lovely world.'

# 33

Reynolds didn't answer his phone, so at lunchtime Stynes drove to his former partner's house, hoping to catch him there or, short of that, leave a note saying they needed to talk. When Stynes arrived at the house, he saw Reynolds in the front yard surrounded by three grandkids tossing a ball back and forth, trying very hard to keep it out of Reynolds's reach. And he was doing his best to pretend like he couldn't intercept their throws.

Stynes stepped out of the car, pushed the door shut, and said, 'Careful, kids, you'll give your granddad a heart attack.'

The kids paused for only a moment to look at the man by the curb before returning to their game. Reynolds told them to go into the backyard with Grandma, and then came over to the street by Stynes.

'I left you a message this morning,' Stynes said.

Reynolds jerked his thumb toward the house. 'I was busy, as you can see. Being retired means I don't have to answer the phone if I don't want to.'

'I see that.' Stynes leaned back against the car. 'You got a minute?'

'A minute. It's almost lunchtime for the kids.'

'I was going to ask you if you wanted to go out and grab something to eat.'

'I can't. What's up?'

The day was hot, the sun high above in a cloudless sky. Stynes felt the heat against his scalp.

'You know all those loose ends with the Manning case?' Stynes said.

'Loose ends for you, you mean.'

'We had two pretty big loose ends. The stories told by the kids, and the questions about the whereabouts of Bill Manning on the morning of the murder. Not to mention the questions about Scott Ludwig.'

Reynolds looked at his watch. 'You better hurry up and get to it.'

'I know those loose ends don't really mean anything to you. Maybe it's because you're retired. I don't know. I hope when I hang it up I'll be able to walk away and turn the switch off as well as you have.'

'You won't.'

'Why do you say that?'

'Because you're different than me, Stynes. When my head hits the pillow late at night, I go right to sleep. I don't give a shit that Dante Rogers says he's innocent or that those kids told one story at the park and another later on. But not you. No, you've got to make sure everything is right with the world. I bet you've been sleeping like crap, haven't you?'

Stynes didn't answer. He didn't have to. Reynolds had pegged him.

Reynolds said, 'I bet you stared at your bedroom ceiling so long you started to see cracks in the plaster you didn't know were there, right?

Well, you can do that with any case. Stare long enough until you see all the imperfections. It doesn't change the facts, though.' Reynolds looked like he wanted to say more, but he swallowed the additional words, whatever they were going to be. 'Do me a favor? Don't come back here anymore. Don't drag your bullshit onto my lawn.'

As he started to turn away, Stynes said, 'We're searching for a man right now.'

Reynolds stopped.

'He's using Justin Manning's name and carrying his identification,' Stynes said. 'He's wanted for assault in Columbus. He beat up a social worker over there, someone associated with child protective services.'

Reynolds raised his hands. *So?*

Stynes decided he didn't really know why he had come to Reynolds's house after all. He knew he wasn't going to change his former partner's mind. He knew Reynolds wouldn't concede any fault or fallibility. He never had.

'You know, you're right,' Stynes said.

'About what?'

'I'm not going to come back here anymore.'

'Good.'

'But I do want to say something to you. I want to apologize to you.'

Reynolds looked puzzled. He tilted his head to the left, almost like he didn't believe the words he heard coming his way. 'What for?'

'*I* should have been a better cop,' Stynes said. '*I* should have been a better partner to you. You said I did a good job back then, but I didn't. I should have stood up to you. I should have asked the tough questions. That's what I was supposed to do, and I didn't. But I'm going to ask them now, and we'll see what happens.'

Reynolds waited a long moment, then said, 'Are you finished, Oprah?'

'With you, yes.'

'Good.' Reynolds pointed to the car. 'Then get the fuck out of here before I beat your scrawny ass.'

Stynes got into the car and started the ignition. As he drove off, he looked back one more time. He watched Reynolds trudging across the lawn, his body a little bent, his posture that of a man in the last phase of his life. Then Stynes caught a glimpse of himself in the rearview mirror, saw the lines around his eyes, the old-man sweat on his forehead.

'You're almost there,' he told himself. 'But not quite yet.'

# 34

Janet was surprised to look up from her desk and see Kate Grossman, the reporter from the *Dove Point Ledger*, entering the dean's office shortly after lunch. Kate waved to Janet and started across the room toward her, and as she did, Janet realized she was about to speak to the only reporter in town who went to work in a skirt and high heels.

Kate's face lit up as she approached Janet, and she held her hand out for a businesslike shake.

'It's so good to see you again, Ms Manning.'

'Janet. Remember?'

'Of course. Sorry. I still feel like a kid, you know?'

Janet couldn't imagine what the reporter wanted with her. Follow-up questions? Another story? Her dad would love that. And Janet's curiosity only rose higher when Kate leaned in a little closer and asked if the two of them could speak somewhere in private.

'Sure,' Janet said.

Madeline watched the proceedings from her desk, not even trying to disguise her curiosity about the visitor. Janet didn't stop to explain but simply told Madeline that she'd be back in a few minutes. She led Kate Grossman out of the dean's office and across the hall to a seldom-used conference room. They went inside, and once Janet had closed the door, the two women sat next to each other at one end of the table.

'What is this about?' Janet asked. During the short walk to the conference room, Janet had reminded herself not to get worked up and not to engage in too much speculation about the nature of Kate's visit. But she couldn't control her own reactions. Janet imagined a little bit of everything and then some before she sat down. She didn't want to wait while Kate warmed up to the topic.

'I have some good news for you,' Kate said.

'What?'

Did they find Justin? Is it him?

Is it over?

Kate smiled. 'We received a lot of positive feedback regarding the stories we ran about your brother's murder. More letters and e-mails than we normally get.'

Kate paused briefly. She seemed to want Janet to say something to this, so Janet said, 'That's great. What are you here to tell me?'

Kate looked a little disappointed. She appeared to want more praise, or a more detailed discussion of her reportorial skills. When it didn't come, she went on. 'A lot of people were moved by your plight. Anyway, this morning, we received something in the mail at the newspaper office. Something addressed to you.'

'What is it?'

'We're not sure,' Kate said. 'We didn't open it.'

'Then how do you know it's good news?'

Kate didn't miss a beat. 'I have a positive feeling.' She bent down and reached into her oversized purse. When she came up, she held an envelope out to Janet. 'See?'

Indeed, it was an envelope addressed to Janet, care of the *Ledger*. A plain white business envelope. Janet wasn't sure what to think, and she didn't understand why Kate Grossman would show up making such a production out of what was probably a note of support or some crank's speculations about what really happened to Justin.

Janet studied the address. It was printed, not handwritten. The postmark said Dove Point, but the envelope lacked a return address.

'Go ahead and open it,' Kate said.

But Janet didn't move right away. She thought about taking the envelope back to her desk and opening it away from Kate Grossman. Or maybe just throwing it in the trash. Did she need to know anything else?

But Janet turned it over and started to slip her index finger under the sealed flap.

'Just one second,' Kate said.

Janet looked up.

'I know it's weird, but I brought a camera with me. Would you mind if I — ?'

'Yes, I'd mind.'

Janet completed the work of opening the envelope and looked inside. She didn't see much. Just a white piece of paper. She drew it out and unfolded the sheet.

*Dear Ms Manning,*

*In response to your stated request to see your late brother and mother buried side by* *side, please accept a donation of $10,000 for that purpose, which has been placed into a fund in your name at Dove Point Farmers Bank and Trust.*

*With our sympathies.*

'Well?' Kate asked.

Janet didn't respond. She didn't know what to say. She turned the paper over. It was blank on the back. The whole thing seemed like a joke. Was it some sort of crank attempting to mess with her again?

'Oh, God, Ms Manning,' Kate said. 'Is it something awful? Did someone say something nasty to you?'

'Why did you come in here and say you had good news?' Janet asked. 'Do you know what this says?'

Kate shook her head. She really did look young, like a kid who thought she might be in trouble. 'I don't know,' she said. Her shoulders sagged, and she lost the shiny, confident smile. 'See, my editor thought coming and watching you open the letter personally would make a good follow-up story. I guess we were just *hoping* it would be good news.'

'Hoping?'

'Is it? Or is it something bad?'

Janet folded the letter and tucked it back into the envelope. 'I need to call the bank.'

'Here, use my phone.'

'I don't know the number.'

'It's a smartphone. I'll look it up.'

Janet told her who to call, and within a few

minutes Janet was speaking with the branch manager. She explained who she was and asked if he could tell her anything over the phone about something being opened in her name.

The manager seemed circumspect at first, reluctant to give out too much information. But Janet insisted.

'If this is some kind of sick joke, then I have to call the police,' Janet said. 'Do I need to call the police?'

After a short pause, the manager said, 'No, you don't have to call the police. This isn't a joke at all, Ms Manning. No joke at all.'

# 35

Ashleigh was sitting at the kitchen table, eating a bowl of cereal even though it was after five o'clock in the evening, when her mom came through the back door. Her mom usually whisked through the world with breezy efficiency. She moved quickly, but always with purpose, her body and movements under her complete control. But that evening her mom seemed out of sorts when she came into the house. She dropped her keys on the kitchen floor. They fell in a rattling jumble against the linoleum. Rather than take her purse to her room, as she always did, she dropped it onto the floor as well. Her face was flushed, and Ashleigh didn't think it was just from the heat.

'Hi, Mom.'

Janet stopped in the kitchen and leaned back against the counter by the sink. She let out a deep breath and then moved to the refrigerator, where she pulled out a bottle of wine. While it wasn't unusual for her mom to have some wine in the evening, it was unusual for her to open a bottle before she was even ten steps in the door. She still hadn't spoken to or looked at Ashleigh.

'Is everything okay?' Ashleigh asked.

Janet filled a glass and took a long first swallow. She came over to the table and sat across from her daughter.

'Would you believe me if I told you someone

gave us ten thousand dollars today?' Janet asked.

'No.'

'I don't believe it either, but they did.'

'Who gave you ten thousand dollars?' Ashleigh asked. She studied her mother's face. Had she been drinking before she came home? Had the stress of the last few days driven her to say crazy, nonsensical things? Her mother's eyes looked clear. She didn't slur her words or seem fuzzy-headed.

'Someone created a fund at the bank in my name,' Janet said. 'An anonymous donor. They set it up because they read the story in the paper about Justin, and they wanted to give us the money to move Justin's grave next to your grandma's.'

'An anonymous donor did this? Someone we don't know?'

Her mother swallowed more wine. 'The bank manager doesn't even know who did it. The whole thing was set up by a lawyer or something. But the money's there. I saw the paperwork at the bank.'

'Have you ever had that much money before?' Ashleigh asked.

'Just in my retirement account. And I can't touch that.'

Ashleigh ignored her cereal. The Cheerios looked fat and milk-swollen. 'You seem pretty upset about this,' Ashleigh said. 'Aren't you happy? You said you wanted this to happen. You've always said that.'

Her mother didn't speak for a long time. She finished her glass of wine, then went to the counter and poured another one. When she came back, Ashleigh studied her mom's face again. Her mother didn't look very old up close. She was younger than most of the other parents of the kids Ashleigh went to school with, and in the slanting late-afternoon light that came through the kitchen window, Ashleigh noticed again how pretty her mother's eyes were. They were light blue, and the sun picked up flecks of a gold color in the irises that Ashleigh had never noticed before. Her mother never dated, but she could. No doubt about it, Ashleigh concluded: her mother could be out on the market finding a nice guy and having a little fun. And Ashleigh wished her mother would do that, would choose to have a little bit of fun. She deserved it.

'I don't know what to make of this, Ash,' she said.

'Someone just wants to help. There are rich people who can write a check for thousands of dollars just like that.' Ashleigh snapped her fingers to demonstrate. 'We don't know any of them, but I'm sure they exist.'

'Isn't it strange that this is happening right when this guy is here saying he's Justin? What if the two are related?'

'You mean that guy might have given the money? No way. You didn't see his sketchy apartment, Mom.'

'I guess I don't trust anyone anymore,' her mom said. 'I feel like there's a trap around every corner. I feel like — '

'Like Grandpa,' Ashleigh said, her voice low. The old man was back in his room, the TV on.

But she still didn't want to risk having him hear her.

'What do you mean?'

'He's so angry. So bitter. He thinks the world is out to get him.'

'I know.' Janet nodded, then said, 'He wasn't always like that. He could be warm and fun when I was a little kid. I can remember him laughing and playing sometimes. He's had a rough ride.'

'No rougher than you.'

Janet smiled. She reached out and squeezed Ashleigh's hand. 'That's sweet of you to say. But he lost a son. Maybe I can't imagine.' Janet let go and sat up in her chair. 'But you're right. I don't want to look at everyone like they're a suspect or like they're up to something.'

'So just take the money and have Uncle Justin moved. You'd feel better — '

But Ashleigh stopped talking. She recognized the problem with what she was saying at the same time the words came out of her mouth.

A chill went through Ashleigh's torso, shaking her upper body hard enough to make her teeth rattle against one another.

'Mom, if that's not Uncle Justin in there . . . '

'I don't know, honey. I don't know.'

# 36

Stynes arrived at the Manning house after nine o'clock. He'd received a call from Janet Manning that afternoon, something about money being donated to her for the purposes of —

He couldn't be sure. He hadn't listened to the message carefully, and he didn't replay it. Other things were cluttering his mind.

He had called in advance of his arrival at the Mannings'. He wanted to tell them in person, before they found out about it on the news or some other way. But he hadn't given many details over the phone. He simply said they needed to talk, that there'd been a development in the case and he needed to speak to them as soon as possible. Was it too late?

Janet Manning assured him it wasn't.

She opened the door for him seconds after he knocked. She was barefoot but otherwise still wearing the clothes she'd probably worked in. Her father wasn't in the room, but Ashleigh was. The two of them sat on opposite ends of the couch, the TV playing one of those shows where they redecorate an entire home for fifty bucks or something like that. Janet turned it off, and Stynes sat in a chair, noting the empty wineglass on the end table by Janet's arm.

'Detective,' Janet said, 'this house has just about exhausted its potential for hearing strange or disturbing news.'

Stynes almost laughed. He looked at the two of them on the couch, the daughter a more petite version of the mother, but undeniably mother and child. He admired them, even liked them. Hell, if it weren't for the complications surrounding the twenty-five-year-old murder of one of their close relatives, he'd really enjoy spending time with them.

'Is your father home?' Stynes asked. 'Would you like him to hear this?'

'He's here,' Janet said. 'But why don't you tell me what you know, and I'll decide when to get him involved.'

Stynes nodded. *Fair enough.*

'We arrested a man today,' he said. 'His identification said his name is Justin Manning.'

The words settled over the room like an enveloping fog. No one moved or spoke. Stynes waited, watching the two Manning women. Ashleigh turned her head toward her mother as well, as though in anticipation.

'Is it him?' Janet asked.

The question — so simple, so loaded — cut to the heart of the entire matter.

*Is it him?*

'I'll tell you what I do know,' Stynes said. He brought out his small notebook, flipped to the right page, and lifted his glasses so he could read the page. He knew some of the details without referencing the pad and spoke without directly referring to it. But it sometimes felt better to have the notebook there as a kind of prop. 'This afternoon we received a call from St Anne's Elementary School. Are you familiar with it? It's over on Roselawn Avenue.'

'That's where I went to school,' Janet said. 'Grade school.'

'They're doing some summer cleaning projects, and one of their maintenance men found a man sleeping in the cafeteria. It looked like he was homeless and had been there for a couple of days, so they called the police.'

'Did he break in?' Ashleigh asked.

'Someone had left a service door open in the back, and he slipped in that way. When the officer arrived and asked for identification, the man produced an Ohio driver's license saying he was Justin Manning of Columbus. The officer knew we were looking for this guy, so he brought him in.' Stynes reached into his jacket pocket again and brought out a photo. 'First things first. Is this the man who came to your house in the middle of the night? And then this same man spoke to you on campus?' He handed the photo to Janet. 'Take your time.'

Janet looked at the photo and said, 'Yes, that's him.'

She held on to the photo, her eyes studying it.

'Ashleigh?' Stynes said. 'Can you look too?'

It took a long moment for Janet to hand the photo over, so long that Stynes had to speak.

'Janet?'

She passed it to Ashleigh without saying anything, and her daughter took the photo. Just as quickly, she said, 'Yes, that's the guy.'

'And just to be clear, where did you see this man?'

Ashleigh said, 'He came to our porch and talked to Mom in the middle of the night.'

Stynes took the photo back and returned it to his pocket.

'What did he say?' Janet asked.

'He hasn't said much,' Stynes said. 'In fact, he's refused to answer any questions. He didn't even ask for a lawyer. He handed over his identification and clammed up. We searched him and the small bag he carries with him. He didn't carry any other identification. Nothing with the name Steven Kollman on it.'

'He must have had something with that name on it,' Janet said. 'How else would he be able to work and get a paycheck?'

'Good question. And one we thought of. Turns out the place he was working, this Mi Casita or whatever it is, has a habit of paying some of its help under the table. They had some undocumented workers in the kitchen in addition to this guy. That's a problem they'll have to deal with, but it doesn't concern us right now, except to say that as far as we can tell, Steven Kollman didn't exist in Dove Point. He paid cash for the apartment and worked without identification. No one there knew him as Justin Manning. They knew him as Steven.'

Janet's face brightened a little. 'Doesn't that mean it's likely — ?'

Stynes held up his hand. 'It's too early to conclude anything. It really is. We're going to search the public records we have access to and see what if anything we can find out about Steven Kollman. In the meantime, we do know

308

that someone — presumably this same guy — has been using your brother's name and social security number for the past decade. He's worked at a series of odd jobs all over the country — some in the South, some as close as Columbus and Cincinnati. He was never in any other trouble with the law, at least not anything that shows up as a conviction or an outstanding warrant beyond the one incident in Columbus. That's the summons that Ashleigh found in his apartment. We've been in contact with local police departments in the places where he lived, hoping that they'll do some legwork for us and ask about Justin Manning at some of the places he worked, but they're strapped for time and resources, so who knows how long that will take to pan out, if it does at all.'

'Can anything else be done?' Janet asked. 'How are we going to find out what's going on with this guy?'

'What we can do is send this photo out,' Stynes said. 'Send it to law enforcement agencies, the media. With the Internet, we can hit all corners of the country. We can hope someone recognizes him and knows something about him. Otherwise, the clock is ticking, and eventually we'll have to let him go.'

'Let him go?' Ashleigh said.

Stynes looked over at the girl. She hadn't said much since he'd come in the door, so her voice sounded discordant. She wasn't content to just let her mother ask the tough questions.

'That's the law,' Stynes said. 'We can't just hold someone as long as we want.'

'But he's using my uncle's social security number. Isn't that identity theft or something?'

'It is,' Stynes said. 'If he's really not your uncle. Do you have any proof that he isn't who he says he is?'

Again, the room fell silent. Stynes understood where Ashleigh was coming from — he felt the exact same way. At some point, he no longer cared what the answer was — yes, this man in the jail was Justin Manning or, no, the man in the jail wasn't Justin Manning — he just wanted a final answer.

But their options for answering that question were limited.

'Look,' Stynes said. 'I know how frustrating this is. I get it. If that man in the jail is your brother, then we convicted the wrong man twenty-five years ago. And that's on me. Big-time. And if he's not your brother, then I want to see him punished for harassing you.'

'He never told me he was Justin,' Janet said. 'Never.'

'He still pretended to be Justin to some extent,' Stynes said. 'People do that. They use the identities of deceased children because they know there isn't much of a paper trail on a child. No arrests, no work history. It's easy to acquire that information through a public record search and then get false identification made. He broke the law by doing that.' Stynes thought about it and chose the right words. 'He raised your hopes. He led you on. That's wrong.'

'So what are our options here, besides just waiting around?' Janet asked.

'Do you mean what options do we have for proving that man's relationship or lack of one to you?' Stynes asked. 'Absent a witness who will swear to something, which I don't think we have, there's only DNA or finger-printing. Your brother didn't have any prominent scars or anything like that, did he?'

Janet shook her head.

'So take a DNA sample,' Ashleigh said.

'From the man in the jail?' Stynes asked.

'Yes. Compare it to Mom. Then you'd know.'

'We already asked him to do that, and he didn't respond,' Stynes said. 'And we can't just force him to do it. It's invasive. We'd have to have a court order, and in a case like this, I don't know if a judge would grant it. They tend to do that with sexual assault and murder cases, but with this — ' He shrugged. 'I don't know.'

'Can't you just get him to lick an envelope or something?' Ashleigh asked. 'Or steal his gum?'

'This isn't TV,' Stynes said.

'What would it take to get a DNA sample from the body in Justin's grave?' Janet asked.

'You'd still need a court order, but there wouldn't be any obstacles to getting it because the family would be making the request. But the judge would have to weigh the cost and time against the potential value that would come out of it. It might be a tough sell. And if I can be perfectly frank, we wouldn't even know how much viable DNA they could get off the body. Remember, he was buried in those woods for a number of weeks. The body was skeletonized when we found it. And there was no embalming,

311

no preservation possible. After another twenty-five years in the ground, who knows?'

'But it's possible?' Janet asked.

'It is possible. They can do great things these days. They may be able to recover some tissue or even something from the bone marrow or the teeth. Then they'd take a cheek swab from you and compare. But you still have to get a judge to agree to have the city take on the cost in a case in which there is no abundantly clear evidence to justify the exhumation.'

Janet and Ashleigh exchanged a look. They knew something.

'What?' Stynes asked.

'Did you get my phone message today?' Janet asked.

'I did, but I didn't have time to call back.'

'Did you hear what the message said?' she asked.

'You said something about a donation and a burial,' he said.

Janet told him, and as she spoke, the words from the message came back to Stynes again. And then he understood the look exchanged between Janet and Ashleigh. They had the money to exhume and rebury the body. Acquiring the court order would be easier than he thought.

They could finally find out who was buried in that grave, if it was Justin or someone else.

'Okay,' Stynes said. 'It should take a couple of days to get the ball rolling. The next big thing for you, Janet, is that they'll take a sample from your cheek. It's quick and painless.'

'Detective?'

Stynes looked up. So did Janet and Ashleigh. Behind them, in the doorway that led back to the bedrooms, stood Bill Manning. Stynes wasn't sure how long he'd been standing there. He must have walked up silently, but he acted as though he had heard a fair amount of the conversation.

'I'd like to give a sample for this test,' Bill said.

'Dad, it's not — '

'Actually, it might help,' Stynes said. 'If the sample in the ground is degraded, having another point of reference would help. Are you sure you want to do that, Mr Manning?'

'I said I did.'

'Then I'll include that in the request,' Stynes said, but he said those words to Bill Manning's back. He had already turned back down the hallway.

# 37

Late that night, after Detective Stynes had left the house promising to call and keep Janet up-to-date as things progressed, and after Ashleigh went upstairs to bed, Janet knocked on her father's bedroom door.

She knew he'd be awake. The TV still droned behind the closed door, and she had noticed over the previous six months or so that he was staying up later than ever before. He used to be an early-to-bed, early-to-rise type, bragging about being able to wake up at five thirty on the dot every day without the help of an alarm clock. But unemployment had shifted his living patterns, and even after eleven Janet knew she could likely catch him still awake, staring at a baseball game or news show.

'Dad?' she said.

'Come in,' he said from the other side of the door.

Janet didn't think she'd heard him correctly. He always opened the door and then treated his room like a private sanctuary, a boundary territory not to be crossed by anyone. She'd grown used to talking to him in the doorway, a far cry from the moments of her childhood when she could climb into bed with her mother in the morning. Her dad would be gone to work, and Janet would sneak in and lie next to her mother, feel her warmth and affection.

Inside the room, her dad lay across the bed, the covers thrown back. He wore a white T-shirt and a striped pair of boxer shorts. Without a regular shirt on, Janet saw that he had gained some weight in the preceding months. His belly bulged against the cotton fabric of the T-shirt more than she would have expected.

*He's also getting older,* she reminded herself. *Even he has to get older.*

He didn't mute the volume on the TV or turn to face her. Janet looked at the screen. In black and white Humphrey Bogart and a band of American soldiers stormed their way across the desert.

'I'm sorry to interrupt.'

'Are you going out?' he asked.

'No, it's too late for that.'

'Well, the other night . . . ' He left the thought unfinished.

The room filled with the sound of tank and artillery fire. 'Dad? Can you turn that down a little?'

He frowned but thumbed the volume control. He still didn't look at her.

'Dad, I just wanted to know why you volunteered to give that sample tonight. You've acted so cold about everything else. It seemed out of the blue.'

He kept his eyes directed to the TV screen. He looked like he was planning on ignoring Janet and hoping she'd go away. But she wouldn't go away, and before she'd said anything else, he said, 'Won't that put the questions to rest?'

'Some of them. Maybe all of them. It depends on what they find.'

'And will that make you happy?' he asked.

Janet thought about her answer to that question. She answered truthfully. 'I'm not sure, Dad,' she said. 'I'm just not sure.'

'Neither am I,' he said. 'But I think it's time we tried to do something, isn't it?'

# 38

Janet wished she could escape from the news, from Dove Point. From everything.

The days waiting for the DNA results to come back from the state crime lab were agony — and they were made worse because everyone in town and throughout the region knew about the arrest of a man who might be Justin Manning. Detective Stynes had released his mug shot to the news media and held a press conference on a Friday morning, explaining the developments in the case. Not only did he speak about the arrest of the man claiming to be Justin Manning, but he also revealed that a DNA test was under way to determine the identity of the body in Justin's grave. He said that the family had decided to relocate Justin's body to the plot next to his mother, not mentioning the anonymous donor.

Janet chose not to attend the press conference. Stynes placed no pressure on her to be there, and rather than subject herself to questions and photographs, she stayed away and read a story about it — written by none other than Kate Grossman — on the Internet.

But staying away from the press conference didn't matter. In the days after the story went public, reporters began to call the Manning house several times a day. Kate Grossman sent Janet a bouquet of flowers and a request for an interview. Janet crumpled the note and threw it away. Then Janet came in to work three days after the press conference to find Madeline waiting for her with a piece of paper in her hand. An Internet news service had picked up the story. But they didn't place it under national news or crime news. They filed it under 'News of the Weird.'

'Jesus, Madeline.'

'I know. It's awful.'

'They're making this look like it's some kind of sideshow,' Janet said. 'My life — my family — has become a sideshow.'

'I'm sorry. Maybe I shouldn't have shown you that.'

Janet sat in her desk chair, her shoulders slumped. She felt tired more than anything else. She hadn't been able to sleep in anticipation of the test results. And just being at home meant a ringing phone — and Janet answered every call, thinking it might be news from Detective Stynes when in reality the calls were only media requests or the occasional crank caller.

'No, it's good that you did,' Janet said. 'I should be prepared for more calls.' Janet looked at the piece of paper again. 'People in offices all over America are going to be sending this story to each other. They're going to say, 'Hey, look at this crazy shit.''

'On the bright side, at least the word will get out.'

Janet wanted to laugh at Madeline's insane attempt to see the silver lining, but she didn't have the energy.

'Why don't you take some personal time?'

Madeline said. 'Hell, you and Ashleigh could take a drive somewhere.'

'Where? Everybody has seen the story.'

'Oh, they don't know who you are. When's the last time you took a day off? By the time you come back — '

'Thanks, Madeline. But I wouldn't be able to think about anything else. I might as well stay here and try to live a normal life. Not that that's possible.' Janet stood up. 'I just wish . . . '

'What?'

'I wish Ashleigh didn't have to get dragged through all of this. I feel like our weird family has put her right in the middle of something.'

'Don't worry about that one,' Madeline said. 'She has a good mother. And a good example of how to be strong.'

Janet walked back to her desk, and Madeline followed. Janet wanted to put her head down, to lose herself in work as long as possible. But Madeline had something else to say.

'I've been meaning to ask you,' she said.

'Yes?'

'I saw that you're getting your wish. They're moving Justin's body.'

'That's right.'

'When is that going to happen?'

'The coroner is holding the body until the state crime lab reports their results. If they're able to use the DNA they got, then the body will be released back to us. After that, I guess.'

'Make sure you let me know. I want to be there for you.'

'Thanks. I will.'

But Madeline still didn't leave. She leaned down and lowered her voice. 'Is your dad going to go to the reburial?'

'I have no idea. Why do you ask?'

'I just remember Justin's first funeral. Your dad didn't shed a tear. I know how men are, you know? But still, didn't shed a tear. I guess I just hoped you could both go. You were so young the first time, and he was . . . Bill. I thought, well, in a way this is working out to give you a chance to really say good-bye.'

'And what if it isn't Justin in the grave, Madeline? What if it's really my brother sitting in a jail cell not speaking to anybody?'

Madeline didn't say anything to that. Janet didn't think anybody had an answer for the question.

# 39

The answer came to Janet later that same day.

She had managed, late in the afternoon, to lose herself in her work for the first time in close to a week. A proposal to change the way faculty compensation was budgeted had landed on her desk in midmorning, and Janet spent most of her day reading it over, entering data into her computer, drafting an e-mail to send to the dean himself about whether the plan was feasible. She didn't even look up from her computer screen until Detective Stynes stood next to her desk, his hands folded in front of him, a worried, pitying look on his face.

Janet could tell he knew something.

And her mind raced to guess.

'Can we talk somewhere private, Janet?' he asked.

Without saying anything, Janet led him across the hall, to the same conference room where she had spoken to Kate Grossman. Janet's thoughts remained unfocused. She felt almost hysterical. She wanted to laugh, then cry. And when they entered the room, she thought, somewhat irrationally, that the drapes were out of date. *What a dreary little room this is*, she said to herself. *I don't think I ever want to come in here again. With anyone.*

They sat down, and Stynes cut to the chase.

'The results of the DNA test are back,' he said.

Janet wanted to cry. She felt the tears welling.

'I'm sorry,' he said, 'but the results show with a high degree of probability that the body buried in that grave is your brother's.'

The tears didn't come. Janet felt some energy slip out of her body. Her spine became loose and springy, like a bouncing, flailing child's toy. She slipped forward, out of the chair and onto one knee on the floor. Stynes reached out, placed his hands on her arms, and braced her. He kept her from going flat on her face.

But she didn't cry.

Had she ever cried for Justin? Really?

Had she cried as a child when he first went missing? Had she cried at his funeral?

For a long moment, they sat like that, Stynes holding her limp body. But she didn't faint or black out. She saw the details in the carpet. The loose threads, a paper clip shining in the fluorescent lights. The energy came back quickly. She felt her spine stiffen, felt the strength return. She pushed against Stynes, lifted herself back into the chair.

'Are you — ?'

'I'm fine,' she said.

She slid back against the chair as Stynes let go. She pushed her shoulders back, lifted her chin. She would be fine. She knew it was likely it would be him. She could accept that.

Justin was gone. He was really gone.

It was over.

'Would you like me to call somebody?' Stynes asked. 'Do you have a friend here?'

Janet shook her head. She was fine. And she

didn't want anyone else in the room. Certainly not Madeline. She could hear the news from Stynes, take the blow, and then figure out what to do next. She had to tell her dad, had to tell Ashleigh. She had to tend to the details of the reburial once they released the body.

'And they're certain?' Janet asked.

'Yes. As close to one hundred percent as they can get. They were able to recover some very usable DNA, and the comparison was relatively easy as far as those things go.'

'And the man in jail?'

'We don't know yet.'

'And Dante?'

'They tried but couldn't recover anything that might be able to prove or disprove Dante's guilt. I don't think this changes much.'

'Thank you for telling me in person.'

'Janet, there's something else.'

'I guess reporters will hear about this soon — '

'Janet? The tests showed something else.'

'Maybe we'll get back to a normal life now. Maybe after the reburial — '

'Janet.' Stynes's voice grew louder. It focused her, brought her back to the matter at hand. She looked at Stynes, saw the pitying look in his eyes. He had something else to say to her. What else could he possibly have to say to her?

'Okay.'

'Janet, they also tested your father's DNA against the sample from Justin. Like I said, they do this to increase the likelihood of an accurate reading. When they received the results from that test, they found that your father and Justin share

323

no genetic material. They're not biologically related in any way. Justin is your brother, but he's not your father's son.'

Janet still felt strong. Something hot and red rose inside her chest. She no longer saw Detective Stynes sitting before her. She saw a small man, an imperfect man, one who couldn't even manage the simple matter of reporting the results of a DNA test.

'No, you're wrong.'

'They double-check their work.'

'You're an asshole,' she said. She wanted to push back from the table, to lash out at Stynes. If she were a man, she'd hit him. He couldn't say these things about her family. About her father. 'That's a lie.'

Stynes didn't look wounded by her words. His expression didn't change. He just looked tired.

'I'm not lying, Janet,' he said.

'Then they're lying. Or they're wrong. Crime labs make mistakes all the time. I see it on the news. The police make mistakes all the time. And so I can't know that what you said about Justin is true. None of it is true.'

Speaking the words allowed her anger to ebb. She heard the irrational tone of her voice, the snapping, bitter quality to what came out of her mouth. Her chest still burned with an internal redness but it was not as hot. This was simply a problem that could be solved. They had messed up the test. How else to explain the nonsense Stynes was repeating to her?

Stynes remained calm in the face of her

outburst. He nodded, his face and demeanor full of sympathy.

'This is something you're going to have to take up with your father. The test results are conclusive. They don't leave room for error. I can go with you when you talk to him if you want.'

Janet tuned him out. She didn't need his pity. She didn't need anyone's pity. Her mind spun. Her father wasn't Justin's father? Justin was her half brother?

And then she had another thought: was her father really her father?

Who was he?

'I have to go home,' Janet said.

She stood up, although that word resonated in her head. *Home.* She thought she knew what that meant. Even after everything that had happened, at least she knew what that word meant. Battered and bruised and complicated, she knew where home was.

Didn't she?

'Let me drive you. You're upset.'

Janet held out her hand. 'I'm fine. I can get myself home.'

'Can I follow you?'

She walked over to Stynes and held out her hand. He looked down at it, his face puzzled. They shook. 'I know it was difficult for you to have to tell me this news,' she said. 'Thank you.'

'I'm sorry I had to tell you,' he said.

'No, I know it's your job.' She let go of his hand. She didn't even know why she shook it, except that she felt like she wanted some kind of

connection, something to show that she recognized the importance of what she had been told.
She didn't want him to think her irrational or
incapable of accepting the worst. She was
capable. She knew she was. And she had to
believe Stynes knew it too. But still ... she
wondered. 'Are you sure, Detective? About all of
this? Are you sure?'

Stynes nodded. 'I'm sure.'

'My brother's dead. Really dead. And my
father ... '

'I'm sorry.'

But she didn't want to hear that, didn't want
to or need to hear those words, so she left,
heading for home.

# 40

'Dad?'

The house wasn't just quiet — no TVs playing, no conversation or music. It *felt* quiet. Still. Like something had been removed. But she worried that the thing that had been removed had always been in her head: her own notion of home. Did the place just feel different because of what Detective Stynes had told her?

Janet went down the hall to the bedroom. The door was open, the bedclothes pushed down. The TV was off. She stepped back into the hallway. The bathroom was empty as well.

'Dad?'

As she drove home from work with Detective Stynes's words spinning through her head, she tried to make sense of it all. And worst of all, it did make sense in ways Janet didn't want to admit. Justin's paternity made for a grand unifying theory of her father — why did he refuse to speak about the past? Why did he not cry at Justin's funeral? Why did he throw those photos away? Because Justin wasn't his? And the fact that it started to make sense made Janet feel even worse.

Her dad had known all along and didn't tell Janet. Her *mom* must have known all along and never told. Who were these people after all?

Janet walked back out to the living room and into the kitchen. The lights were off, the late-afternoon sun slanting in through the back window. The trees in the yard provided shade and made the kitchen darker than the rest of the house during the summer. He was there, sitting at the kitchen table, an open bottle of beer in front of him. He didn't say anything when he saw her, but he studied the look on her face.

'Is Ashleigh home?' Janet asked.

He shook his head. 'She's out with that boy.'

It looked to Janet like he knew, like he was anticipating the very question she was about to ask, but she asked anyway.

'Why did you provide that DNA sample, Dad?'

He nodded his head. There was nothing left to hide. He asked her to sit down across the table from him, and she did.

★ ★ ★

'It's true,' he said. 'That's why I gave the sample to the police. I suspected it was true. Believed it really, all these years. I saw this as an opportunity to end the speculation for both of us.'

'You knew?'

'I *suspected*,' he said. 'Your mother suspected, too. Nobody knew for sure. Nobody ever did a test or anything. Until now.'

'You wanted them to find out? With this test?'

'There's no other way to prove it,' he said. 'And I wanted you to find out. I thought you should know. This business with Justin and this man in the jail, I watch it tearing you apart. And now Ashleigh's getting involved. We don't need it, Janet. It was time to end it, and I hoped this would be the thing to do it.'

'Who's Justin's father?'

'I figured you would be able to guess already. It's someone who was close to us at one time.'

Janet started to speak, then stopped herself. She thought about it.

'Ray Bower,' she said.

Her dad nodded. 'Our best friends, the Bowers. Your best friend, too. Michael. Your mom and Ray had an affair back when you all were little.'

Her father didn't meet her eye. He looked at the table-top as he spoke. She saw the pain etched on his face, something that hadn't left him even after twenty-five years. She thought about backing away and not making him relive all of it. But her desire — her need — to know outweighed any concern she felt for her dad. She'd waited too long to know these things, things she didn't even know she needed to know.

'Did you know about this when Justin was born?'

He sipped his beer. 'No. I suspected something was going on between them before Justin was born. They were awfully cozy, the two of them. More than you would expect from a man and a woman who are just supposed to be friends. But when Justin was born, I tried to put those thoughts aside. Your mother was a good mother — she really was. You know that, right?'

'I do.'

'I don't want that memory to change for you.

329

This story doesn't invalidate what she was to you or what you remember her to be. You got that?'

'I've got it, Dad.'

'She was devoted to both of you, you and Justin. But when Justin was about two, I guess, things started to change again. I noticed the flirtations between her and Ray, just like before. They made jokes that only the two of them laughed at. They shared looks, you know?' He shook his head. 'I hate to even say it. It makes me sound like a goddamned woman. But I knew something was going on there. Hell, maybe I even accepted it a little bit. I thought whatever it was would blow over, that it would cool off. I thought as long as we had the kids, your mother and I, that it wouldn't matter what went on with anything else. I guess I thought that would trump everything. Little did I know.'

'No one could blame you for saying or doing anything.'

'I know. But I didn't do anything. I just stewed. I think I deserve more blame for that, for just sitting there and taking it like an asshole.'

He stood up and placed his empty beer bottle in the sink. He reached into the refrigerator and brought out another one, twisted the cap off, and drank.

'Would you get me that wine?' Janet asked.

He grabbed the wine bottle and a glass and brought them to the table. He sat down with his beer while Janet poured her own drink. She needed it to listen to the rest of his story.

'Remember how fair-haired Justin was?' he asked. 'Completely blond?'

'Sure.'

'Neither your mom nor I were blond, even as kids.'

'But that doesn't mean anything.'

'He didn't look like me, Janet. I could tell. I know you don't like to think about it, but you look like me. But Justin, do you know who he looked like? His coloring, the shape of his mouth?'

'Michael.'

'Right. I wouldn't have thought about it, but my suspicions made me look at those things closely. Janet, this is awful to say, but Justin just never felt like my kid. Not like you did. Not even the way Ashleigh does. Something told me he wasn't mine.'

'But you never asked Mom?'

'Never. I didn't want to know the answer. I came close a hundred times. Lying in bed, sitting at this table.'

'So you never talked about it?'

'We talked about it. Once. One day. That's when I found out everything for sure.'

Janet tried to remember the times she had seen her father cry. She could remember only one — at her mother's funeral. Janet's recollections of Justin's funeral were fuzzy, so she could rely only on Madeline's memories and the words she heard from her father in the kitchen. But it seemed safe to say he'd shed tears only for her mother, and while he silently cried in the kitchen, his shoulders shaking a little, his face buried in his hands, she decided she really didn't know what to do. She stood up and came around to his side of the table and placed her arm around his back. He didn't acknowledge the gesture, but it seemed to bring him relief. His tears slowed and then stopped pretty quickly after that, and Janet returned to her chair after first grabbing a box of tissues off the counter and placing them in front of her dad.

He used one to wipe his face, his big hand making the gesture seem odd and almost comical. He took another drink and cleared his throat.

'I'm still crying over her,' he said. 'Like a fool.'

'I think we can all relate to having strong feelings for someone, whether it's good for us or not,' Janet said. 'When did you talk to her about all of this?'

'About the affair?'

'Yes.'

'The day Justin died.'

'That's when she told you?'

'That morning. Before we knew anything was wrong. That's why I didn't go to work that day. And when the police came, we told different stories. Mom said I was home, but I said I went in to work like any other day. I lied. I knew I didn't go, but I lied to them because I didn't want to have a bunch of questions asked. 'Why didn't you go in to work as usual?' That kind of thing. I tried to keep it simple by not telling the truth. Later that day, Mom changed her story because I told her I didn't want people to know the real reason I was home that day. It was embarrassing. And it really didn't matter, because Justin was gone, and that was everybody's focus.'

'Did the police ask you about the contradiction then?'

'I kept expecting them to, but they didn't. I don't know why. I think once they heard about a suspect being in the park, they zoomed in on that. I know that cop, Stynes, came here the other day because he suspected me. I know that. But they didn't have any reason to suspect me besides that. I had no record. I never hurt you kids.'

Janet didn't argue with him, but she knew her father's detachment and demeanor made him a target as well. These were the same things that made Janet suspect him, the very things they were talking about in the kitchen. Her father felt emotionally detached from Justin his whole life — and that detachment could easily be read as suspicious.

'So she told you that day? Early in the day?'

'First thing. She sent you kids out of the house. She never did that, but she didn't want either of you to hear. I guess she didn't want that to be a memory of us you carried around. There were always a lot of people in the park. Mothers that she knew. She thought you'd be safe.' He sighed. 'Once you were gone, she told me she was going to leave me for Ray. And Ray was going to leave Rose. The two of them were going to be together. I don't know what she thought was going to happen to you kids, but I guess it only mattered for you and Michael. Justin was probably theirs.'

'She told you that during the same conversation?'

'She told me she suspected. She suspected pretty strongly. Around the time Justin would have been conceived, let's just say things were pretty frosty between your mom and me. That's when I suspected her of being with Ray the first time. She told me she didn't think Justin was mine because she thought she'd only been with Ray. We would have had to do a blood test and all that, but pretty soon there's a police car in our driveway. Someone at the park told the police who we were and where we lived. It's safe to say our focus shifted a little at that moment. Your mom fell to pieces because she was worried about Justin. I was, too, I guess, but let's just say that conversation with your mom, as difficult as it was, opened my eyes a little bit, too. I understood why I had felt the way I had about Justin. I guess I felt vindicated. Some things made sense, things that for so long I had thought were just paranoid and stupid fears.'

'But you went along,' Janet said. 'You stood by Mom's side through the whole thing. You didn't leave her.'

'Would you?' he said, sounding almost angry. 'How could I? She needed me. And if I left, I'd be raising a whole boatload of new questions. Remember, the press and the police were following everything so closely. I didn't want to raise any red flags. Besides, I did have a kid to think about. I had you — and I knew you were mine.'

Janet felt the tears stinging her eyes. She held them back. 'You stayed with her after that, though. After they found Justin and the funeral and the trial. It could have been all over then. All of it. You didn't owe her anything at that point. She cheated on you. And you . . . you kept this all hidden away inside you.'

'What was your mother like after that?' he asked. 'You remember, don't you?'

Janet did. It wasn't difficult to summon the memories of her mother in the years after Justin's death. The nights crying, the vacant stares during the day. The slow, steady decline of her health. She was different after Justin's death. She was gone, shattered. She was there, she was present in Janet's life, but Janet often felt like her mother had died that day in the park along with her brother.

'I remember.'

'I couldn't leave her then,' he said. 'She was broken. A shell. Whatever she had planned or had with Ray appeared to be over, too.' He rubbed his hand over his chin, across the gray stubble growing there. 'I loved her, Janet. Always did, always will. I couldn't walk away when she really needed me. She blamed herself for Justin's death, you know? That's what killed her. The guilt more than the grief.'

'She blamed herself because — '

'You kids wouldn't have gone to the park alone that day if it hadn't been for her needing to talk to me. If it hadn't been for the affair, she would have gone with you kids, and she believed she wouldn't have let Justin out of her sight. She was reckless and distracted because of our problems.'

'I was supposed to be watching him — '

'No. No. You were seven years old. No. That was not your fault. The adults were to blame for this one. The adults and that guy who killed Justin. Don't blame yourself for that. Not for one minute.'

Janet heard him, but her mind skipped ahead to other things. Michael. Michael came to town asking questions about Ray's possible involvement in Justin's death. If Ray was really Justin's father, would that make him more or less likely to have committed the crime?

'Dad?' Janet said. 'Did Ray know about all of this? Did he know he was Justin's father?'

Her dad took a drink of his beer. He seemed to be thinking over his answer. 'I know he meant to leave Rose. That very day, the day Justin died, the same scene that was playing out at our house was playing out at theirs. I always assumed that's how Michael ended up in the park that day as well. Ray was telling Rose about the affair and that he was leaving her.' Her dad paused. 'Your mom thought Ray might have been coming to our house that morning, after he told Rose. I guess he had some chivalric notion of telling me man-to-man. But he never showed up, if he even planned to. Justin disappeared, and the police showed up. And that was that.'

'Ray might have been coming over here that day?'

'Yes.'

'From their house?'

'I guess so.'

'Do you know what that means, Dad?' Janet asked.

Her father might be many things, but he wasn't slow. She could see his face as he connected the dots. 'You're saying he would have had to walk through the woods? He would have walked right where Justin was killed?'

'Yes.'

'No,' he said. 'The Bowers almost always drove when they came to our house. Even if he did walk, it doesn't prove anything. Maybe he walked, saw the commotion, and turned around and went home.'

'You're defending this man?' Janet said. 'The man who ruined your marriage, and you're defending him.'

'They arrested a man. They had a trial. He had pornography in his room. You saw him at the park with Justin.' He pointed at her. 'You did. Ray Bower may be a lot of things, but he's not a killer. Why would he kill his own kid?'

Janet already knew she couldn't answer that question. She couldn't answer any of these questions.

But she knew whom she wanted to talk to about it all.

'I'm going to go see Michael.'

'Wait.'

Janet didn't stand up. Her dad didn't look at her. He held his hand to his mouth, his thumbnail between his front teeth. She knew he wanted to say something, but he wasn't saying it.

Then she understood. He was embarrassed.

He had just told her the most painful, embarrassing event of his life, something he had kept to himself for twenty-five years. And she wanted to go tell someone else about it. The whole town would find out if the news broke.

'We have to do this, Dad,' she said. 'We have to find out what happened.'

He didn't say yes or no. He didn't even nod.

But Janet knew he agreed.

# 41

Rose opened the door for Janet. She wore a large smile until she saw the look on Janet's face. Then she knew something was wrong. She didn't move out of the way so Janet could come inside.

'Is he home?' Janet asked.

After a pause, Rose nodded. 'He's in his room.'

'Do you know why I'm here?'

Rose reached up and fiddled with a loose strand of hair. 'I know there was some kind of DNA test being done. I read that in the paper.'

'Did you know?' Janet asked.

'That was so long ago — '

'Did you know?'

Rose pressed her lips together, making them disappear. 'I wondered. Many times I wondered. Ray thought it might be true.'

'And Michael?'

Rose looked behind her. She came closer to Janet, pulling the door shut a little more in an attempt to block the sound of their voices from entering the house. 'I never wanted him to hate his father. I wasn't going to be the person who destroyed what my son thought of his dad.'

'He hated him anyway,' Janet said.

'But that's because of other things,' Rose said. 'Ray cut him off. He was giving Michael money, and he stopped. It's this new girl Ray's dating. Ray wouldn't . . . He loves Michael very much.'

Janet took a step back and looked at the woman's face. Was she really making excuses for her ex-husband, the man who cheated on her, fathered another child, and left her? After all these years, was she still in love with him?

'I'm telling him, Rose. I'm here to tell him.'

Rose started to object but stopped. Finally, she stepped back and let Janet into the house.

★ ★ ★

Janet told Michael most of the story. While she explained everything — the DNA test, the story her father told her about the affair, and the events of the day Justin died — Rose sat on the couch, listening with her head down. Michael asked few questions during Janet's recitation of events. She watched his face carefully, saw his cheeks redden, his jaw set tight, as if his teeth were gripping something strong and desperately trying to tear it away. He did speak once. He looked at his mother and said, simply, 'He did that to you, Mom?'

Rose didn't answer him.

When Janet finished, Michael sat still and quiet. Rose scooted closer to him and placed her arm around his shoulders. He stiffened under her touch, and Rose looked like she had been slapped.

'I told you, didn't I?' Michael said.

Janet knew what he meant.

'What do you mean, Michael?' Rose asked.

Michael didn't answer her. He stared at Janet, his eyes boring into her.

'You need to tell her, Michael,' Janet said.

'Tell me what?'

'Michael?'

When he still didn't say anything, Janet stepped in.

'Michael has been trying to figure some things out over the years, things about the day Justin died. He saw his father in the woods that day, right in the area where Justin's body was found.'

Rose was already shaking her head.

'And,' Janet said, 'we know that he might have wanted to come to our house that day to tell my dad. If he did that, he would have walked right through there.'

'Ray wouldn't. He couldn't.'

'Rose, did he leave the house that morning?' Janet asked. 'Did he want to come over to talk to Dad?'

'It's been so long — '

'Stop protecting him, Mom. Just stop it.' Michael's voice was as flat and hard as a winter road.

Rose removed her arm from around Michael's shoulders and placed her hands in her lap and knotted them together. When she spoke, her voice was barely above a whisper. 'He did leave the house that morning,' she said.

Michael made a low grunting noise. It sounded like a cross between pain and anger.

Rose said, 'He told me about . . . ' Her voice trailed off, but she pointed at Janet. 'The things you just told me about. And he said he wanted to talk to Bill in person.' She looked at Michael.

341

'We fought that morning when he told me. We never fought. Ever.'

'I know,' Michael said.

'That's why we sent you to the park that day,' Rose said. 'We fought about all of this, including Justin. Ray said he thought Justin might be his child. I guess that was the part I couldn't bear to hear, that he might have had a child with another woman.' She looked at Janet. 'We tried to have another after Michael, but we couldn't. I couldn't, I guess.'

'I'm sorry,' Janet said.

'I begged him to stay,' Rose said. She smiled at Janet, but it carried no joy. 'I guess you don't understand that,' she said. 'Girls from your generation, you're more independent. Stronger. Look at you, raising a daughter all by yourself. And working at the same time.'

'Don't feel bad,' Janet said.

'Well, Ray didn't listen to me anyway. He said he needed to talk to Bill about it man-to-man. He wanted to clear the air that one time, get everything out in the open, and then never mention it again. That's the way Ray is. He didn't want to have a long talk about anything. He thought it could be cut and dried. He was done with me, and he could move on. The end. So he did leave to do that, to talk to your dad, to tell him in person.'

'Did he drive or walk?' Janet asked.

'He walked. He went right out the back door and over toward the park.'

'We have to call the police,' Michael said.

'But he came back, right?' Janet asked,

ignoring Michael for the moment. 'When did he come back?'

Rose paused and thought about her answer. 'It wasn't long. Twenty minutes maybe. He came back in the door and said that something was wrong in the park. He said the police were there, so he decided to come home. Then the phone rang.' Rose pointed at Janet. 'Your mom was on the phone. I thought she was calling for . . . I don't know, something else. But she was upset. She said Justin was missing, and she wanted to know if he was over at our house. Ray told her no, he wasn't.' Rose looked down. 'I may have said some awful things then. I said if she was a better mother and wasn't interfering in someone else's marriage, maybe she could keep better watch on her kids. It was a terrible thought, but I didn't know what had happened to Justin at that point. I wouldn't have said or thought those things if I had known.'

Michael stood up. 'We have to call the police.'

'And tell them what?' Janet asked. 'That a man had an affair twenty-five years ago and probably fathered a child out of wedlock? What's the crime?'

'He was there,' Michael said. 'At the scene. He walked through there.'

'Again, not a crime.'

'But the police should talk to him about it.'

Michael paced around the small room. He walked to one end and then the other and back again. Janet saw the tension in his posture, the tendons in his neck stretched taut. Janet waited, hoping he'd settle down on his own. Together, they could decide what to do and what it all meant.

Then Rose said, 'When your father came home that day, his pants were dirty.'

Michael stopped pacing and turned back to her.

'What?' he said.

'His pants were dirty. He said he fell on the path. He came in and threw the pants into the washing machine.'

Janet turned to Michael, but he was already moving. He was through the door before Janet even made it off the couch. She followed him outside. When she came out into the hot night air, she saw the car backing out into the street, then the tail-lights receding into the distance.

She had to follow him.

# 42

Janet called Detective Stynes from her car. She drove with one hand and held the phone with the other. When Stynes came on, she didn't know exactly what to tell him, so she tried to make it as simple as possible.

'Detective, I need you to get to Ray Bower's house.'

'Janet?'

'Ray Bower's house. Can you get there?'

'I can. What's wrong?'

'It's too much to explain right now.'

'I'm on my way to the door and getting my keys. Can you at least give me a sense of what I'm walking into?'

She stumbled a few times trying to find the right words. Finally, she said, 'It's about Justin's murder. I think Ray Bower killed him. And I think Michael is going over there to kill Ray.'

★　★　★

Janet parked in the driveway behind Michael's car. She went straight into the house without bothering to knock. She hadn't been in there for years, not since high school. The Bowers' house had been so familiar to her as a child, almost a second home. Growing up, she attributed the tailing off of the friendship between the families to the sudden shock of Justin's death, to the slow descent of her mother into illness and death. But it was so much more — more than she ever could have imagined.

The living room sat empty. Janet knew the Bowers had a family room at the back of the house, which used to be filled with two large recliners and an overstuffed couch. They watched TV there. As Janet moved in that direction, she heard a rustling and something thumping against the floor.

'Michael?'

An angry voice came from the rear of the house, something like a shout.

Janet stopped, considered turning and waiting outside until the police showed up. But she knew the state of mind Michael was in when he'd left Rose's house. She feared what he might do.

'Michael?' she said again, her voice a little louder.

The rustling again. Quick movements. Janet stepped to the doorway that led into the back room and came face-to-face with Michael.

He reached out with both hands and took hold of Janet's shoulders, his grip so tight she yelped.

He didn't let go. And she stared into his eyes. They were wide and full of tears, as much red as white in the sclera. He looked different. Crazed with some combination of grief and anger.

'Michael,' she said. 'It's me. It's okay.'

'Janet.'

He said her name. It sounded like a plea.

'The police are coming. I called them.'

'Janet,' he said again.

346

'Michael, let go. You're hurting me.'

Her knees started to buckle from the pressure he was exerting on her arms. She felt the pain shoot through her body.

He let go and stepped back.

'Just wait,' Janet said. 'The police are on their way. They'll take care of it.'

He stared at her for a long moment, his eyes turning more hurt than angry.

'They can't help, Janet.'

He dashed away, toward the front of the house. Janet wanted to go after him, but she heard another voice from the back room. A moaning, keening sound.

Janet rubbed her arms as she went into the room.

Ray Bower lay in the middle of the floor. A glass tumbler, liquid spilling out of it and soaking into the carpet, sat on the floor next to him. Janet took two quick steps toward him.

One side of his face was bruised and bloodied, the eye swollen shut already.

'Oh, Jesus.'

Janet dropped to her knees next to him. She leaned in close, listening for breathing. It came, raspy and short.

She started to reach out, to provide a comforting touch on his arm. Then she remembered who this man was. And what he had done.

She recoiled, pulling her hand back. He had killed Justin. This was the man who had killed her brother and buried him in the woods.

Ray's lips moved. They struggled to form

words, twitching like swollen pieces of meat. Janet couldn't make out what he said. She didn't want to know. But she had to know.

She leaned forward, listening.

'Michael . . . '

'He's gone,' Janet said. 'And the police are coming. Did you hear me? The police are on their way here. Right now.'

'Michael . . . tell Michael I'm sorry.'

Janet heard the door open, Detective Stynes's voice filling the house, calling her name.

Janet watched Ray as his head fell back against the carpet.

'Back here,' she called. 'The damage is done.'

# 43

Stynes watched as the paramedics loaded Ray Bower into the ambulance and drove off, taking him to Dove Point Memorial Hospital. A good crowd of neighbors still stared, drawn by the flashing police lights and real-life drama. It beat sitting inside on a hot summer night and watching reruns of sitcoms that had originally aired in the winter.

Stynes went back inside the house and found Janet Manning on the living room couch. She sipped from a glass of water, her face wearing a distant, distracted look. Her eyes didn't track him as he came in and sat next to her.

'Are you okay?' he asked.

She snapped out of it, turning her head to look at Stynes. 'I'm fine,' she said. She looked down at the glass of water in her hand as though wondering how it had ended up there. 'How's Ray?'

'Pretty banged up. He has a concussion for sure. Some broken teeth. They'll X-ray him at the hospital. He'll be out of commission for a few days. But, all in all, I'd say he's kind of lucky. It looks to me like his son wanted to kill him. And might have if you hadn't walked in.'

'I didn't do anything,' she said. 'I just showed up.'

'I had a teacher in high school who said ninety percent of life is just showing up.'

Janet didn't smile. She stared at the glass.

'I have to ask you, Janet — you said something on the phone tonight about Ray Bower killing your brother. Do you want to tell me about that?'

Janet looked up. 'I found some things out.'

'Did these things arise from the news I told you earlier?' Stynes asked.

'Yes,' Janet said. 'I spoke to my father. He told me some stuff I hadn't known.' She swallowed hard. Stynes could almost hear the gulp. 'And then I talked to Rose Bower, and she provided some more details about the time when Justin died.' She stared at the glass again, as though trying to divine some secret meaning from the water. Then she looked back at Stynes. 'It was Ray Bower. He killed Justin that day in the woods. It all goes back to him.'

# 44

It took a few days to make the arrangements for the reburial and the new service. Janet welcomed the distraction of planning and organizing, choosing flowers and passages from the Bible. She tried to think about what Justin would have wanted if he had lived to be an adult, and for the first time since that day in the park twenty-five years ago, she couldn't give in to the fantasy that her brother might still be alive. She couldn't summon an image of him as an adult, a living, breathing person who walked out of the park rather than meeting his death that day in the woods. She had lost something — she knew that for sure. She wasn't certain yet if she had gained anything better to take its place.

They gathered at the graveside at nine o'clock, an attempt to beat the pounding heat. Janet stood next to Ashleigh beneath the thick canvas of the cemetery tent. The casket was small and covered with a spray of flowers. Janet had picked the casket out with Ashleigh's help. They'd opted for something classy and understated.

Janet took a moment and looked around. Madeline was there, standing on Janet's left along with a few others from the office, including the dean. Detective Stynes stood on the opposite side of the casket, his sunglasses clipped to the pocket of his sport coat. His face looked solemn and rigid. A few other friends stood around in a loose circle, including Ashleigh's friend Kevin, who seemed uncomfortable in his tie and button-down shirt. The police didn't make news of the reburial public, hoping to keep the media and any other curiosity seekers away from the cemetery. Janet didn't mind the tiny crowd. She felt that her family had been in the public eye enough over the past few days. She would be happy to have an intimate service.

But as she looked at the small gathering under the tent, she noticed who wasn't there. Michael. She remembered the crazed look in his eye a few nights earlier at Ray Bower's house, the violence he had committed against his own father. Would she ever see him again?

She had even called Rose's house, taking a chance that Michael might still be around and willing to attend the service. But before Rose even spoke Janet knew the answer. Michael was gone.

'I know what he did to his dad,' Rose said. 'He hasn't come back here. I suspect . . . ' Her voice trailed off. 'Well, I guess I don't know when I'll hear from him again. That's Michael.'

Janet reached up and wiped a droplet of sweat off the side of her face. A man from the funeral home, dressed in a dark suit despite the heat, whispered to Janet that it was probably time to start. She nodded.

The priest began the service. He began with a welcome prayer, something he read out of a small, worn missal. While he spoke and continued with what was meant to be a brief service, Ashleigh leaned in against Janet's body.

Janet reached out her right arm and pulled her daughter close, felt Ashleigh return the favor by placing her left arm around Janet's waist.

When was the last time her daughter had done that? Janet wondered.

She looked down at Ashleigh, still six inches shorter than she was. From that angle, it was easy for Janet to feel that Ashleigh was a little kid, one who needed comforting and sought it from her mother. It felt like years since they'd stood that way. Years. Janet pulled her daughter even closer and gave her a gentle peck on the top of the head.

'It's okay,' Janet whispered. 'I'm okay.'

Ashleigh looked up, even managing a half smile despite the occasion. 'I know, Mom,' she said. 'I know.'

# 45

Stynes lingered near the back of the crowd after the brief ceremony. He saw the grave-diggers off to the side, one of them leaning against an earth-mover, smoking a cigarette while he waited for the crowd to disappear so he could do his work. Stynes intended to offer his — what? — to Janet Manning. Condolences? Was that the right thing when someone had been dead for twenty-five years? He wasn't sure what to say, so he decided to try for something neutral when the time came.

Janet spoke to a small group of women. Friends or coworkers, Stynes assumed. He noted that Janet hadn't cried during the ceremony, instead choosing to hold tight to her daughter while the priest spoke. It didn't surprise him. The woman had experienced quite a bit and was no doubt still processing the ton of bricks that had landed on her as the result of the DNA tests. Stynes wished he had something profound to say about all that, but he didn't. Over the years he'd adopted a simple tactic with the victims of crimes and accidents: say as little as possible as sincerely as possible and then move on.

'Detective,' Janet said when she saw him. 'Thank you for coming.'

'I wanted to,' Stynes said. 'I'm — I hope you're doing okay.'

Ashleigh stood by, watching their exchange, and the priest leaned close to the funeral director near the edge of the tent, where they talked to each other in low voices. Everyone else was gone, drifting away to their cars and on to their jobs and their lives.

Janet leaned in close to Stynes. 'Is anything new with Ray Bower?' she asked.

Stynes nodded. 'He's doing better. The doctors say we can talk to him today or tomorrow.'

Janet nodded.

They faced each other in the heat, and Stynes felt Janet had something else she wanted to say.

'I was wondering,' she said. 'I'm worried about Michael Bower.'

'Where is he?' Stynes asked.

'I don't know. I think he must have left town. But he didn't say anything to me before he left. I wonder about the toll all of this is taking on him.'

'Maybe he just needs to cool off and absorb everything that happened. I imagine you're struggling to make sense of these things too.'

'There's something about Michael,' Janet said. 'I've known him my whole life. I've never seen him the way he was the other night.'

'Angry, you mean?'

'Out of control. I guess he's been heading that way since he came back to town. He's seemed . . . edgy. Anxious. Even though it was out of character for him to get violent with Ray, it didn't completely surprise me. I sensed something building in him over the past couple of weeks.' Janet sighed. 'Is he going to face any charges for what he did to Ray?'

'Ray would have to press them,' Stynes said. 'And I have the feeling he's going to have other things to think about besides that.'

Stynes looked past Janet's shoulder. He saw a movement there, someone approaching through the headstones and stopping at a distance. He took the person for a gawker at first, then saw the intensity with which he appeared to be watching the scene. Something about his posture looked familiar to Stynes —

'I wanted to ask you a question about something else, Detective,' Janet said.

'What's that?' Stynes asked, turning back.

'That man in the jail. I want to talk to him again.'

'You do? Why?'

'It's hard to explain,' she said. 'I want to know who he is and why he did what he did. I was so certain I knew him.'

Stynes took a quick look at the man in the distance and saw that he was turning away, perhaps heading to his car and leaving the cemetery.

'We can talk about it further.'

'I just need to know — '

Stynes walked away, looking back over his shoulder to say, 'Call me. We'll see.'

*   *   *

Stynes dodged tombstones, stepping carefully so as not to disrespect the ground he walked over, but also trying to catch up to the man he saw at the edge of the crowd. His task proved to be easy. The man walked with the aid of a cane, and long before he reached his car Stynes had caught up to him.

'Mr Ludwig?' Stynes said.

The man stopped, his body freezing in place about ten steps from his car. He didn't turn around, so Stynes approached him from behind and then went around between Ludwig and the car to talk.

'If you really didn't want to talk to me,' Stynes said, 'you wouldn't have shown up here today.'

Ludwig smiled. 'You're very perceptive, Detective. But I guess that's your job.'

The man looked older than when Stynes had first spoken to him — his cheeks more sunken, his skin paler and almost translucent, like thin paper stretched over his skull. Ludwig reached into his pants pocket and brought out a handkerchief and used it to dab at the sweat on his brow.

'Are you just here to lend emotional support, Mr Ludwig?' Stynes asked. 'Or do you have a more — how shall I put it? — vested interest in the proceedings?'

Ludwig smiled, but it looked like it cost him some effort. 'I can't stay long.' He grimaced. 'I can't even stand very long. That's why I was heading to the car. I heard from my oncologist about a week ago. The cancer that started in my prostate has spread to my bones. Not much they can do about that, Detective. In another six months or so, I'll be back in this cemetery. Eternally.'

'I'm sorry.'

'We'll all go down that road eventually,' Ludwig said. 'I've had more time than the Manning boy — that's for sure.' Ludwig turned and looked back toward Justin's grave site. 'Much more.'

'Is that why you paid for this?' Stynes asked.

Ludwig turned back around. '*Moi?*'

'Yes, you. Who else would have the money and the interest in the case?'

Ludwig tapped his cane against the ground a couple of times. 'I don't have any children of my own. No heirs to speak of. When I'm no longer here, my money is going to go to some charities that my mother chose a long time ago. I thought, why not do something nice for someone who needs it while I'm still here? And you're right. I did want to stop by to see the result of my gift, even from a distance.'

'But you didn't want the Mannings to know?'

'If you'll excuse me, Detective.' Ludwig pointed to his car, a white Lincoln. 'I need to sit if this interrogation is going to continue.'

'It's not an interrogation.'

Ludwig opened the driver's-side door and slowly, awkwardly lowered his body into the seat, his face red from the exertion. He started the engine and fiddled with the air-conditioning dials and vents, creating a stream of cold air that blew against his face. He dabbed at his forehead again while Stynes waited.

'Better,' Ludwig said. 'Much better. What were you asking me about?'

'About the anonymity of your gift.'

'Oh, that.' Ludwig waved the handkerchief

358

dismissively. 'I didn't do it to seek credit, Detective. I had my own reasons. Personal reasons.'

Stynes leaned in closer to the open car door. 'Which were?'

Ludwig's eyes opened wider. 'Well,' he said, 'this does feel like an interrogation now, doesn't it?'

'Tell me why you disappeared in the park that day. Why we couldn't find you after you got home.'

Ludwig tapped his fingers against the steering wheel. 'I'll tell you,' he said. 'But then I do have to get home. I usually nap several times a day. It's funny that when we reach the part of our lives when time is most precious, we sleep it away.'

'Why couldn't we find you?'

'I was in the park for the nature walk that morning, as you know. But I had a routine, a *habit* if you would, that I liked to perform beforehand.'

'Drugs.'

'I'm clean now. I've been clean for many years, but back then I couldn't get enough. Since we had money, I could afford to sustain the habit. There was a man I used to make my purchases from. Never mind who he is — he's long dead. I never bought in the park or around the kids, but on that day, I ended up short. So my provider agreed to meet me in the park before the walk. I was a good client, so he was willing to work with me.'

'You bought drugs before the nature walk?'

'It's a low point for me. But there I was, holding. Do you think I wanted to stick around and talk to the police? You can say a lot of things about me, Detective, but I loved my job at the high school. If the police reported that I was in the park buying or possessing cocaine with schoolchildren around, what do you think would have happened to my career?'

'A child was missing. We wouldn't have cared.'

'You say that now, but how could I be sure? Besides, on my way home, I sampled some of the product. I was paranoid and scared. How do you think I would have responded to the police at my door?'

Stynes studied Ludwig's face. He believed him. He could see no compelling reason not to. But Stynes also sensed there was more, something else the man had to say about the events of that day.

'Where did you meet your dealer?' the detective asked.

'Well, we couldn't do it out in the open.'

'So you went into the woods?'

Ludwig nodded.

'Where exactly?'

'We met as far as we could get from the playground. There's another path over there, one that leads to the homes that border the far side of the park. Not that many people use it.'

'What did you see there that day?'

Ludwig sighed theatrically. 'I guess I should count myself lucky that I'm being given enough time to correct mistakes I've made in the past. We all hope for that, Detective, don't we?'

'What did you see?'

Ludwig dabbed at his head. 'I saw a man, a man I later came to realize was Ray Bower, the father of one of those kids who was in the park and a friend of the Manning family. He was kneeling down in the dirt out there near that gross little pond, and then he stood up. His hands and his pants were dirty like he'd been burying something. He didn't see me. He hustled away back toward the houses on the far side of the park.'

Stynes stepped away from the car. He walked in a large circle away from where Ludwig was sitting and then back again. While he walked, his heart pumped faster and faster. He flexed and unflexed his right hand, and when he came back to Ludwig, he pounded his closed fist on the roof of the car.

'Why didn't you tell us that back then?'

Ludwig jumped but maintained his composure. 'I just told you why. And you all said you were looking for a black man. You had a description and a sketch. I knew what I should have done, but I only saw a man digging in the dirt in the woods.'

'Where we found a child's dead body.'

'Detective, if you want to stand here and try to make me feel guilty, you can't do a better job of it than I have over the years. I know what I should have done, and I know why I didn't do it. I didn't think it mattered until all of this recent attention around the case seemed to open everything back up again.'

'You'll testify to this.'

'I will.'

'It wasn't a question. It was a statement. You *will* testify to this in court if need be.'

Ludwig lifted his left leg and pulled his body the rest of the way into his car. He pointed to his cane. 'If I'm still here, Detective, I will. I have nothing left to hide.'

# 46

Several hours after the graveside service, Janet met Detective Stynes at the entrance of the police station. She followed him inside and back to his desk, which sat crowded in among other desks in the small office. A detective at a nearby desk spoke on the telephone, and two uniformed officers talked near a coffee machine. Stynes offered Janet a seat in an uncomfortable-looking vinyl chair. Stynes sat behind his desk and pulled out his ever present notebook.

'They faxed over some reports from the state welfare office,' Stynes said. 'I've been going over them this afternoon.'

'His name really is Steven Kollman?' Janet asked.

'It really is. I'm not sure of much in this life, but I'm sure of that. Steven John Kollman. Born in Columbus, moved to Dove Point when he was eight, and didn't stay very long. Mother deceased. Father missing in action. Entered the foster system at age five and was in it until he was eighteen. One of his former foster families recognized the photo we sent out and called us. Apparently, they hadn't seen him since he was sixteen or so, but they thought it was him.'

'He lived in more than one foster home?'

'Looks that way.'

'And no one else recognized him?'

Stynes shrugged. 'A lot of kids pass through

363

that system. They either forgot him or they just didn't care to call. A lot of these foster families don't want to have anything to do with the police.'

Janet let that sink in. She thought of Ashleigh and wondered how people could let any child in their care just slip away from them like a lost memory. 'Why did he start all this pretending to be Justin?'

'He won't talk to us,' Stynes said. 'Still won't, even though we know who he is. He's facing some pretty serious identity theft charges, plus the outstanding warrant in Columbus. He'd be wise to do something to protect himself. He goes before the judge tomorrow, now that we know who he is. We won't keep him here. He'll probably go to the county lockup and wait for a trial if he doesn't plead.'

'What did he do when he lived in Dove Point?' Janet asked. 'I mean . . . what kind of life did he have?'

'You might know better than any of us.'

'What do you mean?'

Stynes tapped the notebook. 'He went to school with you in the third grade. Steven Kollman? You don't remember the name?'

Janet shook her head. She didn't remember at all.

★   ★   ★

Stynes brought Steven Kollman into the small interview room where Janet was waiting. Steven slumped into a chair on the opposite side of the

364

scarred wooden table. Stynes looked at Janet.

'Are you okay with this?' he asked.

Janet knew what he meant. *Do you feel safe?*

She did, and she told Stynes she was fine. So he left. She knew he or other officers wouldn't be far away if something did go wrong. But Janet doubted it would. She looked at Steven in his chair. He couldn't meet her eye. He wore an orange inmate jumpsuit and stared at the floor. Janet felt a little angry that she had ever let this man manipulate her.

'Are you going to look at me, Steven?' she asked.

He did, raising his eyes slowly until they met Janet's ever so briefly across the table. Just as quickly he lowered them again.

'Are you being treated okay in here?' she asked.

'It's fine,' he said. 'It's not the worst jail I've been in.'

'Detective Stynes tells me we went to school together in the third grade.'

'Briefly.'

'I don't remember you. Did we know each other?'

'I told you we knew each other a long time ago. Remember?'

'I remember you saying that. But I don't remember you. Like you said, that's been a long time, so maybe you could help me place you.'

Steven lifted his eyes. He scooted closer to the table. 'Do you know what it's like to not be remembered? To pass through people's lives like smoke? That's always been the way for me, Janet.'

Janet told herself not to listen to what he said, to not be absorbed into his self-pity trap. 'I just want to know why you came and did this to my family. Why did you pretend to be my brother?'

'I thought you wanted to know how we knew each other.'

'I do.'

'Okay,' he said. 'I can tell you that. And in the course of telling you that, I'll answer your other question, the one about why I pretended to be Justin.'

Janet thought about leaving. She considered the possibility that just listening to this man, sitting across from him and hearing his story, would draw her deeper into his web. And she'd be better off just standing up and going and letting the police handle him the rest of the way. But she knew it was a bluff. She knew she couldn't turn away. She had to hear. And she suspected he knew that as well.

'Did the detective tell you I was a foster child?'

Janet nodded.

'That's how I came to live in Dove Point,' he said. 'Do you remember a place called Hope House? It was over on Market Street.'

'I do.' She remembered what looked like an average residential home. But the children she went to school with knew differently. Kids from Hope House showed up at St Anne's from time to time, and when they did, the other kids somehow found out the secret. *He's from Hope House. He's an orphan*, they would whisper to one another. And it wouldn't be hard to spot the Hope House kids even without the whispers. They tended to wear less stylish and, in some cases, more ragged clothes. And they never stayed long. None of the kids from Hope House lasted for more than a year or two. They passed through St Anne's and Dove Point very much as Steven described it — like smoke.

'I was one of those kids,' Steven said. 'I came to school with you in the third grade. You were in another class, but I had Miss Stanton. Remember?'

Janet searched, turning the name over in her mind — Steven Kollman. Was it familiar to her? When she thought she saw her brother's face, had she really just been seeing a glimmer of a boy she knew in grade school?

'I want to know what this has to do with Justin.'

'You saved me once, Janet. Don't you remember that? You saved me from the other kids.'

'Saved you?'

'Do you know what it's like to be the new kid? To show up in a school where all the other kids know each other and have grown up together for years? And then I come into that from Hope House. My white shirt is gray. My pants don't fit because I grew so fast I had to wear another kid's. My shoes are scuffed. And I have no idea what's going on academically because I've been in another school for the first part of the year, so I don't know the math or the reading. And they just put me in the lowest track because they don't know what else to do with me. That's what it was like for me, Janet. I don't even know how many times that happened. I can't tell you how many different schools I went to. Public, private. Big and small. I can't even tell you the number.'

'I don't know what that's like. I've lived here my whole life. But I do know what it's like to have people say things about you. Everyone in town knew about my brother. And then my mother. People treated me different sometimes because of that.'

'Exactly,' Steven said. He nearly leapt out of his chair. 'You get it, don't you? We're alike, you and I. We understand each other.'

'I'm not sure we do.'

'You know what it's like to be ostracized. To be on the outside looking in.'

'You haven't told me about Justin yet. You haven't told me anything.'

'I haven't?' Steven said. His tone shifted. A trace of anger slipped into his voice. 'I've told you about my life.'

'You said you were going to tell me why you came here and why you came to me.'

He leaned forward and tapped the table with the tip of his index finger, emphasizing every word. 'Because you saved me, Janet. Don't you remember? You saved me.'

'From what?'

'From the boys at the school. Don't you remember what they used to do to kids like me?'

'Are you talking about — ?'

And then Janet knew. She remembered the segregated playground, boys on one end, girls on the other. She remembered the boys playing rough games — football and dodgeball — while the girls played hopscotch or jumped rope. And Janet knew — they all did — what the boys, even as early as second or third grade, did to kids they didn't like.

Steven nodded. 'You remember now.'

'The football?' Janet asked.

Steven nodded. 'Have you ever known people who can look back on their childhoods and laugh about the awful things they did or had done to them? You know, someone wet their pants in front of the whole class, and they can tell the story as an adult and act like it was no big deal to be embarrassed and humiliated in that way? I can't do that. I don't think I ever will.'

'I remember that day now,' Janet said. 'I remember you.'

'It was wet,' Steven said. 'It was the late fall, just a few weeks after I came to school there, and it had rained and there were puddles all over the playground.'

'It was one of those Nerf footballs. It was like a sponge.'

'Yes. They'd been on me for weeks about everything. I had a buzz cut, remember? They gave all of the boys at Hope House one because it was simpler and saved time. They knew I lived there. They were on me for the clothes and the hair and for not reading that well. I hated coming to school. I woke up in the morning feeling sick and went to bed feeling worse. I would have done anything to get away.'

'What made this day worse than any other?'

'I stood up to them,' he said. 'They were making fun of the way I read in class, and I told Roger Fouts to go to hell. Remember him?'

Janet nodded.

'I said it low and under my breath so the teacher wouldn't hear. But I made sure Roger heard, and he did. And he told me he was going to get me on the playground. I thought about going to the nurse's office and pretending I was sick, but some part of me just said, Fuck it. I didn't care, really. I just wanted them to do what they wanted to do. Maybe I thought if they did that, then they'd leave me alone and go on to someone else. But when we got out there after lunch, they came after me, a group of about seven of them. All boys. All third and fourth graders.'

'Who were they?' Janet asked.

'Does it matter?' Steven asked. 'They gathered around me, and they took that ball, and they rolled it in a mud puddle until the ball was soaked and full of water and mud. And they threw it at me. I remember very clearly — the first one hit me right in the chest. Water and mud splattered everywhere, and I knew my shirt was ruined.'

'I'm sorry.'

'They all laughed,' Steven said. His eyes remained dry, but he bit his upper lip. 'I can see them all standing around me, just laughing. They looked like animals. They were all teeth and grins. They looked so stupid, so mindless. And then they just picked the ball up and they did it again. And again. They even hit me in the face with one of their throws. Right in the face. The mud was in my hair. It was cold and wet.'

'Where were the teachers?'

'I don't know, Janet. Where were they? Where were they?' He rubbed his eyes with both hands. 'I couldn't get away. They had me surrounded. And you see, those boys didn't understand what they were really doing to me. They thought they were just messing up my clothes and teaching me a lesson or whatever they thought of it as. I guess they were making themselves feel better. More dominant or something. But if one of my shirts got ruined, I didn't get a new shirt to replace it. I only had a couple of shirts and a couple pairs of pants. Not only would I not have those clothes to wear, but I'd get in all sorts of trouble at Hope House. I'd ruined my clothes. I was going to get blamed for that. And it wouldn't matter what I said or who I blamed — they were going to hold me responsible.'

'What would they do to you?' Janet asked.

'If I was lucky, I'd miss a meal or two. If I was lucky.'

'Why didn't you tell? Wouldn't someone intercede on your behalf? Wouldn't someone from Hope House go to the school and tell the principal?'

Steven shook his head and laughed. 'Right. Janet, there were so many kids living in that house, all of them going in so many different directions, they couldn't be bothered to go to the school on our behalf. We were pretty much on our own unless the problem was right in their face. My ruined clothes were right in their faces.'

The door opened, and Detective Stynes stuck his head in. He looked from Janet to Steven and then back to Janet again.

'It's okay,' she said. 'We're doing fine.'

Stynes left without saying anything else.

When Janet turned her attention back to Steven, he said, 'The only thing that saved me was you.'

'I didn't save you.'

'You did. You remember, right? You came right into that circle, and you stood right in front of me, and you told them that if they wanted to throw that ball again, they'd have to throw it at you first. And you just stood there, defiant. You weren't going to move. And those boys just turned and walked away. You backed them down. They listened to you like you were an adult. It was like you scared them. At the time, I couldn't figure it out, you know? How did you know what was going on? You must have been with the girls at the other end of the playground. How did you know what was happening down there with us?'

Janet knew. She so quickly saw and responded to what happened to Steven because she had been watching someone involved with the unfolding scene. Someone she always watched.

'But you know why you were watching, right?' Steven asked.

Janet nodded. 'It was because of Michael Bower. Michael was one of the boys who went after you that day.'

# 47

'He was there,' Steven said. 'He was always there with the bullies.'

Michael. Janet didn't see him that way. He wasn't a bully, not by a long shot. Everyone liked Michael. He got along with everyone. Except —

He had a streak in him. A sense of superiority. A meanness. Always delivered with a smile or a joke, but it was there.

'Michael didn't do anything to me,' Steven said. 'He never mocked me. He didn't throw the football at me that day. But he stood on the edge and watched. Those guys wanted his approval as much as they wanted to hurt me. And Michael stood there and he laughed and he egged them on. He always laughed when someone else did something to me. In a way, I think that's worse. It seems like either the coward's way or the two-faced way. But either way, he was involved. And that's how you knew what was happening, because you were watching him, right? And when you asked him to do something, really asked him, he would listen to you.'

'Not often. Usually it went the other way around. Usually I had to do things for him. But you're right — he would occasionally do things for me if I was really serious.'

'When you stepped in that day, when you stood up to those guys, Michael walked away too. If he hadn't, then those guys wouldn't have left me alone. Ever.'

Janet flashed back to the night with Ray, to Michael exploding and attacking his father. Was that anger always beneath the surface? Even in childhood?

'I never forgot you for that, Janet,' Steven said. 'After that, the entire rest of the school year, I kept my eye on you. I watched for you in the hallways or at assemblies or on the playground. I know that sounds strange to say, but it wasn't a creepy thing for me at all. As long as I knew you were around, I felt safe. You were like a superhero to me, a protector. But you know what you were really like?'

'Let me guess — a big sister.'

'Exactly.' Steven nodded. 'I don't have one. I didn't have any siblings. By the time I was six, I didn't even have parents. But I thought about it all the time. I thought about what it would be like to have a family. To have a sister, just like you. Even after I moved away, which was at the end of that school year, I kept thinking of you. I kept it in my head that you were the ideal. You were the family I wanted to have.'

'So you decided to become my brother.'

'I wanted a new start. This was about ten years ago. I'd had some trouble with the police, mostly when I was a teenager but a little when I was over eighteen. I committed some petty crimes, some robberies. Nothing that serious, but I just woke up one day and was sick of myself, you know? I looked in the mirror, and I thought, 'Who the hell are you and why are you such a piece of shit?' It's pretty easy to assume a new

374

identity if a person wants to. You can look up the tips for doing it on the Internet or from the library. And the way people always do it is they find someone who died, preferably a little kid because then there are no real records about them. All you have to do is find the social security number and request a birth certificate. I figured, why not accomplish two goals at once? I could get a new identity and be the person I kind of always wanted to be. Your brother. I knew the story from when I was a kid. I knew this tragedy had befallen your family. People still talked about it in school sometimes — the other kids. I think everyone thought of you as the girl whose brother had died.'

'I don't think of myself that way,' Janet said.

'I get it,' he said. 'You're more than that. You have your own kid. You have a life. I get it. I didn't want people to look at me and just see Hope House. Or foster child. I did what you did — I created a new life.'

'I didn't steal someone's identity,' Janet said. 'I didn't steal an identity and then torment a family. Why did you let me believe, even for a second, that you might be Justin?'

'Because I liked thinking that I might be him. I wanted to be someone else, someone from a decent family. Someone with a home like yours — '

Janet had listened long enough. She got it. Steven Kollman was a messed-up adult who grew out of a messed-up kid. She remembered that day on the playground, her act of what Steven considered heroism and what she considered simple decency, and she understood the impact such a gesture could make on a young life.

But that was as far as she went with Steven Kollman. She couldn't forget the cruel trick he'd played on her, encouraging false hopes about Justin, leading her to believe there were possibilities where none existed. So rather than listen to any more of Steven Kollman's sob story, Janet stood and went for the buzzer near the door, which would summon Detective Stynes and let her out. But before she reached it, Steven spoke, his voice stopping her.

'I ran into Michael about six months ago,' he said.

Janet froze in place. She didn't hit the buzzer.

'I came to Dove Point almost a year ago. I got arrested in Columbus for an assault. I blew the court date, so there was a warrant.'

'You got arrested?'

'I assaulted a guy who worked for the child welfare office. My records are sealed, the ones from when I was a kid. I wanted to see what they said about my parents and if maybe I had any other family members I could look up. Cousins or something. Since they're sealed, I couldn't even see them. They're my records, but I couldn't see them. And this asshole in the welfare office offered to let me see them for a price. You know, some kind of side deal. We met at some dive bar in Columbus, and when I got there he wanted more money. I punched him. It was stupid, I know, but when the cops came and found me I was only carrying the Justin

Manning ID. Some days, that's all I carried, like I really was him. I went into the system that way.'

'They found the summons in your apartment,' Janet said. 'Actually, my daughter found it.'

Steven looked a little surprised, but then he shrugged and kept talking. 'I figured I needed to get out of Columbus, so I decided to come back here. At least it was a little familiar, and I figured you might still be here. I thought you'd be married and all that, but who knows? We could reconnect maybe. We could be . . . I don't know. Something. Friends? Maybe like family even.'

'What does Michael have to do with this?' Janet asked.

'It's interesting the way you snap to attention when his name comes up. I don't even know if Justin's name gets the same rise out of you that Michael's does.'

Janet looked into Steven's eyes, saw the little glint of glee he seemed to be feeling. 'Good-bye.' Janet reached for the buzzer.

'You love him, don't you?'

'He's my best friend.'

'But you love him, right? You sat around here in Dove Point all those years, like I said, raising your kid and making a life. And it was all good, wasn't it? Except you always wondered what Michael was doing. Was he having a good time? Was he having an adventure? Was he having it with someone else?'

Janet looked at the floor, the scuffed, filthy linoleum tile, the harsh glare of the overhead lights showing every speck of dirt. He was right. She carried that image of Michael around with her all those years, using it as more than just a distraction. She used it as a spur, something to urge her forward. She didn't want Michael to come back and find out she'd completely fallen to pieces after high school, that she'd married the first loser who came along and continued to pump out kids. No, she wanted to show him something — anything — if he ever came back. Some might say she lived for him, and would consider this pathetic, but she didn't see it that way. She wanted a better life for Ashleigh and for herself, and if thoughts of Michael helped her get there, so be it.

'Let me tell you about meeting the golden boy when I came back to Dove Point,' Steven said.

But he didn't start talking. He waited for something. Janet understood what he wanted, so she went back to the table and took her seat again. He had something important to say, and he needed his audience in place.

'I ran into Michael about six months ago here in Dove Point. Do you know Rodney's? That bar out on Old Dayton Road?'

'I've heard of it.'

'I guess it's not the kind of place you would frequent. I'm not even sure why Michael was there, except maybe he was feeling sorry for himself. He was drinking a lot, you know?' Steven pantomimed throwing a drink into his mouth. 'I studied him for a while from across the room because I thought I knew who he was, but I wasn't sure. I hadn't seen him in, what, twenty-some years? I wanted to be sure, but after I checked him out for a while, I knew I

378

recognized him. I had all those faces from that day on the playground memorized. He didn't look that different. Just grown-up is all.'

'Did he recognize you?'

'Recognize me?' Steven laughed. 'Janet, people like Michael don't recognize or remember people like me. Hell, did you recognize me when I came to your door in the middle of the night? Or when you saw me in broad daylight on campus? Did you recognize me?'

'I thought you were familiar.'

'You *hoped* I was your brother,' he said. 'Hoped. But you didn't recognize me. You didn't even recognize me when the cops told you my name, did you?'

By not saying anything, Janet knew she was answering his question.

'I told him we went to school together,' Steven said. 'I bought him a drink, told him my name. I told him I moved away after the third grade, which is true. I didn't mention Hope House and all that shit. We started talking. We just shared stories of our lives. And here's what got me, man — here's what really got me. As he talked about his life and I talked about mine, I realized that the paths we'd been on, the way we'd been moving through our lives in the years since high school, really weren't that different. Sure, he had a great time up to a point. The exact opposite of me. But after graduating, the wheels came off for him. He didn't finish college. He tried a few different careers — salesman, store manager, substitute teacher — but none of them panned out. Nothing ever stuck with him. Or he never

379

stuck with anything. Whatever it was, his life just wasn't that golden. Do you understand what I'm saying here? Do you understand what a revelation it was to hear all that?'

'You thought his life would have gone better.'

'That's right. And I bet you thought the same thing all those years you were here and he was out there. Right? Am I right?'

'I did.'

'See, we're just alike in that sense,' Steven said. He smiled, his eyes glowing at what he saw as a deep, connecting bond between them. 'You sat here in Dove Point all those years thinking Michael was out conquering the world, sleeping with every girl who came along, making a lot of money, living a big life. Except he wasn't. He was a nothing, a failure. He was the classic case of a guy who peaks when he's about seventeen, and the rest — ' Steven held his right hand out, parallel to the table, like it was an airplane. Then he dropped his hand, fingers first, against the tabletop. 'It all just falls away.'

Janet thought back to that first day when she saw Michael standing in the parking lot on campus. As soon as she recognized him, she'd noticed the changes the years had marked on him and chalked them up to simple age. But the light wasn't as bright in his eyes, and the force of his personality seemed dimmer. And since then, whenever they talked, he seemed to be a little scared, a little off his game. Not the same Michael at all.

'It's funny the effect alcohol will have on people,' Steven said. 'If you give them enough of

380

it, they'll tell you anything. It helps if they're a little desperate to share their story, especially with someone they think really knows or understands them. Michael didn't see me as the loser kid from Hope House that night. He didn't see me as the kid he watched get smacked with a soggy football. He saw me as a guy from his past, someone who had lived in the same town and gone to the same school. He thought we shared something. It let him open up to me.'

'What did he tell you?'

'What didn't he tell me?' Steven laughed. 'You know, I have to be honest with you — a part of me talked to him because I wanted to find out something about you. I'd taken on Justin's identity. I'd looked you up in the phone book and on the Internet. I knew where you worked. Hell, I'd driven by your old house, the one you used to rent before you moved in with your dad. That's how I figured out you'd moved. But Michael, he didn't want to talk about you. I asked about Janet Manning, but he kept changing the subject. He wanted to talk about something else. Or someone else, I guess.'

'Who?'

'His old man. His dad.'

'What did he say about him?' Janet asked.

'He's not a big fan of his dad. I can tell you that. Apparently, the old man used to support him. He sent Michael money out in California. Michael made it sound like he just needed the money for the short term, but I got the sense it was more than that. I figure the old man was carrying Michael a lot of the time. I guess

Michael's dad left his mom at some point, and he's an only child. You can see that the old man might feel so much guilt he'd shell out whatever he could to keep the kid happy. I wish I had someone who could do that for me.'

'I hear his dad is getting remarried.'

'Right. Well, maybe that's why the old man cut him off. And Michael didn't like that one bit. Who would, right? If you have a nice meal ticket, who wants to see it go away? But I'm not really interested in Michael's ramblings about his dad. I couldn't care less if he hates his old man. I wish I knew my old man so I could hate him, but I don't. So I tried to steer the conversation back to you again. I thought, what's the one thing I could bring up about you that might get him off this riff about his dad? Do you know what that is?'

'The murder?'

'The murder. I remembered from growing up that Michael was there that day. I knew the two of you were close friends. So I ask, what happened that day in the park? Do you mind talking about it?'

'And did he?'

'Did he? No, he didn't mind. He spilled his guts. How you all were playing there and how your brother ran away into the woods and Michael went to bring him back to the playground. He told me all of that. And he said that he saw his old man in the woods that day, right where they ended up finding Justin's body. I guess, from the look on your face, that you've heard all of that before.'

'Michael told me.'

'So the system chewed up another black man, another less fortunate, for a crime he didn't commit.'

Janet couldn't meet his eye then. She felt the guilt twist in her gut, a metal coil that wound through her insides.

'You feel bad about it, right?' Steven leaned forward, trying to resume eye contact.

'Of course.'

'And you understand why I would take that information and use it to get closer to you? Here I was looking for a way to find out about your life and establish some sort of relationship with you, and Michael just handed it to me. What would you want more than anything else except to know what really happened to your brother?'

'Why didn't you just come and tell me that? Or better yet, why not go to the police and tell them?'

'I had a warrant out on me, remember? And what was I going to tell them? Some guy who used to bully me in grade school told me he thinks his dad murdered some kid twenty-five years ago? What would they think of that?'

'You could have tried.'

'I told you.'

'You didn't tell me anything,' Janet said. 'You strung me along.'

'I did. You're right. I figured that was my one chance to get close to you, to give you something, so I tried to make it last. I shouldn't have done that.'

'I'm not sure I believe you,' Janet said.

'I guess you told Michael I came and saw you.'

'I did.'

'He came to see me a couple of times. He came not long after that first night we talked in the bar. And then he came again after I talked to you on campus.'

'Why did he come to see you?' Janet asked.

'Good question.'

Janet waited. 'Are you going to answer it?' she finally asked.

He nodded. 'Sure. Why not?' He licked his lips. 'I guess you told him that some strange guy had shown up at your house in the middle of the night, and Michael wanted to know if it was me. I admitted it was, of course. I didn't have anything to hide, even though I suspected he wanted to chew me out for bothering you. You know, the whole knight in shining armor thing. Right?'

Janet didn't answer, but she did want to think Michael was there on her behalf.

Steven smiled. 'Well, he must have left his white knight suit at the cleaners. He didn't come to tell me to lay off you. Quite the contrary. He was only mad at me because I wasn't pushing his version of the story. See, he wanted me to go to you and tell you that his old man killed your brother. He wanted me to push his agenda instead of my own. When I told him to screw off, we got into an argument, a pretty loud one.'

Janet felt something drop inside her, like a driver in the midst of a long descent.

'He just wanted to use me,' Steven said. 'He wanted me to get you stirred up, to get you to

384

come around to his way of thinking about the murder. He wanted you to believe his dad committed the crime as much as he did.' Steven leaned back in his chair, looking smug. 'He wanted me to be just another pawn in his game.'

# 48

Stynes was on the phone when Janet Manning emerged from the detention area of the station. A uniformed officer guided her out, and Stynes could see, even from across the room, that the conversation with Steven Kollman had left Janet shaken and disturbed. She looked at the floor as she walked, and her step lacked its characteristic energy. Stynes ended the call he was on and wondered if his first instinct hadn't been correct — that he shouldn't have let Janet talk to Kollman.

'Rough going in there?' he asked when she reached his desk.

Janet nodded.

'Here,' he said. 'Sit.' He held out a chair, and Janet sat. When she was settled, he said, 'That's the most he's talked to anybody since he's been in here.'

'I don't know if that's a good thing,' she said.

'Can I get you some water or something?'

'No, I'm okay.'

'What did he tell you?' Stynes asked. 'I don't mean to be so blunt about it, but if he told you something I need to know about your brother's case, then I'd like to hear it.'

'He told me a lot of things,' Janet said. 'I don't know how much is relevant to you. I'm still trying to get my mind around it all.'

Stynes took a seat in the chair opposite Janet.

He needed to tell her a few things before she left the station. He hoped that what he had to tell her would be seen as good news and go some of the way toward mitigating whatever she experienced with Steven Kollman. He decided not to press her on the conversation with Steven, at least not yet. He had other things to tend to, so he decided to give her time to decompress.

'I've been working on something about your brother's case,' Stynes said. 'This morning I found out about a witness who will also testify to seeing Ray Bower in the woods that day.'

Janet looked up, her face alert.

'I can't reveal much more than that, but I can say that his testimony pretty strongly corroborates what Michael Bower has told you. It's someone who was in the park on the day Justin died, someone who was unwilling to come forward in the past but will now. We're not at the point of filing charges yet, but we've been in touch with Ray Bower's attorney. Apparently, Ray is feeling better, but he's still in the hospital, and soon we're going to be able to speak to him and ask him some of these questions.'

Stynes stopped talking. He'd already said too much about the case. He chose to tell Janet only because . . . because things with her and the Mannings just seemed different. After twenty-five years and all the false hopes, they deserved to know something definitive. And he wanted to give that to them — to her — if he could.

But he couldn't read Janet. Her face didn't change. Maybe it was the encounter with Kollman or maybe it was the impact of his words, but she didn't seem to be fully processing what he was saying to her. He had expected a more substantial response. Grief, elation, regret — something.

'Michael,' she said.

'Michael?'

Her eyes cleared a little. 'Does he know? Michael.'

'I was going to ask you about that,' Stynes said. 'We want him to come in and give a statement as well, but he's nowhere to be found. Still. Even his mother hasn't heard from him.'

'It's weird,' she said.

'What is?'

'He was so determined to see Ray punished. Why would he leave now?'

'Maybe it's too hard for him.'

Stynes saw the hurt on her face — and the fear, the fear that Michael left without saying good-bye. His paternal instincts toward Janet kicked in. He made a silent wish that she'd find someone to treat her decently before too long. And if Michael Bower served as a continuing source of pain or anxiety in her life, then he wished he would finally stay away. He just needed him to make that statement — and if Ray Bower felt like unburdening his soul without a trial, he wouldn't even need that much.

'Well, I have another stop to make before I'm able to go to the hospital,' he said. 'I do want to talk to you more about what you discussed with Steven Kollman. We're going forward with the charges against him as well.' Stynes stood. 'Do you need a ride somewhere?' he asked.

'No, I'm fine. I can drive.'

'Are you sure? I can get an officer to give you a lift.'

The steel returned to Janet's posture. She stood up, pushed her shoulders back. 'Really, Detective,' she said. 'I'm doing just fine.'

★ ★ ★

Stynes drove across the tracks into East. While he bounced over the uneven railroad ties and into the neighborhood that didn't want him, he thought about what he was about to do. He may have given a measure of false hope to Janet Manning by telling her about Ray Bower before any confession or plea agreement had been struck. But it was a calculated risk. Stynes weighed her years of frustration against the possibility that he'd spoken too soon about a suspect in the case. What he couldn't be sure of anymore, what he really couldn't decide no matter how much he thought about it, was who had suffered more: Dante Rogers or the Mannings? Which was worse: losing a loved one and spending a life not knowing how it happened? Or spending the prime of your life incarcerated for a crime you didn't commit?

Stynes decided the answer was above his pay grade. All he knew with any certainty was that two halves of the equation, the people suffering over the years as the result of the same murder, could easily make a case that he was to blame for it all. If he'd investigated more thoroughly, if he'd listened to his gut, if he'd stood up to

Reynolds. *If, if, if* . . .

So he really didn't care about jumping the gun. He needed to tell someone like Janet Manning and someone like Dante a little bit of good news, no matter how tenuous it might be.

The Reverend Fred laughed when Stynes came through the door of the church office. He acted like he had just heard a particularly salty joke. He clapped his hands a couple of times.

'Well, well,' he said. 'The great white hunter. What are you here for? Trying to meet your quota of brothers to arrest?'

'I'm here to see Dante. Is he here?'

'Oh, he's here,' Fred said. 'I don't know if he wants to talk to you.'

Stynes started down the hallway to the literature room.

'I got an interesting phone call today,' Fred said. 'A reporter.'

Stynes turned around. 'From the *Ledger*?'

'Our hometown paper,' Fred said. 'Her name's . . . Katie something. Katie — '

'Kate Grossman.'

'That's it. Grossman. She sounded very . . . starched,' Fred said. 'You know, they're only hiring white girls over there.'

'What did she want?' Stynes asked, although he suspected he knew.

'She's just like you. She wanted to talk to Dante. I told her he wasn't taking calls at the moment, but I represented his interests if she wanted to run something by me. So she did. And guess what she told me?'

Stynes didn't answer but wished he could slap

the knowing smirk off the Reverend Fred's face.

'She told me the police had a new witness come forward in the Justin Manning case,' Fred said. 'One who might just be able to exonerate Dante.'

'She can't know everything.'

'I guess she knows enough,' Fred said. 'Of course, I just listened mostly. Except I did say that if it were up to me to give good counsel to a brother like Dante, I would suggest he hire a civil rights attorney and take the city of Dove Point and the Dove Point Police and all the investigators who worked the case to court for twenty-two years of pain and suffering at the hands of our criminal injustice system. That's what I told her I'd do, Detective.'

'I'm not sure I'd disagree with you about that, Reverend,' Stynes said.

For a moment, Stynes found joy in the surprised look on the Reverend Fred's face. If he'd expected a fight, Stynes wasn't going to give him one. And Stynes couldn't blame Dante if he did try to recoup what he'd lost as a result of his years in prison.

'What does Dante think of all this?' Stynes asked.

It took a moment for Reverend Fred to respond, and while he held Stynes's gaze, even more of his certainty slipped away. The Reverend Fred held a strong initial hand, but his lack of an immediate answer told Stynes something.

'We're still working on that,' Fred said. 'As you can imagine, it's just a bit overwhelming for him after all this time of being treated like a pariah.'

'I guess you'll have to keep working on him, won't you?' Stynes asked.

'I will. Don't forget I was a victim here as well.'

'You mean the money from your accounts?'

'Yes.'

'Don't worry,' Stynes said. 'Mr Bower will answer for that if need be. We're already checking to see if other clients of his were stolen from. I suspect they were.'

Reverend Fred leaned back in his chair and folded his arms across his chest. He nodded his head. Stynes took it for a gesture of appreciation.

'I'm going to go talk to Dante now,' Stynes said. 'This is about him, remember?'

\* \* \*

Dante sat at the same sagging folding table as before. Rather than stuffing envelopes, he was surrounded by file folders, and he seemed to be sorting them into stacks. One of the stacks stood so high on the end of the table that it looked like it could pitch over onto the floor at any moment. Dante didn't look up. He kept shuffling the folders around, his lips moving as he did his work.

'Dante?'

He answered without looking up. 'Yes, sir.'

'Do you mind holding off on your work for a minute?'

Dante stopped. He practically froze in place and still didn't look up.

Stynes came farther into the room and pulled

a chair out from the opposite side of the table. He sat down, feeling the uncomfortable metal dig into his back.

'I guess Reverend Fred told you what's happening with the case.'

'He did.'

'Is there anything you want to say to me about it?' Stynes asked.

Dante swallowed, his Adam's apple bobbing on his puffy neck. 'I'm glad that family will have some peace.'

'That's nice of you to say.'

Dante shrugged. He picked up one of the folders and held it in his hand. He looked like he wanted to return to his filing, but he didn't. He just held the folder in his lap, gently tapping it against his thigh.

'Dante, I want to tell you how sorry I am about your conviction. We made some mistakes during our investigation. We . . . There were witnesses, but it looks like their testimony was probably influenced by someone in a position of authority.'

'You mean those children.'

'That's right. If we'd listened to what they said that day, right after Justin disappeared . . . '

'They were scared. Kids get scared.'

In his mind, Stynes had pictured the whole scene going another way. He had imagined feeling differently about everything he would say to Dante. He had hoped to speak to him and then feel a wave of relief and calm wash over his body and mind, a release from the burden of guilt he carried. But nothing like that came.

Instead, he looked at Dante, a broken middle-aged man, and understood the limits of his own words and actions to make any kind of significant difference in Dante's life.

Stynes reached into his suit coat and brought out one of his business cards. He wrote his home phone number on the back of the card and handed it over.

'If there's ever anything I can do to help,' he said. 'If you need a job or anything, let me know.'

'Thank you.'

Dante tucked the card into the pocket of his jeans without reading it. He tapped the folder again.

'Okay, I'll let you get back to your work.'

'Okay.'

'Dante?' Stynes said. 'Why did you keep those newspaper clippings about Justin Manning in your room? Why were you interested in the case?'

Dante stared at the tabletop when he spoke. 'I remembered that boy from the park. I saw him that day. I played with him, carried him on my shoulders and made him laugh. I could do that with some kids, make them laugh. After he disappeared and you all started asking me questions, I started keeping the newspaper stories. I just felt connected to the whole thing, I guess.' He paused, then went on. 'I'm not saying I wanted to, you know, touch him that day. But I might have done it if I'd had the chance. It was a close call for me.'

'Why are you so calm, Dante? If someone put me in jail for something I didn't do, I don't know

394

if I could control myself. You act like nothing happened.'

Dante didn't answer, so Stynes stood up and moved toward the door. But before he left the room, Dante said, 'Prison helped me a little.'

'What's that?' Stynes said, turning back to the table where Dante sat.

'It helped me,' he said. 'I found God there.'

'You can find God out here, too, Dante. You're in a church.'

'I had desires back then.' He started shuffling the folders again and talked while he shuffled. 'I had a desire for small children. Being in prison helped me with that.'

'Are you saying it cured you?' Stynes asked.

'God did. He healed me.'

'So you don't have those desires anymore?'

Dante put his head down and kept working. He acted like Stynes had already left the room.

'You should get help, Dante. Counseling of some kind.'

'The Reverend Fred counsels me.'

'I mean a real counselor.' Stynes tried to correct himself. 'The reverend is fine with the spiritual side of things, and I'm sure he's been a good friend to you. But you have to believe me about this — I've seen other guys like you. Other guys with your . . . desires, let's say. My experience is they tend not to go away.'

'Not without counseling?' Dante asked.

*Never,* Stynes wanted to say. *For guys like you, they never go away.*

But he didn't say it.

'Just keep at it, okay, Dante? Keep fighting the good fight.'

Dante nodded and added the file in his hand to the tall stack, pushing it that much closer to toppling over.

# 49

Janet drove to Rose Bower's house. She turned the air-conditioning off and rolled down the windows, letting fresh warm air into the car as she moved through town. She turned the car radio off as well. She didn't want distractions. She didn't want to hear happy music or sad news or anything really. Nothing except Michael's voice, telling her he hadn't been using her, that he hadn't been trying to use Steven against her. She wanted to hear Michael say they weren't just pawns as Steven had said.

She'd known him her whole life. She hoped she would get to the house and Michael would be there, opening the door to her. And they'd talk the whole thing through, the way they would have when they were kids. And she'd understand, and it would all make sense.

But when Rose Bower opened the door to the little house, Janet could tell by the look on her face — something between surprise and pity — that Michael wasn't there.

Janet followed Rose inside, and the two women sat. Rose wore a housecoat, and her hair looked limpid and dirty, as if she hadn't bathed for a couple of days.

'Did he leave, Rose?' Janet asked. 'Did he leave town?'

Rose didn't answer. She rubbed her hands up and down the tops of her thighs, back and forth across the gray floral-patterned material.

'Rose? Just tell me.'

'He packed some things earlier today,' she said.

'He was here?'

'He was here and gone. He threw his clothes into bags. He said he'd stayed too long as it was, and he needed to get out of town.'

'Where was he going?' Janet asked.

'He didn't say. I didn't ask, I guess. I don't want to be a nag.'

'He's your son.'

'I know, but . . . ' Her words trailed off. She seemed to not have the will to finish.

'Do you know the police are going to the hospital to question Ray?' Janet asked.

Rose's eyes widened.

'They found another witness who saw him in the woods that day. They're going to ask Ray if he's ready to confess to killing Justin. They're hoping to do the whole thing without a trial.'

Rose stopped rubbing the tops of her thighs. She raised one hand to her mouth, covering it as though she might cough or say something inappropriate. But she didn't speak. She held the hand there for a long moment.

'I'm sorry to have to tell you that, Rose.'

She nodded her head. 'It's okay, honey.'

'Why do you think Ray would kill his own child?' Janet asked. 'He knew, or suspected, that Justin was his son. Why would he hurt him like that?'

'I don't know,' she said. 'Ray wasn't violent. He never hurt Michael. He never laid a hand on me. He didn't hurt us that way.'

'Was Michael ever violent?' Janet asked.

Rose scooted back on the couch a little. 'Michael? Why would you ask me that?'

'Because he beat the hell out of Ray the other night,' Janet said. 'And I saw him, right after he did it. He looked . . . different, Rose. There was something wrong with him.'

'I know he did that to his father,' Rose said. 'But that was his father. Michael was gentle — '

'He wasn't, Rose.'

Janet's words came out hard and flat, like a smack against the top of the table. Rose flinched.

Janet continued. 'He enjoyed it when other kids were bullied in school. That man in the jail, the one pretending to be Justin. Michael egged other kids on when they bullied him. He wasn't always peaceful or benevolent.'

'Why do you hate him so much?' Rose asked. 'Michael paid a price for what happened in that park. He's lived with it all these years, too. I know what it was like for him after he came home that day.' Rose fussed with the hair at the back of her head before resuming. 'He was upset. Very upset. He cried and cried because something had happened to Justin.' Rose's eyes grew misty as she thought about her son in distress or pain. 'He told me it was his fault. He said he was right there, and it was his fault that Justin didn't come back out of the woods. I guess he ran after him or something.'

'And what did you tell him?'

'I told him it wasn't his fault, of course. I told him there were bad people in the world, and sometimes they wanted to hurt small children. We didn't believe in sheltering Michael. Not really.'

'And did Ray say anything?'

'He was adamant that Michael not blame himself. Adamant.'

'And did that help Michael settle down?' Janet asked.

It took Rose a long time to answer. Before any words came out of her mouth, she started slowly turning her head back and forth. Finally she said, 'He only calmed down when we agreed to let him see you.'

'See me?'

'He went to your house.'

'Why?'

Again, Rose hesitated.

'Why?' Janet asked.

'Because your dad called and asked if we could bring Michael over to your house.'

'Why would he do that? After everything he knew.'

'You were upset, too. Just like Michael. You know what that's like, to see your child upset or sick or scared. You wouldn't calm down, and you kept asking to see Michael. After everything he found out that morning, of course your father didn't want Ray or any of us coming near his house. And I didn't want your mother coming near us. But, you see, eventually Bill gave in. He couldn't take seeing you so unhappy, so he called over here. He said Michael could come over to your house if I brought him over there. He said if Ray showed up he couldn't be held responsible for his actions. But I could do it if I wanted.'

'And you did?'

'I didn't want to,' Rose said. 'I was sick, too. Just sick. Physically, I felt ill after what Ray had told me that morning. I didn't think I'd even be able to walk.' She shook her head. 'I wish I'd had the guts to kick Ray out — I really do. But I never had them. I never did. It's sick for me to admit this, but if he knocked on that door today, I might just take him back.'

Rose's admission gave Janet a touch of sickness in her gut. 'So you came to our house with Michael.'

'Your dad let me in. The house, your house — it was just crazy. There were police there and reporters outside with cameras. A lot of your parents' friends were over. People your dad worked with. Women from the church who knew your mom. It was a bit of a madhouse.'

'Did my mom see you? Did you talk to her?'

'I don't know where she was,' Rose said. 'Maybe she was lying down or resting. Your dad met me at the door and he led us upstairs. You were in your room, alone. He didn't . . . we didn't . . . '

'You didn't talk about what had happened?'

'No. We were the aggrieved parties. But it seemed petty to mention anything like that when Justin had been taken. We just wanted to settle the two of you down. I remember your dad standing in the doorway of your room after we got there. You and Michael sat right on the floor together and started playing. As soon as you two saw each other, the crying stopped. The look on your dad's face,' Rose said. 'When I saw him at the door, he looked older, worn down. He looked like a very sad man. But for just a moment, when he stood there looking at you in your room with Michael, and because you had stopped crying, he almost looked happy. I know how heavy his heart was, but he did look happy.'

Janet had been there, but she didn't remember any of what Rose was telling her. She felt her emotions catch in her own throat as she thought back, wishing she could have seen that look on her dad's face, a moment of contentment as everything in his world fell apart. She wished she could see that look on his face in the present.

'So you just sat with us while we played?'

'Someone called your dad away. His happiness didn't last long. I don't know if it was the police or a reporter, but someone called his name, and I saw the weight lower onto him again. He left the room and closed the bedroom door. We were in there together, you and Michael and me. For an hour or so, and when we left, we promised we'd let you two play together again the next day if you wanted.'

'And I guess we talked to the police while you were there,' Janet said.

'You remember that?'

'I don't remember it really. But I know it happened because we told them about seeing Justin in the park with Dante Rogers.' Then something occurred to Janet. 'Did you say you sat with us alone in my room after my dad left?'

'For just a little while.'

'Did you tell us what to say?' Janet asked.

402

'That night, did you tell us to tell the police that we saw Dante and Justin together in the park? And did you tell us not to mention seeing Justin run into the woods chasing after that dog?'

Rose didn't answer. But Janet understood. All she had to do was think back just a few minutes to Rose's admission that she would still take Ray back if he knocked on the door right then. If she felt that way in the present, what would she have done for him in the past? Janet had recently begun to wonder how Ray Bower could have reached them if her father knew about the affair. It was simple — he didn't have to. Rose did the dirty work for him.

'Why did Ray not want us to mention Justin running away?'

'I don't know.'

'He didn't tell you.'

'No, he didn't. And I didn't ask. I saw him come home with that dirt on his clothes. I knew what that might mean. But I never asked him about it. He just told me to make sure Michael understood what to say. He told him here at home not to mention running into the woods, but then he wanted me to repeat it at your house. I just assumed it was true. How do I know what you saw at the park?'

'That's witness tampering, Rose. I think that's what they call it.'

'Oh, honey, look at me. Should I even care what anyone does to me or thinks about me now? Does any of it matter?'

'It still matters,' Janet said. 'It matters a great deal.'

# 50

Ashleigh sat on her bed with her earbuds in. The music went on and on, a nearly continuous loop of sound. She barely heard it. She stared out the window, watching the evening fall. The sky glowed red through the large tree in their yard. She did this sometimes, stared into space, felt herself alone, felt her mind drift. It had been a long day. She got up early for her uncle's funeral service, and then made awkward conversation with the few relatives and friends who came back to the house. She took a nap in the afternoon, but rather than making her feel better, the nap made her feel more tired, more sluggish.

She'd felt off her game for a few days. Lazy, lethargic.

Why?

They finally knew the answer. The man on the porch wasn't her uncle. There was no prize to bring home for her mother. Ashleigh thought all along that just knowing something for sure would help, but she saw that for what it was — a falsity. A lie. Only one thing could make everything better: bringing her uncle back. Short of that, she had failed. Even the reburial had felt a little hollow. When she stood next to her mom, leaned in against her, felt her warmth and comfort, Ashleigh understood how tough her mom really was. She had been through so much, and still Ashleigh could do little to change it all.

Her grandfather must have knocked more than once. He always acted like such a freak about coming into her room. She knew he wouldn't just barge in without knocking, so when he opened the door and appeared at the foot of her bed, she knew he must have knocked several times, but she couldn't hear him over the sound of the music.

She sat up, pulled the buds out of her ears.

The old man stood there, looking down at her. Something showed on his face. Was it fear? Was the old man scared?

'What's wrong?' Ashleigh asked.

He didn't answer right away. For a moment, he looked like he couldn't talk, like he spoke and understood a different language and had no idea what the gibberish coming out of her mouth amounted to. 'Grandpa?' she said.

'You should come down and see this,' he said.

★ ★ ★

The local news was playing on the TV. Neither one of them spoke. They took their spots — Ashleigh on the couch and Grandpa in his chair. What they saw shocked Ashleigh. She had wrongly assumed a plane had crashed or some nutjob had blown up a building. What else would have prompted her grandpa to come to her room and ask her to watch TV with him? But it was bigger than anything she could have imagined.

The screen showed a blond-haired guy, a reporter, holding a microphone and reading off a yellow legal pad. Ashleigh recognized the backdrop. The brick building, the traffic moving in a circle behind the reporter. He was standing near the courthouse and police station downtown, and he was talking about her Uncle Justin. It took her a moment to catch up to the words, to really hear them and register them in her brain . . .

'Sources tell us that the break in the case came about as the result of a witness coming forward, someone who had this information for quite some time but only now chose to reveal it to the authorities. Police are keeping that witness's name and identity a secret from the media now. And I want to emphasize that no charges have been filed against Raymond Bower, the local man now inside the police station talking to authorities, but sources are saying charges could be filed sometime soon . . . '

Ashleigh looked at her grandpa. He held one hand to the side of his head, like something or someone had delivered a strong blow. But his eyes remained wide-open, staring at the screen.

'Grandpa? Are you okay?'

He nodded but didn't speak.

'That name,' Ashleigh said. 'Raymond Bower? That's Michael's dad, right? I mean, he's a friend of yours, isn't he?'

'Used to be. A long time ago.'

Ashleigh looked back at the screen. The reporter was gone. In his place was the photo Ashleigh had seen so many times, the one she kept on the shelf near her bed. A portrait of her Uncle Justin, smiling, his head turned slightly to his left. It was the only image Ashleigh carried in her mind of him, the only way she ever had and ever would see him.

'Did you — ?'

She meant to ask if the news surprised him, if he thought all along that Raymond Bower might be involved in Justin's death. Surely he suspected something, right? Did things like this ever come out of the blue?

But she broke her words off and stopped. Her grandfather was still staring at the screen, but his eyes were full of tears. That sight shut Ashleigh up, froze her. She didn't know what to do or say. She'd never seen her grandpa cry.

'I loved that kid,' he said, his chin quivering. 'I loved him like my very own.'

# 51

When Janet came in the door, she saw Ashleigh sitting on the couch, the television playing a game show. Ashleigh never watched that kind of mindless television. She hardly ever watched television at all. But there she sat, her eyes glued to the screen. She looked up when Janet came in.

'Mom?'

Janet heard something in Ashleigh's voice, a hint of a plea. Or fear. Something not quite right, not quite normal. Or was it just Janet herself superimposing her own emotions onto her daughter's? Janet had driven the whole way home thinking about what she had learned that day and evening. Michael was gone, Ray with the police. Would it end right there? Would Michael just walk — run — away from her and the town and never look back? Never say good-bye?

'What's wrong?' Janet asked.

'Did you hear all this?'

Janet understood. Whatever was happening at the police station was playing out on the news. Ashleigh knew. Everyone knew. Ray Bower was talking to the police. He might be charged.

But what about her dad?

Ashleigh read the look on her face, saw the question there.

'He's in his bedroom,' Ashleigh said. 'I think you need to talk to him.'

'He knows?'

Ashleigh nodded. 'We watched it together. He came and got me out of my room. It's weird, Mom. I don't think he wanted to watch it all alone.'

Janet looked past Ashleigh and down the hallway toward her dad's room. 'Thanks, honey. I'll go talk to him.'

'Mom? Do you think Ray Bower killed Justin?'

Janet didn't look at Ashleigh as she answered. 'I do, yes, but I have to go talk to your grandpa now.'

★   ★   ★

Her dad was seated on the side of his bed, his feet on the floor. The TV was off — a rarity. He didn't look up when Janet came into the bedroom. He remained seated, his head in his hands. Janet closed the door behind her.

'You know?' he asked, his head still down.

'I heard about it.'

'I'm going down there.' He didn't stand up, but he rocked back and forth a little, creating motion with his body. 'I have to.'

'To do what?'

He didn't answer. He kept rocking.

'Dad? What do you think you can do down there?'

He said something, the sound muffled by his hands.

'What?'

'I don't know.' He lowered his hands and stared at the wall. 'I don't know.' His rocking stopped. 'He took away everything I had. One

409

man. He took it all away.'

'Let the police handle it, Dad.'

'He killed my . . . he killed Justin that day.'

Janet came farther into the room. She moved around the end of the bed to the side near the wall. She sat next to him and placed her arm around his back. 'Dad?'

He didn't resist her touch. He didn't move closer to her, but he didn't move away.

'Dad, I thought that since you knew all along, ever since that day, that Justin wasn't your son . . . You never talked about him. You never cried for him.'

'Did what you found out about your mother make you love her any less?' he asked.

They both knew the answer without Janet saying anything. Janet had spent many hours thinking about her mother, turning the news about her and Ray over in her mind. No matter how long she worked at it, Janet couldn't reconcile the two things: the way she felt about her mother and her mother's infidelity. In the end, she split her mother into two. The woman who raised her and the woman who loved Ray Bower. It was the only way she could do it. To do anything else threatened to strip the gears from her mind.

'Did knowing that I'm not Justin's father make you love him any less? Or make him any less your brother?' he asked. 'I raised him. For four years, I raised him. That makes him mine. I guess I spent twenty-five years trying to pretend he wasn't, but he is. He's mine.'

'He's ours,' Janet said.

Her father's body still felt rigid under her touch, so she brought her arm down and folded her hands in her lap. She didn't know where to go next, what to say or do to help her father. She didn't even know how to help herself.

'Don't go anywhere, Dad. Promise?'

He brought his hands together, intertwined the fingers and moved them around. They tangled up like knotted roots. The pressure he exerted by squeezing his fingers together looked painful and almost made Janet wince.

'What am I going to do anyway?' he said. 'I couldn't protect Justin from him back then. I couldn't keep my wife away from him. I couldn't protect you from . . . '

'From boys?'

'From a boy,' he said.

'And we have Ashleigh because of it.'

'I know,' he said. 'I've had to absorb a lot. And accept a lot. It's not easy for me, with you moving in. I know you had to move in when I lost my job, but it's not easy for me.' He sighed. 'Just do me a favor.'

'What?'

'I know you love that Michael Bower, and I know he's back in town. Maybe for good. Just promise me something. Promise me that if you have to be with that guy, if you love him and want to be with him, promise me he's a better man than his father. Can you promise me that?'

'Michael's gone, Dad. He's gone, and I don't think he's ever coming back to Dove Point.'

# 52

The noise brought Janet out of her shallow sleep. In her dreams, she saw the faces of Michael and Justin. But it was the noise — something faint, something distant — that woke her.

'Ashleigh?'

She thought someone had knocked on her bedroom door. She never kept the door locked, a habit left over from Ashleigh's childhood, when Janet felt she always needed to be within reach of her daughter. Janet rose from the bed, pushing the covers away. She walked to the door and pulled it open. The darkened hallway was quiet. The entire house was still. Janet moved down the carpeted hall to the door of Ashleigh's room. She listened outside until she heard faint, regular breathing sounds.

Had it been her dad?

No, Janet decided. He wouldn't come to the door, knock, and then disappear. A dream. She concluded it was a dream.

But when she returned to her room and slipped back beneath the covers, the noise came again. A light ticking against the windowpane. Janet moved quickly. She tossed the drapes aside and lifted the window. The thick darkness prevented her from seeing anything. Not even shapes or figures. But then she caught a glimpse, a movement at the edge of the yard. A light-colored fabric darted and then disappeared.

Janet wanted to call out, but didn't want to wake everyone else in the house.

Steven Kollman was in jail.

It could be only one person. Janet dressed and set out to follow him.

★ ★ ★

The park was quiet.

Janet hoped, as she approached, that she would find Michael waiting in one of the public areas — a picnic shelter or the jungle gym. Tall sodium arc lights lit portions of the park, some attempt by the police to keep unsavory elements away after dark, and in their hazy glow Janet saw no sign of Michael, no sign of another soul. The absence of any other people set Janet even further on edge. She didn't expect anyone to be in the park, and when they weren't there, she felt even more alone. She knew where Michael would be waiting. Back in the woods at the scene of Justin's murder. All she needed to do was turn around and go back to her house. If he really wanted to see her or needed to see her, he could knock on the door in daylight. But he would not do that.

Janet couldn't deny the fundamental truth — she couldn't walk away and risk not seeing him again. Her dad was right: knowing certain things about certain people didn't change Janet's feelings about them. Janet wondered if she was going into the woods to prove that her feelings about Michael hadn't changed — or to make sure they did.

413

Janet moved down the path. The humid night stuck to her skin. As she walked, she listened for Michael, but she heard nothing except herself. Every step she took seemed magnified. The rustling of the leaves and branches she passed sounded like the shifting of tectonic plates. While she walked, Janet thought of home, of Ashleigh and her dad. She hadn't left a note, hadn't told them she'd gone out of the house. With Steven in jail and Ray in custody, they should be safe. Then she had to ask herself, were they safer than she was?

Janet passed the pond. In the darkness, something plunked into the water. Janet gasped, raised her hand to her chest. Was it just a fish? A turtle? She looked ahead in the darkness. The opening to the clearing came into view. Janet approached slowly, squinting into the night, trying to make out a shape or a human figure. Anything, really.

'Michael?'

She listened. She thought she heard breathing.

'Michael? It's me. I can't see you.'

'Over here.'

His voiced sounded faint, a little worn and cracked.

'Where?'

'Keep coming,' he said.

Janet entered the clearing and still didn't see him. 'Michael, I can't — '

'Over here,' he said.

He sounded insistent. She tracked the sound of his voice and went through the clearing and out the other side where the vegetation grew thicker and denser. Several yards off the clearing, she made out Michael's figure, his white shirt glowing in the darkness.

He sat on the ground, Indian-style. The shirt hung open at his throat, and his olive-colored pants blended into the darkness, appearing to become one with the earth. Janet let her eyes take him in. He looked tired, ragged. He breathed heavily, as if he'd just run a distance, even though he looked to have been sitting in that same spot for quite a while.

'What's wrong, Michael?'

'You talked to Steven, didn't you? You had to. I know he's in the jail. He must have told you and the police what I said to him in that bar.'

'He told me that you wanted him to get me thinking about the murder again,' Janet said. 'He said that you told him about Ray, and you wanted Steven to come to me and get me to think Ray did it. Why did you do that, Michael?'

'I wanted him punished.'

'You're getting your wish, aren't you?' Janet said. 'I talked to Detective Stynes, and he has Ray at the police station. He was hoping for a confession so it can all be over with.' Then Janet thought to add, 'And he says they're not really worried about pressing charges against you. I guess if you beat the crap out of a murderer they don't worry about charging you for it.'

Michael didn't look up.

'Do you understand what you did to me? To my family? You got our hopes up. That guy came to the house, and I . . . I thought he was Justin.'

'I didn't make you think that.'

'But you set it in motion. I thought everything was going to be different. And that man, Steven, he could have been dangerous. How was I to know what he intended? We're supposed to be friends, Michael. We're supposed to care for each other after all these years.'

'What do you remember from that day, Janet?' he asked.

The question took Janet off guard. His voice sounded flat, wooden. It came out with a rasp, as though the words had passed through barbed wire.

'Your dad killed Justin,' she said. 'Isn't that what we've all found out?'

He didn't answer.

'Michael? What is it?'

He still didn't lift his eyes. He started to speak, stopped, and then said, 'I heard my parents argue that morning. I could tell by the way they were fighting that it was different than other fights they'd had. They seemed like they meant it, like they were building up to something final. You know?'

'They were. Your dad was leaving your mom to be with mine.'

'I know,' he said. 'They said one name over and over before they sent me out of the house. Can you guess what name they said?'

It took Janet a moment, but then she said it: 'Justin.'

'Yes,' he said. 'Justin. That name over and over. And it made me mad, Janet. Angry. I understood, at that time, that somehow Justin was the cause of what was going wrong between my parents. It just seemed that way to me.' He chewed on his lower lip for a moment. 'It makes sense now, knowing what we do about the DNA test. Why else would they be fighting about a four-year-old boy?'

'And?'

'So I was angry. Angry about Justin, even though I didn't know why. And then he ran off into the woods and wouldn't come back, when I came back here and told him he had to go back to the park with us . . . and he wouldn't — I . . .'

Janet's breathing shortened. She found herself struggling for air, as though something thicker than the surrounding humidity had been placed across her nose and mouth. She was choking.

'Michael . . .'

'He wouldn't go back to the park, Janet. And his name, it was in my head.'

Janet opened her mouth. The words were slow to come.

'What did you do to him?'

He hesitated. 'I pushed him. Shoved him. I took hold of his shirt with both of my hands and I shoved him down to the ground. This spot right here. I shoved him as hard as I could, and he hit his head on a rock.' Michael reached out and patted a stone, one that was half sunken into the ground. 'It might be this rock right here for all I know. It might very well be.' He leaned back. 'I could tell he was hurt. It knocked him right out, although there wasn't any blood. Not that I could see anyway. I didn't know what to do, Janet. I knew I'd get in trouble. I was scared.'

'What did you do?' Janet asked. Her words came out steady, but she felt the world turning beneath her, a great shifting of the ground beneath her feet. She thought she might topple over to the side.

'I wanted to run. I was going to. I guess I was hoping no one knew what I'd done, although, of course, they would have. But then — '

'Ray showed up.'

Michael nodded. 'He was just there, all of a sudden. My dad. He stood over me — and Justin. It was like he knew what I'd done, and he came out to find me. I don't know why he was there in the woods that day. It was like magic.'

'He was on his way to our house.'

'He told me to leave. He told me that he would take care of it, that it was an accident, but we couldn't tell anyone, ever, what happened in the woods that day. So I left. I just left and went back to the playground.'

'And after that he told you to never mention being in the woods that day?'

'I don't remember all of this clearly,' he said, his voice rising. 'Remember that first night I saw you in the coffee shop? I told you about going to therapy and trying to remember things. I've been working on that for years, and some of it isn't clear. Is it clear for you?'

'No.'

'See?' He threw out his hands. *See?* 'I could only remember bits and pieces. I thought I remembered my dad here. For a number of years, I remembered that and came to believe it was true. That's why I told you that in the coffee shop. I wasn't lying to you.'

'Why is this coming back now?' Janet asked. 'Why are you saying these things?'

'I was angry, Janet. So angry. When I went to therapy and they asked me to remember that day, that's what I felt. Not fear. Not sadness, really. Anger. Just anger. And it was always directed at Justin. Just Justin. And I didn't understand why. I knew he ran off that day. I knew I was mad at him about that, but it didn't explain the level of anger I felt sometimes. Gut-churning anger. It boiled just below the surface of my mind. I even thought it might be a form of grief, you know? I was mad at him for dying maybe. Does that make sense?'

'I understand.'

'But it was too strong for that. And it wouldn't go away.'

'How do you know what really happened?'

It took Michael a long time to go on. Janet waited, her arms folded across her chest. Her eyes were completely acclimated to the dark, and she watched Michael, trying to be patient, trying to let him tell the story at his own pace.

'I came back here after I lost my job. I moved back to Dove Point, and I started coming out here.' He ran his hands through his hair. 'I had a therapist who said that sometimes long-dormant or repressed memories come back if the person is placed in a situation similar to the original event. Maybe they return to the exact place where the memory was formed or maybe they experience a similar, intense emotion. So I came back here after I returned to town. And I felt it when I was here. The anger. The confusion, I guess.'

'Then?'

Michael didn't answer.

'Then, Michael? What changed?'

'That night . . . the night I went to Dad's house.'

'You lost control.'

'I wanted to kill him, Janet. I wanted to — to choke the life out of him. I can't remember being that mad any other time . . . '

'Except?'

'My dad told me. He told me what happened that day in the woods. He told me I killed Justin. And that's when I went after my dad. I would have killed him too if you hadn't come into the house and called my name.'

# 53

'I thought it was Ray all this time,' Michael said. 'I really did. And here he was getting remarried and moving on with his life. He wanted to act like what happened in these woods didn't happen. That we could all just go on with our lives and be happy.' Michael's voice caught. 'He was going to have a new wife and pretend like I wasn't his son anymore. I wanted him to know it wasn't that easy to just leave the past behind.'

A chill passed up Janet's back. 'You really thought he didn't want you to be his son?'

'He cut me off, Janet. He cut me off.'

Janet paced back and forth. Something welled inside her, a hot mixture of anger and grief. 'My God, Michael. You killed Justin. You killed him.'

'An accident — '

'All these years. A man went to jail. All these years . . . we didn't know. We didn't do anything. I thought . . . '

'Janet.'

Janet bent double at the waist, as though racked by a sharp pain. She felt sick, nauseated. She stayed like that, hands on knees, breathing deeply, trying to regain her equilibrium. She didn't know how long she remained in that position before she was able to straighten up again. Her sides hurt.

'Oh, Michael.'

It was all she could say.

'Janet, it was an accident.'

Janet took a couple of steps closer to Michael. She worked up to it. She didn't know if she could bring herself to do it, to reach out to him. The man who killed her brother. But he was Michael, too. Always Michael. Always the boy she knew and loved. She knelt down next to him and placed her hand on his shoulder.

'What do you want to do now?' she asked.

He took a moment to answer, then said, 'I came to say good-bye. I wanted you to know all of this before I left, but I need to go.'

Janet took her hand away. 'Go?'

'I have to,' he said. 'Ray's talking to the police right now. Whose hide do you think he's going to save? Mine or his? It's his fault this happened, Janet. All of it. Do you think your mother instigated the affair? Do you think she started it?'

Janet stood up. 'Michael, you have to tell the police. Let's call Detective Stynes and clear this up. An innocent man went to jail.'

'I can't do that.'

'You were seven years old. You didn't mean it. We'll tell Stynes, and they'll work it out. You have to face what happened.'

Michael shook his head. His eyes were on the forest floor, the intensity of his shaking growing. It looked mechanical and regimented. 'I won't go to jail, Janet,' he said. 'Not even a little bit. I've had a taste of that before.'

'You have?'

'I can't,' he said. 'Not for something Ray did.'

'You did it, Michael. Yes, Ray is to blame. He should have helped you. He's to blame as well.

He manipulated us, told us not to tell the whole truth about that day. But you have to come clean.'

Michael buried his head in his hands. He rubbed his hands over his face, then spoke in a muffled voice. 'Let me go, Janet. I'm just going to leave. You can get out of here and make it back to your life and your kid and even your dad. You have your job and your benefits and the whole thing. Right? I don't have any of that. I have to go. Just get out of here, and come tomorrow, I'll be gone.'

'Gone for good?' Janet asked.

Michael lowered his hands. He didn't speak, but he nodded.

They didn't touch or hug. Janet just turned and walked back up the path, out of the clearing and the woods.

# 54

Janet saw figures coming down the path, at least five of them. She thought she recognized something familiar about the one in front, something about the way he walked with his shoulders a little slumped. They all came closer to her, and despite the darkness and isolation of the woods, she didn't feel afraid.

'Janet?'

'Detective Stynes?' she asked.

'Are you okay?'

Behind Stynes stood four uniformed officers, their thick frames looking like solid blocks in the dark night.

'I'm okay,' Janet said.

'Are you alone?' Stynes asked.

Janet didn't hesitate. 'Michael Bower is back there.'

Stynes turned to the uniformed officers and made a gesture with his hand. Without saying anything else, the four of them moved past Janet in the darkness, heading down the path toward Michael. She turned and watched them go, almost wishing she could stop them. But they had to do what they had to do. And Michael had to face his past.

'Janet?' Stynes said. 'Is there something wrong?'

She turned back to the detective. 'How did you know where I was?'

'Ashleigh called me,' he said. 'She woke up and saw you weren't in the house, so she got worried. She thought something happened to you.'

'How did you know to find me here?' Janet asked.

'We saw the car wasn't gone,' Stynes said. 'Ashleigh thought you might have come over here. It seemed like a hunch worth following. We thought Michael Bower might be here as well.'

'It's strange. I never come here,' Janet said.

'Maybe it's different now,' Stynes said.

Janet agreed. It was all different.

Janet pointed down the path. 'Michael,' she said. 'He's . . . he told me something. He told me a story about the day Justin died.'

Stynes reached out and touched her shoulder. 'I heard the same story from his father this evening. We'll take care of it.' He paused. 'And I'm sorry. I know it's a hell of a thing to find out after all these years.'

'Do you think it's true?' Janet asked. 'Just because Ray said it . . . '

'And Michael just corroborated it, right?'

Janet nodded. The dark made it difficult to see Stynes's face. He seemed to have his head lowered, to be looking at the ground.

'I think that's it,' he said. 'I do.' Stynes started down the path. He turned and looked back at Janet. 'Are you sure you're okay?' he asked. 'Do you need anything?'

'I'm fine. Can I just go home?'

'Go ahead,' Stynes said. 'But you'll be hearing from us soon. Okay?'

As the detective disappeared, Janet started up the path. When she emerged from the woods, she saw Ashleigh.

'Mom? Are you okay?'

Janet folded Ashleigh into her arms, kissing the top of her daughter's head as they hugged.

'Thanks for looking out for me, kid,' Janet said.

'Somebody has to,' Ashleigh said. Then she said, 'You've always done it for me.'

Janet pulled her close, felt the girl's warmth against her body. 'I guess we need each other, don't we?'

'It looks that way.'

They started for home, walking arm in arm.

'I told Kevin you want him to come over for dinner,' Ashleigh said. 'He's up for it, so long as you know he and I are just friends.'

'For now?'

'For now.'

When they reached the house, they found Bill waiting in the front yard. He came across the lawn to them.

'I woke up and no one's in the house,' he said. He looked at the two of them, his eyes taking them in from head to toe. He looked like — he looked like he wanted to reach out and hug them. 'What the hell is going on? Are you hurt?'

'No, Dad, we're not hurt.' She almost smiled seeing the concern on his face and in his body language. 'It's a long story. Let's go inside.'

★　★　★

426

The three of them sat at the kitchen table while Janet told them about Michael's confession in the woods. Her father didn't say anything. He didn't ask questions or show emotion. When Janet was finished, he stood up from the table, acting as though he wanted to go to bed.

'Dad?' Janet said. 'Don't you want to talk about this more? Do you have anything to say?'

He hesitated, then said, 'No, I don't think I do. I guess I hope they both go to jail, Ray and Michael.'

'I don't know, Dad. I don't know what they'll do to Michael.'

He turned to go, but before he left the room, Ashleigh said, 'Wait!'

Her grandpa stopped in the doorway and turned around.

Janet looked at Ashleigh. 'What's wrong?'

Ashleigh jumped up from the table. 'I have something — something for both of you to see. A surprise, I guess.'

'In the middle of the night?' Janet asked. 'In the middle of all this?'

'Just wait.'

Ashleigh ran up the stairs, her steps making muffled thumps. Janet sat at the kitchen table, staring at the familiar space, staring at her father. It still felt like home. He had been right: some things, some feelings never changed. Our knowledge about them changed, but not the fundamental feelings. She was home. She and Ashleigh and her dad. Home.

Ashleigh was carrying a familiar box as she entered the kitchen. Janet recognized it right

427

away, even as her tears formed. 'Where did you — ? How did you — ?'

'I knew you'd want it,' Ashleigh said. 'I saved it from the trash the day Grandpa threw it out.'

Janet looked at her dad, who still didn't speak.

Ashleigh said, 'I figured you really didn't mean it, Grandpa. You were probably just pissed off or something.'

Janet flipped open the top of the box. She reached in and took handfuls of pictures. Justin. Her mom. All of them as a family. Before it all changed. Before.

But some of it was still there. And not just in pictures.

Janet took one out of the stack. It showed the four of them the year before Justin died. They looked happy in the photographer's studio. They looked like a family.

Janet held it up.

'Remember this one, Dad? Remember going there that day? We tried to get Justin to wear that little bow-tie, and he kept taking it off.'

Her dad came forward, took the photo out of her hand. He studied it a long time before one side of his mouth raised, the tiniest hint of a grin.

'I remember,' he said. 'I remember.'

# Acknowledgments

I want to begin by thanking my colleagues and students in the Western Kentucky English Department and the Potter College of Arts and Letters, especially Tom Hunley, David Lee, David LeNoir, Mary Ellen Miller, Dale Rigby, and Karen Schneider. Thanks also go to James Weems, Glen Rose, and their crew for the amazing book trailer. For friendship and psychological insights about memory and trauma, I am indebted to Drs Sherry Hamby and Al Bardi. Big thanks to Kara Thurmond for her work on my Web site. And I owe so much to my family, especially my mother, Catherine Bell, my late father, Herbert Bell, and my in-laws, Mike and Penny McCaffrey.

As always, thanks to the booksellers, librarians, reviewers, readers, book club members, and bloggers who buy, borrow, sell, and talk about books.

I would be nowhere without the great efforts made by everyone at NAL/Penguin. Special thanks to my publicist, Heather Connor, and her amazing team. Thanks for getting the word out.

I can't say enough nice things about my brilliant editor, Danielle Perez. Her sense of humor, great skill, calm demeanor, and vast knowledge have made all of this possible. Thanks for making me look good, Danielle.

I also want to thank everyone at Markson

Thoma Literary Agency for their dedication and professionalism. And a special thanks to Julia Kenny and her foreign rights team.

My amazing agent, Laney Katz Becker, has worked tirelessly on my behalf and has perhaps set a world record for answering an endless stream of questions in a timely fashion. Thanks for everything, Laney. I'm lucky to have you as my agent.

And finally, special thanks to Molly McCaffrey for years of good times, movies, and long car trips. Can you believe we pulled this off?

We do hope that you have enjoyed reading this large print book.

Did you know that all of our titles are available for purchase?

We publish a wide range of high quality large print books including:
**Romances, Mysteries, Classics**
**General Fiction**
**Non Fiction and Westerns**

Special interest titles available in large print are:
**The Little Oxford Dictionary**
**Music Book**
**Song Book**
**Hymn Book**
**Service Book**

Also available from us courtesy of Oxford University Press:
**Young Readers' Dictionary**
**(large print edition)**
**Young Readers' Thesaurus**
**(large print edition)**

For further information or a free brochure, please contact us at:
**Ulverscroft Large Print Books Ltd.,**
**The Green, Bradgate Road, Anstey,**
**Leicester, LE7 7FU, England.**
**Tel:** (00 44) 0116 236 4325
**Fax:** (00 44) 0116 234 0205

*Other titles published by*
*The House of Ulverscroft:*

**PRETTY GIRL THIRTEEN**

**Liz Coley**

Angie Chapman was thirteen years old when she went missing. Three years later, she reappears, and she doesn't remember a thing. But some people do — people who could tell Angie every terrifying detail, if they weren't locked inside her mind. With help, Angie slowly begins to unravel the darkest secrets of her own past. But does she really want to know the truth?

723
5013
1010